TEXAS NEIGHBORS

TEXAS
NEIGHBORS

Grace for New Beginnings Abides in
Three Endearing Romances

DEBRA WHITE SMITH

BARBOUR
PUBLISHING

The Key © 2003 by Debra White Smith
The Promise © 2003 by Debra White Smith
The Neighbor © 1998 by Debra White Smith

ISBN 1-59789-111-8

The Key and *The Promise* previously published as *Take Two*.

Cover art by Getty Image

All scripture quotations are taken from the HOLY BIBLE, NEW INTERNATIONAL VERSION®. NIV®. Copyright © 1973, 1978, 1984 by International Bible Society. Used by permission of Zondervan. All rights reserved.

Published by Barbour Publishing, Inc., P.O. Box 719, Uhrichsville, Ohio 44683, www.barbourbooks.com

Our mission is to publish and distribute inspirational products offering exceptional value and biblical encouragement to the masses.

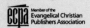

Printed in the United States of America.
5 4 3 2 1

DEBRA WHITE SMITH, author of the best-selling historical series, *Texas*, continues to impact and entertain readers with her life-changing books, including *The Jane Austen Fiction Series*, the *Sister Suspense Series*, *Romancing Your Husband*, *Romancing Your Wife*, and *It's a Jungle at Home*. She has been an award-winning author for years with such honors as Heartsong Presents Top-10 Reader Favorite, Gold Medallion finalist (*Romancing Your Husband*) and Retailer's Choice Award Finalist (*First Impressions* and *Reason and Romance*). Debra has about 50 book sales to her credit and, since 1997, has been blessed with over a million books in print. Her book, *The Neighbor*, which is a part of this collection, was the second book Debra published.

The founder of Real Life Ministries, Debra speaks at events across the nation and sings with her husband and children. She has been featured on a variety of media spots, including The 700 Club, At Home Live, Getting Together, Moody Broadcasting Network, Fox News, ABC Radio, Viewpoint, and America's Family Coaches. She holds an M.A. in English.

Debra lives in small-town America with her husband of 23 years, two children, and a herd of cats.

To write Debra or contact her for speaking engagements, check out her website:

www.debrawhitesmith.com
or send mail to
Real Life Ministries
Debra White Smith
P.O. Box 1482
Jacksonville, TX 75766

The Key

Dedicated to my all-time favorite boy,
my son, Brett Smith.

Chapter 1

Brendy Lane gaped at Ezekiel Blake. Zeke, her high school sweetheart. Her first love. The man for whom she had promised to wait when he went off to Vietnam some thirty-three years ago. The man she had jilted for Mack.

Her cheeks flashed hot, and then chilled just as quickly as they'd heated. She gripped her coffee shop's counter and swallowed an exclamation. Her father had always attributed her spontaneous tongue to the presence of her fiery locks. Problem was, her natural hair color had been a long way from fiery for several years. Nevertheless, her former fiancé's presence evoked a storm of emotions that would have produced a barrage of nervous babbling if she were still in her youth. Instead, Brendy left all babbling to the mockingbird, whose song floated from the oak near the open door.

"Ziggy!" She croaked the old endearment as if she had seen a ghost from the halls of Jacksonville High School.

The year had been 1970, and they were voted the senior class sweetheart and beau. By the time the two walked across the stage for their award, the boys' basketball team was chanting, "Ziggy. . . Ziggy. . .Ziggy."

"Hi, Brendy." Zeke tilted his head to one side, and the morning sun highlighted silver threads in his thick, black hair. A smile, tentative yet teasing, increased the lines around one of his eyes. A white patch covered the other, and Brendy stopped herself short of asking what happened to his eye. She hadn't seen him since that teary moment she waved as the Greyhound bus whisked him out of Jacksonville, heading for boot camp. In her youthful sorrow, she dreaded the thought that he might land in the Vietnamese jungle. Minutes before his departure she pledged her undying faithfulness. . . no matter what.

"Mom mentioned you'd opened a new coffee and gift shop." Zeke hooked a thumb in his jeans belt loop and scanned the shelves, lined with specialty coffees and a wide array of country gifts. "I wondered when you called if it was you."

"C—called?" she questioned and wrinkled her brow. An over-stuffed, striped feline rubbed against her legs, and Tiger-Higer produced a pitiful meow that sounded like a high-pitched echo of Brendy's word.

"Yes—for a locksmith," Zeke answered. He rested his weight on his left leg in a gesture that suggested he was settling in for a long conversation.

"Oh! A locksmith!" Brendy blurted. "Yes—I—I—you mean that would be you?"

"Yes, that would be me." His deep voice floated around the quaint store like liquid satin, and Brendy shivered against a delightful chill that danced up her spine. She had heard through the grapevine that Zeke was back in town. She'd even picked up the news that he opened a locksmith business. But that information hadn't crossed her mind when she snatched the phone book and dialed the first locksmith who was listed—B and B Locksmith Service.

"Well, uh, th—thanks for coming so—so s—soon." Brendy released the counter and began stroking her oversized apron. The smells of gourmet coffee and chocolates mingled with the scent of the vanilla candles she'd just placed near the cash register. Brendy sucked in a deep breath and reveled in the sudden rush of expectation that assaulted her from nowhere. All at once, she wondered if the smell of vanilla would forever remind her of the day Ezekiel Blake stepped back into her life.

"So, this is your little place?" Zeke asked. He closed the door, and the bell merrily clanged against the glass panes of the door.

"Yes, this is The Friend-Shop!" She awkwardly waved her hand to encompass the quaint home-turned-shop that represented a six-year dream to own her own business. The polished hardwood floors and knotty-pine walls served as a perfect backdrop for the 1950s-style coffee bar where Brendy served hot coffee and homemade cookies.

Presently, a klatch of four retired locals sat in the corner, sipping their coffee and playing checkers. But the main thing they usually accomplished was gossiping about the "latest" around the sleepy town of Jacksonville, Texas—where, for the past fifty years, time had seemingly stood still. One of those checkers warriors looked up from a time-intensive move, slipped his narrow reading glasses down his nose, and eyed Zeke as if he were the latest piece of juicy news. Mr. Narvy's three checkers partners followed their *compadre*'s lead, and all paused to examine Zeke.

Brendy's stomach did flip-flops, and warmth oozed from her midsection into her limbs. When the checkers brigade shifted their focus from Zeke to Brendy, she resisted the urge to shrink to her knees and hide behind the counter. Brendy wondered how long it would take for this meeting between her and Zeke to spread along the social grapevine. Brendy had long ago ended the hallucination that she could ever keep secrets in a town with a population just over thirteen thousand. She figured the seniors' Sunday school class would be abuzz with all manner of conjectures, and that was exactly forty-eight hours away.

"So. . ." The hardwood floor creaked as Zeke neared.

Brendy snapped her attention back to him. Yet all she could think of was their first kiss—which was Brendy's *very first* kiss.

❦

At the age of sixteen, she and Zeke went on a picnic with her parents. The summer sun glistened across Lake Jacksonville like a shower of glitter. Zeke asked Brendy's dad for permission to take a walk around the lake, and she despaired that her father would say no. When he agreed, the sun shone a little brighter, the breeze seemed a bit more refreshing, the birds sang just for Zeke and Brendy. When Brendy first noticed the weeping willow, the summer wind whispered through its limbs and summoned them closer. Zeke tugged her trembling hand, and the two of them walked toward the willow. She hoped Zeke might kiss her there. Oh, how she hoped. Soon they paused under the weeping willow. . . .

"You said you were having trouble with a lock?"

Zeke's words seemed to float across the lake upon a balmy zephyr that lifted her hair and christened her cheeks. Brendy started and blinked. "Uh. . .a—a lock. Yes—yes, I have a lock. I mean, I have a *problem* with a lock." Her knees wobbled as fiercely as they had years ago when Zeke's lips brushed hers in a chaste caress that tilted her world. "It's—it's the back—the back lock," she said on a snatch of breath.

Zeke rubbed slender fingers along the edge of the bandage that covered one eye, and a tender smile revealed the twin dimples she had adored as a teenager. She held his gaze a fraction longer than the checkers brigade would claim was decent. Then she looked a little deeper into his soul, and Brendy would have pledged that she saw the weeping willow. . .the lake. . .and the undying flames of first love.

Get a grip! she admonished herself. *You're a woman over fifty. You aren't a teenager, and neither is Ziggy. He's probably married anyway!*

Brendy couldn't stop herself from glancing at his left hand, where no gold band claimed his ring finger. Her pulse pounded at the base of her throat, and she touched the inside of her own wedding band. The wedding band she had refused to stop wearing even after ten years as a widow. Her pledge of loyalty to the memory of her children's father had been the force behind the continued presence of the wedding ring.

But in the face of Zeke's warm appraisal, Brendy realized with aching poignancy that loyalty to a memory did little to keep her warm at night.

Tiger-Higer plopped his striped self atop the counter and stuck his nose squarely into the midst of the vanilla candles. "No, no," Brendy admonished. "It's time for you to go out anyway." She grabbed her grandchildren's pet and clung to him as the most logical diversion available. *And, heaven help me, I need a diversion,* she thought. *The checkers brigade is going to have enough fodder for the gossip chain for months if I don't cool it!*

"Come on back, Zeke," Brendy called over her shoulder and applauded her ability to finally sound as if she were getting down to business. "The lock with the problem is back here."

❧

Zeke followed Brendy behind the counter. As he neared the doorway to the other rooms, the skin along his spine crawled with the sensation of being watched. Zeke darted a glance toward that checkers gang. As if they were one, the knot of men simultaneously shifted their attention to the checkerboard. With a shake of his head, Zeke followed Brendy past an office and into a storage room that opened to the backyard. Along the hallway, he stepped around a Barbie cash register and a Hot Wheels race car set. *Must be grandchildren,* he thought, yet the observation served as a spear to his heart. Undoubtedly when Brendy jilted him to marry Mack Lane, she found the man of her dreams. *They're probably still dreaming together.* He couldn't stop the twist of unexpected jealousy that shot through his belly. Even after his own marriage and raising his children—even after all these years—he couldn't deny he'd never completely gotten over his first love.

As they paused beside the door and Brendy tossed out the striped tomcat, the familiar scent of Shalimar overshadowed the smell of cappuccino. He had introduced Brendy to the fragrance the Christmas of their senior year.

The aroma now evoked memories of those carefree days. A time before war and loss. A time when they nearly married, yet separated forever. A time that seemed so close, yet so far away.

Brendy inserted her hand into the pocket of a butcher's apron that covered most of her slacks and hand-painted T-shirt.

❄

Thirty-three years ago, at Lake Jacksonville, Brendy held out a supple hand. Zeke then slid his senior ring on its fourth finger. The smooth skin yielded as the sign of his pledge slipped into place.

They had attended the athletic banquet at school, and a klatch of couples drifted out to Lake Jacksonville. Young love filled the sweet autumn night. The pairs scattered, leaving Zeke free to extend his ring to Brendy. Then, holding hands, they walked toward their favorite spot. A weeping willow grew beside three large iron ore rocks at the edge of the lake. The rising moon shed circles of light upon the rippling water like bands of glowing satin strung by fairies of the deep. The two exchanged no words. None were necessary. The gentle pressure of her hand told him volumes.

They stopped. She turned. He answered by a caress of her cheek. Zeke tilted her chin upward until their lips met. The delicate kiss lasted only a moment but was filled with an eternity of commitment as his ring glistened in the moon's luminescence.

❄

Now, her hands were showing wear, and there was a band of gold where Zeke's ring had been.

"When I arrived this morning, the key opened the lock, as usual, but it froze up, and I can't get the key to come out now." Brendy bent over the ornery lock, and her fingers flitted around it.

Her honey-toned voice woke Zeke from his reverie. More than anything he longed to say, "I've still got the key to your heart." He dared not. The wedding band meant she still belonged to Mack Lane.

The shop's bell rang. She rose and looked back the way they had come. "Oh, rats," she whispered; then her face brightened with a smile that seemed to light up the whole musty hallway. The smile Zeke would never forget. The smile that had implanted itself upon his heart and refused to release him.

"Would you believe it?" she asked and shook her head. Her copper curls danced delightfully around her cheeks. "I've been praying for more business, and now that it's here, I'm saying 'rats.' "

Zeke rested a hand on the doorknob and leaned into his good leg. "Look," he said, "go on and take care of your business. I'll see to this problem. As soon as I figure out what you need to do, I'll meander back up front."

"Okay." Brendy's eyes, as green as the finest Vietnamese jade, turned toward him, and she seemed ready to hang onto his every word. Zeke wasn't prepared for the longing stirring her soul. Longing—and a hint of remorse. He stopped himself from taking in a hissing breath and felt as if the tidal wave of attraction would take him under. If Zeke didn't know any better, he'd say he was eighteen again.

She tried to step past him in the narrow hall. Yet their attempts to keep from bumping into each other resulted in the two of them doing something akin to the jitterbug. Indeed, by the time she was sashaying up the hallway, Zeke's pulse *was* doing the jitterbug.

But she's married! he reminded himself and stared at the gold band on her ring finger until she disappeared into the store.

Zeke purposefully stepped from the shop and into the morning sunshine, hoping to remove himself from the magnetic pull of the woman within. Yet a lattice full of honeysuckle hugged the back of the house and reminded him of their senior prom. Someone had thought it clever to lay branches of fresh honeysuckle along the center of the round tables. Brendy loved the idea and had even tucked a strand behind her ear.

As a cool spring breeze danced through the pines, oaks, and maples, Zeke scowled at the honeysuckle. *I need to get out of here*, he decided. *As in move back to Houston while I still have some pride left.* A squirrel's scoffing bark seemed a response to his thoughts. Zeke glanced over his shoulder and into the inky gaze of a gray squirrel who protested his interruption.

"I hear ya. I hear ya. I'm not after your babies," he responded and purposed to focus upon the task at hand. After examining the doorknob, Zeke pronounced the thing worn-out—irrevocably and completely. He eyed the repaired eaves of the home-turned-store and figured the lock was the original. "The thing is probably seventy years old," he diagnosed.

Zeke stepped back into the hallway and peered toward the store. In the distance, Brendy chatted with a lady who deliberated over two candles. For a flash, he was tempted to just go around the store, get a new knob out of his van, fix it, and mail Brendy a bill. While that route seemed the safest and most sane, Zeke knew he couldn't compromise his usual business procedures. He never made a change unless his customers approved and understood the cost. The only way Brendy could approve his diagnosis would be if he discussed the problem with her.

He scraped together all his courage and ambled up the hallway, doing his best to hide his slight limp. Zeke hadn't felt self-conscious about his missing leg in years. Being near Brendy somehow reawakened those first feelings of inadequacy after the terrible battle that also took his eye. He touched the patch the doctor had placed on yesterday. "Wear this a day or two and keep the socket clean. Make sure you use this antibiotic ointment three times a day. I know this is irritating, but it's a simple infection. Your socket should be cleared up in a day or two, and you can put your prosthesis back in." Zeke had agreed and gladly followed the doctor's instructions.

He wondered if it would make any difference to Brendy that he had not only lost a leg in the jungles of Vietnam but an eye, as well. He stroked the thin scar that coursed the edge of his right jaw. The horror of the firefight at Phong Din—a little-known but deadly battle—traced its way through his memory.

When he regained consciousness three days after the battle, his eye and leg were gone, and a row of neat stitches dotted his jaw.

Zeke stepped into the store as Brendy finalized the sale. She graciously smiled at the snowy-haired lady and even threw in a sample bag of French vanilla coffee. Zeke had longed for that smile during those months of convalescence. Looking back, he wondered if thoughts of Brendy were what kept him alive.

Buckets full of morning sun spilled through the line of windows along the east wall and illuminated the locks of Brendy's auburn hair. In another life, she had caught the wavy locks into a bouncy ponytail that swayed with her every step. Now the fiery ringlets hugged her ears and neckline in a full, easy-swing style that suited her just as much as the ponytail. She'd kept her figure nicely, as well. Her shoulders sloped a bit, and her waist didn't pinch at the middle quite like it had at age eighteen. Still, as Zeke matured, he preferred a woman with some meat on her bones anyway.

Brendy bade her customer farewell, and the aging lady with spry blue eyes looked Zeke up and down. "You Ezekiel Blake?" she asked.

"Yes," he answered. "Yes, I am." The angle of the lady's arched brows and firm jaw struck him as familiar, yet he couldn't place her. Zeke rested a hand on the rustic counter and leaned off his prosthesis.

"Eloise Thom," the lady said and tugged on her lavender sweater as if she were the authority at large. "When you were a freshman,

I sent you to the principal's office for pulling a girl's ponytail," she said as if the very memory made her want to repeat the punishment.

"Oh, Mrs. Thom," Zeke said and extended a hand to his former English teacher. "Yes, I *knew* you looked familiar."

She clasped his hand and winked. "I believe the girl with the ponytail was she, if I'm not mistaken." Mrs. Thom nodded toward Brendy.

Zeke chuckled. "Yes, I believe you are right." He stole a glimpse at Brendy, whose cheeks now matched her hair. She busied herself with a pile of receipts that crackled with the activity. A cursory glance toward the checkers brigade revealed they were processing more information for later discussion.

"I was so sorry to hear of your dear wife's death, Ezekiel," Mrs. Thom said, and Zeke was almost certain she was projecting her voice over the sound of the rattling receipts.

"Well, that was five years ago," Zeke supplied.

"Hmm, and I guess Brendy's dear husband had been gone a good five years before that." She shook her head and turned toward the door. "It's all a crying shame."

Zeke dashed a glance to Brendy's ring finger, and his attention was drawn to her candid eyes. She didn't look away. No, indeed. Brendy Lane tentatively held his gaze. Without a word, she confirmed Mrs. Thom's statement.

"Toodles," Mrs. Thom called before reaching the door. Zeke would have sworn in court that the old lady sent an exaggerated wink to the checkers guards.

Brendy made a monumental task of counting those crinkled receipts again. At the rate she was going, Zeke calculated the things would disintegrate. The doorbell jingled, Mrs. Thom stepped outside, and Brendy called after her, "Thank you, Mrs. Thom. Come back."

"Come back. . .come back. . .come back." Her words reverberated from the past and tore at his heart.

The month after graduation, the draft board sent Zeke a notice. College and a deferment were the best choice, but he needed the money the army offered. Imagining himself a mighty warrior, Zeke stepped up to his responsibility to serve his country.

Brendy cried when he told her about the army. Even his arms failed to hush her weeping. "Promise me you'll come back," she begged. And between sobs, she pledged to be waiting when he returned. His heavy class ring upon her finger pressed into the back of Zeke's neck as if she were trying to keep him from the dreaded departure. She kissed him until desperation blended into heartache. Each kiss evidenced her vow. All so long ago.

Boot camp was a blur, yet Zeke would never forget the sight of South Vietnam as they descended toward their battleground. He recalled those initial days, frenzied and full of overwrought nerves, wondering if he'd been crazy to imagine himself as a military hero. Bemoaning the agony of living without his Brendy. Only her letters kept Zeke sane. He remembered standing in mud or drizzle or blinding sun as Sergeant Myles called the names of those getting mail. The mere mention of his name always assured Zeke he could make it another day. The letters did come every day for a season. Then they dwindled: three per week, four a month, once every six weeks, and then finally, none. Several of his buddies experienced the same, and they silently bore each other up while pretending they didn't care. Deep inside, the despair almost crushed Zeke.

Now, with her closeness palpable, all the plans and hopes of those lost days rushed upon Zeke. The fragments of dreams fell at his feet. He stood close enough to touch the woman he once yearned to marry. Now, years later, they had both loved. . .and lost.

And Zeke wondered if Brendy Lane remembered. Did she remember the weeping willow. . .the moon's satin ribbons on Lake Jacksonville. . .the honeysuckle. . .the promise of eternal love? Or was it all dashed aside the minute she met Mack Lane?

"I'm going to need to replace your lock," he said and was amazed at the calm timbre of his voice.

"Y—yes. Yes, of course." As she rearranged the cookies in the glass display case, a lock of her copper hair grazed the apple of her cheek—a cheek his lips had brushed. Zeke rubbed his callused thumb against his fingers and wondered if her skin was as soft as when she was eighteen. The faint hint of Shalimar beckoned him to caress her face, and Zeke decided this was a locksmith job he was doing for free.

When Mack Lane entered the church that fine September Sunday, Brendy hadn't stopped herself from taking a second, third, and fourth look. His blond hair, mysterious brown eyes, and finely chiseled features sent the whole row of teenage girls into gaping fits. The grapevine was alive and well as always. Word had it that Mack Lane was the nephew of their pastor and had come to live with him while attending Lon Morris College.

By the time Brendy sneaked a fifth look at the newcomer, she realized he was looking back at *her*. So she took a sixth look! Despite the presence of Zeke's senior ring evoking a cloud of guilt, Brendy strategically placed herself by the back door after service. She simply didn't bother to shy away when Mack paused to chat.

The rest was history. A whirlwind courtship. Married by spring. Their first child a year later. And somewhere in the middle of it all, Brendy tucked her promise to Zeke in a corner of her soul. She told herself he'd find someone new, just like she had, and that he'd be as happy as she. Despite her rationale, Brendy never shook the nagging sense that she would have walked down the aisle for Zeke if he hadn't been drafted.

❦

Brendy dared read the note again, and tears welled in her eyes. Tears that refused suppression. She stepped back up the hallway and called to Sylvia, "I'm going to be in my office awhile," and didn't deny that her voice sounded strained. She could only imagine what the checkers brigade must be thinking.

She moved into the office that looked like a tornado had struck. Along with a pile of papers covering the desk, an overflowing toy box claimed one corner. Her grandchildren's art projects decorated the opposite wall, and an array of their play clothes had been scattered near the closet. When their mother abandoned the children and Brendy's son two years ago, Brendy found herself filling the role of mother once more. Her son Kent moved back home with his children, and they all struggled together the best they could. As always, Brendy wondered if that vixen of a mother of theirs, way out in California, ever thought of them. She clenched her teeth and suppressed the bitter bile welling from her soul. Never had Brendy so struggled with the temptation to retaliate against a person.

Yet today another broken relationship demanded precedence in her thoughts—a relationship *she* had ended. Brendy scrubbed the back of her hand against a tear trickling down her cheek and picked a path through the clutter. She settled into her leather chair, laid Zeke's note on the desk, and covered her face with her hands. The smell of Shalimar perfume filled her senses.

The year was 1969. Christmas Eve spirit hugged her parents' frame home like a cozy blanket. The trees, barren and gray, strained against the cold breeze. The misty clouds predicted the coming of a long-anticipated white Christmas, a rare treat in east Texas. Zeke arrived promptly at ten of five and bustled Brendy into the black Mustang his parents helped him buy. The two lovebirds didn't really have anyplace to go, and the small town of Jacksonville certainly didn't offer a wide array of choices.

So Zeke drove out to Love's Lookout, a scenic roadside park that overlooked the east Texas rolling hills and provided a breathtaking view of Lookout Valley. The two bundled up and walked hand in hand near the rock wall, poised on a precipice that descended straight into clumps of pines. Brendy and Zeke paused and absorbed the miles and miles of trees and hills as well as the occasional peek at homes nestled amidst the woods. The crisp winter breeze smelled of evergreens, and Brendy imagined that, if Zeke ever got around to proposing, they would be in their own home, with their own Christmas tree, by this time next year.

Zeke cleared his throat and dug his hand into his coat pocket. He pulled out a tiny red box, too big for a ring, but too little for anything Brendy could imagine. The green velvet bow shivered in the breeze, and Brendy leaned into Zeke as he spoke his heart. "I couldn't wait a minute longer," he said. "I. . .hope you like it."

She gazed up into his vulnerable blue eyes and reverently took the package. Looking back, Brendy understood now that, somewhere along the way, Ezekiel Blake had irrevocably lost his heart—lost it to her.

Brendy wasted no time in unwrapping the package. In her haste, the paper and ribbon fell to their feet; and Brendy was left holding a box of perfume—*real perfume!* Breathless, she had thrown herself into his arms, and the two rocked as she squealed with glee. Zeke pulled away and bestowed a gentle kiss upon her waiting lips. He helped her remove the cellophane from the box and dabble just a touch of the perfume upon her wrists and behind her ears.

That evening, Brendy declared Shalimar her favorite perfume, and a scattering of tiny snowflakes falling like white diamonds seemed to christen the moment.

The day she met Mack, Brendy stopped wearing the cherished fragrance. She didn't start wearing it again until a year after her husband's heart attack and subsequent death. Brendy stumbled across the cherished bottle tucked in a keepsake box at the back of her closet. Surprisingly, the fragrance was still sweet. After she'd used the rest of it, Brendy placed the empty bottle back into the box and bought herself more Shalimar. She'd been loyal to the scent ever since. Deep inside she wondered if, perhaps, she'd worn the fragrance in the hopes that Zeke might one day return and understand she never forgot him. Such whimsical notions had seemed far-fetched—until today.

❧

Brendy lifted her face from her hands, now damp with the essence of her poignant reverie. She pulled open her oak desk's bottom drawer, dropped to her knees, and reached beneath the clutter to the back. Her fingers encountered a small padded box, covered in satin, once royal blue, now nearly gray; topped with a rose, once peachy, now pale. She shoved aside a mound of paperwork on her desktop. As if she were handling the rarest of treasures, Brendy settled the oval box upon the desk, lifted the lid, and absorbed the essence of the treasures within. The empty perfume bottle. A dried corsage from the prom. A senior ring, swathed in tape. A yellowed photo of Zeke in his letter jacket. And underneath it all, a golden locket, strangely lacking tarnish. Zeke had presented her with the locket on Valentine's Day of their junior year. They placed a photo of themselves inside, and Zeke kept the key while Brendy wore the locket.

Now Brendy pressed the locket to her lips and wondered if Zeke still had the key. Before she had the chance to analyze her motives, she clasped the necklace around her neck and tucked the heart beneath her decorative T-shirt.

A shaft of morning sun pierced the windows and glimmered against her gold wedding band. Brendy eyed the symbol of her vow and pondered her deceased husband. Mack had been good to her. Really good. He adored her and lavished her with the love, loyalty, and respect many women crave their whole lives but die never knowing. Brendy had been devastated when the call came that he was the victim of a massive heart attack. He'd been dead upon arrival at the hospital, at the age of forty-one. All these years Brendy wore the band as a symbol of loyalty to the man whose son and daughter she bore. The golden band twinkled up at her as if to say its purpose had been fulfilled. *Mack would want me to be happy,* she thought. With a sense of deep peace, she twisted the gold band off her finger and examined the tan line left behind. Before she could change her mind, Brendy dropped the ring into the padded box.

"Oh, Lord," she breathed, "Mack always said You work in mysterious ways. I'm mystified, to say the least. Guide my steps. I don't want to make any mistakes. But You know there's always been a place in my heart for Ziggy, and if I'm not badly mistaken, he feels the same."

❧

Zeke Blake parked his van by the duplex he rented from Major Purvis on Cherry Street. His landlord imagined himself a big man around Jacksonville. He wasn't a big man in any sense of the word. His parents gave him the name *Major*, not the military. The only distinction Major carried was being the owner of more junk property than anyone in town. Zeke found him a good man to do business with, so Zeke handled all the security problems of Purvis's rental property. They had struck a work-for-rent agreement, and since the amount of work was moderate, Zeke considered the deal advantageous. His plan included banking his disability payments and supporting himself with the income of his locksmith business. When he added all this to the equity received on the home he had sold, the sum was tidy.

Moving back to the town of his birth had been a necessity to help care for his aging mother, who lived only two streets over. During the last nine months, he'd become involved in his small community church. But in a town the size of Jacksonville, most singles groups were tailored to college-aged people. Therefore, the downside of his move proved to be loneliness.

Zeke checked his watch. He'd been out answering calls most of the day, and now three thirty steadily approached. He secured the lock on his van, which housed thousands of dollars in equipment. After limping toward the aging duplex, he unlocked the door and shuffled into the frame home, filled with his deceased wife's country decor. Yet this afternoon his thoughts weren't with the woman who nursed him through his physical recovery. Instead, they were with the woman who broke his heart.

Nostalgia was taking him under. With purpose in his step, Zeke strode through the house toward the spare bedroom. He rummaged under the heavy four-poster bed until his worn hands rested upon the box, taped tight for years. He tugged the box across the short-piled carpet the color of plums, then reached for his pocketknife. Zeke wasted no time slitting the tape and gazing upon the musty contents. He'd told himself when he found the dust-laden box in his mother's garage that he was a sentimental old fool for hanging onto it. Nevertheless, he couldn't allow himself to discard a single item within.

Zeke dug past high school annuals, a few chipped trophies, and a basketball jersey. At the bottom of it all rested a scratched-up cardboard box the size of a business card. Zeke opened the box and pulled out a gold key attached to a short chain long enough to wrap around a couple of his fingers. He held up the key and watched it dangle in the afternoon light as if dancing with glee to be out of the box.

Zeke pressed the keepsake against his palm. As he closed his fingers around it, more memories he'd thought long forgotten bombarded him. But most of all, the words he and Brendy pledged reverberated through the corridors of his lonely heart. *Undying love. Always for each other. Nothing can come between us.* A hundred worn-out clichés that never came true.

His cell phone emitted the beginning of "America the Beautiful" from his belt. Zeke rocked back on his heels and sighed. Today was Friday. The weekends were usually the busiest days for a locksmith. He and his jovial mother usually joked that people weren't any good on their own. Once they started getting off work for the weekend, they began locking themselves out of their cars and homes.

He stood, kicked the box back under the bed, and retrieved his cell. Still clutching the key, he pressed the answer button and spoke the usual greeting. This time, the words sounded less than enthusiastic.

"Uh, Ziggy?" Brendy's hesitant voice sounded over the line, and the key seemed to warm in his grasp.

"Yes?" he rasped. Was his voice cracking like a fourteen-year-old, or was he imagining things?

"I. . .uh. . .you said in your note to call you if I needed you again."

She needs me! he thought. *Yes!*

"Of course," he responded. "Is there another problem with your lock?" *I love you*, he thought. *I never stopped, you know.* "I meant to tell you in the note that I placed the old one on the back steps."

"No. It has nothing to do with *that* lock," she said on a sheepish note. "I'm here at Jacksonville Christian School." The sound of a child's high-pitched squeal attested to her claim. "You two stop it now!" she admonished. "Sorry, Zeke, I wasn't talking to you."

He chuckled and gazed out the room's window toward a circle of dwarf crepe myrtles in his backyard.

"It's my grandchildren. I'm helping raise them. They're trying to wrestle each other to the floor right here in the principal's office," she continued in a harassed voice. "Listen, I've locked my keys in my car. Would you please come—?"

"I'll be there in five minutes," he agreed and acknowledged the location and color of her Chevy minivan.

As Zeke disconnected the call, he was tempted to leap out back, snatch a handful of crepe myrtle blooms, and present them to Brendy after he unlocked her car. Instead, he decided to behave like a fifty-one-year-old man instead of an adolescent. So he dropped the old key into his shirt pocket, fastened the button at the top, and marched off to rescue the woman who'd been his high school sweetheart. His leading lady. The woman who was now his damsel in distress.

Chapter 3

H ere he comes." Brendy sighed as Zeke's gray Chevy van pulled into the parking lot of Jacksonville Christian School. He gassed his vehicle into the drive that circled through the parking lot and headed straight for her van. Her straw-headed, blue-eyed grandchildren jumped up from the short brick wall under the portico and dashed toward the driveway just as Zeke's van drew parallel with them.

Brakes screeched.

Gravel flew.

And Brendy screamed, "Stop!"

The children halted. Pete glared at the locksmith while Pat hovered close beside him.

"You two almost got run over!" Brendy scolded and covered her heart with her trembling hand. "You know better than to run out into this driveway."

"He should have been watching better," Pete retorted and marched toward Brendy's cobalt blue minivan. Her head hung, Pat followed in his wake.

"Pete," Brendy threatened, "watch your attitude, young man."

He shot her a glare, and Brendy wavered between gathering him in her arms and sentencing him to time-out when they got to the store. Filling the shoes of their mother kept Brendy in a constant state of upheaval. They were hurting, and there wasn't a thing she could do to erase their past.

Indeed, that very day Brendy had been summoned to a teacher's meeting. There she had been informed that Pete was continuing to disrupt his second grade class. On top of that, he started a fight that day during recess. Pat was a different story. Now in all-day kindergarten, the child seemed to be recessing deeper and deeper into a shell. Her teacher was looking for ways to encourage Pat to speak up more.

At last, her grandmother's heart won. With a sigh, Brendy moved between the children and placed an arm around each of them. She figured Pete had been through enough discipline today without her heaping more on him.

This morning, the May sunshine had tenderly caressed the countryside, but an unseasonable warm spell caused the temperature to hit ninety. Now the beads of perspiration upon the children's upper lips matched the moisture along Brendy's neckline. *I'd probably be grouchy too,* she thought, *if I was only eight and hot as a pistol.*

Zeke's van crunched to a stop beside hers. When his door slammed, Brendy recalled the locket still around her neck. She fumbled with the chain and made certain the heart rested beneath her painted T-shirt. The second she was confident of the locket's covering, Zeke rounded his van wearing a smile the size of Texas. The lines around his eyes crinkled, and that lone patch over his eye nearly prompted Brendy once again to inquire about his problem. Nevertheless, she refrained. *Probably just an irritation or something,* she mused. In his hand Zeke held a device that strongly resembled a blood-pressure-cuff ensemble—except an inflatable pillow, rather than a cuff, resided at the end of the air hose.

Brendy stepped beside him and tried to concentrate on how he would open her door. Of course, that was nearly impossible when his dancing blue gaze silently adored her. She glanced at his lips, tilted in that boyish grin, and Brendy was nearly certain he whispered, "I want to kiss you." Yet his lips never moved.

Her heart began pattering as it had when they nearly did the jitterbug in the hallway. Nearby, a woodpecker hammered a tree, and

Brendy started babbling in staccato rhythm with the bird.

"I was distracted because Sylvia called me on my cell. Sylvia, that's my part-time employee." Brendy waved her left hand. "Anyway, she called me on my cell about the time I was getting out. As soon as I shut the door, I knew my keys and purse were locked in." Her fingers flitted through the air. No matter how many times Brendy told herself to quit talking, her mouth kept moving. "But I had a teacher's meeting, so I decided to just wait until after the meeting to call."

Without a word, Zeke shifted his focus from her face to her left hand. His brows knitted, and a clever light twinkled in the baby blue eye that wasn't patched. When he got around to looking back into Brendy's face, she was breathless. "I, uh, I—I decided to take, er, to take it off. . .um. . .this morning," she stammered as a warm flush crept up her neck and burned her cheeks.

He winked and nodded, and they might as well have been sitting across from each other in algebra. "So I guess that means you might be free tomorrow night?" he queried. Zeke reclined against the mini-van and propped his arm upon the top. The lock was forgotten.

Brendy stopped herself short of a gape.

"The chamber of commerce is holding a chili supper to help raise money for beautifying downtown. I thought that maybe if you weren't busy. . ." He toyed with the strange mechanism in his hand, and Brendy sensed they had an audience.

She darted a glance to her grandchildren, who both observed this new man as if they didn't know whether he was friend or foe. Torn between the love from her past and the responsibilities of her present, Brendy wracked her brain for any reason she shouldn't accept Zeke's invitation. Her son Kent was scheduled to work at the hospital tomorrow night, and she debated whether to ask her mother to watch the children. At the age of seventy, Lila Angle could still work circles around Brendy some days. She seldom imposed upon her mom, despite the fact that Lila frequently offered her assistance. Perhaps the time had come to accept the help. Besides, Brendy needed a break. After today's teacher's conference, she was on the verge of despair over what to do with Pete.

"I'd love to go." As a gentle warmth tickled her tummy, Brendy wondered if she sounded a bit too enthusiastic.

Zeke's baritone laughter, warm as the east Texas sunshine, dashed aside any worries. "Great! Then I'll pick you up about five thirty; is that okay?"

Brendy looked at the scattered gravel, dared another glance at him, and tugged on an auburn curl. At once she felt like a coy sixteen-year-old accepting her first date. Her vague nod seemed all the answer Zeke needed.

"Good," he said. "Then it's a date."

"Hello–o–o, people!" Pete's abrupt interruption from the front of the van shattered the magical moment. "Some of us are tired of standing here."

Zeke's brow furrowed as he glanced toward the children, and Brendy thought about dissolving into an embarrassed heap. *"Pete!"* she exclaimed. "You're not supposed to address your elders like that. What is *wrong* with you?"

His bottom lip protruded while Pat walked around the van and slumped against her grandmother. A pathetic whimper reminded Brendy that she had others to consider besides herself—children who were hot and tired and ready to leave.

"I guess I *did* make the little guys stand in the sun, didn't I?" Zeke asked and directed a charming smile to Pete. "When I was growing up, after a long day at school, all I wanted to do was hit the couch and have myself some milk and cookies."

Pete eyed the friendly newcomer, and Brendy was almost certain he came close to a smile. Yet he hardened his lips and chose a glare instead. Pete hadn't been the same since his mother left, and Brendy wondered if he'd ever learn to trust again.

"This is called a Jiffy Jak." Zeke held up his interesting contraption for Brendy to see. "This little air pump inflates this pillow, like so." He pumped the ball, and Pat's attention was riveted upon the plastic pillow that began to expand. Brendy sneaked a glance toward Pete, who was trying to act disinterested.

"Here"—he extended the instrument to Pat—"hold this for me. I need to get a few more things out of my van." Pat took the gadget, and Pete could stand the suspense no longer. He trudged around the vehicle and examined this new oddity called a Jiffy Jak.

Zeke retrieved a short bar and petite wooden wedge from his van. "Brendy, I'm going to pry your door open on the side with this." He held up the bar. "I'll place the wedge in the door first so nothing is scratched or bent. In the end, there will be a space just big enough for me to insert this little air bag. Then I'll inflate the air bag, which will give me a space in the door big enough to use this." He held up a long metal rod. "This is what I'll hit your lock with, and you'll be all free. It's as simple as one, two, three," he said.

"And it won't bend my door?" Brendy asked and hated that she sounded so doubtful.

"No, ma'am." He raised three straight fingers. "Scout's honor."

"That's all I needed to hear." She lifted her chin as if she had the utmost confidence in his pledge.

Just as Zeke claimed, he had her van door opened in a few seconds. Pete even forgot to be hostile as he helped the locksmith return the fascinating tools to the van.

Finally, Zeke snapped his vehicle's sliding door in place. The kids tumbled into Brendy's van. Yet she hesitated to get in the vehicle as Zeke focused solely upon her.

When he spoke, the nuance of his voice suggested they were sharing the most intimate of secrets. "I'm really glad you called me," he muttered, and his heart was in his eye. Zeke reached toward her cheek and stopped. With an apologetic smile he dropped his hand to his side, and Brendy restrained herself from begging him to stroke her cheek anyway. She would have closed her eyes and leaned into his touch and maybe, just maybe, he would have kissed her.

"Stop it! Stop it! Stop it!" Pat screamed. "Grandmom, he's pulling my hair!"

"Well, she took my ruler!"

Brendy shook her head and tossed aside all those latent yearnings from years gone by. "I guess it's time for me to go," she said.

"Right." A ribbon of disappointment crossed Zeke's features. Features forever etched upon Brendy's heart.

A straight, prominent nose, generous mouth, and high cheekbones. Everyone in his family said he took after his paternal grandfather, who was one-half Native American. Nevertheless, he'd inherited his mother's baby blues, which contrasted handsomely with his dark hair and skin tone. Only the thin white scar from ear to chin marred his mature features. Fleetingly, Brendy wondered if the scar was related to the problem with his eye. She started to ask but didn't. Maybe tomorrow evening he'd explain.

"I. . .guess I'll be seeing you tomorrow night, then?" he asked.

"Yes, tomorrow night," Brendy agreed and hated the thought of driving off and leaving him.

"Okay then, tomorrow night," he repeated.

Brendy made no move to depart. The years since they'd shared those last stolen kisses seemed to throb between them with the poignancy of long-lost love.

Some lonely voice deep within bade her linger with this man who still seemed so much a part of her. "Unless. . . ," Brendy began. She cast a furtive glance toward her grandchildren, who were jostling into their seats and snapping seat belts. "Unless you'd like to eat with us tonight." She spoke the words as soon as they entered her mind.

"I'd *love* to," Zeke said with the same eager acceptance she'd voiced.

"Great!" she said on a breathy note and leaned against the van to keep from collapsing. "I—I've still got to go back to the shop and work until five," she rushed on. "So, um, does six sound fine?"

"You bet," he agreed. "And, instead of you cooking, why don't I run by Stacy's Barbecue and pick up the works—diced beef, plenty of sauce, coleslaw, and potato salad. I'll even dart into the Wal-Mart Super Center and get us a bag of hamburger buns."

"But I don't mind cooking—"

"Nonsense," he said and shook his head in a manner that broached no argument. "You'll be tired—just like I will. Besides"—he threw in a sly wink—"if you make a mess in the kitchen, I'll feel obligated to help clean up." His face dropped into a piteous mope. "And I don't want to wash dishes half the night. Do you?"

Brendy giggled as if they were sharing straws over a soda at the Dairy Queen. "I've got paper plates and cups. Does that work?"

"Deal." Zeke extended his hand. Brendy inserted her hand into his. As she remembered, her fingers slid into his palm as though they were made for each other. The contact that started as a handshake soon turned to a caress, and Zeke's fingers stroked her skin. His hand trembled. Brendy caught her breath. Helplessly, she gazed into the soul who had once pledged his undying faith in her. This time, when he reached to touch her cheek, he didn't stop. As the backs of his fingers grazed her face, Brendy felt as if she were sucked into a tide of what-might-have-beens, all wrapped up in a warm sheath of what-could-bes. She closed her eyes and shamelessly tilted her head into his caress.

"Hello—o—o, people!" Pete's bellow shattered the moment.

Brendy's eyes popped open. Her shoulders slumped, and she whispered a remorseful, "I'm sorry. He's got a lot to be angry about. It's a long story. I'll explain tonight."

"Well, they've got to be hot in there," Zeke said and gazed across the sunbathed countryside full of rolling hills and plenty of pines.

"Summer seems to think it's time to move on in—even though it is just the beginning of May." He squeezed her upper arm. "I'll see you in a bit. You take care of those kiddos, you hear?"

Brendy conjured her most dazzling smile and then shamelessly hoped she knocked his socks off. "We'll look for you and your barbecue at six then."

"We'll be there!"

It wasn't until after Brendy flopped into the driver's seat, cranked the engine, and turned on the air-conditioner that she realized she hadn't paid Zeke for opening her door.

I'll write him a check tonight, she thought at the same time Pat's tentative voice pierced her romantic musings.

"Grandmom, who was that man?"

"He, uh, he's just a friend from a long time ago," she answered and waved as Zeke's van rolled in front of hers. Brendy started to put the vehicle in drive but stopped at her grandson's question.

"Are you going to marry him?" Pete accused.

She looked in the rearview mirror. "Pete Lane, whatever gave you *that* idea?" she asked and felt like nothing short of a Benedict Arnold. For Brendy *had* pondered those possibilities. She had pondered them all afternoon.

In response, Pete shrugged and slumped farther down into his seat.

"Because that's what happened with Mommy," Pat answered. Pete attempted to hit her. She glowered at her brother and continued to describe what Brendy suspected but had not yet had confirmed. "She kept meeting that man she said was just a friend. But he looked at her just like that man looked at you. And then she left us to go be with him. Are you going to leave us, too?"

A stab of dread punctured Brendy's romantic musings. So her daughter-in-law *had* met her boyfriend with the children present. From the start of that horrific separation and ultimate divorce,

Brendy imagined the children might have witnessed their mom flirting with her boyfriend. Once again, Brendy wished the vixen were present so she could receive an overdue tongue-lashing from a livid mother-in-law.

She turned around and looked both children in the eyes. "Listen," she said, "nothing would *ever* make me leave you—*ever!* Understand?"

Pete's stern mouth relaxed a fraction, and Pat rubbed her nose. "Yes, ma'am," the little girl answered as if by rote. Pete looked out the window. A cloud of uncertainty emanated from them both.

With a helpless shroud encompassing her, Brendy turned back around. Out of the corner of her eye, she caught a final glimpse of Zeke's van cruising up Corinth Road.

As she put the vehicle in gear and steered the van from the parking lot, a silent war raged within. She was no longer so certain she should have readily accepted Zeke's invitation for chili or even invited him for dinner tonight. Brendy glanced in her rearview mirror and wanted to weep over the blond-headed heartaches in the backseat. Indeed, her every decision now involved more than just her. Fleetingly she wondered if she had any business reliving a past that insisted she fantasize about the future. A future that belonged to her grandchildren.

Chapter 4

The next two months swelled into a sea of stolen moments, clandestine meetings, and late-night dates. The children's welfare consumed Brendy, and Zeke honored her request to keep their relationship low-profile. Yet during that season of getting reacquainted, Zeke told Brendy of Vietnam. . .of his eye, his leg, the facial scar. . .of those awful days in recovery. . .of his trip back home. . .of the rehab nurse who became his wife. He proudly showed her pictures of his twin sons, now living in Houston, both successful businessmen; and he didn't bother to suppress the swell in his voice when he spoke of his four grandchildren. He also mentioned his wife's untimely death, although many details were too painful to recount.

Likewise Brendy shared with Zeke. She told him of her marriage to Mack. . .of her daughter, a teacher living in Henderson. . .of the daughter's rowdy-yet-delightful boys. . .of her daughter-in-law's desertion. . .of her son's hectic work schedule. She even explained her struggle against bitterness toward her former daughter-in-law. And Brendy wept through the story of her husband's heart attack and how the small Texas town had mourned the death of the favored banker and churchman.

In the midst of all the sharing and romance and support, Brendy and Zeke discovered the balm of companionship, the essence of love, the promise of matrimony. So fiercely did they fan the flames of their long-lost love, Zeke decided the time had come to propose. Neither Brendy nor he were spring chickens, by any means. They both were lonely. They had never stopped loving each other. And each hinted that they believed God Himself was restoring unto them that which had been lost.

"So why wait?" Zeke whispered to himself that Saturday night as he slid from his van on El Paso Street. He walked across the cracked sidewalk toward Brendy's house—a rambling two-story Victorian affair with more rooms than she could use. In precise fashion, he answered his own question. *Actually, I can think of two reasons to wait to get married. Their names are Pat and Pete.*

Zeke clutched the stuffed shopping bag and slowed his uneven gait. He eyed the remodeled white house with fashionable blue trim that oozed early twentieth-century character. Zeke imagined Brendy's grandchildren skipping along the wraparound porch—a porch that welcomed all with the added appeal of hanging ferns. The porch swing even danced in the hot breeze as if Pat and Pete were enjoying the ride.

Zeke shook his head and wondered what he was going to have to do to win them over. While they hadn't been overtly hostile by any means, the two still scrutinized him with the suspicion of the betrayed—and that was only on the occasions they'd *known* he was going out with their grandmother. He could only imagine their reaction if they understood the wealth of time he and Brendy were enjoying together.

The night that Zeke had taken Brendy to the chamber of commerce chili supper, Brendy explained the children's situation and even detailed the conversation at the school. "I think they're afraid you're going to take me away," she'd explained.

"I just might," Zeke had teased with an exaggerated wink and marveled at his own bravado so early in their renewed relationship.

"Oh, stop it!" Brendy slapped at his arm as if they were still going steady. "We need to be cautious about this; that's all I'm saying. I want to make sure the kids feel as secure as possible under the circumstances."

So we've been cautious, he thought. *If you call sneaking out for mid-night drives cautious.* Zeke yawned and covered his mouth. "Something's got to change," he said, "or this is going to kill me."

When Brendy invited him over to dine with her grandchildren and son, they both hoped that the children might grow accustomed to the idea of their grandmother's suitor. Yet a low rumble of thunder from the west that predicted a much-needed rain also sent a ripple of dread through Zeke.

Pete was a hard kid to reach and didn't mind sassing Brendy. Over the last couple of months, Zeke decided Pete's most pressing need was a firmer hand with discipline. The person to offer that security should have been his father. Yet Kent Lane, an RN, worked a double shift many days at the hospital. Zeke even suspected that the young man he'd only met in passing might be trying to escape his problems rather than face them. That left Brendy bearing the brunt of the responsibilities. Those issues aside, he often wondered if his attempts to win Pete would prove a loss.

As a redbird zipped between him and the house, the July heat, oppressive and humid, weighed upon him. Summer was at its height, and Zeke's thigh even perspired against his prosthesis. Mere feet from the porch steps, he maneuvered around Pat's Barbie bicycle, which had been dropped and left in the walkway.

Now that little girl was a different story. While Pete's distrust was more overt, Pat was most apt to cling to Brendy's leg and stare at Zeke with owl-like blue eyes—too big for her face, too wise for her years.

Zeke clutched the shopping bag all the tighter, climbed up the porch steps, and knocked on the front door. He was hoping maybe the toys he'd just bought would convince the children he was friend, not foe. Usually, he didn't have to resort to such measures with little ones. His own grandchildren often begged to come stay with their Pa Blake. But he was falling deeper in love with Brendy by the day and wanted nothing more than to place his wedding band on her finger. Indeed,

Zeke was a desperate man—desperate enough to prowl the aisles of Discount City until he found the perfect gifts, a new ball glove for Pete and a Barbie for Pat.

He repeated the knock, this time louder, and strained to hear signs of life. At last, the tromping of small feet paused near the door. Pete called, "Who is it?"

"It's. . ." Zeke paused and wondered if there was another name he could encourage the children to call him besides "Mr. Blake." The formality of the surname suggested he was not a part of their family. "It's Mr. Zeke," he said and hoped one day to change that to Grandpa Zeke—and then maybe just Grandpa.

The door creaked open, and Pete observed him through the screen. Pat hovered behind as usual, and Zeke felt as if he were a bungling nineteen-year-old, being examined by a prospective father-in-law. *The years certainly have a way of changing the roles,* he thought with a hint of frantic humor.

"Grandmom's in the kitchen," Pete said as he unlatched the screen door. "We'll tell her you're here."

Before Zeke had the chance to even mention his gifts, the straw-headed twosome turned as one and darted from the doorway. Zeke opened the screen door that squawked on resistant hinges. Before the night was over, he planned to retrieve the can of WD40 from his van and spray those hinges. The smell of smothered steak sent a growl through his belly as Zeke secured the door and meandered into the den. The spacious room with high ceilings and a marble fireplace appeared to have once been a decorator's paradise. Yet the shades on the brass lamps now hung crooked. A tea stain ringed the mauve love seat. And the center of the floor looked like a glorified playroom, replete with building blocks scattered all the way to the recliner, where he gratefully dropped.

Shaking his head, Zeke remembered the days of raising kids. In fact, he and his wife decided there was no use buying new furniture until the boys were grown. The country decor Zeke now used had been the product of Madeline's shopping spree the week their nest was officially empty. Yet she hadn't lived much longer to enjoy it.

A melancholic ache pierced Zeke's heart as he flipped the recliner's handle and relaxed into the chair's comforting folds. He hadn't thought of Maddy's untimely departure in days. And he thanked the Lord that this time the pain wasn't quite as sharp.

As he gazed toward the gurgling goldfish tank atop a Queen Anne side table, his drowsy mind drifted to Brendy. An evening listening to her melodious voice and touching her soft face promised the balm to heal all hurts, all disappointments, all lost dreams. His heavy eyes closed, and he pondered the possibilities of making her a permanent part of his world. . .waking to her laughter, sharing her love for gourmet coffee and chocolate, delighting in the union that would make them man and wife.

In the middle of his fantasies, Zeke's skin crawled like it had the day those checkers kings were giving him the once-over. He barely lifted one eyelid and attempted to validate his suspicions of two short spies. To his left, he noted a couple of half-faces peering around a hallway door. Both had silky, blond hair, light tans, and keen blue eyes. Neither made a sound.

Zeke struggled to contain his amusement over the intensity of their gazes and hoped this might be the beginning of a friendship. "Hi, Pete and Pat," he said without a move. "Come on in."

With a jerk, the youngsters disappeared. Zeke kept watching. After a couple of minutes they came back. He figured his eyes, barely opened, appeared to be closed to the kids. He could only imagine their minds racing with how he could see them. He fumbled for the shopping bag and found it near the recliner's handle. "I brought you guys some toys." He lifted the bag yet didn't alter his position.

Pete's face disappeared again, but Pat crept out and stood in the doorway. Her face glowed with hesitant curiosity, and she inserted her index finger into her mouth. Zeke nearly roared with victory. He opened his eyes and slowly lowered the recliner's leg rest. As he was floundering with the bag, a hand reached out and tugged on the back of Pat's short set. She stumbled from sight.

Zeke's momentary victory deflated to despair when he caught a snatch of their hushed, yet urgent, argument. "But I want to see my toy," Pat's little voice pleaded.

"It's a trick! Don't you see?" Pete reasoned. "Now we're going back out there and telling him. . ."

The rest jumbled into urgent hissing, and Zeke peered into the blue plastic bag. The gifts he so hoped would speak his heart now seemed foolish and trite. He dug to the bottom in search of the receipt and tucked it into the pocket of his dress shirt. *Looks like I might be returning these,* he groused. Zeke patted the shirt pocket on a final note and felt the bulge of the tiny chain he'd placed there before leaving home.

Somehow in the rush and thrill of this raging romance, Zeke had failed to mention the key he still owned. Only when he'd seen the locket around Brendy's neck yesterday had he recalled that he placed the key in the porcelain dish on his dresser. Zeke had planned to give her the key tonight after dinner—when he proposed. He smiled and hoped the locket still opened after all these years.

A movement near the doorway diverted his mind back to the present problem—two motherless children who looked at him like he was the boogeyman. Pat hedged into the living room with Pete close behind. Her head bowed and lips pursed, she stopped so abruptly that Pete ran into her.

Zeke clasped the store bag and tried to decide whether to hold firm to the front line or retreat.

"We don't want your gifts," Pete proclaimed as if he were a secret agent rejecting the assistance of the enemy.

Zeke's shoulders slumped, and he grappled for something to

say—anything. Despite all his good intentions, his frustration mounted to aggravation. The child's torn jeans and smudged T-shirt looked like he'd been duking it out with the boy next door. And Zeke wondered if the child thought he could bully him as well. *Not in my lifetime,* he thought with a twist of his lips. *I'm tired of being pushed around by a half-pint!*

"You're just trying to fool us!" Pete accused, his brows furrowed.

"No, I'm not!" Zeke denied, and every child-rearing book he'd ever read disappeared from memory.

The boy's chest protruded as if he were bravely enduring the enemy's camp. "You want us to forget what you're doin'."

"Exactly *what* am I doing?" Zeke pulled on his pants leg and leaned forward. He told himself he really wasn't heading into hand-to-hand combat. Still, his hackles rose as if he were facing the front line in Vietnam.

"It's about Grandmom!"

Pat retreated to Pete's side and hovered behind him. Zeke wondered if the little girl were trying to get out of the line of fire.

"You're always botherin' her." A furious flush tinged Pete's tanned cheeks.

"Bothering her?" Zeke responded and felt like a brainless parrot.

"She spends all her time fixin' up for you!" He stomped his foot.

"Sounds to me like she *likes* me to bother her, then," Zeke claimed and narrowed an eye at the boy. The army never taught him how to deal with enemies this short.

"And she cooks special stuff for you, too." As if to punctuate the child's claim, the scent of freshly brewing coffee mingled with the smell of smothered steak. Like a warrior upon the brink of victory, Pete crossed his arms and glowered at his foe.

Zeke, grappling for a defense tactic, dashed a glance at Pat, whose giant orbs drifted toward the store bag now at Zeke's feet. He didn't stop the slow smile from lifting the corners of his mouth. "I got you a Barbie set," Zeke explained and focused on the little girl. He withdrew the doll, replete with three changes of clothing and extended it toward Pat.

"Don't take it!" Pete commanded like a desperate general. He turned on Zeke and hurled a stream of words like the fire of a machine gun. "You think you can make us like you with gifts, but it *won't work!*"

"Pete Lane!" Brendy's breathless gasp reverberated around the room. Zeke looked at the woman of his dreams. Flour dusted her floral apron and copper curls. Her rounded eyes, at first bewildered, ultimately glared bullets at her grandson. Any minute, Zeke expected her to crouch, run forward, and pluck him from the enemy's mortal trap.

Zeke didn't give her the chance. Instead, he stood and moved to her side. He knew a good rescue team member when he saw one, and Brendy Lane was as skillful as *any* he'd welcomed in the army.

Chapter 5

Brendy scrutinized her grandson's hostile face. A barrage of options hurled themselves at her. She didn't know whether to send him to his room, try to ease his fears, or cry. Brendy felt that the more she tried to encourage Pete to like Zeke, the more he resisted. The more he resisted, the more Pat was likewise hindered. Last night, when she told Pete that Zeke was coming for dinner, he stomped to his room, slammed the door, and didn't come out for an hour. This morning at 2:00 a.m., a sobbing Pat crawled into bed with Brendy. She claimed she'd had a nightmare in which Brendy threw her away. And Brendy, groggy and angry, had wanted to share a piece of her mind with that mother of Pat's.

As Brendy stroked her apron, Zeke placed a hand in the small of her back and leaned toward her. "Let's go into the kitchen," he whispered, and his mint-tinged breath tickled her nose. "I'll help you finish."

"But. . ." Brendy gazed into Zeke's eyes. The patch was long gone, and he now wore the prosthesis. The blue eye so resembled his other eye that Brendy had to remind herself that he couldn't see out of it.

Zeke's response was a jerk of his head toward the kitchen. "I have a plan," he mumbled, as if they were dropping behind enemy lines and pausing to orchestrate their strategy.

With a nod Brendy led the way through the dining area and into the room she adored because cooking was one of her favorite pastimes. The smell of smothered steak, candied carrots, tomato basil soup, steamed wild rice, and broccoli made even *her* mouth water. Before turning to Zeke, Brendy grabbed a spoon, stirred the steaming carrots, and flipped off the electric burner.

His eyes rolled, and he clutched his gut. "Forget the kids. Let's just *eat!*"

Brendy giggled as a warm glow infused her being. "Here." She lifted the lid off of a pot of broccoli and cheese, dipped a sample into a bowl and extended it to Zeke. "You can eat while we talk."

"A woman after my own heart," Zeke purred. He set the plastic bag on the kitchen counter, cluttered with a cutting board and carrot tops, and he took the bowl without a hint of protest. His gaze trailed toward the neckline of Brendy's denim jumper, and he broke into a smile that would have stopped traffic in downtown Dallas.

She touched the locket hanging around her neck by a new gold chain. Brendy had taken the piece to Lang's Jewelry last week to have it polished. To her surprise, the jeweler told her the heart was actually ten-carat gold. The chain, however, was only gold plated and too far gone to be salvaged.

"It's time for me to set the table," Brendy said and dared to dash him a saucy wink. Her womanly intuition suggested that Zeke was on the verge of proposing. She wanted tonight to be extra special, and she even set out her best crystal, along with polished silver and Noritake china. Once before, she had squandered an opportunity with Zeke. Brendy was not about to do that again. Therefore, she had designed this evening to show how deeply their renewed love permeated her heart.

"Wait!" Zeke snared her hand and tugged her back to his side. "We need to talk about *them*," he insisted and jerked his head toward the living room.

"Oh! I'm so scattered I was distracted the minute I got in here. I've lived from one crisis to another today, and I'm starting to get ditzy." She touched her temple. "Maybe it's just that, these days, Pete lives from one blowup to the next, and I'm starting to tune it all out once I leave the room." She shrugged and shook her head. "I guess maybe it's just my way of surviving all this."

"Here's what I think," Zeke said. "You might be onto something smart. Let's ignore his negative behavior. I think if we major on it, we're validating it. Let's continue with our plans, and when he erupts, we'll just smile and keep on truckin'."

Brendy concentrated on his advice, and the longer he talked, the more the idea made sense. "I guess it's like ignoring a child who throws a fit," she said. "What they want is attention, and they're trying to get it no matter what. If you ignore the fit, then they aren't successful."

"Exactly."

Brendy nodded and examined the stack of pots and pans piled in the kitchen sink. "Might work," she said and toyed with the hem of her apron. "And maybe we haven't been doing anybody a favor by sneaking around so much. Maybe the thing that would be best for the children is to see us together as often as possible. Eventually, they'll *have* to realize you're safe, and I'm not going anywhere."

Zeke set the bowl of broccoli on the counter and gripped Brendy's upper arms. "Those are the most beautiful words I've ever heard," he said as if she'd just uttered a melodic poem. "This crazy courtship is going to *kill* me if we have to keep sneaking around. I can't do very many more late-night trips to the Dairy Queen." His forehead wrinkled, and the dark circles under his eyes validated his claims.

A burst of laughter erupted from Brendy, and she laid a hand on his face. "I'm tired, too," she admitted and massaged the small of her back. Brendy didn't elaborate on the fact that she was not only physically exhausted, but mentally and emotionally spent as well. Add to that the perpetual spiritual battle against bitterness toward her daughter-in-law, and Brendy wasn't certain she could take another crisis without falling apart.

He pulled her into the circle of his strong arms, and Brendy relished the faint scent of Brut. She believed he'd worn that after-shave when they were dating. Brendy rested her cheek on his chest, closed her eyes, and imagined them standing near the weeping willow tree at Lake Jacksonville. They were both eighteen. . .care-free. . .and looking forward to a fulfilling life together. If she fantasized enough, Brendy could nearly convince herself she really didn't have the responsibility of two heartbroken grandchildren—that she and Zeke could elope any day they wished.

The creak of the hardwood floor preceded someone clearing his throat. Brendy jumped away from Zeke as if she'd been caught in the most heinous of crimes. She glanced toward her son who entered from the hallway, toweling his hair dry. Kent offered Zeke a cool greeting, and Brendy couldn't deny the trace of caution in her son's eyes. She busied herself around the stove as if she were a teenager caught necking on the front porch.

Kent moved toward his mom and paused by the oven, as if he were ravenous. The look on his face said enough. Brendy smiled up at him. "Dinner's on in about five minutes," she explained.

"Great. I'm starving," he admitted and eyed the mound of wild rice sitting in the middle of the stove. He draped the damp towel around his neck, and the ends settled upon the front of his Jacksonville College tank top.

Everyone said Kent was the spit and image of his father—the blond hair, the full lips, the brown eyes, the developed physique, lean yet muscular. All that was a big part of the problem. Kent had had his share of ladies after him from the time he was in junior high school. Brendy often wondered why, of all the sensible girls he could have chosen, he wound up with the one who was fickle, foolish, and more in love with herself than her family.

"Where are the kids?" Kent asked.

"I think they're in the living room," Brendy said and cast a cautious gaze to Zeke.

"No. I just checked in there," Kent said. "I couldn't find them anywhere in the house."

"Think they went outside?" Zeke asked.

Kent moved to the back door and tugged aside the cheerful checked curtain, the color of currants. "Yep. That's exactly where they are. They're playing in the dirt."

"Oh, no, not now," Brendy moaned. "Dinner's only five minutes away." She moved toward the doorway. "I'll call—"

Zeke gripped her arm and shook his head. "Let *him* take care of it," he whispered. "They're *his* kids."

Brendy blinked and stared at Zeke as the implications of his words penetrated her scattered mind. In a instant, she relived the tension since Kent's wife deserted the family. From the day her son moved in and started working insane hours, she'd been both mother and father to those children. Even when Kent was around, she stepped forward to parent them. Maybe Zeke was right. Perhaps the time *had* come to enable her son to be their father.

"On second thought," Brendy said, "I really need to set the table, Kent. I'll let you go ahead and get them cleaned up, okay?"

"Sure," he said and opened the back door.

Zeke gave Brendy the thumbs-up sign and then said, "What can I do to help?"

❁

Zeke settled at the oval oak table he and Brendy had set. He admired her ability to create divine dinners and make the spread look like a centerfold from *Good Housekeeping*. Zeke knew for a fact that her love of cooking began in the kitchen with her mother, who never minded when Brendy brought him home for dinner. During their high school courtship, Brendy often sat across the table smiling at her beau while her brothers silently eyed him, as Kent was doing now.

One Saturday evening Brendy even stated, "I helped Mamma

make the shrimp gumbo." A monstrous stainless steel pot had commanded the table's center and issued the exotic aromas of peppers, onions, celery, and garlic. Brendy's mom was a Cajun girl from southwest Louisiana, and one of Brendy's favorite dishes was still gumbo.

But tonight she had prepared a different kind of feast. Instead of gumbo, a steaming bowl of tomato basil soup claimed the center of each of the exquisite china plates. She even remembered to place a sprig of parsley in the center of each bowl. Zeke gazed upon the spread and realized he had not yet tasted a bite of the broccoli and cheese that Brendy had spooned out for him earlier. He spotted the broccoli, residing in a crystal bowl on Kent's side of the table, and decided to get an extra helping when it came his way.

Meanwhile, Zeke toyed with the tiny key he'd retrieved from the pocket of his dress shirt. Seeing that locket had made him decide a different way to give the key to Brendy. He hoped she'd be as delighted with his clever plan as he was. Zeke had never considered himself a romantic, but lately he was doing well by anybody's standards. Brendy hinted a time or two that if she ever got married again she would prefer a simple gold band, so Zeke had refrained from buying an engagement ring. However, he wanted to do *something* to commemorate the moment. The key was his answer.

"Where are Pete and Pat?" Brendy asked. She placed a basket of home-baked rolls near the smothered steak; then she claimed her spot between Zeke and her son.

Kent rose from his high-backed chair. "I left them washing their hands and told them to make it quick," he mumbled.

He hadn't taken one step before the two children hurried from the hallway and clambered into their chairs. "There they are," Kent said and dashed a smile as the two sat across from each other. Pete, settling beside Zeke, smiled back as if he'd received the best prize of the whole evening.

At once, Zeke figured Pete would turn down a whole truckload of ball gloves for a little time with his father. His heart went out to the troubled eight-year-old, and he despaired that he would ever break through the child's barriers.

Brendy, at the head of the table, looked at Zeke and said, "Would you give thanks?"

He smiled at Pete and Pat, who returned his appraisal with near-angelic gazes. Suspicion set bells of caution pealing through Zeke's mind—much like the shriek of a horn during an enemy's raid. Pat wiggled like she had a bug in her drawers, and Pete shot her a stare that would freeze a bonfire. Zeke glanced to Brendy. One of her finely penciled brows cocked upward, and a glimmer of speculation marred her jade green eyes. Zeke's quick look toward Kent revealed a father who was innocently placid.

Or maybe so out of touch he's oblivious, Zeke thought, then scolded himself. *I'm probably just imagining things.* With no more deliberation, he decided to go ahead and pray. Out of habit, he began reaching to hold hands and stopped himself from reaching toward Pete. *He probably would rather eat a skunk than hold my hand,* he thought.

With the key in his palm, he extended his hand toward Brendy. When she slipped her hand in his, the symbol of their past warmed between them. He detected her faint gasp as he began the simple prayer. When he pronounced a resounding "Amen," he cut her a glance and winked at her.

She smiled back, examined the tiny scrap of metal, and looked at him as if he were the most wonderful man alive. On an impulse Zeke nearly stole a kiss but thought better of it—especially when he noticed Kent eyeing him like a disapproving father-in-law. While Zeke wanted to run around the room and shout, *I'm in love! I'm in love!* he chose instead to refrain and eat his soup like a respectable guest.

First, he indulged in a slow drink of the iced tea from his crystal goblet and reveled in the cool southern sweetness. When he replaced the goblet, Zeke noted the children were attacking their soup with more urgency than he expected—especially considering they were kids and this *was* tomato basil. Indeed, their little faces were nearly buried in the creamy liquid. Zeke's gaze met Brendy's, and the two of them shared a private communication as strong as any spoken word. The suspicions from before the prayer were surfacing again. Those two were up to something.

Zeke decided his best bet was to eat and mind his own business. As he prepared to remove the sprig of parsley from the center of his soup, he noted that the parsley had disappeared. *That's strange*, he thought. With an inward shrug, Ezekiel dipped his soup spoon into the creamy mixture, and the parsley surfaced with an extra bit of protein. In fact, a writhing night crawler the size of a small snake hung on either side of his spoon.

"Oh, my word!" Brendy gasped.

A deathly silence settled upon the table—a silence broken only by the clank of the children's spoons against their bowls as they continued gobbling the soup at lightning speed. After the initial surprise, Zeke eyed the creature and debated his options. His recent speech to Brendy about ignoring negative behavior flitted through his mind, yet Zeke somehow couldn't bring himself to pretend this incident hadn't happen.

As silence reigned, the worm turned until it lay across the handle's shank. Like a snake captured on a hook, the poor thing had maneuvered to a position of hanging equal parts of head and tail on either side. No amount of squeezing its tiny muscles made a difference.

Zeke eyed the intruder and jumped into a dialogue he'd never planned. "Well, I'll be switched. Where you been, Willie?" he exclaimed. "I've looked all over the house for you." Zeke extended the night crawler toward Pete.

Pat stopped eating and, with a horror-struck expression, stared as Pete scooted to the far edge of his seat. Sensing he had the element of surprise to his favor, Zeke moved the spoon to his ear and pretended to be listening. "What's that you say?" he asked, and his attention rested upon Kent, who had begun a low snicker.

Pete gaped at Zeke, his face covered with a mixture of dread and shock. Certainly, this turn of events was obviously not what he had anticipated.

Zeke, pointing at Willie, leaned toward Pete and whispered, "He says he wants to be your friend, Pete." He stopped and held up a hand. "No, wait! Now he's saying that's not what he meant. He's saying he wants you to eat him."

Kent's snickers exploded into outright laughter as Zeke stood and held the spoon over Pete's head. The worm sashayed back and forth as if he were in the midst of a delightful swing. The child looked up and screamed, "Nooooooo!" at the same time the worm slipped off the spoon. The creature landed with a splat of tomato soup on Pete's upper lip and flopped into his mouth.

An ominous hush claimed the table for but a second as the realization of what just happened sank into one and all. About the time Zeke started to stutter out an apology, Pete spat the worm into his soup bowl and began gagging. His face grew scarlet as the gags turned to near-convulsions.

Pat screamed as if Zeke were threatening to cut off her head. She yanked on her hair and started howling. "Don't let him, Grandmom! Don't let that mean man make me eat a worm!" A hysterical fit followed with such shrieks that anyone from miles around would assume the child was being beaten to death.

Brendy rose from her chair and scooped the little girl into her arms. She scowled at Zeke and crammed the locket key back into his hand. "How *could* you?" she demanded.

"Wait a minute!" Zeke responded. "I didn't do that on purpose. You should know me well enough to know it was an accident. I didn't mean any harm. I wasn't going to—"

A desperate gurgling interrupted his disclaimer, and Zeke looked at Pete. The child was chugalugging his crystal goblet full of tea as Pat snuggled her head against Brendy's shoulder and whimpered. Her face flushing, Brendy clutched her granddaughter, pushed past Zeke, and neared Pete.

Zeke, ready to convince the world of his innocence, silently beseeched Kent with the most virtuous expression he could muster. But Kent didn't even notice. He was doubled over his soup, laughing so hard he was heaving. Brendy cleared her throat and cut another glare to her son. After catching her eye, Kent possessed the decency to stumble from his chair toward the kitchen. As Pete doused his mouth with the remaining tea, Zeke decided he was safer with Kent than Brendy.

Yet the minute he stepped into the kitchen, he knew he had miscalculated the equation. Kent collapsed against the kitchen door and held his gut. "I can't stop," he gasped. The spacious kitchen reverberated with guffaws as Kent swiped at the tears streaming his cheeks.

Despite Zeke's desire to remain serious, Kent's laughter proved contagious. He started with a mild chortle. Zeke scratched the back of his neck and tried to compose himself in the face of unexpected hilarity. Indeed, the more he thought about Pete's expression when he realized a worm was in his mouth, the less self-control he possessed.

"Did you see the look on his face?" Kent gasped.

And Zeke could contain his laughter no longer. "It was like—like something on *The Little Rascals*," he finally said and rested his heaving body against the cluttered counter.

Kent pointed at Zeke and nodded his head. "Exactly. All—all he needed was a cowlick, sticking straight up, and—"

"He could be Alfalfa!" Zeke finished. He pressed his eyes and told himself he needed to get a grip, but the more he tried, the harder he laughed.

That is, until Brendy came into the kitchen. "Excuse me!" she demanded, and both men went rigid as if snapping to attention for the most demanding of generals.

Chapter 6

Wiping his eyes, Zeke was reminded of a mother bear ready to take on an army for the cause of her cubs. *Oh boy*, he thought, *we're heading for trouble.*

First, Brendy looked at her son and snarled, "If you have no more respect for your children than this—"

"Mom," Kent said and raised his hand, "he had it coming." A low-key chuckle rumbled out. "If he's going to put worms in people's soup, then he should expect some consequences. Maybe—" He pressed his lips together until they wobbled. "Maybe it was an act of God!" The very idea hurled both men into another fit of hilarity.

"Go to your room!" Brendy yelled.

"What?" Kent responded and pointed to his chest. "I'm nearly thirty, and those kids are *mine!*"

"Fine, then," Brendy growled. "Go somewhere else where they can't hear you laughing them to scorn! This is probably the most humiliating moment of Pete's life. The last thing he needs is—"

"If you think he's humiliated, think how the worm must feel," Kent said and howled at his own joke.

Struggling to contain his laughter, Zeke turned his back, crammed his knuckles against his lips, and hunched his shoulders.

Zeke figured the joke only added fuel to Brendy's rage, but he couldn't stop the snickers. When he felt her turn on him, he decided he'd rather face the fire than take a hit from behind. As he swiveled, Zeke encountered the worst feminine weapon of them all—*tears!* He groaned within and knew he'd just lost the battle.

"And you!" Brendy pointed at his nose. "A grown man, a grand-father yourself, terrifying—"

"Wait a minute, honey," Zeke said and rubbed the key between his forefinger and thumb. "You know I didn't do any of that on purpose. It was an *accident*." The back door slammed. Zeke glanced over his shoulder. Kent had left him to face the interrogation alone. *A fine backup you turned out to be,* he thought.

"Well, the least you could do is have the decency not to laugh at them. They've been through enough already without—" She stopped and scrubbed at her eyes.

"Ah, Brendy," Zeke said and tried to place his arms around her.

"No!" She pushed him away and shook her head. "I think it would be best right now for you to just *go home!*"

"What? But I haven't even eaten!" Despite the upheaval, his stomach rumbled.

She crossed her arms. "Just leave," she repeated and pointed toward the door through which Kent had exited.

Mutely, Zeke extended the key toward her in an attempt to at least symbolize a future reconciliation.

"No." She pushed his hand away. Her copper curls swayed around her cheeks. Her chin jutted forward.

And Zeke knew arguing with her would be like trying to argue with a rabid bulldog. Never one to back down from a challenge, he decided to argue anyway. He wasn't afraid of bulldogs and never had been. "Brendy, I think you're overreacting here," he began on a serious note. "It was just a *worm*." He bit down hard on the end of his tongue as he recalled Pete's chugalugging the tea.

"J—just a worm?" She pointed toward the dining room. "Pat is scared stiff you're going to make her eat one, too! She even had a nightmare last night, Zeke! She dreamed I threw her away! She's worried sick that I'm going to choose you over her, and now she'll probably have nightmares about you forcing worms down her throat!"

"Why didn't you *tell* me about her dream?" he asked. "I didn't have to come tonight if—"

"Because. . .because. . ." Brendy moved toward the stove and placed a hand on the ledge. "Because I thought—thought that maybe we could work through it all. But now, I just don't know," she agonized. Twining her fingers together, she pivoted to face him again. "You and I both know this is about much. . .much more than just tonight, Ezekiel!" She took a deep breath, fumbled with the clasp on the locket, and Zeke's heart nearly hit his feet. "It's about the well-being of two tormented little souls who've been abandoned once." The locket hung from her fingers and sashayed between them like a pendulum ticking off the seconds until their relationship was over. "And I can't stand the thought of them being abandoned again. I just can't!" she wheezed out.

"Who said anything about abandoning them?" he reasoned. "I can move in here! We'll all be one happy family."

"Yeah, us and the worms!" she huffed and tossed the locket at him.

Zeke caught it, and the scrap of gold seemed as cold as ice. "Well, I'm not planning on any more worms," he said and couldn't quite believe Brendy was actually breaking up with him.

"I was crazy to think this would work." She shook her head as cascades of moisture christened her cheeks.

"But, Brendy. . ."

"The thing that's important here, Zeke Blake, is those children." She pointed toward the dining room again.

Zeke looked past her to see one of Pete's eyes peering around the facing. *Déjà vu,* he thought and detected a glimmer of triumph in the child's eye.

"And I cannot allow them to suffer due to my own selfishness."

"Suffer?" Zeke squeaked. "The person who's suffering here is *me!*" He ground all five fingers against his chest and couldn't quite absorb the pain. Zeke suspected that would all come later. "I'll tell you what's happening, Brendy Lane," he added and squared his shoulders. That little scamp might *think* he was winning, but Ezekiel Blake didn't plan to go down without a fight. "I'll tell you what's happening," he repeated with deliberation. "That child is ruling your life, and you're letting him. He gets what he wants anytime he wants, and you think because he's—he's 'injured'"—Zeke drew invisible quote marks in midair—"that he shouldn't be disciplined."

"I discipline him," she shot back.

"Not like he needs!" Zeke boomed. "I've seen enough to know—"

"This is not the army!" she declared.

"Nobody said it *should* be." Zeke raised both hands. "I just don't think it's right to reward a child for a prank by running off the victim."

"Oh, so now *you're* the victim." She crossed her arms and raised her eyebrows.

"Well, yeah! That *was* my soup!"

"Grandmom," Pete said from the doorway, "Pat's cryin' again."

Without a word Brendy turned toward the dining room. When she passed through the doorway, Pete popped his head around the facing and stuck his tongue out at Zeke. His pug nose crinkled, and his cherry red lips formed a perfect *O* around that pink tongue.

A flash of heat exploded from Zeke's gut, and he took a step toward the brat. "Why, you little. . ."

With a yelp, Pete ran after his grandmother, and Zeke decided to stomp out before he did something he would later regret. No sooner had the door banged after him than he nearly ran over Kent. The young man stood with his hands in his pockets, gazing at the row of pine trees along the backyard fence. Zeke resisted projecting his ire for Pete's behavior upon Kent, but the temptation nearly proved too strong. He came within a breath of blurting, *That imp you call your son just stuck his tongue out at me!* Yet Kent spoke before

Zeke opened his mouth.

"Mom's really stressed out," he said without ever looking at Zeke.

"Yep," Zeke said, and the simple response hid his exasperation. He settled onto his good leg and wished the mosquitoes weren't so fond of humid climates. He swatted at one of the pests already nipping at his arm and figured he'd be sweating like a sow by the time the next mosquito struck. The clouds that had been on the horizon when he arrived were now boiling across the sky. About the time Zeke was ready to tell Kent the time had come to be the father his children needed, a particularly nasty cloud blotted out the sun and offered a hint of relief from the evening heat.

"I guess. . ." Kent rubbed his hands together and cut a look at Zeke. "I guess I've been leaving most of, well, everything to her," he said.

"Yep," Zeke agreed and decided this might be one of the easiest conversations in which he'd ever participated. As his irritation began to wane, he examined the locket against his palm and thought about throwing the thing away. Zeke didn't want the golden heart around the house, tormenting him every time he saw it. And he sure wasn't going to be sentimental enough to keep the locket or key this time. Perhaps Brendy was right. Maybe they were both foolhardy to think they could impose their relationship of the past upon the problems of the present.

"Maybe I should give her some time off," Kent mused and noticed the gold glimmering against Zeke's callused palm. "Did she, like, break up with you?" he blurted.

"Yep," Zeke answered.

"Oh, man, I'm so sorry." Wide-eyed, Kent looked squarely into Zeke's face. For the first time Zeke sensed the young man saw him—actually saw him—as more than just an irritation in his life.

Yeah, I'm a real human being just like you are, Zeke wanted to say. *And I hurt just like you did when your wife left you.* Nevertheless, the hollow spot in his heart offered only numbness; and Ezekiel hoped he didn't start hurting—*really hurting*—until he got home.

"She's just mad right now," Kent said on a consoling note. "She'll get over it."

This time, Zeke couldn't answer yep. Indeed, all his yeps were gone. He sighed and trudged past Kent. "I guess I'll head on over to the Sonic and get me a hamburger," he mumbled. The thought of fast food after seeing Brendy's meal was anticlimactic, to say the least.

"Wait!" Kent grabbed his arm. "Wait here—just a minute." He held up his finger. "I'll go in and fix you the best take-home meal you've ever had. I know where Mom keeps the paper plates. She's got some really *big* ones too." He produced a sizable oval with his hands.

Zeke figured the decent thing to do was politely decline, but his stomach thought otherwise. "Okay," he heard himself say. "And go heavy on the steak and broccoli, will ya?"

"Sure thing."

Kent was as good as his word. He came back in a jiffy with a plate piled high and covered with Saran Wrap. The curtain on the back door inched aside as if someone were checking on him. Zeke wondered if Brendy helped with the platter. He decided her helping was merely the humanitarian thing to do. After all, he was now a prisoner of war, banished from the home he wanted to be a part of. Even POWs deserved to eat.

"I appreciate you, Kent," Zeke said. "I really do."

"No problem." He laid a hand on Zeke's shoulders. "Sometimes, we men need to stick together." He smiled, and the two made eye contact long enough to remember the worm splattering tomato soup on Pete's upper lip, then flopping into his mouth. Both men burst into a spontaneous guffaw.

"He really looked just like Alfalfa." Zeke coughed over the words.

"I'll never forget that as long as I live." Kent groaned. "I think my stomach's probably going to be sore tomorrow."

Narrowing his eyes, Zeke decided that since they were doing all this male bonding he ought to usher in a heavy dose of brutal honesty. "Well, put this one in your hopper," he added, "and it's really not funny."

"Okay, what?" Kent asked.

"Pete just stuck his tongue out at me."

"No way!" Kent's heavy brows furrowed over astonished eyes.

"Yep," Zeke said. "He heard your mother tell me to get lost, and I guess he figured he'd won."

"Did Mom see him?"

"Nope. He made sure she couldn't see. But. . ." Zeke nudged a rock with the tip of his boot.

"What?" Kent prompted.

"Think she would have done anything if she *had* seen him?" Zeke continued.

Kent placed hands on hips and glowered at a wild rosebush near the back door. The winds off the approaching storm whipped through the trees and ushered in the smell of rain.

"Well, I, uh, guess I need to go on home before I get drenched," Zeke said. A fat raindrop crashed into his forehead, and the sound of approaching rain propelled him to action. "See ya later," he called over his shoulder as he raced around the house toward his van. He hoped he really *did* see Kent later but somehow doubted the likelihood.

Chapter 7

Tuesday morning, Brendy dragged into the Friend-Shop at 7:30 a.m. The store didn't open until nine, yet Brendy came in early just to have some peace. Yesterday, Kent labored a double shift, and Brendy took Pete and Pat to work with her. When the two started wrestling and knocked over a display of homemade jelly, Brendy decided to go home. She left Sylvia in charge of the store. The day went downhill from there. Pete, bent on a fight, wound up taking down the next door neighbor's son. Pat, on the other hand, refused to do anything but follow Brendy around the house all day as if she were terrified to let Brendy out of her sight. By the time Kent arrived home last night, Brendy was ready to pull her hair out.

"I'm off for a week now, Mom," Kent had said. "And you need some free time." He'd scooped the children up and headed toward the front door. On his way out, Kent called, "And just so you know, come this weekend I'm taking them to Six Flags." Pat and Pete had gone into an excited screaming fit while Kent whisked them away. Brendy had no idea where they went for the next few hours, and she was asleep when they came back home. This morning when she awoke, Brendy still experienced the overwhelming urge to escape—even though she had spent the previous evening alone.

I think I'm chronically exhausted, she mused and decided that was the only reason she could feel so draggy after ten hours of sleep. She fumbled through the walnut-stained cabinets for the raspberry mocha coffee and prepared to make her favorite brew. After spooning the grounds into the coffeemaker, Brendy folded her arms, and then rested her forehead on her fingertips. Soon the smell of raspberries and chocolate filled the small kitchen. Brendy eyed the stainless steel appliances she scrubbed down nearly every night and wondered if she'd make it until the end of this day.

She filled her cup and meandered toward her cluttered office. As she entered, Brendy stepped over the pile of clothing she told Pete to take home yesterday. Shaking her head, Brendy wondered if her body had waited until the minute Kent took off work to flop. She also wondered about the various influences that propelled him to that decision.

Kent never mentioned what he and Zeke talked about Saturday night, and Brendy hadn't asked. *Probably me.* She took a deep swallow of her coffee, shoved back a section of wayward hair, and settled into her desk chair. A dabble of irritation marred her spirit, and she could only imagine what the two men must have said. While sneaking a peek out the back window, Brendy felt nothing short of betrayed by the both of them—as if Kent and Zeke were siding against her. After preparing that plate for Zeke, she'd been sorely tempted to take it out to him herself and set them both straight again. Nevertheless, Brendy had refused. *There's no reason to pick another fight,* she'd thought that night.

Now, Brendy wondered if she overreacted Saturday night. She had been so frazzled she wasn't certain she dealt rationally with the whole ordeal. By the time she tucked Pete and Pat in for the night, Brendy had still been aggravated at Zeke and Kent. Yet the brunt of her fury had been directed toward her ex-daughter-in-law.

She balled her fists. *This whole mess we're in is her fault!* However, dwelling on the abandonment did little to relieve her fatigue. Indeed, her negative thoughts only heaped more stress upon her drained spirit.

Massaging the back of her neck, Brendy was engulfed in a cloud of loneliness, dense and unrelenting. She rearranged the folds of the denim jumper she had worn Saturday night and couldn't deny she missed Zeke—missed him as bad as she had the weeks after he left for boot camp.

The oak desk's bottom drawer was lodged open, and Brendy eyed the stack of receipts she'd dropped in last night. The edge of a keepsake box peeked from behind the pile. Brendy hadn't looked inside the box since that day two months ago when she retrieved the locket, and her heart bade her revisit the contents.

Grinding her teeth, Brendy slammed the drawer closed and turned instead to the worn Bible atop her desk. A lone dog yapped nearby as their striped cat, Tiger-Higer, sashayed into the office as if he were the king of the joint. He plopped his overstuffed self squarely in the middle of Brendy's desk and attempted to rub his face against hers. Without a smile, Brendy scratched the purring cat's ears and placed him back on the floor. She then turned to the rare treat of reading her Bible without an interruption.

But for some reason Brendy couldn't open the Word of God today. She laid her hand upon the leather-bound book and stared at the gold letters until they blurred. Instead, all she could think of was the keepsake box in the bottom drawer. She grabbed her coffee and marched to one of the spacious windows. Brendy rested her forehead against the cool pane and stared blindly at the flower shop across the street.

Out of nowhere a gray van cruised down the street beside her shop—a gray van with B AND B LOCKSMITH written in black on the vehicle's door. For a wrinkle in time, Brendy thought Zeke was going to pull into her parking lot. Instead, he kept moving and never bothered even looking her way. Brendy touched the windowpane while cradling the warm coffee cup to her chest. She touched the neckline of her jumper, right where that golden locket should have been. Zeke slipped her the key Saturday night, and Brendy secretly hoped he'd planned something special for later. Something like a proposal.

She bit back a sob, and the keepsake box wouldn't be denied a moment longer. Brendy left her coffee cup on the ledge and moved toward the desk. After a hard yank on the stubborn desk drawer, she retrieved the faded symbol of her first love, opened it, and scratched through the contents until she found the tape-swathed senior ring. The green stone glistened back at her, and she remembered what Zeke had told her, "I got green because it matches your eyes," he said, explaining why he didn't choose blue, the school's color.

Tears staining her cheeks, Brendy slipped the ring in the spot her wedding band once claimed. She closed her eyes, pressed the ring to her lips, and wondered how she could have ever betrayed Zeke's pure heart. "The bad part is," she whispered, "I've done it again."

The whole worm episode rushed through her mind, and Brendy couldn't stop the impish chuckle that mingled with her tears. Pat's reaction aside, Pete's punishment had indeed fit his crime. Last night, Kent had taken a firmer hand with the child, and for the first time Brendy didn't try to interfere. She was beginning to think that maybe Zeke was right. Maybe Pete *did* need a different discipline tactic. Last night when Kent told her Pete actually stuck his tongue out at Zeke, Brendy began to doubt her methods.

A light tapping interrupted Brendy's thoughts, and she looked for Tiger-Higer, fully expecting the cat to be up to mischief. However, the feline had stretched himself out on a pile of dirty clothes and was snoozing. The tapping continued. This time, the noise sounded as if it were coming from behind her. Brendy turned to see a person peering through the window. She jumped and released a scream.

"It's just me!" Zeke called.

On second glance, Brendy recognized the man whose senior ring rested on her finger. With a rush of adrenaline, she jumped toward the window and unlatched it. The vertical pane swung outward. "You scared me to *death!*" she said, her hand upon her heart. For a moment their companionable laughter dashed aside the issues between them.

"What are you *doing*, anyway?" she asked.

"I was out on a job. When I drove by, I thought I saw you looking out the window. So I decided to stop and say, er. . ." He shuffled his boot against the pavement. "Say 'hi.'" Zeke looked back up at her, and his vulnerable expression nearly knocked her to her knees. Brendy's heart began to pound out a desperate tattoo. When Zeke's attention riveted upon the class ring still on her hand, she went breathless.

Brendy rested her fingers against the top of her coffee mug and stared at the gold ring as if it were from outer space. She hadn't put the thing on since taking it off when she met Mack.

"Ah, man," Zeke said. He shook his head and backed away.

"What?" Brendy prompted.

"Here I was, trying to act like Romeo and court you at the window, and I see you're already going steady."

She giggled and snagged her bottom lip between her teeth. The urge to apologize for Saturday night overtook her, and Brendy didn't bother to analyze the implications. "You know, Zeke," she began before she could change her mind, "I'm really sorry about blowing up on you the other night. I guess. . ." She trailed off and wondered if she were daft to try to make up.

Even if everything were resolved between her and Zeke, she still had the children to consider. Thankfully, Pat hadn't been harassed by any more bad dreams. And Pete did act a little more civilized last night after Kent took away his TV privileges for two days. Nevertheless, they still didn't like Zeke and still viewed him as a threat.

Brendy dared a glimpse at the man who had once stolen her heart. His adoring expression nearly melted her every resolve. Brendy knew she didn't look half as good as his gaze suggested. She'd barely run a comb through her hair and applied only lipstick that morning. She gulped some of her raspberry coffee and hoped the warm jolt would give her the courage to continue.

"I guess I'm just—just exhausted," she explained.

"Well, I have the perfect remedy for what ails you." He narrowed his eyes, glanced downward, and then darted a sly smile at her. "Let's get married."

Wide-eyed, Brendy looked at the man and tried to convince herself she was hearing things. "Wh–what did you—did you say?" she stuttered.

"I said, 'Let's get married,'" Zeke repeated and tugged her hand to his lips. "I can't stand being without you. And, if you want the truth, I've driven by this shop half a dozen times since yesterday. I kept telling myself I was acting like a love-struck teenager, but I can't seem to stop. This morning when I drove by, I thought it was just going to be another time to pass, but when I saw you standing in the window. . ."

A shower of tears blurred the view of the man who had always been a part of her. At once, Brendy understood part of the reason she was so exhausted after a good night's sleep. She was as lovesick as he. Brendy hadn't eaten a solid meal since Saturday night. And while Pat wasn't having any dreams about Zeke, Brendy had been haunted by images of the blue-eyed Vietnam veteran who held the key to her heart.

"We could go to Rusk this morning and get the marriage license," he continued. "You could be back at the shop by nine thirty."

"But Sylvia doesn't get here until ten, and the shop opens at nine." Brendy felt as if her head were spinning with details.

"So, put a note on the door that you'll be here at nine thirty."

"But what about Mr. Narvy and—"

"They can wait," Zeke said. "All they're going to do is sit around and play checkers until lunch anyway."

"This is crazy," Brendy said. She tugged her hand from his and deposited her coffee on the windowsill once more.

"No, it's not." Zeke placed his hands on the windowpane and leaned toward her. Given the elevation of the hardwood floor, Brendy stood eye-to-eye with Zeke. "It's not crazy," he said. "It's love."

His face neared hers, and Brendy was drawn by the magnetism that had reignited the moment Ziggy Blake stepped back into her life. Common sense issued two suggestions. First, Brendy shouldn't kiss him because a kiss would signify their relationship was back in swing. Second, if that officially happened, she would again be facing choices that affected her grandchildren.

Nevertheless, Brendy couldn't resist the thought of Zeke's lips upon hers. Not only did she let him kiss her, she kissed him back. She flung her arms around his neck and kissed him with the abandon of a woman irrevocably in love.

As he trailed a row of kisses toward her ear, Brendy whispered, "Kent says he's taking the kids to Six Flags this weekend," and didn't bother to expound upon her meaning.

"If we get the license today, we can get married Friday. We'd have the whole weekend together—*alone*." Zeke sounded as if he'd been given a pot of gold.

"But what are we going to do once they get home?" she worried.

"I don't have the foggiest idea," Zeke answered.

He followed that with a kiss that left Brendy without recollection of her own name. And within fifteen minutes she found herself being whisked away to the Cherokee County Courthouse, thinking they were indeed crazy or this was what her daughter called a "God thing."

Chapter 8

From Tuesday until Friday Zeke felt as if he were caught up in a whirlwind of expectation, plans, and mystery. The expectation nearly rivaled his emotions when he and Brendy had talked of getting married the first time. His plans involved getting his best suit cleaned and picking up the set of matching gold bands from the jewelers.

Brendy's plans, however, proved more complicated. Indeed, Zeke only got a few minutes alone with her between her flitting all over town. According to Sylvia, her plans involved getting her hair and nails done at Rainbow's End, or arranging a makeover with Debbie and Cheryl at Merle Norman Cosmetics, or purchasing the perfect suit from Elaine's. How she kept their wedding a secret in a town as small as Jacksonville was a mystery to Zeke.

By the time he picked her up Friday evening at five of six, Zeke decided all her preparation had been worth it. "You look great," he whispered as he helped her into the front seat of his van. Her jade green, two-piece suit made her hair appear as if it were on fire—a fire that matched the blaze in Zeke's veins. "And you smell great, too," he added before placing a lingering kiss on her lips.

"Mmmm," she purred, "it's Shalimar."

"I know. I would recognize that scent from ten miles away," he said. "You're wearing your locket?" he asked and glanced toward her neck.

She touched the gold heart and smiled. "You have the key?"

He pulled the tiny key from his suit pocket and held it up for her inspection.

"I guess we're all set, then," she said.

"Yes, all set," Zeke said and wanted to stand and look at her until the sun set and they were surrounded by shadows that resonated with their love. But, alas, the Reverend Crandall Henderson was awaiting them at First Church on the corner of Beaumont and Bryan Streets.

Within half an hour they would be husband and wife. Zeke had planned for a private meal to be catered at his home. After that, he hoped they could come back to her place and spend the weekend in marital bliss. What they would do when the kids came home was still an enigma. Neither of them spoke of that problem. As he climbed into the van, Zeke sensed they had somehow made a silent pact to enjoy the weekend and let tomorrow take care of its problems.

Five minutes later, Brendy and Zeke stepped along the sidewalk of the small church he attended. They passed a bed of multicolored impatiens and begonias before Zeke tried the glass door. When he tugged on the handle, the door didn't budge. He frowned, cupped his hands, and gazed into the modest foyer. Only the whir of intermittent traffic bespoke any activity.

"No sign of life," he muttered and wondered what they would do if his pastor forgot. He was known for his "absentminded professor" syndrome, and Zeke checked his watch. "Six o'clock on the dot," he said. "We're right on time."

"What if he forgot?" Brendy asked, and her voice wobbled.

Zeke turned toward her, covered her hands with his, and couldn't deny the tremor in her fingers. "You're nervous," he said and searched her guileless gaze for any hint of uncertainty. All he saw was excitement.

"And you're not?" she provoked with a flirtatious smile.

"Nervous? Me? Not in the least," he teased, and Brendy laughed. Zeke tugged on the stifling neck of his starched white shirt. He couldn't deny that his perspiration was as much from nerves as July humidity.

"Look, let's walk around the church," Zeke added. "The side door is often left open. The pastor lives right next door. Maybe you can at least go in and sit in the cool while I see if I can find him."

❦

Brendy walked around the church with Zeke, and they discovered the side door open, just as he predicted. He ushered her in, flipped on the lights, and promised to be back with the absentee minister. Once Zeke closed the door and Brendy had the cozy sanctuary to herself, she thrilled in the holy silence.

Sunlight streamed through the stained glass windows, creating a feeling of walking inside a rainbow. A large vase filled with eucalyptus and dried flowers stood on a table behind the altar. The smell of hymnals and carpet deodorizer tinged her senses as Brendy moved toward the flowers.

Near the vase, she touched the pages of an open Bible. The displayed passages were from Jeremiah, chapter twenty-nine. An unknown hand had underlined verse eleven. " 'For I know the plans I have for you,' declares the LORD, 'plans to prosper you and not to harm you, plans to give you hope and a future.' "

Brendy considered the whirlwind of activity since she'd recklessly accepted Zeke's proposal. Her sneaky shopping had led up to Kent's departure that afternoon. He had driven off with the kids chanting, "Six Flags! Six Flags! Six Flags!" She only hoped Kent could maintain his new upbeat persona once he realized his mom had gotten married behind his back.

She moved to the altar and knelt. Her knees cracked as they touched the short-piled carpet, and Brendy was reminded she was no longer a carefree eighteen-year-old. Nevertheless, her soul soared with the hope of a rewarding marriage. And the words from Jeremiah 29:11 became her own. Slowly, she placed her hands upon the altar and rested her forehead upon her hands. A prayer sprang from her heart: thankfulness for the gift of Zeke, petition for her son and grandchildren, joy for her place in God's love.

Upon the heels of her thanksgiving, a tender voice nudged her to also pray for her ex-daughter-in-law. Brendy stiffened. Her head rose, and she gripped the edge of the altar. Thoughts of that fickle female nearly banished all Brendy's joy. Even though she had often said something like, "All we can do is pray for her," the words were a mere sentiment. For she seriously struggled with speaking a sincere prayer for the betterment of the woman who had abandoned those innocent children.

The men's footsteps nearing the side door banished the moment. Relieved, Brendy stood from the altar and watched Zeke enter with the portly pastor.

"I don't know why, but I put this wedding on my schedule for six thirty," Reverend Henderson was saying as they came in.

"No problem," Zeke acquiesced. "I understand. You have a busy schedule. We're just thankful you could perform the ceremony on such short notice."

The reverend slowed as he neared Brendy. The two had met numerous times around town, and she welcomed the handshake of the kind minister. "I always say the smartest men are the ones who marry higher than themselves." The fiftyish pastor smiled at Zeke. "Looks like you're probably about the smartest man I've met."

Brendy warmed, and Zeke offered a jovial protest.

"I guess I should say, aside from me," Henderson added. "I somehow managed to marry a woman twelve years younger than I. She's tall and blond and way prettier than I am. It's nothing short of a miracle." He rubbed the top of his balding head and chuckled.

After the humorous exchange, Reverend Henderson suggested the three of them hold hands and pray. Brendy marveled at the presence of the Lord as the skilled pastor closed the prayer and began the ceremony, keeping it brief yet meaningful.

As they exchanged wedding bands, the years melted away, and Brendy felt as if they were standing beneath that weeping willow tree on Lake Jacksonville. The summer sun still glistened across the water like a shower of glitter. Brendy wasn't so certain she didn't hear the mockingbird's sweet song, and she could almost smell the fresh summer breeze whispering through the weeping willow.

Finally, the pastor spoke the long-awaited words, "I now pronounce you husband and wife." Brendy beamed up at her handsome husband as the minister added, "I understand the two of you have something special you'd like to do now."

"Yes." Zeke pulled a key from his suit pocket as Brendy fumbled with the locket's clasp. After removing the chain the two of them worked to unlock the tiny heart that had been closed over thirty years before. At last, the spring released, and they gazed upon a diminutive black-and-white photo of themselves. They were sitting upon the hood of Zeke's black Mustang and smiling with the cheerful assurance that the future was nothing but bright. Yet that photo had been taken before the cruelties of Vietnam. . .before loss. . .before the heartaches of life.

As if the locket released the essence of their first love, Brendy felt as if she were swept away in a tide only matched by that moment when Zeke first kissed her. As if he too were whisked into the waves of first love, Zeke pulled Brendy close and didn't wait for the minister to tell him to kiss his bride. She threw her arms around his neck and pressed her lips against his with the enthusiasm of a married woman.

The enthusiasm increased as the night progressed, through the catered candlelit meal, during the time they softly swayed to the music in Zeke's living room, all the way to the moment they pulled into Brendy's driveway.

The weekend blurred into a home-based honeymoon that left Brendy's head spinning and raised the eyebrows of a few neighbors.

Finally, she was forced to tell their next-door neighbor that she and Zeke had secretively wed. Otherwise, she didn't think her reputation would have remained intact another two days.

By Saturday night around nine thirty, the two lovebirds decided what they needed now was a good night's rest. Kent was due home Sunday by supper, and both Brendy and Zeke were stressed with how to share the news of their marriage. While Zeke suggested the bold approach, Brendy thought they ought to keep a low profile for as many weeks as possible.

After brushing her teeth and running her hairbrush through her curls, Brendy snapped off the bathroom light and glided toward the four-poster bed. She'd taken special pains to enhance the room's classic Victorian atmosphere, so they each felt more like they were at a bed-and-breakfast than at her home. The smell of the buttercream candle that had burned most of last night still clung to the air. And Brendy suspected she would never smell buttercream again without thinking of the night that she and Zeke fulfilled the dreams of over three decades.

Zeke, stretched on his back, observed her through heavy lids. He had the covers pulled up to his chin, and Brendy snickered. "Still trying to hide those threadbare pajamas?" she asked and slipped out of the silky robe that covered her sensational peach negligee trimmed in Belgian lace. Last night Zeke had told her she resembled a queen.

"Well, compared to *your* nightclothes, I look like a vagabond," he admitted with a roll of his eyes. "I guess I needed a coach for this wedding thing. I was in Beall's department store Thursday working on their security equipment. I could have bought a whole drawer full of pajamas, but it never even crossed my mind."

"That's okay, honey," Brendy soothed. "I love you even though you *do* wear pink pajamas." She clicked off the lamp, and a nearby streetlamp filled the room with an unforgettable luminescence.

"Now she's mocking me," Zeke teased as Brendy slid against the cool sheets. "They're not pink! They're *red,*" he insisted. "Or they were when I bought them!"

Brendy giggled and settled her head against his shoulder. His hand descended upon her curls, and his fingers lovingly caressed her forehead. "And when was that?" she asked with a honey-sweet tone, "*1975?*"

"Well, I oughta—" Zeke raised up on his elbow and began tickling her tummy.

With a delightful squeal, Brendy tried to squirm away, but to no avail. Finally, she grabbed the only defense she could clutch and whacked him over the head with her pillow.

"Ugh!" he croaked and clutched his chest. "She got me!" He flopped onto his back, and the laughter of two souls knit as one spun a musical chant into the room.

He tugged her close again, and Brendy settled her head upon his shoulder. "I love you, Ziggy Blake," she whispered.

"And I love you," he echoed. "I wish—" He halted, and Brendy waited for him to finish.

Chapter 9

Finally, she propped herself up on one elbow and scrutinized his profile. Brendy rested a hand against those infamous pink pajamas and finally said, "You wish?"

"How do I say this?" His eyes glistened in the streetlamp's silvery highlights, and Brendy expected he was grappling for words. At last, Zeke propped his hand under his head and looked straight at her. "Can I be honest?" he asked.

"Of course." Brendy stroked the side of his face and took in the faint scent of Brut. She would go to her grave loving that stuff.

"Okay," Zeke finally said like a brave soldier. "Let's see how we survive brutal honesty."

"Shoot," she encouraged.

"I. . .hmm. . .how do I say this?"

"Just say it!" she encouraged. "Say it or I'll go insane!" Brendy touched her temple.

"Right. Well, you asked for it, then. I. . .already know that you and I have something Madeline and I never had." Zeke's words reverberated around the room like a phantom of the past. "I was going to say I wish I could have had this kind of marriage with her, but then that sounded *really stupid*. So I started to say I wish I'd married *you* in the first place, but—"

"But that was a decision I made for both of us," Brendy inserted, and she couldn't keep the regret from marring every word.

"That's *not* what I was going to say," Zeke insisted. "I was going to say that if I hadn't married Maddy, then I wouldn't have my sons,

79

and I can't imagine life without them."

"Did you call them about our marriage?" Brendy asked, ready to grab at any diversion from the well of guilt springing from her soul. Strangely, amid the guilt came thoughts of her daughter-in-law.

"Actually, yes."

"I still haven't even met them," she said and tried to force all images of that vixen from her mind.

"They're in shock," he admitted.

"I wonder if they'll like me."

"Who knows? I'm certainly not winning any popularity contest with *your* relatives, so. . ."

"I told my mother this morning," Brendy continued. Somehow, she hoped the repartee would extinguish the humiliating conviction from her spirit that grew the longer she pondered her daughter-in-law. For the first time, Brendy was faced with the fact that she had done to Zeke what her ex-daughter-in-law had done to Kent and the kids. And Brendy had yet to forgive her—truly forgive her. *But I'd never leave my children*, she argued. Nevertheless, the still small voice that urged her to pray for Tamala now insisted *Brendy* had also violated a promise that broke a man's heart.

A realization hit her smack between the eyes. She had allowed herself to think the name Tamala for the first time since Kent and Tamala's ugly divorce. Brendy had been so hurt by what that woman did she hadn't even wanted to hear her name.

Now the mere echo of the word. . .*Tamala*. . .ushered in a holy comparison—a comparison of Brendy's betrayal of Zeke with Tamala's betrayal of Kent. *But we weren't married,* she thought and wanted to shrink from sight under the fragrant sheets. Even so, Brendy knew she couldn't escape the reality. She had broken a promise that ripped out a man's heart. *How can I hold a grudge against Tamala?* Brendy wrestled with the intrusive thought and wished she could escape the brutal truth.

"Zeke?" she whispered.

"Hmm?" he asked.

"I'm sorry."

She hadn't realized he was tense until his arm relaxed against her shoulder. "What for?" he crooned and stroked her hair again. "Here I was worried you were angry, and—"

"No, not angry in the least," Brendy said, her voice cracking. "I just. . ." She sniffled.

"Hey." Zeke rose to his elbow. "Why all the tears?" he asked, his face only inches from hers.

"I'm just so sorry about—about jilting you," she admitted. "And I'm not sure I ever even told you—not until now."

"It doesn't even matter. I forgave you years ago. As a matter of fact—" He stopped again.

Sensing his hesitancy once more, Brendy laid a hand on his face. "Go ahead. We might as well tell all," she encouraged.

"Well, Maddy and I didn't have what you and I have," he admitted, "but she *needed* me, Brendy. Her father was a drunk who beat her half to death. Her mother didn't do a thing to stop him. By the time I met her, she had somehow managed to struggle through licensed vocational nursing school and was pretty much an emotional version of my physical problems. The two of us together were a wreck, I can assure you. I think maybe that's what attracted us to each other. We were both pretty much chewed up, but we had somehow managed to survive." Zeke settled back onto his pillow. "Or I guess *I* survived better than she did."

Brendy rested her hand under her head and watched the shadows chase across the ceiling as a car cruised down the dark street. She grappled for any words to help ease the forlorn echo in his voice, but nothing came. Finally, Brendy said, "I don't know what to say."

"I didn't tell you the whole story of her death, Brendy, because, well. . ." Zeke shifted under the covers, and Brendy looked at him through the shadows. He placed his forefinger and thumb against his eyes, and her pulse responded to his anguish. "She committed suicide," Zeke finally blurted. "I came home one day from work, and she'd done the old car-in-the-closed-garage routine."

"Oh, no!" Brendy gasped and her eyes stung. "Oh, Zeke. I—I'm so sorry."

"It was a couple of years after our sons left for college. She wrestled with depression most of our married life. I think she just couldn't handle the fact that they were gone—for good."

Brendy laid a hand on his chest and pressed her lips against his cheek. She came away with a trace of dampness and salt.

"Really, Brendy," he continued, and she marveled that his voice revealed little sign of tears, "I've spent the last five years hurting because I—I somehow think I failed her. I'm not sure my sons are over it all either—"

"I don't see how they ever *could* be."

"I hope you'll be patient with them. They both hinted that they thought you might be after my nest egg."

Brendy laughed outright and rolled toward him.

"That was my exact reaction. I think it aggravated both of 'em. I'll tell you what, people who don't have identical twins just don't know what they're missing. What one thinks, the other one thinks. You just might as well get ready for it." He shook his head.

"I guess the Lord has brought both of us through a lot, huh?" she asked.

"Seems that way," Zeke agreed. His arm slipped around her once more and pulled her closer. Brendy reveled in the security he emanated. Already, she loved being the wife of Ezekiel Blake.

The sound of summer crickets singing the joys of night ushered in a hush between the newlyweds. A hush that took Brendy back to the altar of that church where they married. Back to the point of praying for Tamala. Back to the point of realizing that she was no better than

Tamala. Nevertheless, her chest tightened with the mere thought of what the woman had done to Brendy's son and grandchildren.

"Ziggy," she finally said, accompanied by the distant siren of an ambulance. "I need you to pray for me."

"Oh?"

"Yes. I, uh. . ." Brendy swallowed. "I'm having trouble forgiving Tamala."

"Who?"

"Tamala. Kent's ex-wife."

"I can't imagine why," he said with a twist of irony.

Brendy thanked God that her husband understood as she continued her explanation. "It would appear that the Lord is showing me I'm no better than she is. I abandoned *you*. Now, how can I hold a grudge against Tamala?" She balled the freshly laundered sheet in her hand. "But it's still so hard to release the pain."

Zeke remained silent, and Brendy wondered what he might be thinking. At last he said, "I know from experience that sometimes forgiveness comes in layers—kinda like an onion. Right now, you've come to the first step of realizing the need to forgive. From here, it's all about releasing the memory to God every time it comes to your mind and allowing Him to heal your hurt until He takes the healing all the way to the core. For some people that takes several years; for others, it's more of a deliverance."

"You sound like you've done this." Tears seeped from her eyes, for she already knew the answer.

"I have," he said, and the rumble of truth vibrated against her cheek resting upon his chest. "I was one of the slower ones," he admitted.

"That would be. . .when you forgave me?" she asked.

He stroked her cheek with his thumb. "That would be. . .when I forgave you," Zeke affirmed.

Brendy wrapped her arms around her husband and held on tight. *Oh, Jesus,* she finally prayed, *teach me to forgive Tamala like Zeke forgave me.* The instant the words left her heart, a warm assurance flowed into Brendy's soul. For the first time in months she rested—truly rested—in the presence of a holy God.

Brendy didn't have all the answers. And she wasn't about to pretend she would stop hurting for her grandchildren. Nevertheless, she knew God had heard her prayer and was beginning to answer in His own way, in His own time. He had heard and was extending to Brendy the desire to begin praying for Tamala, and Brendy would—for her own spiritual well-being.

The sound of a car pulling into the driveway pierced the moment with a hint of intrigue. Zeke stiffened. Brendy clutched his arm. They looked at each other, nose-to-nose, through the shadows.

"When was Kent supposed to be home again?" he whispered.

"Not until tomorrow evening—around dinner," Brendy hissed back.

A car door slammed. The ebb and flow of children's voices preceded the clatter and creak of the front door being opened.

"Oh, my word," Brendy said, "he's brought them home early! What are we going to do?"

"Look, maybe they won't even suspect I'm here," Zeke reasoned.

"Are you *kidding!*" Brendy shot back. "Your van is parked at the curb."

Zeke groaned. "My van. How could I have forgotten?"

"Grandmom!" Pat's shrill voice floated up the hallway.

"Mom? Zeke?" Kent called. "They've got to be here somewhere," he mumbled as he neared the bedroom. "Zeke's van is at the curb."

"Maybe they went somewhere in Grandmom's van," Pete said, and his words dripped disapproval.

"Her van is in the driveway," Kent answered, and his voice now held a hint of concern. "I hope there hasn't been an emergency." A hesitant knock reverberated upon her door. "Mom?" Kent called. "Are you in there? Is everything okay?"

Brendy gulped in a decisive breath and snapped on the lamp.

"Might as well face the music," Zeke mumbled.

"Brace yourself," Brendy said with a wince.

The two partners exchanged a flash of silent communication and simultaneously nodded as if they were preparing to head into the most fiendish of enemy fire.

"Come in," they said in unison.

Chapter 10

As the door swished open, Kent gaped at his mom as if she were the most wanton of women. Brendy held up her left hand to display the wide gold band. Zeke followed suit.

"We're married," they said together.

"Married!" Kent yelped. By that time, two tired faces, smeared with candied apple, appeared behind their dad. "When?" he demanded.

"Last night," Brendy said. "After you left."

Pete clutched his father's arm and gazed at Zeke as if he were a space alien. Bursting into a wail, Pat reached for Kent. He scooped her into his arms while keeping a firm hand upon Pete's shoulder. Pat snuggled against her father's neck and reduced her crying to whimpers.

Holding her breath, Brendy counted the seconds until the inevitable explosion. Yet no explosion came. Only silence. Silence and relief. Relief and a new realization. With her own eyes, Brendy watched as Kent's children turned to him for solace rather than insisting upon her.

"Well!" Kent finally said, and his full lips twisted. "I guess you two really pulled one over on *me.*"

"Uh. . . ," Brendy started and looked to Zeke.

"We. . . ," Zeke began and glanced at Brendy.

"An apology might be in order," Kent huffed as if he were Brendy's offended father. "The kids wanted to come home early because we thought you might be lonely!"

Pete glared at Zeke. Brendy, tense and ready for anything, noticed Zeke wasn't flinching from the child's hostile stare.

"Does Grandmother know?" Kent asked.

"Yes. I called her this morning," Brendy explained.

"So I'm the last to know?" His brown eyes rounded, and the dark circles beneath matched the tired state of his T-shirt and pleated shorts.

"No, I still haven't told Leandra," Brendy admitted, referring to her daughter.

"I'm sure *she's* going to be thrilled to be the last to know." Kent settled onto the end of the bed, lowered Pat to his leg, and pulled Pete into the circle of his arm. "This is just too *weird*," Kent mumbled. "The last I knew, worms were flying around the dining room table, and you guys weren't speaking."

"Well, I guess we just realized that nothing could keep us apart." Zeke cut a humorous glance toward Brendy. "Not even worms," he added.

Kent's tired chuckle seemed to relieve his aggravation.

"I don't like worms." With a shiver, Pat covered her mouth. She reached for Brendy, who gathered the child into her arms.

Zeke stroked the little girl's hair, and she didn't move from his touch. "I wouldn't have put a worm in your mouth the other night, sweetie," he said. "And I was just fooling around with Pete. I didn't mean for that worm to fall in."

Pat eyed Zeke as if she might want to believe him.

"I missed you, Grandmom," she finally claimed, and Brendy lifted a brow as she pieced together the rest of the reason they'd come home early. "Can I sleep with you tonight?" Pat asked.

"Of course," Zeke answered before anyone else could.

"But—" Kent started.

"We don't have to—" Brendy began.

Zeke held up his hand. "Now that I'm a part of this family, we might as well act like it."

"She snores," Brendy mumbled.

"Put her over there on the other side of you, and I'll never know it," Zeke said with the gallant air of an honorable knight.

"Oh, and one more thing." He turned to Pete, who didn't offer even the hint of a smile. "I left that shopping bag here the other night. Your grandmother told me she put it in the top of the hall closet. There's a ball glove in there for you, if you want it, and I really like to play catch."

Pete looked down. And while he offered no acceptance, neither did he reject the idea.

Kent extended his hand to his new stepfather. "You're all right," he said as the two men shook hands.

"So are you," Zeke responded, and Brendy covered their hands with hers.

The Promise

Dedicated to my all-time favorite girl, my daughter, Brooke Smith.

Chapter 1

"Y ou've got brownie mix all in your hair!" Pete Lane's candid declaration matched the conviction in his sister's guileless blue eyes. The two of them nodded with the sage wisdom of a six-year-old and an eight-year-old.

With a chortle, Sylvia Donnelley ruffled the children's hair, as blond as hers. "So do you two," she said. She pulled her hand away from Pete's hair, and the dot of chocolate on her index finger verified her claim.

Sylvia gazed around her boss's tiny Victorian-style kitchen and began a slow giggle. Specks of brown goo marred the cabinets and even the side of the refrigerator. The electric mixer dripped a puddle of chocolate near the plastic bowl that held their creation.

"We've got a mess!" Pat dug her index finger into the brownie mixture.

"It's amazing there's anything left in the bowl," Sylvia said as the smell of chocolate proved too tempting for even her. She joined Pat, dipped her finger into the thick mixture, and inserted it into her mouth. The taste of double-Dutch-chocolate delight urged her to forego the baking.

"Hey! I want some," Pete chirped.

Sylvia opened the silverware drawer, retrieved three spoons, and handed one each to the children. "Dig in!" she said with glee.

The blue-eyed siblings clutched their spoons and gazed at Sylvia as if they'd seen a heavenly vision but were afraid to embrace it.

"Grandmom never lets us eat the mix," Pat said, as if they were about to break one of the Ten Commandments.

"Well. . ." Sylvia shrugged and debated how best to handle the situation. She didn't want to encourage the children to break their grandmother's rule, but neither did she envision ruining this masterpiece with baking. "I don't see what it will hurt this one time. I bought the mix, so it's mine. We can eat it however and whenever we want. And I, for one, want it now!" She jabbed her spoon into the bowl and prepared to fill her mouth with brownie mix.

A movement from the kitchen door snared her attention. While the children wasted no time gobbling the rare treat, their father paused inside the doorway. His gaze swept the splattered mess and landed on Sylvia.

She lowered her spoon and tried to feign nonchalance as she observed the man whose features had haunted her dreams for over a decade: the prominent nose, the heavy brows, the square jaw, and the lips that hinted at a roguish grin. The only differences between Kent and his kids were that his fair hair was wavy, rather than straight, and his eyes weren't blue. They were brown—a dreamy brown that had arrested Sylvia's attention twelve years ago. That had been before Kent married Tamala who eventually abandoned her family.

When Kent's mother, Brendy Lane Blake, left for her Hawaiian honeymoon with her new husband, Zeke, she asked Sylvia to take care of Kent's kids for the next two weeks. Sylvia readily agreed—despite the fact that she had also planned a vacation away from Brendy's coffee shop where she served as a part-time clerk. Little did Kent know, Sylvia would gladly sacrifice her vacation or anything else if she thought it would help him.

Sylvia offered Kent a cautious smile—the same smile she had learned to temper with mild detachment that hinted at polite coolness. She had used the smile with Kent the day he got married. It had served her well for twelve years—had hidden her true feelings and somehow protected her heart.

Initially, Kent didn't return the grin. Instead, he crossed his arms as if he were about to announce a grave sentence upon their sticky mess. The dark circles under his eyes attested to his weariness. He'd just completed a twelve-hour shift that started at 7:00 a.m.—thirty minutes after Sylvia arrived to watch the kids. She wondered if he might have expected something a little more substantial for supper than brownie mix. His gaze slid from Sylvia as he, once again, observed his children. His face softened into an indulgent grin.

"You guys have that mix all over you," he said and moved closer. His surgery scrubs whispered with every move.

"Daddy!" the kids chimed in unison.

After placing her spoon in the sink, Sylvia eased away from the trio. Kent hugged his children, both dressed in park-weary shorts and T's. He dipped his finger into the mixture and wasted no time tasting the chocolate masterpiece.

"Mmmm. . . This is *great!*" he mumbled against his finger.

Sylvia's heart warmed, and she stifled a satisfied grin. Twelve years ago, during her freshman year at Jacksonville College, she had started clutching every hint of a praise Kent Lane might toss her way. Like a connoisseur of fine diamonds, she carefully placed each compliment into a special alcove of her heart—an alcove she visited often, particularly on those lonely nights when she despaired of never being able to give her heart to another man. Over the years, the alcove had become a place of reverence so exclusive that Sylvia suspected she might have prohibited even God access. With a cringe, she reached to turn off the oven as the silverware drawer rattled.

"Here's you a spoon, Daddy," Pete offered.

Sylvia swiveled from her task and silently observed the trio. Since five o'clock that afternoon, the children had repeatedly asked the same question, "How much longer 'til Daddy's home?" Sylvia had tried her best to keep them distracted after their foot-long sandwich dinner. The brownies were her last effort.

Brendy often said, "That hospital must think Kent's the only RN in Jacksonville." Sylvia had heard that claim so many times, it almost echoed in her sleep. But anybody who knew Kent understood he'd been working too many hours ever since his wife divorced him. . .and the kids. He'd recently arranged to work four days of twelve-hour shifts and be off three days every week. Tomorrow started his three-days-off stretch, which meant Sylvia would also have three days off from caring for the kids. Next week, she'd stay with them four more days, then her season of helping Kent would end.

Unbridled laughter danced around the kitchen as Kent dotted his daughter's nose with brownie batter. He followed suit with Pete, and they both blessed Kent with a dollop on his nose. Sylvia toyed with a button on her embroidered shirt and debated if Kent realized just how much his children needed a full-time mother. Brendy had certainly poured out her grandmother's heart in an attempt to take the place of their mom, but she was foremost a grandmother. *They need a mother in their own home,* Sylvia thought.

For the first time, hope flared within Sylvia—a hope that the appreciation in Kent's haunted brown eyes might be the start of something that would last a lifetime. When Sylvia learned of Kent's divorce, she left her missionary position on an Arizona Indian reservation and moved back to Jacksonville with the specific intent to marry Kent Lane. At last, Sylvia dared expect that her dream was on the verge of being fulfilled. She slid a hand down the side of one thigh and wondered if Kent still longed to have a wife with a perfect figure, or if he'd value commitment and character so much he wouldn't mind Sylvia's extra pounds.

Her focus drifted back to Kent. Fully expecting to view his interacting with the children, she made no attempt to mask the unbridled admiration pouring from her heart. When she encountered his contemplative gaze, Sylvia glanced away and did her best to mask the truth from her features. Once she dared glance back at him, her knees weakened. A spark of awareness glimmered from Kent's soul— awareness, mixed with uncertainty.

Chapter 2

Kent commanded himself to look away from Sylvia. But the command went unnoticed in the wake of what he thought he'd read on her finely made-up features. Her eyes reminded him of the Caribbean Sea—a sea that tugged him into serene waters and beckoned him to swim deeply into Sylvia's awestruck soul. The impression of her awe was so swift in disappearing that Kent debated if perhaps he'd imagined it. Other than brownie mix speckling her abundance of blond curls, Sylvia looked as meticulously groomed as if she'd just stepped out of the beauty parlor. As of yesterday, he began to fight the urge to compliment her on her appearance. After spending all day with Pat and Pete, few women would look as fresh. Kent could no longer deny that Sylvia Donnelley was an attractive woman whose golden character seemed to match her becoming appearance. Baffled, he wondered why he hadn't noticed before this week. Yesterday, he suspected he might have been looking forward to seeing her at the end of the day a little too much for comfort.

Get a grip. He forced his attention back to his children, who were in the process of overextending their chocolate allotment for the whole week. Kent had let one woman with bewitching eyes break his heart, and he wasn't about to give another one the chance.

Time to politely tell Miss Sylvia Donnelley to "get lost," so I can have three days of peace, he decided.

"Thanks for your help today," Kent said with an impatient edge and dared another glance in Sylvia's direction. This time, he had the good sense to peer past her into a glass-front cabinet that held his mother's china.

"Oh. . .uh, sure," Sylvia stammered. "I—I guess I'll, uh, be leaving then." She prepared to step past Kent. The space between him and the stove proved too narrow as Sylvia edged by, and Kent caught a whiff of the raspberry body spray she'd left in the bathroom the day before. He'd secretively smelled it last night. The effect was as pleasing now as then.

Shoulders slumped, she turned to leave, and Kent couldn't deny the impulse to soften his abrupt thanks. There was no need to make her suffer because of his anxiety. Kent touched her shoulder. Head bent, she paused.

"Sorry I'm a little snappy," he said and mumbled something about the day being long and hectic.

"Oh, sure," Sylvia said and turned to face him, a brittle smile firmly in place. The tinge of pain in her almond-shaped eyes couldn't be denied.

Kent battled the wave of longing that demanded he move closer to this woman who'd been in and out of his life for over a decade. But a steel wall within his heart seemed to trap him forever behind its cold control.

"Thanks again," he rasped and wondered if his voice sounded as husky to her as it did to him. He toyed with the chocolate-streaked spoon and placed it on the kitchen counter with the click of stainless steel against tile.

"Oh, sure," she replied and fidgeted with the clasp of her wristwatch. "I guess I'll see you Monday morning, then, as planned."

"Yeah." Kent eyed the floor, which sported a splatter of brownie mix against blue tile. His attention wandered to Sylvia's toes, ensconced in brown leather sandals. Her toenails were the exact color of the red Capri pants she wore, and Kent wondered if the woman even color coordinated her food pantry.

She turned to leave, and Kent kept his focus firmly on her feet. Yet she stopped and pivoted back to face him. "Oh, I almost forgot," she said.

Kent purposed to look past her again—this time into the Victorian dining room that housed an antique upright piano.

"We had foot-long sandwiches for supper," she said. "There's one in the fridge for you."

He forgot the piano and looked into her eyes. No hint of pain remained—only the mildest nuance of a soft invitation, veiled in azure mist.

"You didn't have to—" he began.

"I know. But. . ." She shrugged. "I knew you'd be as hungry as they were."

"You're going to spoil me." Kent failed to stop the appreciative smile as he admired the way the blond ringlets framed her face. The evening sun spilling through the dining room's lace sheers seemed to ignite her curls with silver fire. "That's three nights in a row you've fixed my dinner," he said and all at once hated to see Sylvia go.

She nodded and one corner of her mouth lifted. "Your mom told me to take good care of you while she was gone. She's my boss, you know." Sylvia rubbed her palms together. "I have to do what she says."

He leaned against the counter, crossed his arms, and propped one ankle on the other. "I believe she was referring to the kids, not me." Kent jerked his head toward Pat and Pete who simultaneously looked up from their chocolate pursuits. Both had dark rings around their lips.

"Ah, well." She placed the tip of her manicured pinkie between her teeth. A tinge of pink flushed her light tan before she moved her hand to her hip. "It's really not that big of a deal," she added, and Kent was certain he hadn't imagined the admiration earlier. This time, it was wrapped in appreciation. . . respect. . .and a hint of longing.

Whoa! A blast of awareness socked him in the gut. *Have I been blind or what?*

Pete's aghast voice dashed aside every mental musing, "Oh, gross! Are you two about to kiss or something?"

Kent's eyes widened as quickly as Sylvia's face went scarlet. He whirled to face the child who seemed bent upon speaking his mind at the most inopportune moments.

"Pete!" he gasped. "Whatever gave you *that* idea?"

"Because you're looking at each other like Grandmom and Mr. Zeke do!" Pat proclaimed as if she were Pete's defending attorney. She punctuated her remark with a lick of her spoon.

"Yeah!" Pete added and placed his hands on his hips. "And then *they* got married. Are you two going to get married? Because if you are, I think we need to know about it now!"

"Right!" Pat affirmed, and her ponytail swayed with her nod. "We don't want you to do what Grandmom did and be sneaky about getting married!" She wrinkled her nose as if her grandmother were the most blatant of criminals.

Chapter 3

Kent gaped at his children and grappled with some debonair means of ending the awkward moment. He'd never been prone to blushing, but a warm wash crept up his neck and invaded his eyes as the seconds stretched his nerves to the point of a scream. The click of sandals against hardwood tapped from the dining room. . .and then the living room.

"Oh, kids," he groaned and covered his face.

"What?" they chimed together.

"Please. . .please don't. . ." He struggled against lambasting them. Only an understanding of their innocence stopped the flow of heated words. He stared at their blameless faces and wondered why nobody ever told him how hard parenting would be.

When the front door clapped, Kent knew he must do something to right this awful turn of events. He fumbled with the kitchen's door that opened up onto the backyard. Kent succeeded in stumbling outside, trotting past his mother's plethora of rose bushes, and bursting upon the front yard in time to catch Sylvia opening the door of her compact Nissan, parked on El Paso Street's curb.

"Sylvia!" he called. Not certain exactly what he should say, he strode toward the street, lined with aging homes similar to his mother's. Next week would prove a long one indeed if he didn't somehow correct his children's assumptions.

She stepped between the car and door then paused. As if she were using the door as a shield, she rested her arm on the window frame and gripped the edge. While Sylvia appeared to be observing

Kent, she was the one looking past him this time.

"I don't know why the kids. . . ," he began, his breath short after the swift sprint. "I can't imagine what. . ." He faltered, and the whir of the vehicles on the nearby highway filled the pause. "My children at times are a mystery to me, and they can really come up with some whoppers. Their imagination is—"

"It's okay," Sylvia said to the hood of her silver sports car as she fiddled with the keys. "I guess with your mom getting married like she did—when you guys were out of town—they must be jumping to all sorts of wild conclusions at every turn."

"Exactly," Kent agreed and laughed. The smell of someone grilling burgers sent a rumble through his belly. "The very idea of. . ."

Sylvia studied her keys.

And Kent decided his children might very well have provided him a wonderful opportunity to set some boundaries for himself. Despite his growing attraction to Sylvia, the last thing he needed was a new relationship. He was barely recovered from the devastation of divorce. His kids, who both had suffered with issues of abandonment, were doing better than they had in months. When his mother started dating Zeke, both of them were worried that she would leave them, just as their mother did. Kent didn't need to threaten their growing peace with a new woman in his life.

"The very idea of you and me," he continued and laughed again. "We've known each other so long, we're like old news, I guess."

"Old news," Sylvia echoed. "Yes, I guess you're right." She plopped into the driver's seat, closed the door, and didn't look at him again. In a flash, she was pulling away from the curb as if a pack of wolves were after her.

He rested his hands on his hips and kicked against a clump of St. Augustine grass. The evening heat insisted that August in east Texas was going to be as hot as July. Beads of perspiration broke out along Kent's upper lip. He dashed aside the moisture and released a muffled edict. A sickening realization insisted he had said the wrong thing at the wrong time. His wayward mind contended he cared too much.

Shaking his head, Kent strode back toward the house. The front porch steps creaked with the echo of decades past. His mother's antique home had once been the epitome of immaculate grace. . .until he and his kids moved in. With a grimace, he picked up one of his mom's better bowls, filled with dirt from her flowerbed—a flowerbed that once held a wide array of tulips and irises. Now the thing was barren.

He sighed and wondered how long it would take the newlyweds to get tired of him and his children under the same roof. So far, Zeke had acted like nothing short of a sterling knight. But the kids had yet to disassemble Zeke's electric shaver or use his best socks for slingshots or scatter his arrowhead collection all over the house. Kent would give them exactly two months to conquer all of these feats and many more.

Kent didn't bother suppressing the mammoth yawn that threatened to take him down. The day had been beyond hectic, with a long line of scheduled surgeries plus two emergency surgeries thrown into the middle of it all. Neither he nor Dr. Vonduval had taken a lunch break. After a long day when he lamented his decision to forego med school years ago, the last thing Kent needed was a trying talk with his children. He opened the front door, stepped into the classically decorated living room, and welcomed the blast of cool air that chilled the sweat along his hairline. Squaring his shoulders, Kent decided he might as well set his children straight now before they conjured up who-knew-what in their wild imaginations.

He marched into the dining room, plopped the bowl of dirt on the oak table, and charged the kitchen. But Pat and Pete were nowhere to be seen. The only evidences of their presence were the two spoons lying near the brownie mix. Kent narrowed his eyes and swiveled back toward the dining room.

A giggle tottering from the front of the house prompted him to retrace his steps. When his feet encountered the living room's Oriental rug, the front window's floral drapes wiggled.

"Okay, you two spies," he said. "It's time to come out."

Pat edged out first, and Pete soon followed. Their shoulders squared, they stood side-by-side as if they were glued together. Both had as much chocolate on their faces as they probably had in their stomachs, and their straight hair stood out in baby-fine spikes after their behind-the-drapes excursion. Kent stifled a chuckle and purposed to remain firm.

"I want both of you to listen closely," he began. "You just embarrassed me and Miss Sylvia something awful. Do you understand?"

"Well, we—" Pete began.

Kent held up his hands. "I want you two to get one thing through your heads. I am not about to marry Sylvia, and I don't ever want you to say anything about kissing or marrying in front of her again."

"But—" Pat attempted.

"No buts!" Kent glowered. "Just because your grandmother hauled off and got married, that doesn't mean I'm going to." His face softened as he recalled the first night his mother was away on the honeymoon. Pat woke up three times during the night, terrified that her grandmom wasn't coming back. Now that some of his embarrassment was abating, Kent held no doubts that the children's comments in front of Sylvia must have been driven by the terror of his abandoning them. He couldn't imagine what they must feel at the thought of their father getting married, too. Kent rubbed his gritty eyes, sighed, and neared them. Kneeling in front of his children, he clasped their hands and stroked the backs with his thumbs.

"Listen," Kent began, "you don't have to worry about me leaving you. Ever." He knitted his brows and grappled for the right words to say.

"Don't you even *like* Miss Sylvia, Dad?" Pat asked.

Kent squinted and tried to anticipate the nature of this conversational turn. He averted his gaze from his daughter's scrutiny and observed a new candle, the color of butter, flickering on the Queen Anne coffee table. The smell of vanilla seemed to whisper the essence of Sylvia's presence. She'd done much more this week than just care for the children. Much. . .much more.

"Huh, Daddy?" Pat prompted.

"Yeah, I mean, don't you like her even a little?" Pete asked.

Their voices echoed from a distant canyon as Kent tried to drag his attention back to the problem at hand.

"Well. . .I don't *not* like her," he hedged.

Both children puckered their lips and drew their brows as if they were attempting to process exactly what "don't not like her" meant.

Kent gave each of their hands a reassuring squeeze. "I don't *dislike* Sylvia," he added. "But I don't want to marry her, nor will I be, uh, kissing her. Okay?"

"But we *want* you to marry her!" Pat blurted and bobbed her head. Her ponytail swung in merry celebration of her claim.

"Pat!" Pete wrenched his hand from his father's and stomped his foot. He placed his fists on his hips and turned on his sister. Silently, he glared at her as if transmitting a hostile ESP message that only Pat would understand.

"Woops!" She covered her lips with the end of her fingers and focused on her sneakers.

"Okay, what's going on?" Kent narrowed his eyes and crossed his arms. From the day these two conspired to put a worm in Zeke's soup, he had stopped underestimating their schemes.

Pat fidgeted with the hem of her stained T-shirt while Pete dug a rubber lizard out of his pocket and examined it.

A car's distant horn proved the only noise to break the tense silence. As Kent continued to stare at his children, he grappled for a logical explanation for their behavior. As his tired mind processed the clues, he concluded that they must have been planning the opposite for him that they planned for his mother. While they tried to break up Brendy and Zeke, perhaps they were plotting to play matchmaker with Kent and Sylvia.

Kent rubbed his throbbing temple and debated his options. When Tamala walked out, he vowed never to make himself vulnerable to another woman again. Despite the fact that Sylvia had worked magic with his children, she was still a woman. *And you'll do well to remember that, you dimwit,* he chided himself. For a few minutes in the kitchen, he'd seemed to lose all resolve in his resistance to the opposite sex. *Perhaps she's weaving the same spell on me she has on the kids.* He scowled.

He stared at the children, who had nearly run out of things to fidget with. "I want both of you to listen to me, and listen closely," he said in a voice that invited no argument.

Kent peered at Pat, then Pete. "Whatever you're cooking up in those little brains of yours, it's time to stop!" His voice boomed, and Pat jumped. Kent sucked in a steadying breath and shook his head. "I'm sorry I hollered," he said, "but this is serious. I am *not* going to marry Sylvia." Images of Sylvia wearing white lace and satin tantalized his imagination. "I'm *not* going to kiss her." Thoughts of his lips on hers warmed his veins. "I'm *not even* going to hold her hand. Understand?" He rubbed his palms together and refused to imagine her supple fingers twined with his.

Shaking his head, Kent stood. He yanked on his ear lobe and clenched his jaw. "Now, I don't know *what* you two have planned," he began, "but the time has come to unplan it."

He narrowed his eyes and stared at the vanilla candle whose merry flicker orchestrated a welcoming array of light and shadows against the darkened corner. "As a matter of fact. . ." Kent marched to the candle and blew it out with a gust that sent a ripple through the melted wax. He whipped back around and faced his children.

"I've just decided to take some vacation time until Mom and Zeke get home," he announced. "I've got a whole month built up, and I think next week is as good a time as any." Kent squared his stance and silently dared the children to argue. "Do I make myself clear?" he asked and loaded every word with a double message.

"Yes, sir," they mumbled in unison. Like two defeated warriors, Pat and Pete lowered their heads and trod from the living room.

Kent picked up the candle, stomped into the kitchen, and dropped the offending intruder into the trash can.

Chapter 4

"Keep goin', Pat!" Pete urged. He gripped the ring of the tree house ladder and pushed against his sister's bottom with his head.

She stretched one thin, tanned leg to the next rung, but the other leg remained fast. "I'm tryin' to, but my shorts won't go with me," Pat whined.

"You're caught on somethin'. Hang on, I'm moving my head so I can see better." Pete spotted the trouble. A thick splinter in the board above had fastened itself right in the middle of a yellow buttercup on the short's printed fabric. "Back down a little, Pat, and I can getcha loose."

Pete fumbled with the fabric as a pair of bees buzzed past his ear. The August breeze was nearly as hot at seven thirty in the evening as it had been at the park at noon. "Got it," Pete said.

At last, Pat started climbing again. "You're the best brother I've got!" she exclaimed as she scaled the last three rungs.

He followed close behind to make sure she didn't fall. "I'm the *only* brother you've got," Pete reminded her.

Pat giggled and crawled through the narrow doorway. Pete scrambled in behind her. He claimed the tree house as his own but didn't mind his sister's company—as long as he didn't have any friends over or she didn't get too bossy. He and Mr. Zeke built the whole thing with scraps left over from the remodeling job his grandmother did on her coffee shop. Zeke taught him how to saw boards and use a hammer. The project was always fun because Zeke let him do most of the work.

The little room still had the smell of pine lumber. The golden sunlight, bright and penetrating, seeped past gaps in the wall planks. Pat squinted, shielded her eyes, and scooted from one side of the tree house to the other.

"You gotta sit still, Pat, or the splinters will be in your rear instead of your pants," Pete said and plopped down with his back to the sun. "Move over this way with me. The sun won't be so bad on your eyes then," he said.

Pat crawled beside him, sat down, and crossed her legs. The tree seemed to whisper about their recent defeat in the kitchen. Pat listlessly watched as Pete reached for a rust-streaked lunch box marked with faded images of *The Fox and the Hound*. As if he were handling the rarest of jewels, he removed a large amber colored marble, a fishing lure with a hook missing, and a golf ball with a nasty gash. He placed each treasure on a ledge near his left shoulder.

After closing the box, he clicked the bent clasp into place. "I think Daddy really wanted to kiss Miss Sylvia—I don't care what he says." He rattled the lunch kit's plastic handle and glanced at his sister. "Whatcha think?"

Pat's eyes narrowed as if she were Sherlock, Jr. "He was lookin' at her just like Mr. Zeke looks at Grandmom," she said and nodded.

"Yep! That's what I'm figuring," Pete answered, rubbing his chin as he'd seen his Dad do. "And Miss Sylvia was lookin' back."

"I saw her, too," Pat said.

"But Dad says he's not going to hold her hand or kiss her—none of that stuff Mr. Zeke and Grandmom do." Pete waved his hand, and a long shadow played across the tree house wall.

"Well. . ." Pat tugged on the end of her ponytail. "Do they have to do all that to get married? Why can't they just get married?" Pat hit her bent knee with her fist.

"I don't know." Pete grimaced and ran his finger along one of the scented timbers. "If I ever get married, I'm not going to kiss—that's for sure. I just wish Dad would do whatever for them to get married. Miss Sylvia's way more fun than Grandmom."

"But I love Grandmom." Pat's bottom lip quivered.

"Well, so do I! But we need a mom! Everybody else has one. Besides all that, Grandmom won't play Twister or tackle football or—"

"Let us eat brownie mix," Pat finished. She swiped a strand of hair away from her chocolate-smeared cheek.

"Right," Pete agreed, glad he had convinced Pat to see things his way.

He stood and moved to the far corner. Pete tugged on a rope that wound around a pulley and fastened to the roof. A bucket holding a rubber-grip hammer, nails, and a foil packet dangled near the floor. While the container inched up, he pondered their predicament. Recalling the mother they once had became more difficult with each passing day—unless he remembered to look at the picture he'd hidden in the drawer beneath his socks. Sometimes he saw her in a dream or a whiff of perfume reminded him of her. Pete grabbed the bucket handle and released the snap on the rope's end. During those memories, she was always doing something to herself—combing her hair, adding lipstick, fretting over a dress. The vision contained no smells of cookies baking or playing baseball together—nothing like Sylvia.

"I really like Sylvia," Pete said.

"She makes the best brownies ever!" Pat rubbed her turned up nose and squinted her eyes. "And I like it when she fixes my hair." She touched the wilting yellow ribbon dangling from her ponytail.

Pete put three nails in his mouth like he'd seen Zeke do and examined a board that had come loose during last week's storm. "Hold the bottom of this board while I nail the top," he mumbled through the metal between his teeth.

Pat stood up and assisted her brother. The hammer's weight offered a struggle, but he tapped two nails in the top then nudged Pat aside in order to drive in the third nail. "Scoot over," he said. "I'm going to really whack it." With a grunt, he pummeled the lower nail until it inched into the wood and bent double.

"Stop it!" Pat screamed and covered her ears.

Pete rolled his eyes. "Girls," he huffed.

"Well, Sylvia's a girl!" Pat claimed in a singsong voice.

"She's a *woman*," Pete corrected. "That's different."

"She used to be a girl—so *there!*" Pat stomped her foot and dashed aside a trickle of moisture that made her bangs stick to her forehead.

"Whatever," Pete replied like a long-suffering adult and turned his back on his sister. "She's a lot like Vic's mom," he mused.

"What does Vic know about anything? I don't even *like* him."

"So what. . .who cares!" He pivoted to face his sister. "Hello, people!" Pete tapped his temple with his index finger. "I'm not talking about Vic anyway. I'm talkin' about his mom, okay?"

Pat rolled her eyes and crossed her arms.

Pete ignored her on purpose and kept talking. "She's really great, like Sylvia—hand me another nail—even if she does make him wash a lot and sit straight at the table. She's not even afraid of his pet grass snake."

"Hrrumph," Pat mumbled. "Grandmom would throw a fit if we brought a grass snake in the house." She fumbled in the bucket and pulled out a spike.

"That's too big!" Pete exclaimed.

She dropped the nail back into the bucket. "Get your own nail then. It's hot out here. I'm going in."

With a growl, Pete shoved the nails around until he found one that suited him. "You can't go in," he said without ever looking up. "We gotta figure out how we're gonna make Dad like Sylvia enough to marry her."

"How can we do that?" Pat asked. "Dad was really mad awhile ago."

With both hands wrapped around the hammer, Pete tackled the

final nail and didn't stop until it, too, was bent double. He sat down and wiped his nose on the hem of his baggy shorts. "I don't know, but we gotta think of somethin'."

When Pat settled beside her brother, he forgot he'd been aggravated at her, and the two sat in silence for several minutes. The breeze whipped through the opened door and offered the first hint of the approaching evening's coolness.

"Maybe we could think better if we ate a cookie," he suggested and reached for the foil pouch lying near the nail bucket.

Pat eyed the pouch with a mixture of suspicion and anticipation. "If they've got green stuff growing on them, I'm not eating them," she claimed.

"I just put 'em out here this morning," Pete said and opened the pouch with the crinkle of foil. "They're not green—unless you count the green M&Ms." He extended a cookie toward his sister. "Vic's mom made them last night."

For several minutes, Pete nibbled the chocolate-infested treat. All he did was chew and think. Think and chew. Finally, the cookie worked its magic, and an idea sprang into his mind. He jumped up. The floor planks squeaked in protest. "I've got a plan!" he announced.

Pat looked up and popped the last sliver of cookie into her mouth. "I want another cookie," she said and reached for the foil packet.

"No!" Pete dropped to his knees, snatched the packet from beneath her hand, and opened the lunch box. He dropped the cookies inside and slammed the lid shut. "We better save the last two—in case we need more ideas," he said.

Pat frowned and acted like she was going to howl, so Pete started talking fast and loud to drown out anything she might say. "I was thinking. . .what about us being sick all the time?" He watched for her reaction, ready to defend himself if she thought the idea was stupid.

She eyed him critically. "That sounds stupid! Besides, I don't like being sick."

"It's not stupid!" He crossed his legs and pretended as if he didn't care what she thought. "Anyway, we'll only be *playing* like we're sick. First, you get a bad stomachache, and nobody but Sylvia can help you. Then I start havin' pains in my head and cry for Sylvia."

She looked skeptical. "Then what?"

Pete rested his chin on his fist and grimaced. "What do you mean?"

"Do you think just *that* will make them get married? Besides, how do we know Dad would even call her?"

"Well, I'm workin' on more sick things. We might have to keep goin' for two or three days. But don't you see. . .if we won't let anybody 'cept Sylvia help us. . ." He let the notion trail off because the steam behind it was leaving fast.

"It's still stupid, and I don't know how to *pretend* to be sick."

Deflation grabbed Pete. He flipped open the rusty lunch box and took out a pocketknife with a broken handle. He picked up a dead stick he'd left yesterday and began to whittle.

Pat put her hand on his arm. "I've got an idea," she offered. "Wanta hear it?"

"Not really," Pete grumped. He cut her a sideways glance. Her mouth drooped. If it weren't for the fact that she'd just said his idea was stupid, he would have felt sorry for her. "Okay, I'll listen," he grudgingly agreed.

Pat's smile preceded a flood of words. "You know how Grandmom is always having dreams, and she sometimes talks about dreams in the Bible. I heard her tell Mrs. Raskin in the coffee shop that she had a dream about Zeke—before he came back to Jacksonville—and in a few weeks he came." She paused for a breath. "What if we started having dreams about Sylvia being our mom and told people at the shop. Daddy would hear about it and want to marry Sylvia."

Dreams were not a place where Pete cared to go. While his were not frightening, they could be less than pleasant—especially when he dreamed about his mom leaving.

"I don't know." He rested the knife blade against the stick. "Sounds to me like a lot of work. Anyway, Dad would get really mad if we started tellin' stuff like that at the shop. You saw how he got awhile ago." He resumed chipping slivers of wood off the stick.

Pat rested her elbow on her knee and cupped her chin in the palm of her hand. She stared at the growing pile of wood. In Pete's estimation, she needed a mom more than he did—even if he *did* enjoy playing football with Sylvia. There must be *something* they could do.

He dropped the knife and stick near the lunch kit, jumped to his feet, and paced the tiny tree house. Pete paused by the north wall, rested his head against a board, and peered out the gap. A squirrel scurried along a branch and paused long enough to release an offended bark.

"Hey, I've got it!" Pete whirled to face his sister. "What do we do best?"

She stared at him a few seconds then her gaze roved to the foil packet lying in the top of the lunch box.

Pete snatched up the cookies. "We're good at being *bad!*" he claimed. "Nobody can be badder than us. Remember when we put the worm in Zeke's soup? And how Grandmom said we were poor kids without a mom. Maybe Dad would think the same, and ask Sylvia to marry him! Man, oh, man, think of all the stuff we could get into! We won't obey Dad, Grandma, or Zeke. . .only Sylvia. We're mean to everybody but her. Dad would know for sure he needed her to keep us in line." With a satisfied grin, he nodded as if he were the president.

Pat shook her head until her ponytail snapped at her cheeks. "We got grounded from the TV for two weeks because of that worm, and we had kitchen duty every night, too! This idea is even more stupid than the other one."

"Can't you take a little punishment for a mom like Sylvia?"

"No! I *hate* doing dishes every night!" Her bottom lip stuck out like Vic's bulldog. "Besides, your plan might take a long time. . .maybe a week. Can't you think of something else?"

Pete opened the foil packet and pulled out the last two cookies. He extended one to his sister. "We'd better eat these. I'm out of ideas." He took a bite and tried to make it last. The second taste went faster, the third and fourth too quickly to remember. He sighed. A small gurgle from his tummy signaled that he'd downed too many sweets. He looked at the last two bites of cookie. The M&Ms weren't sitting too well after all that chocolate brownie mix.

"Want this?" he asked and extended the rest of his cookie to Pat.

Her upper lip curled, and she tossed half of her cookie into the lunch box. "Nope. I'm through," she said.

Ready to give up on any new ideas, Pete shoved the rest of his cookie out a crack in the wall and listened as it rustled through the leaves. He sighed and decided to go inside. This was getting them nowhere.

A tingle twittered in his mind as a thought stirred. He loosened the bucket rope from its cleat and dropped the container through a saucer-size hole in the floor, just like Zeke taught him. When the bucket hit the ground, the idea erupted in his thoughts like a roman candle, all bold and strong and brilliant.

"I've got the best plan ever," he whooped. "It will guarantee that Sylvia will come over quick, and when Dad sees how much she loves us and we love her, he'll be *glad* to marry her!"

Chapter 5

The next morning, Sylvia snuggled against the mattress's soft folds and wondered what time it was. Eyelids droopy, she gazed at the alarm clock on her nightstand. Her eyes popped open.

"Already nine thirty," she groaned. A shower of sunshine assaulted her eyes. She covered her head with a sheet and attempted to turn on her side. A dull ache zipped through her side and trailed her waist. Sylvia moaned.

Whatever possessed me to play tackle football with Pete? "I must have lost my mind," she breathed against the sheets and contemplated her pleasingly plump figure. Sylvia spent most of her teen years pining to be slender. By her midtwenties, she had accepted herself the way she was. And while she hadn't gained any new weight, she had done nothing to keep herself physically fit either.

Without a hint of warning, images of Kent's first wife sashayed from the recesses of her memory just as Tamala Searcy had sashayed into the choir room the first day of Sylvia's sophomore year of college. She imagined every male student momentarily abandoned all academic pursuits and forgot his own name. Tamala had been the epitome of the California girl, in every measure of the word: tall, blond, tanned, with generous lips begging to be kissed.

Sylvia would never forget the resigned expression two of her friends exchanged. However, Sylvia had simply looked down at her abundance of curves and prayed that Kent wouldn't be the one. But he was the one. Kent and Tamala got married a year later. A year after their marriage, Tamala was expecting their first child, and Kent abandoned his plans for medical school to become an RN. Two years ago, a man more wealthy proved too much of an enticement for Tamala. According to Brendy, neither Kent nor the kids had heard from her after the divorce was final.

Upon the heels of those musings, Sylvia recalled yesterday's kitchen fiasco and tightened the covers around her face. *I have never been so embarrassed and humiliated in my life.* When Sylvia moved back home to pursue her master's degree at the University of Texas at Tyler, her academic goal had concealed her matrimonial objectives. Nobody knew that, not even her parents, and especially not Kent. The very idea that he would discover the truth left Sylvia mortified beyond words. Sylvia had planned to move in gently and gracefully make herself available. When Kent expressed interest, he would believe the whole thing was his idea and never suspect Sylvia's plans. The deed had taken nearly two years, but her patience was beginning to pay off.

Yesterday, when the children had voiced their concerns about matrimony, Sylvia almost melted into a sea of mortification. *Out of the mouths of babes.* She frowned as another suggestion nibbled at the edge of her mind—a suggestion that she should have at least prayed about her decision to move back home with schemes of marrying Kent.

I've loved him since college, she defended. *Why shouldn't I marry him if he's willing?*

Inside, Sylvia rushed through the doorway of that sacred alcove and reveled in her internal shrine to the man of her dreams. Memories hung upon the walls like phantoms of yesteryear. . .the first time Kent smiled at her. . .the day he offered to carry her books in college. . .six months ago in church when they shared a hymnal. . .his recent appreciation of her help with his children. No one. . .no one was allowed entry into this haven. No one but Kent.

A whisper of a thought wisped through the alcove's doorway and disturbed the waters of her soul, *What if marrying Kent isn't God's perfect will for you? What if the Lord were to ask you to move back to Arizona and be a single missionary your whole life?*

Sylvia slammed the door on the alcove and refused to listen to those disturbing whispers another second. She tossed aside the bedcovers, clenched her teeth, and swung her feet to the floor. An involuntary gasp accompanied her abdominal muscles' raging protest. A hot shower was in order—*soon*. She stood, hobbled toward the end of the bed, nabbed her satin housecoat, and inched toward the window by her dresser. Stifling a yawn, Sylvia peered into her parents' backyard and noticed their striped cat, Tom, lying near the pool.

After several years teaching English as a second language on an Arizona Indian reservation, Sylvia had decided to pursue graduate school. Her parents had gladly allowed her to clean out the quaint garage apartment and make it her own for two years. The part-time job at Brendy's Friend-Shop supplied Sylvia with enough income to support herself while giving her the freedom to attend school. . .and pursue Kent.

The longer Sylvia gazed upon the pool, glimmering in the brilliant sunshine like a cache of rare sapphires, the closer her mind wandered to the broken family that lived only three streets over. The first day she cared for Pat and Pete, Sylvia had brought them home with her. They spent the morning in the pool and had a splashing good time. Sylvia gripped the edge of the window and braced herself against the dull ache that assaulted her spirit. After four days with those two, the apartment seemed too empty and too quiet.

Even though she valued her professional accomplishments and was thrilled to be wrapping up her degree by Christmas, a nagging voice deep within perpetuated a longing to be a mother. . .especially to Kent's children. Everywhere she went with Pat and Pete, someone assumed she really was their mother. Her hair was as blond as theirs, her skin the same lightly tanned hue.

Her cell phone released a series of croaks that sounded like a happy bullfrog in a puddle of mud. When Pat and Pete discovered her cell phone's alternate signals, they insisted on changing the ring several times a day. . .until they discovered the frog tone.

She shrugged her protesting arms into the flimsy robe and hobbled toward the phone, lying atop a lace doily in the dresser's center. Before pressing the answer button, Sylvia examined the displayed phone number. Her breath caught. Either one of the children was calling her. . .or Kent.

Despite her decision to avoid thoughts about yesterday's embarrassment, Kent's final words echoed through her mind, "We're old news." A boulder of despair had crashed through all Sylvia's hope. Perhaps Kent only viewed her as a leftover from his past. *But what he said doesn't match the way he looked at me in the kitchen,* she assured herself.

The blue-lighted phone's continual croaking would no longer be denied. Sylvia cleared her throat and hoped she didn't sound as if she'd just awakened. She barely spoke her greeting when Kent's urgent voice broke over the line.

"Sylvia, have you seen Pete?" he rushed.

Her fingers tensed against the top of the dresser. "Uh, no. . ." She trailed off and glanced around her three-room apartment as if the child might appear. The only evidence of Pete hung on her small cork bulletin board. Pete and Pat's drawings of flowers and sunshine stood out among a collection of similar drawings from her Indian students.

"Oh great!" Kent growled.

"Why? What's going on?" Sylvia demanded, and yesterday's awkward moments blurred in the face of Kent's urgency.

"He's gone," Kent explained. "Pat said she saw him heading toward your house."

"Gone!"

"Yes." His raspy voice squeaked over the word. "I slept late this morning. They got up without my knowing it. Now. . ." A shrill voice floated from the background. "Just a minute. Pat's trying to say something."

"No, Daddy, Pete's been *kidnapped!*" Pat claimed.

"Kidnapped!" Kent hollered.

Sylvia grimaced, moved the phone away from her ear, and dropped to the edge of the bed.

". . .man with a hook on his hand," Pat's certain tones drifted over the line. "And—and he had a patch on his eye. . .and—and he wore a scarf. . .yeah, a scarf around his neck like a *really nasty* cowboy. . ."

Sylvia bit down on the tip of her fingernail between her teeth and her feet tensed against the thick, gray carpet. A thousand possibilities crashed into her mind as she grappled with comprehending this awful news.

"Pat's getting hysterical now," Kent rushed. "I'm calling the police."

"Police!" Pat's shriek barely preceded the phone's decisive click.

A slow tremor started in Sylvia's midsection and rippled to her limbs. A knot of nausea pushed against her throat. The last four days flashed through her mind like a fast-forward movie, highlighting Pete's laughter, his hugs, his love of ice cream.

Kidnapped. . .kidnapped. . . The word ricocheted through her mind, and Sylvia tried to piece together the bits of information. Pat must have witnessed a man nabbing her brother.

Choking back the tears, Sylvia stood, bolted toward the closet, and her aching muscles reminded her of Pete's love of sports. She gripped her side and slowed her pace. As she turned the closet's handle, a suspicious proposition posed itself as a definite possibility. Sylvia inched open the closet and propped her forehead against the door's edge. Pat's description of the kidnapper strongly resembled a cross between Captain Hook from Peter Pan and the villain from a

Bonanza rerun. They had watched both this week.

Sylvia's trembling subsided. She narrowed her eyes. Those two mischief makers might well be up to one of their famous schemes. *But why fake a kidnapping?* she thought. *Well, what if Pete really has been kidnapped, and Pat is so hysterical she's describing the abductor in terms of the most recent villains she's viewed?* Images from the Missing Children's Network bombarded her mind. The last face that posed itself was Pete's. . .on the side of a milk carton.

Her eyes stung. She stepped into the closet, snatched a short set off its hanger, and dressed as quickly as her stiff joints allowed.

Chapter 6

Kent stopped pacing the front porch when Sylvia's silver Nissan whisked to a stop at the curb.

Pat, who had been huddled in the porch swing, jumped up and squealed, "Miss Sylvia!" The second Sylvia rushed onto the sidewalk, Pat hurled herself into her arms. Her uncontrolled sobs instigated a round of barking from the neighbor's backyard mutt. A gardener across the street turned his concerned appraisal toward Kent.

The man must think I'm beating her, he thought as Pat's wails escalated.

Sylvia wrapped her arms around the child and stared at Kent with a desperate tear trickling down her cheek. Kent, feeling as if the bottom had dropped out of his world, neared the two. He'd been trembling all over since the second Pat told him Pete had been kidnapped. Truth was, Kent wanted to wail even louder than Pat, but he couldn't allow himself the luxury.

Sylvia gathered Pat into her arms and stood. "Have you talked to the police yet?" she asked. Her ruffled hair and sleepy eyes, haunted against her makeup-free complexion, testified that Kent wasn't the only one who'd stayed in bed late.

"I expect them any second now," he said.

A black and white car with flashing lights whipped around the street's corner and purred to a swift stop behind Sylvia.

"Here they are now," Kent said and rushed toward the car.

". . .didn't—didn't get—get kidnapped. . ." Pat's broken words, punctuated by weeping, penetrated Kent's frenzied mind.

"What did you say, sweetie?" Sylvia asked as a pair of concerned police officers stepped from the car.

"Pete didn't—didn't get kidnapped." Pat hiccoughed, and the mutt next door yelped.

Kent stopped in his tracks. Both police officers gazed past him, toward Pat. Kent swiveled to eye his daughter, then Sylvia. "Did she just say what I think she said?" he asked.

Sylvia nodded and grimaced as Pat's fingernails dug into her neck.

"Pat?" Kent prompted. His trembling subsided as her claim's significance penetrated his mind.

The child buried her face more tightly against Sylvia's shoulder and refused to look at her father.

"Pete and me didn't—didn't want you to call the police—just M—Miss Sylvia." Her muffled words hurled a blast of relief through Kent. He looked toward the police officers. Hands on hips, they observed Pat with "That's what we figured" expressions. In a town as small as Jacksonville, Texas, a kidnapping was about as common as space aliens.

Kent stepped around Sylvia and tapped on his daughter's head. Cautiously, she raised a guilty gaze to her father. The second she encountered his scrutiny, Pat pressed her face into Sylvia's shoulder.

"Pat," Kent said in a no-nonsense voice. "Tell me what's going on here."

Her silence dripped with the culpability of a scheme gone awry.

"Sweetie," Sylvia's soft voice contrasted with Kent's less patient tones and only heightened his growing irritation. "You need to tell your daddy exactly what's happened to Pete. The policemen are here and everything. If he's in trouble—*really* in trouble—then we need to know."

"He's not." The words drained Kent of all remaining panic and ushered in a higher degree of exasperation. His two children were undoubtedly up to one of their grand schemes. This time, they had succeeded in nearly causing Kent to have a nervous breakdown.

"Exactly where is Pete?" Kent demanded.

"You're just going to upset her more," Sylvia mumbled.

"Upset her?" he snapped. "She didn't mind upsetting me!"

"It was *Pete's* idea!" Pat whined.

"Where is Pete?" Kent bellowed.

Sylvia shot him a glare over her shoulder, and her azure eyes held the same glint of maternal protection he'd seen in his mother's eyes.

"In the tree house," Pat whimpered.

On a whim, Kent looked at the police officers. "Would one of you like to accompany me to visit with my son?" he asked with a tight grin.

"Of course," the taller one agreed. The man was every bit of six-ten. Kent had noticed him more than once around town. A silver bar pinned to his shirt bore the name J. Stuart. Kent figured he'd do nicely.

"What are you up to?" Sylvia hissed.

"Nothing," Kent shot back. He motioned for the police officer to follow him. Kent marched around the house, past his mom's rose bushes, and toward the tree house. The August heat stung his skin, even at 10:00 a.m. But the sun's rays were a mild manifestation of the heat stirring his gut.

"Pete!" Kent demanded and halted in front of the tree house. He scrutinized the hut's narrow doorway, swathed in lush oak leaves. "I know you're up there! Pat told me. I want you to come down—and I mean *now!*"

A dreadful silence cloaked the tree. Only the scurry of a squirrel and a distant crow's call broke the moment. Kent glanced up at the police officer. "I want you to scare the pants off him. Got it?" he mumbled.

Stuart nodded. One corner of his mouth lifted, and his brown eyes held the strength of granite. "If this was my son, I'd skin him alive."

"Exactly." Kent glanced back at the tree house and encountered Pete's forlorn face poking from the opening. The child's blue eyes bugged when he noticed the policeman.

"Your little game is over," Kent stated and wondered what rationale the kids would use to justify faking a kidnapping.

The size of J. Stuart alone was enough to strike Pete with awed panic. When Stuart detailed the penalties for lying to the police, the child was trembling with dread. Kent silently stood by, arms crossed, and decided that this punishment was matching the crime far better than anything he could ever dream up. At last, the police officer finished his spiel. He straightened to his full height, winked at Kent, and strode back toward his car.

Feeling as if he'd worked a twenty-four-hour shift, Kent nudged Pete toward the kitchen door. He didn't say anything to his sniffling son because he was afraid of what all he might say were he to get started. His anger had subsided enough for Kent not to want to over-correct Pete. However, he wanted the boy to understand fully that his elaborate pranks had to stop.

Silently, he opened the back door and followed his son into the kitchen. Sylvia stood near the sink with Pat seated on the counter next to her. A box of spilled Corn Pops and a gallon of milk surrounded the little girl. Undoubtedly, the kids had helped themselves to breakfast. Sylvia turned from the waterspout. With a damp paper towel, she gently sponged Pat's swollen eyes.

Fleetingly, Kent wondered if he should pull Pat aside for a stern reprimand, until he recalled her panic at the sight of the policemen. He decided Pat's mental torture had far better punished her than he ever could.

The infinite care Sylvia continued to bestow upon his child far exceeded that of her own mother. The sight of her in the tiny kitchen somehow made Kent feel as if she belonged exactly where she was, in his home, with his family. Overwhelming appreciation, unexpected and stunning, halted any comments Kent might make. A spiraling curl clung to Sylvia's cheek, and he was tempted to move closer and nudge the curl back in place.

Kent's fingernails dug into his palms, and he scowled. With every exposure to Sylvia, he slipped closer to the precipice of unbridled fascination.

Chapter 7

Resist. . .resist! A voice of sanity urged Kent. *She's a woman! She'll take you down just like Tamala did!*

"Have you gotten to the bottom of anything in here?" His taut tones increased the room's tension.

Sylvia shot him a wary look. "What did you find out?" she asked and examined Pete, who scrubbed at his damp cheeks.

He moved toward Sylvia and rested his forehead against her side. Pete's action left Kent strangely hollow—almost as if his son had chosen Sylvia over him.

"Nothing. . .yet," he answered and crossed his arms.

Sylvia stroked Pete's straw-colored hair. Pat looked at her father as if he were a three-eyed monster. Kent stepped toward Pat and extended his arms. She reached for him, and he hoisted her against his chest. Whimpering, Pat toyed with the neck of his tank top, and Kent was reminded that he wore the same jogging shorts he slept in.

"Now, would you two please tell me why you thought it was such a good idea to fake a kidnapping?" Kent made certain his words left no room for tolerating duplicity.

Pete muttered something against Sylvia's T-shirt. Kent cast her a questioning glance. The wash of red creeping along her cheeks was her only answer. Sylvia turned toward the sink and doused that paper towel in water again.

The alluring scent of raspberry body spray reminded him that Sylvia Donnelley was all woman. . .cuddly and receptive and warm.

Kent tightened his gut. "What did you say, Pete?" he prompted while a cautious voice assured him they were about to be toppled into a difficult moment.

The water came to a splashing halt as Pete's guarded words grew clear. "We wanted to see Miss Sylvia again—and—and we, uh, figured you'd call her if you thought I was kidnapped." He tugged on the silverware drawer and bumped it shut with a clang. "And then when she came over, we, uh, hoped that if you saw how much she—how much she loved us that you'd, uh. . .well. . ." The boy shrugged.

"That you'd marry her!" Pat interjected.

Her back turned, Sylvia gripped the side of the counter.

Kent groaned and covered his eyes. A dozen possible responses tripped through his mind, none of them appropriate. No wonder Sylvia blushed at Pete's first words. He slid his hand to his stubble-laden jaw and refused to look at Sylvia. Instead, he focused upon his son, whose head was still buried against her side. Without a hint of warning, his wayward mind wondered what it would be like to wrap his arms around Sylvia's curves every day of his life and feel her sigh with contentment.

I am going nuts! he scolded himself.

On the heels of his embarrassment, a new onslaught of aggravation assaulted Kent. Sylvia Donnelley had somehow won a landslide victory with his kids. They were so enamored with "Miss Sylvia," he was beginning to think their allegiance to her might even rival their loyalty to him. As Kent examined her curly locks, all soft and blond and inviting, the flame of his aggravation gained furor and flashed into full-blown ire.

She's snared them in her web of charm and is moving in on me!

Matrimonial images from yesterday bombarded his mind. Images, that took on a disconcerting twist. Today, Sylvia was dressed in that same bridal lace. But this time, she was marching down a candle-lit aisle with a triumphant smirk that said, "I won! I won!"

Kent's fingers flexed against Pat's leg. He clenched his teeth and glared at Sylvia's creamy cheek that invited his touch as she "pretended" to scrub at the sink. *Undoubtedly, she wants me to fall all over myself trying to fix this goof as well. Well, she can think again!* he barked to himself. *I am not getting married again—to her or anybody!*

The heat of resolve wafted off the flame of his anger and hurled the words from ready lips. "Whatever you've done to them, Sylvia, you can stop now!" he declared.

"What?" she gasped and pivoted to face him.

Kent didn't hide his resolve. "You have apparently,"—he grappled for the right word—"seduced them into believing that you'd make them the perfect mother, but I have news for you—"

"Excuse me?" she squeaked, and her mouth fell open.

"Don't act like an innocent, Sylvia," he stormed. "These two don't fall in love so easily. They're tough! I know! I've lived with 'em their whole lives." He waved his hand. "They were ready to burn Zeke at the stake when they thought he was going to marry Mom. And somehow you've managed to dupe them into—"

"To dupe them?" she repeated, her eyes brimming with tears.

Kent didn't try to stifle the sarcastic moan. "Now if you think you're going to use the old tears trick on me," he accused, "it's not going to work!"

She scraped at her cheek, and the tears abated as quickly as they'd arisen. "Listen you. . .you. . .you jerk!" Sylvia stomped her foot.

Kent raised his hand and shook his head. "Just stop right there, Sylvia. Don't even try to tell me I'm off base. I know better! You've got matrimony up your sleeve, woman, and you're pointing it at the wrong man! I'm *not* available! Got it?" He shifted Pat to his other arm as the morning sunshine peaked through a matte of limbs to splash the room with silver light behind Sylvia. For an instant, she took on an ethereal glow that beckoned him to move into the center of her web.

Kent stumbled backward. "And just for the record," he crowed, "I'm taking a vacation next week, so you won't be here to—to *influence* the kids any more."

"You are the most infuriating. . ." Her face crumpled into a hostile mask.

"What all did you do with them anyway, Sylvia?" he demanded. "What did you do to make them like you so much?"

". . .the most self-centered. . . ," she ground out and balled her fists.

"She took us to the pool," Pat chirped.

"And played football with us," Pete explained, tightening his grip on Sylvia.

". . .the most hardheaded. . ." Sylvia snarled.

"And we went to the park," Pete added.

"And to the mall," Pat added.

". . .man I have ever met!" Sylvia shrieked and slammed the soggy paper towel into the sink. "If you want to know what I did, then I'll tell you!" She placed both hands on her hips and glared at Kent. "I spent *time* with your children, Kent Lane!"

Pete backed into the kitchen cabinet and gazed up at Sylvia as if she'd sprouted an extra head with orange antennae. Pat dug her blunt fingernails into Kent's shoulder, and he winced.

Sylvia pointed her finger at Kent's nose. "Something you should try to do more often!" She marched past him, head high as if she were the queen of Texas.

When Sylvia entered the dining room, Kent gingerly deposited a bewildered Pat beside her sullen brother. He stomped after Sylvia, not certain why, other than he wanted to see her *gone*—for good!

When she stopped on the edge of the living room and pivoted to face Kent, he was caught off guard and nearly ran over her. At such a close range, her cheeks were as inviting as ever. His fingertips tingled with the potential of stroking her skin. He balled his fists and fanned the flames of fury all the more—his only defense against her feminine wiles.

"And one other thing," she hollered into his face. Her sea green eyes were as turbulent as the Pacific during a hurricane, and an audacious voice challenged him to ride the tempestuous waves. "I wouldn't marry you if you were the last man on the planet!" Sylvia finished with an irate scream that bounced off the walls.

"Good!" Kent barked and noted that the fire of her anger only accented her beauty. Some daredevil whim drove him to kiss her. . . to kiss her in a way she'd never forget. Kent's heightened emotions mingled with his growing attraction and spun him into a whirlwind of action. He had no idea what Sylvia Donnelley had planned to say next. None. For his fingertips hushed her rebuttal as they encountered her heated cheeks. Just as he'd imagined, her supple skin sent a rush of pleasure through his hands.

She gasped. Kent gazed into the depths of her soul and saw the admiration that couldn't be denied. Admiration mingled with pain and the agony of rejection. Recklessly, he decided he'd gone too far to turn back. He wanted to kiss her, and the desire could no longer be abated—even with anger.

Seconds before his lips would have brushed hers, Sylvia shoved hard against his chest and stumbled into the coffee table. After stopping herself from a fall, she released a pathetic whimper. Kent reached to steady her, but she hit his hands and refused to look at him. She lunged for the door as if she were running from a rabid dog. Sylvia whipped open the door, rushed through, and banged it shut.

The resounding clap sent a shock of reality through Kent. Reality, mixed with mortification. He'd just acted like a Class-A moron.

"I am *going crazy*," he mumbled and covered his face with his hands. But no amount of self-incrimination could blot out the feel of Sylvia's cheeks against his fingertips. An unrepressed longing erupted from within. . .a longing to discover the real Sylvia Donnelley. . .a longing to have and to hold.

The triumphant giggles from the dining room sounded as if they were gurgling past mouths full of wedding cake icing.

Chapter 8

Cars covered the farmyard's lot like dimples on a golf ball. Sylvia wheeled her silver Nissan into an open spot and found the last parking place between Rev. Henderson's sedate maroon sedan and Bobby Plum's yellow convertible. Directly in front of her Barry Ray Wheeler's camouflage pickup with a row of lights on the cab roof took up room for two vehicles. The annual October hayride brought out even the most delinquent church members. The last few participants were scuttling across the farmyard near the sprawling white home where a hay-covered trailer waited to take them on an evening of fun.

Rats! I'll be left to sit on the tongue. Sylvia grabbed her light denim jacket lying on the passenger seat, locked the doors, and jogged toward the waiting crowd while cramming her arms into the jacket. She smiled to herself when she noticed how loose her jeans were. That body-wrenching football experience with Pete had encouraged her to try to get in better shape. Her new treadmill had certainly helped.

The crisp evening air, cool and still, seemed to usher in a night perfect for the hayride. The first star was already twinkling near the full moon that peeked over the eastern horizon while the sun's final rays made the western horizon look like the waters of a mysterious blue sea. The smell of freshly cut hay and a fireplace's smoke mingled with the soft lowing of cattle and invited Sylvia to, one day, live in the country. One of the things she had loved about the Arizona Indian reservation was the long evening walks out in the open. While city life was fine, Sylvia had dreamed of living in the country since grade school. She stopped near the hay-laden trailer and relished the faint whiff of ripened apples drifting from the nearby orchard.

Sure enough, Sylvia was the last person to the rendezvous point. Good-natured laughter mingled with urges for her to stop holding up the group's departure. She scanned the hay-covered trailer for a place to sit and spotted the one person she never anticipated would be present—Kent Lane. What was worse, the only vacant place was smack beside him.

The last two months, she'd noticed him at church only on Sunday morning. A couple of times, he'd spoken to her, but Sylvia remained coldly polite. She had made a decided effort to avoid him since that horrible August morning when he accused her of manipulating his children and trying to get him down the aisle. She touched her cheek and couldn't deny the delicious memory of his hands upon her face, which had rocked her, even in the midst of her fury. Sylvia had spent the last eight weeks in a state of ecstasy and turbulence. Turbulence and dread. Dread and anticipation.

Even though Kent had been wrong about her desire to "seduce" his children into loving her, he had been right about Sylvia having "matrimony up her sleeve." The very idea of his discovering her secret filled her with dread. Brendy hinted a few times that perhaps Kent was interested in Sylvia, but she believed he was afraid of a new relationship. Every one of Brendy's sly comments hurled Sylvia into a state of ecstasy. Each time Sylvia glimpsed Kent she couldn't deny the fear in his eyes, which would throw her into mental turbulence. But even the turbulence couldn't drown her anticipation when she ran into Kent at Wal-Mart and then spotted him staring at her in the checkout line.

But in the midst of it all, Sylvia's sacred alcove, her internal shrine to Kent, was filling with doubts about the constancy of his intentions. Although Sylvia would love nothing more than to start a new relationship with Kent, she didn't want him to view their friendship as only a passing fancy. Sylvia moved back home with one desire in her relationship with Kent—*permanence.*

Despite her goals, Sylvia's pride had hurt so much she distanced herself from Kent and the kids as much as possible. Once Pat and Pete started to school in late August, Brendy allowed Sylvia to change her working hours from afternoon to morning. Sylvia didn't tell Brendy her reason was to avoid being present when the kids arrived at the Friend-Shop after school. Their absence from her life left her aching for eight weeks. But she would never allow Kent to see just how much she adored his children and him until she was certain he wouldn't feel as if she were trying to trap him into marriage.

Meanwhile, Sylvia's feelings still stung nearly as bad tonight as they had the day he hurled those appalling accusations at her. Frantically, she searched the trailer for another spot to sit. The only other opening was smack beside Charley Flaugherty who was a former professional basketball player. He relived every game to anyone who would listen. And, if you were female, he just might make a move or two in between slam dunks—despite the fact that he was married! If forced to make the choice of whom to sit by, Sylvia decided there was no choice. She would either sit beside Kent or stay behind.

Finally, Oris Granes, the church's source of all humor, yelled, "Sylvia, would you hurry and get on? Kent's saved a spot just for you."

Her eyes widening, Sylvia dashed a glance to Kent, who boldly appraised her. He didn't even attempt to deny Oris's claim. Within two seconds, she counted five pairs of lips that would be spreading this juicy tidbit over the phone tomorrow morning. . .and those were the slow ones!

So the spot beside Kent wasn't a coincidence after all. She wondered if anyone would notice if she ran back to her car.

The truck cranked, and a few church members looked at her with raised brows. Hoping the twilight shadows were hiding her internal debate, Sylvia jumped onto the trailer and squeezed into the narrow spot next to Kent. *Okay,* she thought as a hay straw pricked through her jeans, *the deed is done. Now what?*

She peered past the group of laughing friends toward a pile of wood, shaped like a teepee, which would be burning when they got back. The plan was to make s'mores and drink hot chocolate after the hayride. Sylvia drew her knees to her chest and wrapped her arms around herself. She stared at the sprawling farmhouse, replete with wraparound porch. As the trailer began to roll, Sylvia focused upon a bale of hay inches away, but all she could think about was the man sitting next to her. The man she had longed for all her adult life. The man who had taken great pains to deny his interest in a relationship with Sylvia.

But he wanted to kiss me—despite what he said. The memory had possessed her dreams and sent her into daytime distraction. She missed two test questions last week because she'd been thinking of Kent when she should have been focusing on the lecture. Several times at work, Brendy had been required to repeat instructions—on one occasion even three times.

"Nice night," Kent's rhythmic words sounded as if they were laced with an unheard melody.

Sylvia pressed her lips together and pretended she didn't hear him. Half of her wanted to warmly welcome his overtures. Yet the voice of caution warned her not to act as if she were too eager for his attention. Another thought bore upon her feminine musings—a thought that insisted her grandmother would have told her she wasn't being completely honest with Kent. She forced herself to listen to the conversation on her left.

". . .then you just dump the cake mix on top of the pie filling, sprinkle the top with pecans, and dot it with butter. It's called Dump Cake, because that's all you do is just dump stuff together—right in the pan you bake it in." Mrs. Loretta Grayson waved her hand as she detailed the specifics of her latest hit at the church social.

"Okay," Mrs. Heart repeated. "All I need is cherry pie filling, a yellow cake mix, pecans, and butter. Right?"

"That's right."

"That sounds wonderful and easy," Sylvia interjected.

Both ladies turned their attention to her, and Sylvia would have testified in court that they each slid a glance to Kent as well.

"It is," Mrs. Grayson agreed and bobbed her head as the breeze teased a lock of her snowy hair.

"You're just the source for all quick and easy recipes, aren't you?" Sylvia smiled.

The aging women returned her warm smile. "When you've raised as many kids as I have, you learn to take all the shortcuts you can get."

Mrs. Heart nodded and adjusted her glasses. "And when you've got as many grandkids as I do, you do the same."

"I've got an easy recipe or two," Kent chimed in as if he were desperate for Sylvia's attention.

She hid her pleasure and wondered how the ladies would respond. Mrs. Grayson appraised Kent with sympathetic kindness and said, "I'm sure you do, seein' as you're a single father now. I'd marry you myself and take care of those babies, but I'm just too old." She looked straight at Sylvia, who considered melting into the hay.

"I appreciate that offer, Mrs. Grayson," Kent said with a round of chuckles.

Mrs. Heart's keen brown gaze pierced Sylvia, and she would have vowed the old lady wanted to say, "Stop wastin' time, honey!"

If Sylvia hadn't been the brunt of all these not-so-subtle hints, she would have laughed out loud. But laughing was miles removed from the nervous jitters that assaulted her extremities.

Mrs. Grayson and Mrs. Heart fell into another round of dialogue that Sylvia found impossible to follow—especially when Kent laid his hand on her shoulder.

"I saved this spot for you because, well. . .I—I wanted to talk to you," he said.

Sylvia looked at his chin and didn't dare go higher. Instead, she shifted her attention to Kent's cowboy boots that jutted from beneath a pair of long, lean jeans.

The truck and trailer bumped onto the country lane and began its chug-a-lug along Lookout Valley's winding roads. A trio of coon-hounds charged the trailer as they neared the next farmhouse. Sylvia wondered if their incessant barking would put an end to the conversation with Kent. Her stinging pride insisted that she hoped he stopped talking to her, but her heart drank in his every word. As soon as the hounds' barks were trailing in the distance, Kent continued.

"I can understand why you aren't speaking to me, Sylvia," he said.

"I never said I wasn't speaking to you." The strained words matched the knot of anxiety in her midsection. She picked up a piece of hay and began bending the straw at one-inch intervals. The evening breeze snapped at her cheeks and invaded her oxford shirt's open collar. Sylvia shivered and wished she had brought something a little heavier than a jean jacket.

"Of course you haven't said that," Kent finally said. "How could you? You weren't speaking to me." He chuckled.

A smile tugged at the corner of her mouth, but Sylvia stiffened her lips and snapped the fragrant hay straw in two. She picked up another one and started tormenting it. The rest of the group had become engrossed in their own worlds—some caught up in conversation, like Mrs. Grayson and Mrs. Heart, others preoccupied with excited children. For the first time, Sylvia noticed Pat and Pete's absence. She came within a breath of asking Kent where they were but stopped herself.

The choir director's mellifluous voice floated from the front of the trailer with the first stanza of "How Great Thou Art." When the group burst upon the chorus with, "Then sings my soul, my Savior

God to thee," Kent gripped Sylvia's arm and whispered in her ear. "I'm sorry, Sylvia—for all those horrible things I said. I was wrong."

Sylvia gulped. And this time, she couldn't stay the impulse to peer into his eyes. His face was only inches from hers. The full moon's mellow glow mingled with the illumination of a nearby streetlamp to highlight the sincerity in Kent's contrite brown eyes. Sylvia pressed her tongue to the roof of her mouth and tried to will the stinging in her eyes to abate. The effort was wasted. And she wondered what Kent would think if he knew he had been right about her plans to marry him.

"I really hurt you, didn't I?" he asked and lifted his hand toward her cheek. Before the backs of his fingers grazed her face, he stopped, glanced around the group, and lowered his hand.

The trailer continued its rhythmic bump along the narrow road while producing an occasional squeak. A clump of hay toppled over the side rail, and Sylvia watched it hit the road and scatter. The sting in her eyes produced twin puddles that trickled beside her nose.

"You don't have to answer me," Kent said. "I know hurt when I see it."

"I didn't purposefully. . .seduce your children into loving me, Kent," Sylvia choked out and was glad that at least that part was the truth.

"I know," Kent admitted.

"I just did what your mom asked and tried my best to keep their minds off the fact that she wouldn't be home for two weeks."

"I know," he repeated. "And you did a bang-up job."

"I was so embarrassed by what they did. If I had ever imagined they would have tried to play matchmaker between. . .between you and me. . ." She couldn't think of anything else to say. The truth was, Sylvia was delighted the kids wanted her as a mother.

"Oh? So does the idea of a match with me revolt you?" he asked with a saucy grin.

"I didn't say that," Sylvia responded and scrambled for a means to escape this conversational whirlwind with her dignity—and secret—intact.

"So, then you *would* be interested in a match with me?" His eyes twinkled through the shadows as he delivered an audacious wink.

"I didn't say that either." An unexpected giggle gurgled up her throat as she realized Kent was actually flirting with her.

"So, what *are* you trying to say?" Kent tilted his head.

"I was just trying to—to affirm that I wasn't behind their schemes, that's all," she explained.

"Well, why didn't you say so?"

"I just did, okay?"

"Okay." He released another chortle, and Sylvia laughed with him. Every trace of irritation evaporated in the face of Kent's warm appraisal. The moonlight's golden gleam bathed Kent's longing gaze with the kiss of promise. A river of warmth washed Sylvia's spirit and whisked away every trace of anxiety.

"I guess it's no secret—I really wanted to kiss you that morning," his sonorous voice was barely discernible over the group's shift into "I'll Fly Away." "I think that's part of the reason why I was so. . .so. . . uptight, I guess." He shrugged, and his padded jacket shifted. "The truth is, I guess I'm a little, well. . .uh. . .scared."

Sylvia kneaded a clump of hay and debated how to respond. An awed voice suggested that her dreams were finally becoming a reality—dreams she had believed forever unreachable the day Kent married Tamala. Yet a more rational thought insisted that Sylvia not jump to conclusions. Despite the light of attraction in Kent's eyes, they still bore the pain of the wife who betrayed him. Sylvia wasn't so naive that she believed he was fully healed from his disastrous marriage or that he was ready for a commitment. The last thing she wanted was for him to use a relationship with her as a passing flirtation.

But what about what the Lord wants? The question broke through her feminine musings like an overwrought river, violating the serenity of her sacred shrine to Kent. *God wants me to be happy,* she argued and tried to ignore the memory of never praying about her relationship with Kent. *And I want Kent more than anything.*

Kent covered her fidgeting hands with his. "You probably don't find it surprising that I'd like to kiss you now as well"—he darted a sidelong glance toward the church group—"if it weren't for all our, uh, friends here."

"But. . ." Sylvia gulped as images of flinging herself in his arms and pressing her lips against his nearly drowned out common sense. Nevertheless, the voice of reason persisted. *But what if he does kiss me? What then? Is Kent interested in a lasting relationship or a light flirtation?*

He tilted his head again. "But?"

"Aren't you moving a little, uh, fast here?" She left the rest unsaid and hoped he understood her implied meaning enough that he would dash aside all her doubts.

Kent's eyes narrowed. "Fast?"

"I mean, after your divorce," she explained and prayed that he would declare he was thinking of starting over with a new wife and home. *Kent, if only you would, I'd do anything in the world for you. I'd even do whatever it took for you to go back to med school.* Sylvia had listened to Brendy bemoan her son's choice to abandon med school so many times, she could only assume that Kent regretted that choice as much as his mother did.

After the truck had chugged along an eighth of a mile, Kent finally mused, "It's been two whole years since my divorce."

"Yeah. . . ," Sylvia hedged and finally blurted, "but are you ready for commitment?"

"Who said anything about commitment?" he said with a flippant wink. "I just wanted to steal a kiss or two."

Sylvia examined the features of the man she had loved so long she could barely remember not loving him. The heavy brows, the prominent nose, the roguish lips. The winds off that lonely alcove in her heart whispered that she should take Kent's interest at whatever level he offered and let tomorrow take care of tomorrow. She stroked the third finger of her left hand and wondered if she would be sealing her own doom in regard to marriage if she appeared too easy a conquest. Furthermore, after he stole a kiss or two from her, would he move on to another woman?

Her heart pounded in her ears. Her hands trembled. And for the first time since she chose to pursue Kent, she released a heavenward plea for help. As the seconds ticked on, no divine inspiration posed itself. At last, Sylvia decided she would follow her sage grandmother's advice, offered when Sylvia became a teenager, "Men don't value what comes too easy."

Sylvia rubbed her damp palm against her jeans leg. The next words she stated were some of the hardest she'd ever spoken in her life. "I'm not interested in stealing a kiss or two, Kent," she said. "If this is about a shallow flirtation, or. . .or. . .a means to help you get over the past, or"—she waved her hand—"something you have no plans to take seriously, then you've got the wrong woman." Sylvia held her breath, scrutinized his face, and desperately prayed that Kent would assure her he was interested in commitment, not flirtation.

At first, Kent's right brow arched into an incredulous peak. His eyes widened. He tightened his lips and tugged on his ear lobe. "Well," he finally said, "I guess we can say I've been put in my place."

"I'm not trying to put you in your place." Sylvia gripped his arm. "I'm just trying to tell you that. . .that. . ." She shook her head and grappled for the right words. "I'm just trying to tell you that I—"

"That you're playing for keeps, and if I'm not, you aren't interested." The words fell between them like precisely aimed bullets that hit the heart of the target.

"Well, if you put it like that. . ."

"I didn't put it like that. You did," he snapped.

Sylvia winced and cast a cautious glance around the group whose musical fancies were fading. Nevertheless, no one seemed to notice that she and Kent were locked in an intense conversation.

Kent bent his knee, and his boot scraped through the hay as he pulled his leg closer to his torso. He propped his elbow on his knee and had the audacity to laugh out loud.

As a warm wash crept up her neck, Sylvia scowled.

Kent's chortles subsided. He cut a glance at Sylvia out of the corner of his eye and winked. "You beat all I've ever seen, woman," he drawled with a hint of a Texas accent.

"Excuse me?" Sylvia asked.

"The last thing I expected tonight was a proposal."

Sylvia held her breath and was tempted to tumble into an ocean of anger. The man was making a mockery of her concerns and didn't seem bothered about her feelings in the least. In the heat of tension, Sylvia scrambled for some brilliant retort that would stop him in his tracks, but at the same time pique his interest in her.

"In your dreams!" she finally quipped and didn't flinch from his shocked appraisal.

Chapter 9

The next morning, the smell of brewing coffee tugged Kent from the folds of his tangled sheets. He meandered into the bathroom and scratched at his unshaven face. The whiskers made him itch like crazy, and that only aggravated him all the more. He slammed the door to the petite bathroom and stepped on Pat's damp Barney bathtub toy. The cool moisture oozed between his toes and onto the short piled carpet. He growled under his breath. Kent scooped up the offender and slammed it into the bathtub. It landed with a splat and squish.

Kent gripped the sides of the sink and peered at himself in the mirror. The dark circles under his bloodshot eyes testified to the grand total of three hours sleep—tormented by dreams about Sylvia. Dreams in which her exotic eyes nearly hypnotized him.

The other five hours Kent was in bed, he relived that hayride until he worked himself up into a frustrated fit. After Sylvia delivered that flippant challenge, she turned her attention to Mrs. Grayson and Mrs. Heart. The three ladies enjoyed a roaring good time while Kent sat in silence and reflected over how this whole excursion had blown up in his face.

"All I wanted to do was tell her I was sorry," he said to his reflection. "And maybe ask her out or something. But. . ." Kent yanked on his ear lobe and scrubbed at the end of his nose. He whipped open the medicine cabinet and snatched his shaving cream. After crashing the can on the sink side, he grabbed his toothbrush and toothpaste and plopped them next to the shaving cream. Kent slammed the cabinet door and looked at his reflection again.

"Women!" he huffed.

Sylvia had barely cast him another look the whole hayride. After arriving at the farm, she left so discreetly he lost her in the jumble of the crowd. Only when Kent saw her sleek Nissan purring up Lookout Valley Road did he realize she had slipped past him.

"What an idiot I was," he groused and picked up the can of shaving cream. He covered his fingertips in the lime-scented froth and began swathing his face in white. "Who said anything about commitment?" He reproduced his flippant wink from the night before. "I just wanted to steal a kiss or two." *How old are you, anyway, you idiot? Thirty or thirteen?*

Sighing, Kent wondered what Sylvia must think of him. *Probably that I'm a flirting skirt chaser who wants a few cheap thrills and nothing more.* He grabbed the disposable shaver and tackled his prickly beard. While that assumption would be far from true, Kent hadn't been able to tell Sylvia he was interested in a relationship—no matter how he might try to force himself. The very thought of stating those words had hurled him into a blinding spiral of panic.

He flexed his bare toes against the bathroom carpet and relived the day he and the kids came home from church early one Sunday morning. Tamala had stayed home, claiming she had a headache. Kent planned to take the kids to McDonald's after church, so Tamala wouldn't have to cook. But Pat had thrown up during Sunday school and altered the whole plan. Kent assumed that perhaps the reason Tamala didn't feel well that morning was because she was coming down with the same bug. . .until he walked into their bedroom and found her in Skylar's arms.

The irony of her getting involved with that Californian doctor was that Kent had gladly tossed aside his own dreams of med school when Tamala became pregnant with Pete. She had insisted his changing majors would be the best choice for their family, even though an RN's salary wasn't as much as he could have earned as a general practitioner. Somehow, he imagined the betrayal might have been less bitter if Tamala hadn't thrown him aside for a man in the very profession Kent had felt called to himself.

The razor nicked Kent's chin. He grimaced and examined the dot of blood oozing from beneath the skin. After dashing it away, he completed the last three strokes and doused the razor in warm water. *If only I could wash away the memories as easily,* he thought as the final dregs of shaving cream slipped down the drain.

Part of the reason for his late, great insomnia attack lay in the fact that he didn't blame Sylvia for her caution. She had every right to be cautious. Kent gave his eyes a hard stare and wondered if Sylvia saw as much pain and confusion as he saw. Truth was, he wouldn't take Tamala back if she lay at his feet and begged. He was over her, but he couldn't honestly say he was over the pain she'd inflicted.

"Women," he mumbled again and decided the time had come to evict them all from his mind for the entire day.

Last night, Pat and Pete had wanted to go to the hayride, and Kent promised them they could have his whole Saturday if they'd give him Friday night alone. They traded the hayride for a Saturday trip to Kid's Depot in Tyler—an indoor playground, full of tunnel-slides and mazes. He'd done that in hopes of having plenty of time to talk to Sylvia without those two scheming matchmakers watching his every move. Now Kent was duty-bound to honor his promise to his children.

He took a shower as hot as he could stand it, dressed in the first set of sweats he laid his hands on, and meandered into the kitchen in search of a bowl of cereal. His mother looked up from a pan of biscuits she was setting on the kitchen counter.

His surprise at seeing his mother was dashed aside by his growling stomach. Kent groaned and clutched his midsection. "My word, Mom, you're going to kill me with that smell. I hope you fixed enough biscuits for me to have a dozen or two."

"Sorry, kid, you're going to have to share." Smiling, Brendy grabbed a spatula and began lifting the fluffy works of art from the pan into a basket. A dot of flour blessed the top of her cloud of red curls. A dollop of gravy clung to her chef's apron, which covered a snazzy pantsuit in royal blue she usually wore to work.

"Why aren't you at work already?" Kent asked and checked his watch, which announced that nine o'clock was upon them.

"I wanted to hang around a bit this morning and cook a big breakfast for all you guys. Zeke didn't argue one bit. He's gone to the store to get some orange juice."

"So, where are the kids? Still in bed?" Kent asked.

"Not on your life, Buddy. They were up by seven. They're at the store with Zeke."

"Oh, well, I hope he took his big checkbook! Those two could con a miser out of a fortune in five minutes flat. Last time we went to Wal-Mart together, I came home with about thirty dollars worth of stuff I never intended to buy."

Brendy snickered. "I love it!" she said with a little too much gusto as she placed the last biscuit in the cloth-lined basket. "They're just like you and your sister when you were little. You two drove me nuts in the store!"

"Ha, ha, ha," Kent mocked as a cool breeze whipped through the open kitchen window. He gazed upon the sun-kissed yard as hundreds of yellowed leaves floated toward the earth. "Too bad I'm going to Kid's Depot," he mused. "I won't be around to rake any today."

"Oh yeah, you're really sorry about that, aren't you?" Brendy's lips twisted into a sarcastic smirk as she shoved the basket full of biscuits into Kent's hands. "Here, put these on the table, will you?"

"You're going to trust me with these? I might hit the front door and not come back." Kent sneaked his hand under the cloth, extracted one of the biscuits, and headed toward the dining room, aglow with the morning sunlight.

"You won't go far. I've got three-cheese omelets, sausage, and gravy as well."

Brendy's words sent another rumble through Kent's stomach, and he took a mammoth bite of the biscuit. The masterpiece proved as fluffy and savory as it looked. "Mmm," he mumbled and followed the first bite with another one. He set the basket of biscuits on the sprawling oak table and checked under the cloth to see if there were enough for him to steal another. He thought of the last time his mother made her famous Saturday morning biscuits. Pete had eaten two. With a swift shake of his head, Kent decided he'd filched enough.

By the time he returned to the kitchen, the last bite was sliding down his throat.

His mom looked up from pouring a pan full of brown gravy into a large, glass bowl. "Don't think I didn't see you get that biscuit." She leveled a daring, green gaze at him.

"You knew I would," Kent shot back and smacked his lips. "I always do."

Brendy chuckled and checked her watch. "I hope Zeke hurries. I've got to get to the shop before the Saturday crowd hits."

"Did Sylvia open up for you?" Kent made a monumental task of lifting the last three sausage patties from the iron skillet in an effort to hide his soaring curiosity about Sylvia. His mouth watered with the mellow smell of cooked spices and meat. As he clicked off the burner, the back of his neck prickled. Kent could always feel his mother's scrutiny.

"You know she did." Brendy's voice held a humorous edge that made Kent wish he'd never even mentioned Sylvia. He frowned at the plate full of omelets, left to warm in the stove's center, and wondered what happened to his vow to evict all women from his mind for the day. The very mention of Sylvia's name resurrected the images of her sea green eyes from his tormented dreams.

"Annie Mobley called this morning," Brendy said.

"Oh, really?" Kent questioned. He turned from the stove and wondered where this was leading.

"Yes, she was on the hayride last night." Brendy handed Kent the bowl of gravy and shoved at the side of her hair with the back of her hand.

"She was? I didn't see her."

Brendy smirked. "She sat right next to you."

"Oh," Kent said and decided this conversation was heading to a zone he'd rather not visit. He hurried to the dining table and placed the gravy next to the basket of biscuits. Squinting, he decided to lower the blinds. The sunshine was threatening to put his eyes out. He took his time and hoped his mother would be distracted by a culinary emergency and would drop the hayride subject.

Kent thought of retiring to the living room, but dismissed the idea. There were days he felt as if he and his kids were nothing short of a pain to his mom and Zeke. The newlyweds never acted that way, but still Kent worried. Therefore, he purposed to help Zeke and his mother whenever he could. After stalling as long as possible, Kent meandered back into the kitchen.

His hopes about Brendy forgetting Sylvia were dashed the second he entered the kitchen. She plopped the platter of sausage in his hands and acted as if they'd never missed a beat in the hayride conversation. "Annie said you saved a spot for Sylvia and the two of you were mighty cozy."

"Ah, Mom," Kent complained and rolled his eyes. "What's the deal with all you women? You think just because a couple of people talk for a while, they're heading down the aisle the next day."

"Don't 'ah, Mom' me!" she said with a cocked brow. "I have eyes, you know. I can see, and what I see is a couple of people making eyes at each other."

He waved his hand. "You're just so awestruck over marrying Zeke you think everybody's in love."

"Tell me you're not attracted to her." Brendy challenged and placed her hands on her hips.

"Okay, I'm not attracted to her." The admission filled the kitchen with no hint of conviction.

Brendy laughed out loud. "You're so pathetic." She lifted her chin as if she were the source of all knowledge.

"What?"

"You're as smitten as Zeke Blake." Her head bobbed from side to side.

"My, my, aren't we sure of ourselves." Kent shifted the platter in his hands.

"I know love when I see it."

"Well, you don't see it in me," Kent denied. This time no doubt traced his words. He wasn't in love with Sylvia Donnelley. Strongly attracted maybe, but not in love. He'd tasted love and was still miles removed from that falling-all-over-himself experience he'd lived through with Tamala.

"Besides," he added and searched for any means of denying his mother's claims. "Sylvia really isn't my type."

"Oh, really?" Brendy filled the teakettle with water, set it atop the stove, and clicked on the burner.

"No. . .her eyes are awfully big and she's, well, you know"—he shrugged—"overweight."

"Aren't we all." Brendy patted her rounding tummy. "I've gained ten pounds since Zeke and I got married." She lowered a sharp gaze at his stomach. "And you aren't as thin as you were a year ago yourself."

Kent sucked in his gut and decided not to enjoy another biscuit. "Yeah, but—"

"And Sylvia's got the most gorgeous pair of eyes I've ever seen on any woman my whole life, and you know it, Kent." Brendy shook her finger at his nose. "Tamala would have given her life's savings for eyes like that."

That's part of the problem, he thought.

Kent looked past his mother to the glass-front cabinets that held an askew mixture of cups and plates and saucers. Tamala's figure had been model perfect. Of course, she spent hours at the gym perfecting her body, even after the kids were born. That's where she met Skylar-the-doctor. Kent would be lying if he said he didn't appreciate the benefits of Tamala's dedication to physical fitness. But he'd come to a point in his life where if he ever married again he would choose sterling character over body perfect any day. Not only were Sylvia's eyes gorgeous, they shone with the light of an honest soul who would never betray a man she promised to love, honor, and respect until the day she died.

"So, are you going to answer me?"

"Huh?" Kent asked and refocused upon his mother who was wiping the dollop of gravy from her apron with a stained dishtowel. As Kent waited for her to repeat her question, the sweet autumn smell of crisp maple leaves wafted through the opened window and mingled with the rich aromas of coffee and the Southern breakfast.

"I said, 'Don't you believe God can help you with your fear?' "

"What fear?" he rushed.

Brendy gave him the "You-know-exactly-what-I'm-talking-about" look Kent would recognize in a crowd of hundreds. His mother had been using that expression on him since the day he sneaked her keys out of her purse and drove to the corner store when he was fourteen.

"All you have to do is ask Him, Kent." Brendy began fumbling with her apron's ties. She paused long enough to peer into Kent's soul. "Have you asked Him?"

He squirmed inside and searched for a way to change the subject. The thing his mother didn't understand was that the fear was his protection. As long as he was afraid to trust again, he *couldn't* trust again. If Kent never trusted again, he would be safe from the risk of more heartache for the rest of his life.

Brendy slipped the chef's apron over her head, folded it into a neat square, and placed it on the counter. She reached to take the platter of sausage from her son when a chorus of raucous giggles erupted from the open kitchen windows. A resounding "Boo!" followed as three faces appeared on the other side of the screen.

Kent jumped and clutched the platter. Brendy released a sharp squeal. Pat, Pete, and Zeke laughed all the harder.

"What are you three up to?" Brendy demanded. She hurled her apron at the window. The limp cloth bounced off the screen and landed on the sink's edge.

"We're scaring you!" Zeke howled, his blue eyes dancing. The kids shrieked with merriment.

"Well, breakfast is ready!" Brendy declared. "And if you scare me again, I'll eat it all myself."

"Oh, no, you won't!" Zeke challenged as the sun glistened off his dark hair, streaked with gray. "Come on, kids!"

The three struggled passed the bushes, and gurgles of joy drifted through the open window as they ran to the kitchen door. Kent set the sausage on the dining table and stepped back into the kitchen to grab the omelets. When his children burst into the kitchen, a sickening thought slammed into him.

What if the kids heard what I said about Sylvia's eyes and weight? As his mom repaid Pat and Pete with a plethora of tickles and bestowed a playful kiss upon Zeke, Kent plopped the omelets on the table and made a decision. Before they ate, he'd discover what all Pat and Pete heard and then make certain they understood they were not to repeat a word of it to anyone—especially Sylvia.

Chapter 10

A lull in the stream of customers at the Friend-Shop gave Sylvia and Brendy an opportunity for the much-needed, pre-Christmas inventory. An hour into the count, Sylvia felt as if she were drowning in a blur of items and numbers. She stuck her pencil into the loose twist in her hair. The pencil's added weight proved too much for the fine curls. The coil relaxed and flopped free of its clip.

"Oh, great," Sylvia growled as the pencil toppled to the polished, hardwood floor with a click and snap. She bent to retrieve the pencil, straightened, removed the clip, and fluffed her shoulder-length hair around her face.

Sylvia laid the clip on the checkout counter and listlessly gazed at the shelves she had yet to count. Since the opening of the trendy coffee-and-conversation house nearly a year ago, Brendy had added numerous new items. All but two were selling well. The pre-Christmas inventory was important in determining what last-minute orders they should place; but on a drizzly Saturday afternoon in early December, a good book to doze by took precedence over *counting* things!

Sylvia gazed through the front window at the beads of water trickling down the large, single pane in odd intervals. Last week's decorations of plump turkeys and golden pumpkins were gone, replaced with a wreath of holly in the center and ivy around the frame. The smell of wassail added an aura of homey welcome to the whole shop and tempted Sylvia to enjoy a second cup of the sugary treat.

She contemplated her figure. Since August, Sylvia had lost fifteen pounds, simply by avoiding sugar and walking on her treadmill. The last thing she wanted to do was use the holidays as an excuse to overindulge.

The patter of rain cast an aura of gloom upon memories of the weeks since the hayride—weeks filled with dashed hopes. After that nocturnal conversation with Kent, he and Sylvia had exchanged nothing more than trite pleasantries. Sylvia suspected Kent was purposefully avoiding her at every turn—including the church Thanksgiving dinner.

Shortly after the hayride, she had even fallen into a desperate heap beside her bed several times and begged God to make Kent love her. But each time she petitioned heaven with such requests, the same disturbing thoughts entered her mind: *Whom do you love more? God or Kent? Would you release your dreams of marrying Kent if that was God's will?* Each time these questions crashed into her cries for help, Sylvia would race into her internal shrine, dedicated solely to Kent, and refuse to answer.

She tapped her pencil against the clipboard and glanced down at her jolly, red sweater, decorated in tiny bells and cheery green Christmas presents. Christmas was as near as her next dream, but she wondered if the holidays would end in bliss. For even in the midst of all her love schemes, a sickening realization plundered the fields of her soul. Somehow, Sylvia had placed her love for Kent higher than her love of the Lord. Last week, during a particularly touching church service, Sylvia had faced the fact that those disturbing thoughts during her prayer time had been true. She wanted Kent Lane, even if that meant going against God's will.

She placed the tip of her pinkie between her teeth and pondered the crumpled letter in her slacks pocket. The message from Arizona arrived last week. The school's superintendent was asking Sylvia to consider returning to her former position as soon as she finished her master's degree program. She would wrap up her final class next week—Studies in Shakespeare. Then, Sylvia would be perusing the job market. Returning to Arizona proved to be the exact opportunity she hadn't planned to pursue. Sylvia was more than an employee on that reservation. She was a missionary. The pay was atrocious, despite the fact that they offered a furnished apartment with all utilities paid. Furthermore, the position would put too many miles between her and Kent.

But what if that's where God wants me? The internal war that started the day she received the letter began anew. Her shoulders tensed, and Sylvia gripped the clipboard as if it were her weapon.

She reached into her wool slack's pocket and tugged on the slip of paper she'd placed there this morning. The handwritten note from her favorite student, Mark, tugged at her heart. Mark, a child with a speech impediment, was eight now—the same as Pete. The words, "I miss you," scrawled in black crayon accompanied a precocious pencil drawing of an eagle. Sylvia stroked the note and wondered if the Arizona offer was God's way of telling her the time had come for her to stop pining for Kent and start living, truly living, for His glory.

I've kept tabs on Kent since college, Sylvia thought and aimlessly wondered how much further her spiritual life would have progressed if she had spent half the time thirsting for God that she had spent dreaming of Kent.

This is too convicting.

With a grimace, Sylvia shoved Mark's art back into her pocket and decided the task of taking inventory was now an attractive option. She pressed her lips together and rapped her pencil against the tops of her favorite vanilla candles by House of Wax Specialties.

Before Sylvia entered the count, a crash and a cat's howl resounded from the storeroom. "Oh no," Sylvia groaned and tugged on the neck of her sweater. Pat and Pete had been at school all week. Today they were here with Brendy because Kent had to work. She laid her clipboard next to her hair clasp and hurried down the narrow hallway. The aging floor creaked with her every step. Tiger-Higer, the store cat, darted past Sylvia, his striped, brown fur dotted in glistening moisture.

Brendy stepped from her office, a few feet in front of Sylvia. "What's going on?" Her redheaded boss held a pair of reading glasses in one hand and a mug of wassail in the other. "Where are Pete and Pat?"

"Beats me," Sylvia responded. "I've been up front for the last hour."

They rushed down the hall like a pair of Green Berets. Brendy arrived at the open storage room door first and nudged it wide open. Sylvia raised herself on tiptoe and gazed over her boss's shoulder. Brendy caught her breath, and Sylvia figured she was counting to ten as she so often did.

The children were in the middle of a pool of pickle juice, mixed with broken shards of glass, sliced sweet pickles, and strips of red peppers. Just yesterday, Brendy had purchased the jumbo jar of gourmet pickles from a salesman. Since Zeke loved pickles so much, he often proclaimed himself the "King of Pickles." Brendy thought the sweet-hot pickles would be a perfect Christmas gift for her husband. Pete looked up at his grandmother as if he thought the roof might be caving in. Pat sat in the middle of the mess, her bottom lip quivering. They both appeared to be helpless street waifs in the canyon of boxes marked GLASSWARE and HANDLE WITH CARE.

Sylvia swallowed hard. Brendy huffed, and Sylvia suspected that counting to ten didn't work this time. "Can't I leave you two five minutes without—"

After a touch on Brendy's shoulder, Sylvia said, "Let's get them out of danger; then we can scold." Her calm voice contrasted with Brendy's frazzled question.

"You're right." Brendy stuffed her reading glasses into the pocket of her green blazer and set her wassail on an empty shelf. "Would you get the broom and dustpan, please?" she prompted. "I'll try to keep them still."

"Sure," Sylvia agreed.

Soon she deftly swept up the sticky mixture and led the children to safety. As Brendy marched the kids off to her office, Sylvia applied the mop to the syrupy coating. Despite the mess, the sweet-hot smell tempted Sylvia's taste buds. The words "dangerous, expensive, and hurt" echoed from the office. She smiled to herself as she pictured Brendy hugging Pete and Pat while trying to maintain a stern fuss. *A grandmother's way*, she mused, and *a mother's, too*, her heart threw in.

Sylvia was turning out the light in the storage room when Brendy neared from behind. She held a twenty-dollar bill, and Sylvia guessed she must be up to her normal patterns. Usually after a necessary scolding, Brendy indulged the kids to "make up for" having been so firm. Sylvia had often heard Zeke complain that Brendy's lack of consistency would neither get nor keep Pete and Pat on the right track.

They need a mother. Sylvia despaired that Kent would ever view her as the perfect candidate.

"All through with terrorizing the kids?" Sylvia teased as she snapped the storage room's door shut.

Brendy shrugged. "I don't think I can be mom to them much longer. At fifty plus my energy is kaput!" She pointed her thumb down, and her lopsided grin suggested she was brewing mischief. Sylvia had witnessed the same grin with Kent and both his children. "Would you know of a good candidate to take over the job?" Brendy cocked her head and eyed Sylvia as if she were a piece of prime rib.

Sylvia wanted to scream, *Yes! I'm the perfect candidate!* Instead, she said, "There are a lot of women who'd be thrilled to fill that job." She could count three at church who seemed more than eager every time Kent stepped through the church doorway. *And if I go back to*

Arizona, who's to say Kent won't marry one of them? The disturbing thought made her want to rush back home and pen an immediate rejection of the job. She'd already wished Kent well at his first wedding. Repeating the gesture would undoubtedly kill her.

"Well, I'm not voting for 'a lot of other women.'" Brendy drew quotation marks in the air, and the twenty-dollar bill crinkled with her gesture. "I'm rooting for you." She scrunched her nose. "If that harebrained son of mine would only straighten up and see the perfect opportunity right under his nose."

With a hard swallow, Sylvia examined her comfortable loafers. While she and Brendy hadn't discussed her feelings for Kent, Sylvia felt that Brendy's women's intuition had clued her in on plenty of information. If nothing else, the church gossip mills after that hayride enforced what Brendy probably already suspected.

Sylvia had yet to mention the letter from the Indian reservation. Perhaps now was as good a time as any. They were asking her to come back right after the New Year. That was only a month away. But as much as she tried to voice this new piece of information, Sylvia couldn't conjure the courage. She tried to straighten her shoulders from their melancholic droop, but the effort was lost.

"I'm going back to my counting," she said.

"No, you aren't!" Brendy insisted. "I've got something more fun for you." Brendy grabbed her hand and started for the office where Pat and Pete were still incarcerated. "The kids need a break," she said as they entered the cluttered office, "and so do you. I want you to take them to the Dairy Queen, get them a snack, and let them loose on the indoor playground. Kent called about thirty minutes ago and said he's taking off early. I'll call him back and tell him to just pick up the kids at the DQ." She turned a scheming smile upon Sylvia whose heart did a flip-flop.

"I don't want to see you back here until Kent picks up the kids. Got it?"

The children looked up from the pile of blocks they were tackling. Both their eyes sparkled. As one, they hopped up, squealed, and jumped around like a couple of kangaroos.

Chapter 11

Within minutes, Sylvia ushered the two ecstatic children from the folds of a dull drizzle into the local Dairy Queen. Despite the Christmas season, east Texas was as warm and humid as ever. That morning, the weatherman predicted the high to be seventy-five degrees. Sylvia swiped a trickle of moisture from her forehead and scoffed at all hopes of a white Christmas.

Despite the weather's lack of cooperation, every table sported a miniature Christmas tree, and inexpensive wreaths adorned the row of windows along the west wall. All the staff wore Santa hats, and Bing Crosby's, "Silent Night," played over the speaker system.

Sylvia glanced across the crowded restaurant and understood why no one was at the Friend-Shop. They were all here. . .even the weathered Mr. Narvy and his buddy, Fred, who were usually waiting on Brendy to open the Friend-Shop every morning so they could play checkers and sip coffee. The checkers brigade would often show back up midafternoon for a rematch, but not today.

Sylvia glanced at her watch. "Three o'clock," she mumbled and shook her head. Usually the Dairy Queen was deserted at this hour.

Pat and Pete darted past a pair of teenage girls toward the playground as if they owned the place. "Hey!" Sylvia reprimanded. "Wait while we place our order!"

"But Brandon and Amanda are here!" Pat and Pete crowed and hit the playground door as if they just won the jackpot.

Sylvia strained to see through the door and noticed her blond pastor's wife, Amanda Henderson's mother, sitting in the corner of the crowded room.

With a sigh, she placed her order for a Diet Coke and two ice cream cones. The savory smell of freshly cooked onion rings almost beguiled Sylvia to add a large order of the crisp, fried treat to her Diet Coke. Nevertheless, she thought of Kent's pending appearance and resisted.

Visions of chocolate dipped ice cream cones lured Pat and Pete from their pursuits of play. Sylvia settled into the booth and tousled Pete's blond hair. When she pulled away her hand, a dot of clear goo clung to her index finger. *Pickle juice.* She chuckled to herself and took a draw of her soda. The aftertaste of artificial sweetener did little to appease thoughts of those onion rings. She glanced toward the restaurant's glass door, expecting Kent to arrive any moment. Resisting would be well worth the effort if he noticed her weight loss.

Pat toyed with their table's tiny Christmas tree between bites of her ice cream cone, but Pete was too intent upon devouring the whole thing with as few bites as possible. All at once, Pete stopped and looked at Sylvia. A white circle of ice cream ringed his mouth.

"You don't like Dairy Queen much, do you?" he asked.

"Excuse me?" Sylvia prompted. She scrunched a napkin, decorated with a red ice cream cone, and searched for any clue to Pete's conclusion.

"Nobody comes here and just gets a Coke." He crunched his ice cream cone and chewed as if he hadn't eaten in weeks.

"Yeah," Pat chimed in. She abandoned the Christmas tree and observed Sylvia as if she were an unusual insect under a microscope. "Why didn't you get an ice cream cone, too?"

How do you explain wanting a body a man finds attractive to a six-and eight-year-old? Sylvia wondered. "Well, guys, it's like this." She placed her elbow on the table and rested her chin in her hand. "The foods you like—and me, too, for that matter—have an awful lot of calories in them."

"What are calories?" Pat inquired.

"Things that make ya fat." Pete injected.

Sylvia winced. "That's right," she continued. "Things like ice cream have lots of calories, and if you're a grown-up who has a weight problem like me, they can make you gain weight." She touched her diet cola. "Diet drinks don't have any calories."

"It figures," Pete declared with enough volume to be heard three tables away. "Dad said he couldn't marry you 'cause you're overweight!"

A distinct silence fell over the neighboring tables. A hot wave flashed across Sylvia as she inched down in the booth. A panicked glance to those nearby attested that their table had become the focal point of the moment. Several patrons discreetly leaned forward as if they were being clutched by an intense movie's cliffhanger.

Pat clamped a hand over her mouth. Between separated fingers she hissed, "You promised not to tell, Pete!"

Sylvia hunched her shoulders. Her heart turned inside out as she realized the veracity of Pete's comment. The conviction in the child's eyes insisted that Kent really had remarked about Sylvia's weight and the kids must have overheard. The blurring diet cola seemed to mock her efforts at losing weight. Kent married "body perfect" once, and he undoubtedly expected as much if he were ever to marry again.

Even if I lose some weight, I'll never have a body like Tamala.

A trickle of fury mingled with her mortification. Sylvia wondered how she could have fallen for a man who was so shallow he would never see her good traits just because she wasn't thin. His claim on the hayride of wanting to kiss her only added heat to her ire.

He obviously sees me as some pathetic plaything he can use and toss aside! I have been a fool! Sylvia stormed. The last few months of God's dealing with her about releasing her desires to marry Kent played through her mind. *Maybe the Lord knows Kent will never truly love me and only wants what's best for me.* The realization both lent her peace and heartache. Her fingertips slid across the outside of her slack's pocket to encounter the imprint of that note from Arizona. Perhaps going back to her missionary work was the only sensible option for her future. There the children loved her, and she was like a mother to them all.

Sylvia gulped a quick sip of her soda and swallowed against a tightened throat. The last two years of her life spun before her like a fruitless goal that offered mockery instead of fulfillment.

"Was there anything else your dad didn't like about me?" she choked out and couldn't imagine what prompted that question. *I must be a glutton for punishment,* she thought.

"Not much, except your eyes are too big." Pete wiped a dollop of ice cream from his sweater sleeve and poked his index finger in his mouth.

"Pete, Dad is gonna kill you!" Pat insisted, her eyes like blue beacons of prophesy.

"I guess he must think they're like cow's eyes," Pete continued.

"Cow's eyes?" Sylvia croaked.

"Now you're lying!" Pat fumed and plopped her ice cream cone on the table. The treat fell over with a soft squish. "Dad didn't say that!" Her ponytail snapped at her cheeks as she shook her head.

"Whatever." Pete rolled his eyes as if he were a jaded adult, tired of the whole conversation.

"I think your eyes are *beautiful,*" Pat said in awestruck wonder.

"Thank you, sweetie," Sylvia choked out and wondered that she ever imagined Kent might have agreed with Pat's compliment.

"Oh, gross," Pete said before shoving the last bite of cone into his mouth.

A hum of conversation suggested their table was no longer the focal point of half the restaurant. Sylvia, feeling as if her world were caving in, cast a discreet glance around her to confirm that everyone had lost interest in the "fat woman" with two loudmouthed children.

Her initial trickle of fury gained the strength of a devouring river. She blotted the corners of her eyes and drained the pooling tears, as ache became action. Sylvia clenched her fists. Visions of confronting Kent instigated her jumping to her feet.

"Wipe your face, Pete; we're leaving!" she said.

Pat's mouth fell open. "But we wanted to play with Amanda and Brandon some more!" she bleated.

"Yeah, you promised that after we finished our ice cream, we could play some more," Pete whined.

"Oh, great," Sylvia mumbled and checked her watch. They had only been here about fifteen minutes. Brendy asked her to keep the kids here until Kent arrived. She wilted back into the booth and debated the reactionary choice to confront Kent. Despite her fury, the option now held little wisdom. He was probably still at work anyway.

She straightened her spine and took another swift draw of her soda. The day had arrived for Sylvia Donnelley to stop listening to her heart, start listening to the Lord, and begin to live her life like Kent Lane never existed.

"Hey, there's Dad!" Pete chirped.

"Dad? Where?" Pat asked and squirmed in her seat.

Sylvia looked at the children's animated faces with cold horror. She had yet to regain her equilibrium and didn't think she was capable of making small talk with Kent.

"Right there." Pete pointed toward the front door. "He just walked in."

Clutching the Styrofoam cup, Sylvia forced herself not to follow the children's gazes.

Chapter 12

Kent maneuvered through the crowded restaurant and neared the table where Sylvia sat. An unexpected thrill zipped through his gut when he saw her tousled blond curls. After he arrived at the Friend-Shop, his mother told him Sylvia had just left with the children. So he'd fully expected to see her. Nevertheless, his heart was hammering as if her presence were a total surprise.

An elderly couple rose from their chairs in his pathway. Kent halted his progress as he recalled the events of the last two months. Several times, he had been tempted to strike up a conversation with Sylvia, but he'd been overtaken with fear and backed away each time. A couple of weeks ago, Kent realized that while his fear was protecting his heart, it wasn't doing much to keep him warm at night. So he'd cautiously begun to pray that the Lord would give him the strength to overcome the terror of another marriage.

Kent hadn't considered how or if the Lord was answering his prayer until his mother told him Sylvia had taken the kids to the Dairy Queen. The only reaction he had experienced was anticipation and the hope that perhaps Sylvia would agree to a romantic evening. The chamber of commerce was sponsoring a holiday flotilla next week, which involved a bonfire and a cozy, nocturnal barge ride on Lake Jacksonville. From what the advertisement said, the lake houses would be blazing with Christmas lights and holiday decor.

As the aging couple shuffled out of the way and Pat and Pete squirmed past them, Kent glanced down at his surgery scrubs and wondered if perhaps he should have gone home to splash on some aftershave and change into something a little more attractive. As the weeks had rocked on, Kent finally admitted to himself that he was far more deeply moved by Sylvia than he'd ever admitted to his mother. At this point, he could honestly say that he was interested in more than stealing a few kisses. He rubbed a flattened hand across the front of his tired, green smock. Kent shrugged and decided that his charm would have to make up for what his appearance lacked.

"Dad! Dad!" Pat and Pete squealed in unison as they hurled themselves around his legs.

"Whoa!" Kent exclaimed and struggled to keep his balance. He bent and patted both their backs. "You two act like you haven't seen me in months, and I tucked you in last night."

"Sylvia bought us ice cream," Pat exclaimed and peered up at him with twinkling blue eyes.

"I already ate mine," Pete said.

"Oh, really?" Kent rubbed his thumb along Pete's cheek. "Looks like you're wearing part of it, too, champ." He hoisted Pat into his arms, tousled Pete's hair, and glanced toward the table to see Sylvia hastening to clean up the remains of their ice cream cone experience. Her lips were set in a line that looked less than pleasant, and her hunched shoulders and abrupt movements suggested she wasn't the happiest woman on the planet.

Kent furrowed his brow and eased Pat to the floor. Without a glance his way, Sylvia dumped the scraps into the trash can and marched toward the doorway.

"Sylvia?" Kent called and stepped toward her.

"Looks like she's mad," Pete said with a nod.

"It's because of what Pete told her," Pat claimed.

"Uh-uh!" Pete said and stiffened his spine.

"You did, too!" Pat demanded and screwed up her face into a reddening banner of truth. "You told her Dad said she was fat and had eyes like a cow!"

"I did not!" Pete denied and shoved his sister.

Pat never had allowed Pete's size or gender to stop her from tearing into him when duty called. Without a word, she kicked him in the shin and grabbed the top of his ear.

Pete howled and grabbed for her hand. Before Kent could stop his petite daughter, Pat scooted behind her brother and said, "You tell Dad the truth, or I'll twist your ear off!"

Kent glanced around the crowded restaurant in hopes that nobody had noticed their little family upheaval. But his hopes were dashed. Every person within ten feet of them was more interested in Pat and Pete than their treats and eats.

"Would you two stop it!" Kent demanded and scooped Pat into his arms. Another glance toward the exit offered a view of Sylvia with the glass door closing in her wake. Her back stiff, she rushed across the parking lot.

"Oh, great!" Kent groaned. He glared at his frowning son, who fingered his reddened ear and glowered at his sister. Kent deposited Pat into a vacant booth and knelt in front of Pete. "What exactly did you tell Sylvia?" Kent asked, his voice low. He narrowed his eyes and silently dared Pete to hide the truth.

"He told her you said you couldn't marry her because she was overweight and her eyes looked like cow's eyes," Pat repeated.

Kent ignored her and focused upon his son, who shot Pat an "I'm-gonna-get-you-good-for-this" look.

"Pete?" Kent demanded.

Without a word, the boy stared at his feet and produced a barely discernible nod.

With a growl, Kent gripped Pete's upper arms. "Why in the name of common sense did you tell her that?" he asked. "I told you not to repeat that. I thought you *wanted* Sylvia and me to get married."

"I do!" Pete said, his eyes wide.

"Well, if that's what you wanted, then why did you—" Kent

stopped and decided now was not the time to dissect his son's logic, or lack of it. All he could think about was the last glimpse of Sylvia marching toward her car.

"Is everything okay out here?" a pleasant voice asked from the playroom.

Kent glanced up to notice their pastor's wife, Joy Henderson, standing just outside the doorway. Graceful and blond, Joy had charmed their congregation from the day she and her husband had arrived five years before.

"Uh. . ." Kent glanced toward the restaurant exit and saw no signs of Sylvia. "Would you mind keeping an eye on the kids for me for a few minutes?" he asked. "We've had an, um, emergency."

"Oh, sure," Joy agreed and extended her arms to the children. "They can play with Amanda. I've got Brandon with me, too," she added. The children trotted toward Joy who paused before entering the playroom. "Is there anything else I need to do? I've got my cell phone if you need me to call someone about the emergency. . ."

"No, it's not *that* kind of emergency," Pete explained as he trotted into the playroom.

"Yeah," Pat added. "It's all because of Pete's big mouth." She stuck her tongue out at her brother, and he tried to sock her in the shoulder.

Kent stepped toward his bickering children but stopped himself. He could deal with them later. Right now, he had a more pressing problem.

Chapter 13

S ylvia, wait!"

She rested her hand upon the door handle as Kent's urgent cry pierced her anger and pain. Sylvia debated whether to jump in the Nissan and zip out of the parking lot or acknowledge his call. The tepid drizzle had grown into a gentle sprinkle. Droplets of moisture beaded upon her eyelashes and trickled down the side of the car. After two seconds, Sylvia realized she really had no choice. There was nothing left to say to Kent Lane—and nothing she wanted to hear from him.

With a flick of her wrist, she popped open the door and scrambled into the driver's seat. Fingers trembling, Sylvia inserted the keys into the ignition and cranked the engine. Her eyes blurred as she fought back the ocean of tears that choked her. She ground her teeth and blinked against the moisture. *The last thing you need to do is start crying.*

But a thud against the window sent a shock through her, and she jumped. An involuntary glare to her left revealed Kent's hands pressed against her window and his face only inches away.

"Sylvia, please stop!" he said, his words muffled by the glass. "We need to talk," he continued, his brown eyes pools of anxiety and remorse.

"I. . . ," Sylvia began and stopped. The sight of Kent so near muddled her every thought, and she couldn't conjure a logical means of rejecting his request.

"Look, why don't I get into the passenger seat, and—"

"No!" Sylvia said and shook her head.

"Then at least lower the window," he pleaded as rivulets of rain trickled down his cheek.

Sylvia smashed the electric window button and stopped when the window was half down. "Where are the kids?" she asked, and her voice sounded as if it were full of jagged ice. She tensed her spine and examined the steering wheel's leather cover.

"Joy Henderson was in the playground. She's watching them."

Sylvia nodded.

"Pat told me what Pete said," he continued.

She toyed with the floor gearshift and remained silent.

"Sylvia," he began, "would it matter if I said I didn't mean any of what Pete said the way it was repeated to you?"

"Which part, Kent?" she squeaked out. "The part about my being too fat or my eyes being like a cow's?"

"In the first place, I never said you had eyes like a cow's," he said with tired resignation. "That was Pete's vivid imagination at work."

"So what exactly *did* you say?" Sylvia dared turn her misty gaze to his and silently demanded the truth.

He hesitated and looked down. "What I meant was—"

"I want to know what you *actually said*, Kent. Was there any truth in what Pete said? Any at all?"

"Well. . . ," he hedged. A rumble of thunder from the west issued in a flash of lightning and a closer boom. "Looks like another Christmas storm," he mumbled with a sarcastic lift of his mouth. "I just love this weather. Mind if I get in the passenger seat?"

"Well. . ." By the time Sylvia tried to conjure an excuse to prohibit Kent from joining her, he had rounded the car and was tapping on the passenger window.

Doubting her own judgment, Sylvia pushed the electric lock button. Kent crawled inside and slammed the door two seconds before a deluge fell from the heavens. Sylvia shoved the window button up and switched off the ignition.

"Okay," Kent said. "I guess maybe all isn't lost after all." He turned to face Sylvia with his roguish grin. "I convinced you to let me in, didn't I?"

Sylvia didn't answer. Instead, she narrowed one eye and looked at him while the word *overweight* echoed through her mind in Pete's candid tones.

Kent rubbed a hand across his damp forehead and lowered the corners of his mouth. "Let's see. . .where do I start?" he said as if he were standing before a merciless judge.

"Maybe it's time for both of us to start by being honest with each other." Sylvia didn't expect her own admission or the sad laugh that followed. Neither did she anticipate the growing need for the truth to be out between them. Sylvia gripped the gearshift handle and prayed for the courage to come clean with Kent. "I have a secret, Kent Lane," she said and stared past the wash of water pouring across the windshield. "Something you don't know and have never known."

"Oh?"

She nodded and looked him square in the eyes. "Yes. I've been in love with you since college—and I mean *really* in love with you."

He blinked. His eyes widened. He slowly shook his head. "What?" Kent finally gasped.

Sylvia nodded. "Yeah," she admitted, and the word sounded as tired as her soul. She propped her elbow on the door ledge and rested her forehead against her fist. "I can't believe I'm telling you this," she rasped as the smell of her dampened hair spray released the essence of tropical flowers. *Might as well tell all now,* she thought and plunged forward. "The day you married Tamala. . ." She smiled, yet the gesture felt as if it lacked even a trace of joy. "I thought I would die inside."

Avoiding eye contact, she shifted her elbow from the window ledge and restlessly clicked her key backward in the ignition. Sylvia pressed her index finger against the CD button. Listlessly, she watched as the drawer slid out to reveal a disk of worship music.

Sylvia stayed focused upon the blue-labeled disk. Nevertheless, Kent's astounded scrutiny pierced her mind.

"When I heard the two of you were divorcing, I came back home to pursue grad school—at least that's what I told everyone. But really, it was to pursue you." She shrugged as a choked sob erupted into a pathetic squeak. "Oh, heaven help me. . . Why am I *telling* you this?"

Sylvia pressed the CD button again, and her finger trembled against the button. Through a blur, she watched as the drawer slid back into place. Sylvia dashed at a rebel tear that refused to be abated. "The day you said what you did about my having matrimony up my sleeve. . ."

Kent's ironic chortle filled the vehicle.

"Part of the reason I was so upset was because I was terrified you'd learn the truth." She clicked her keys back into the neutral position and removed them from the steering column. They clinked with her every move. "I don't know what I was thinking when I came back to Jacksonville," she whimpered. "I guess. . .I guess I had some sort of fairy-tale hopes that one day you'd wake up and—"

"But I have," Kent said. "Don't you see? That's the reason I chased you out here."

She shook her head and closed her eyes as if he'd never spoken. "I've spent my whole adulthood dreaming of you, Kent, and pining for you, and what has it gotten me?" She raised her hand. "A verdict that I'm too overweight from you, and God telling me I'm out of His will."

"Sylvia," Kent began, "listen to me! I *did* say that! Yes, I did, but I didn't mean it. Don't you see. . ."

She dared gaze at him.

He shook his head. "I was looking for anything—any excuse to get my mom to back off. She wouldn't stop teasing me about the hayride, and I just blurted out any excuse I could find to make her think I wasn't attracted to you, because. . .because. . . Believe me, your weight doesn't bother me in the least. I like you, Sylvia. . .just the way you are. I like you *a lot*—so much that it's scared me half crazy." The sincerity in his words matched the earnestness in his eyes.

"Really," he added, "I guess that's the reason I said what I did to my mom and what I said to you on the hayride about, well"—he shrugged—"just stealing a kiss or two. When you mentioned some kind of commitment, I panicked."

Sylvia rested her forehead against the steering wheel and gripped it as if the thing were her lifesaver in a sea of conflicting emotions, churned by doubts and confusion. At long last, the desires of her heart were being granted. The ring of truth in Kent's words attested that her weight really wasn't an issue with him.

Nevertheless, she could no longer deny the haunting conviction that God's perfect will for her lay in Arizona. The note in her pocket seemed to warm with the passing of every second. While Pat and Pete might need her, so did a school full of children in Arizona. She gazed past the steering wheel at the odometer, which registered exactly 55,238.9 miles. A new rumble of thunder accompanied the distinctive ping of ice on her windshield.

"Oh my word, it's hailing now," Kent said.

"Figures," Sylvia said and raised her head to view the tiny balls of ice, mixed with water. "Somebody in east Texas will probably get a tornado out of this."

"Merry Christmas," Kent injected.

"For sure," she said and continued without missing a beat. "I've been given an offer to go back to Arizona. They want me back after the first of the year, but I've thought about maybe heading that way next week," she said and wondered if the Indian reservation would have a spot for her so soon.

"You mean right now—right before—before Christmas?" Kent stammered.

"Yeah," Sylvia answered.

"Please don't go." The pressure of Kent's cool fingers upon her hand wavered Sylvia's resolve to follow the Lord's voice. "I was just. . ." He hesitated, and Sylvia moved her hand from his in order to pinch the pleat in her slacks. "Believe it or not, I was planning to ask you out for next week," he added on a wry note.

"Even though I have eyes like a cow's?" Sylvia asked and couldn't hide the smile from her voice. Now that she was sitting here with Kent, Pete's claim sounded far-fetched and childish.

"I never said that, Sylvia." Kent reached to stroke her cheek.

"I believe you," she breathed. Sylvia closed her eyes and leaned into the gentle pressure of his touch. The wash of warm tingles that trailed down her neck beckoned her to run headlong into this opportunity and forget the still, small voice that persisted about her belonging in Arizona.

"You have the most gorgeous eyes of any woman I have ever seen. They're the color of the sea. Did you know?" Kent's hand trailed to her ear and slipped to the base of her neck.

Catching her breath, Sylvia fluttered open her eyes to see that Kent's face was only inches away. "So I've been told," she croaked.

"Hmmm," he said as his gaze trailed to her lips. "Mind if I kiss you?" he asked.

"Please do," Sylvia responded seconds before his lips moved upon hers. Everything Sylvia had ever imagined about a kiss from Kent was exactly what occurred. She felt as if she were dashing down the daring slope of a runaway roller coaster that wasn't about to stop. She clung to him and prayed that God would let her fully embrace the man of her dreams. But in the middle of it all, the exhilarating roller coaster crashed into a solid wall of opposition.

The words, *No!* and *Arizona!* bombarded her mind. As the kiss lingered, Sylvia cleaved to Kent and stood at the door of that sacred alcove, ready to guard it from the eyes of the Lord Himself. She had carefully built the internal shrine to the man of her heart. Going back to Arizona would mean destroying the shrine and closing the door on her heart's desire, never again to return. A merciless band of anxiety squeezed Sylvia's heart, demanding that she forever make her choice: either Kent Lane or God.

Despite all her pining and all her desires, Sylvia realized she had little choice. If God wanted her back in Arizona without Kent, then she would go. Still clutching the front of Kent's shirt, she broke the exhilarating kiss.

"No," Sylvia rasped as she inched back. "I—I can't."

Only a breath away, Kent scrutinized her eyes with an intensity that pierced her soul.

Sylvia looked down. "I—I can't," she repeated, and Kent released her.

"Okay," he said, his voice unsteady. "So, maybe. . .maybe I'm not the best kisser in the county."

"No, it's not that," Sylvia wailed. She balled her fist in her lap and focused on her tense fingers. "I just don't think this—you and me—is God's will for me, Kent. I really don't. The closer I get to you, the more I feel as if God is asking me to release you. It's the craziest thing." She gulped. "I've longed for this moment since—since college." She raised her head and watched the wash of water flooding her windshield. Another rumble of thunder accompanied a swish of wind. A row of oaks along the restaurant's east side bowed and shuddered as if shaken by an invisible hand. Sylvia slumped deeper into the seat and traced her finger along the electric lock button.

Kent released a resigned sigh, and she darted a glance to him. "Oh man, I can't believe this," he drawled. Kent propped his elbow against the window's ledge and pressed his fingertips along his brow.

"I've been doing some praying, too," he said and rubbed the top of his thigh. "I've been so scared of a relationship with you, or any woman for that matter." He peered out the window, and Sylvia drank in his profile. "And, well," he shrugged, "I asked the Lord to do whatever He had to do to make me less fearful. Over the last few weeks, it's as if I have felt these chains dropping from my soul. I'm not sure if that even describes it. All I know is, I was eaten up with fear last August when the kids pulled that kidnapping stunt, and now I'm not afraid at all—at least, not where it concerns you."

He turned his attention back to Sylvia, and she gulped. The soft adoration spilling from his soul was enough to make her wish she had never even gone to Arizona in the first place. Kent reached for her hand and tugged on it. He pressed his lips on the backs of her fingers, and Sylvia couldn't deny the electricity that rippled through her veins. When he lowered her hand, Kent eyed her with a solemn humor that suggested she wasn't the only one affected.

"I want you to go back to Arizona, if that's what you really believe the Lord wants you to do," he said. "But I want you to promise me something."

"Okay," Sylvia whispered.

He eyed the front windshield as the deluge began to diminish. Sylvia clung to his hand and wavered on the precipice of indecision. *Perhaps I could stay here until summer, and then go back to Arizona in the fall.* But the very idea of delaying her journey knotted her stomach in dread.

"If you get out to Arizona, and you and the Lord work out whatever it is you need to work out. And, if you decide you'd like"—his lips tilted into a daring smile, and he threw her a saucy wink—"some company. Would you call me?"

"Of course," Sylvia squeaked out.

"You promise?" he asked, and his brows lifted a fraction.

"Yes. . .yes, I promise," she said. Yet her heart twisted as she wondered if she would ever be able to do what he was asking. Presently, Sylvia sensed that the Lord was asking her to release Kent. . .forever.

Chapter 14

So Sylvia Donnelley left the man of her heart. She journeyed back to her calling, to the place where God asked her to deconstruct that shrine inside and allow Him, once and for all, to become the Lover of her soul. For the first time in her life, Sylvia learned what it meant to release all of herself to her Holy Creator. She abandoned herself to Christ and held back not one shred of her own desires. Until at last, she came to the realization that, despite all her longing, Kent Lane could have never been her everything. Only the Lord could fill those deepest longings of her soul.

At that point, Sylvia was at peace with whatever God wanted for her—whether she should remain single for life or marry and have a house full of children. And that is when God impressed her to contact Kent.

She thought of calling him, but determined a visit in person would better suit the situation. With excitement building, Sylvia decided the best time was during a brief school break, the weekend before Valentine's Day. Driving all the way to Texas for such a short trip proved illogical. When a fellow missionary at the reservation offered to donate her frequent flier miles to what she dubbed "Project Romance," Sylvia grabbed the opportunity.

After an uneventful flight, she arrived in her austere garage apartment. Sylvia dropped her overnight bag on her bed in the middle of a shaft of noon sunshine and waited half an hour while her mother fussed over her and supplied a platter full of chocolate chip cookies with a six-pack of diet soda. Once the front door clicked shut in the wake of her mother's departure, Sylvia finally found herself alone in the musty-smelling flat she'd called home for two years.

She kicked off her low-backed loafers, pulled her cell phone from her purse, and paced the modest apartment. The route was a short one, a mere three rooms, and Sylvia found herself back where she started in less than a minute—in the center of the room that offered both a kitchenette and a den. Cell phone in hand, she adjusted the wicker-framed mirror over the striped love seat but realized it was straighter before she bothered it. She gave up on the mirror and moved three steps to the tiny bar. Sylvia whipped open a drawer and pulled out an oversized vanilla candle that reminded her of the one she'd placed in Brendy's living room while keeping Pat and Pete. She lit the candle with a butane lighter and wondered if Kent had enjoyed the homey smell when he came home from work.

"That was the day the kids and I were making brownies," she whispered and the candle's cheerful flame seemed to dance to a melody that incited her to call Kent.

She looked at the cell phone and fidgeted with the antenna. On an impulse, Sylvia foraged in the white cabinets until she found a coffee tin full of raspberry mocha from Brendy's Friend-Shop. As she scooped the fragrant coffee into the filter basket, her mind filled with hundreds of doubts. Doubts about the wisdom of the trip. Doubts about Kent. Doubts that he would still be interested.

What if he's started dating someone at church? She dropped the spoon on the counter, and a bit of coffee scattered across the yellow tile. Sylvia shoved the filter basket into place and toyed with the hem of her cheerful, red sweater. She looked down at the brand new outfit she'd found at Goodwill—both pieces still had Neiman Marcus price tags on them, and they were a size sixteen. Sylvia hadn't fit into a sixteen since she was a junior in high school. She tugged on the pants waistband and reveled in the loose fit.

While wondering if Kent would appreciate her trimmer figure, she worried if he'd lost interest in her by now. *Maybe I was a fool for flying all the way here without calling him.* Sylvia reached for the plate of chocolate chip cookies her mother had brought and snatched back the cellophane wrap. She crammed one in her mouth and held a second one. Months had passed since she ate a cookie without restraint. The chocolate and nuts only left her taste buds aching for more.

After the pot started percolating and the rich aroma mingled with the smell of vanilla wax, Sylvia looked at her cell phone and pressed in the speed dial number for Kent's cell, which he supplied the first day Sylvia cared for the children. As her finger hovered over the *send* button, a tremor passed through her hand, and Sylvia hit the *end* button. The number disappeared.

She scrolled through her phone book until she highlighted Brendy's Friend-Shop. Without reserve, she hit the send button as the final traces of the first cookie slipped down her throat. This phone call posed itself as the only logical choice. Brendy would clue Sylvia into the climate of Kent's life and hopefully dash aside all her doubts.

After the sixth ring, Brendy's cheerful yet strained voice floated over the line. Sylvia tossed the other cookie back onto the plate and berated herself for the weakness.

Oh, great! Sylvia thought. *Brendy's probably so busy she can't talk right now.*

"Hello," Brendy repeated.

"Hello, Brendy, this is Sylvia," she said on a breathless note.

"Sylvia!" Brendy chirped. "Oh my word, it's so good to hear your voice. I wish you were here now! The gal I hired in place of you just quit, and I've been swamped all morning!"

"Oh, well, then. . .I. . .I won't keep you," Sylvia said and watched the coffee pot as it filled drop-by-drop to the four cup line. "I—I was just going to ask you. . ."

"Thank you and have a good day," Brendy's muffled words were punctuated by the ring of a cash register.

"Sorry, Sylvia," she said. "That was a sale I needed to wrap up."

An expectant silence permeated the line, and Sylvia snatched one of three mugs from the petite cabinet. She snapped the cabinet door shut and began to question the intelligence of even calling Brendy.

"Sylvia, is everything okay?" Brendy prompted.

No! she wanted to wail but didn't. Instead, she prayed for the strength to pose her question. "How's Kent?" Sylvia finally asked and gripped the top of the empty mug.

"Uh. . . ," Brendy hedged. "He seems okay, I guess."

The undercurrent in Brendy's words implied a whole host of scenarios, none of which Sylvia would enjoy. She grabbed the coffeepot and sloshed the dark liquid into the mug. The steaming aroma that once seemed so inviting now repelled. With a grimace, Sylvia slid the pot into place and debated exactly what to say next.

"Sylvia? Have I lost you?" Brendy prompted.

"No. I'm still here," Sylvia answered. "I was just debating whether or not I was prepared for the whole truth," she added with a nervous chuckle.

"Who knows," Brendy said, and Sylvia imagined her waving her hand and widening her eyes. "The man certainly won't talk to me. I brought up your name last week, and he nearly bit my head off."

"Oh?"

"Uh-huh, and then last night. . ."

"Last night?" Sylvia leaned against the counter and closed her eyes. The darkness in no way illuminated her apprehension or slowed her heart's hard, heavy beats.

"Oh, never mind," Brendy said.

Sylvia's fingers flexed tighter around the cell phone. "Brendy," she said, her voice low and shaking. "I'm in Jacksonville. I flew home this morning to see Kent. If there's something I need to know—"

"Oh no, you poor dear," Brendy breathed. "Oh dear, then I guess you need to know."

"Know what?" she croaked.

"He went out last night with Pam. You know, at church—"

"The youth director?" Sylvia rasped, as if she needed affirmation that they were both talking about the lithe redhead who was about six dress-sizes smaller than she.

"Yeah," Brendy admitted.

Sylvia opened her eyes and grabbed the mug of coffee. She gulped the hot, black liquid in hopes it would cure her eyes' stinging. The only thing accomplished was scorched taste buds.

"Well, would you say they're an item, then?" Sylvia asked and resisted a sniffle.

"I don't know, Sylvia," Brendy said. "Like I said, Kent won't talk to me." The faint chime of a bell preceded Brendy's cheerful welcome and a promise of, "I'll be with you in just a minute."

"You've got to go," Sylvia said.

"Where are you?" Brendy rushed. "I'll call you back."

"I'm at my apartment here in town. You can reach me on my cell."

"Will do," Brendy offered, and the phone clicked.

Sylvia laid her cell phone on the counter and covered her face with unsteady hands. Her first reaction was to begin a heartfelt outcry to the very God who had asked for all or nothing. After several minutes of begging for the Lord's intervention, Sylvia finished with a resolved, "But, oh, Father, you know I have released Kent to You. . .completely. If this whole thing with my flying out here has been a mistake and You are finally ending this chapter in my life, then not my will but *Your* will be done."

The unfathomable peace of heaven sprang from the center of Sylvia's soul. She wiped her damp eyes and gazed into the inky coffee. Sylvia reached for the discarded cookie and had it halfway to her lips when she frowned.

"I don't need this," she told herself and placed the treat back on the plate. *Kent or no Kent, I don't want to gain more weight.* Sometime during the last few weeks, Sylvia's treadmill experience had grown from a means to nabbing a husband into something she was doing for herself. . .and her Lord.

She gingerly sipped the raspberry flavored coffee and welcomed the calorie-free explosion of flavor. Sylvia eyed the spotless apartment, void of the clutter of human habitation, and wondered what she would do with her afternoon. In her romantic fancies, she had envisioned Kent welcoming her with opened arms and the two of them enjoying their first Valentine's Day together. Instead, she could only look forward to the plane flight back to Arizona. The last thing she wanted to do was interfere in Kent's new relationship and endure his pity-filled apology.

She stepped toward the lone love seat and settled into its folds. Her mind wandered to Brendy and her busy day. *At least I could go help Brendy. That way the trip won't be a complete loss.* She set her mug on the simple end table with a decisive thud. Sylvia marched to the counter where she left her cell phone and hit the redial button. In a matter of seconds, she informed Brendy that help was on the way within the half hour.

Chapter 15

When Sylvia arrived at the store, a frowning customer was walking back toward her Suburban. As Sylvia climbed from the car into the cool February air, the immaculately groomed woman shot a scowl at her and said, "You might as well go back home. There's a note on the door that the place is closed for the next hour."

"What?" Sylvia gasped.

"Yep! And I have a package I'm supposed to pick up, and my schedule is tight." With her red lips in a tight line, she pressed a button on her key chain, and the Suburban's door produced a faint thump.

As the woman climbed into her vehicle and pulled from the driveway, Sylvia relived the last hour of her life. *Brendy said she desperately needed my help,* she thought. *It's odd that she'd close up shop on such a busy day—especially so close to Valentine's Day.* Sylvia considered driving back to her apartment but decided to check out the note herself.

Sure enough, a note was taped to the front glass. Brendy's relaxed scrawl proclaimed her message.

> *It's 1:00 p.m. I am closing the shop until 2:00 p.m., due to an unexpected errand. Please forgive me. I will remain opened until 7:00 tonight to compensate my customers.*

Underneath the note to her customers, a PS snared Sylvia's attention.

Sylvia, go ahead and let yourself in and keep the shop closed.
Feel free to start any housecleaning you see needs to be done. Thanks!

Sylvia glanced at her Timex. The hour was half past one. Brendy had left only fifteen minutes after talking to her. "This is so strange," she whispered. Shaking her head, she lifted her hand. "I don't even have a key."

A cold breeze wheezed around the front porch of the antique home-turned-shop, and Sylvia glanced up at the low-hanging clouds. The first traces of snow drifted from the cottonlike blanket and settled among the faded mums in the flowerbeds. Sylvia stood on the porch, pulled her wool jacket tighter around her torso, and watched a stream of vehicles hum along the small town street. Silently, she debated whether to call Brendy and remind her she didn't have a key.

When the fifth car purred by, Sylvia recalled the spare key Brendy kept beneath the huge rock in the mum bed. She trotted off the steps, into the ever-increasing sprinkle of snow—an unusual event for the balmy east Texas town.

Sylvia gripped the cold rock and lifted its edge. Beneath it lay a key to the shop alongside a pink plastic key that looked like it might belong to one of Pat's Barbie toys. A sentimental tinge gripped her heart, and Sylvia couldn't resist the indulgent smile. Thoughts of Pat and Pete, speckled with chocolate brownie mix, sent an ache through her soul. Kent wasn't the only one she'd missed these past weeks.

She dashed aside an icy snowflake that lodged in her lashes and trotted up the stairs. Soon she was stepping from the grip of cold air into a warm welcome, bearing the scent of hot cocoa and a hint of cinnamon potpourri. A quick glance testified that Christmas was over and the Valentine season had arrived in all its glory. Red hearts and white streamers now replaced holly wreaths and the manger scene.

Sylvia wasted no time depositing her coat and hat in the office and stood near the hallway, trying to decide exactly what housekeeping needed to be done. "This place is immaculate," she said as she scrutinized the polished wood floor, void of clutter. *Brendy must be staying after hours to clean.* She ran her finger along a glass shelf, stacked with packets of gourmet mints used for flavoring tea.

As she examined her fingertip for any sign of dust, the old railroad station clock on the wall behind the cash register signaled 1:45 with its deep-throated chime. At the end of the last note, the front door handle rattled. The rattle escalated into frantic bumping that grew into a forceful battery of knocks.

❧

Kent peered between the small red and white hearts covering most of the frame door's window. He caught a glimpse of someone moving inside, and he wondered if the person were his mother. Her urgent call from only minutes before had sent Kent running from the house without so much as grabbing a coat. "Kent, there's an emergency at the shop," Brendy said. "I need you here now!" During the brief drive, he had imagined all sorts of tragedies, including fire. A gust of wind swished across the porch and tossed a few snowflakes upon Kent's cheek. He scowled at the weather as he'd scowled at everything since Sylvia walked out of his life.

He pounded the door again and bellowed, "Mom!" That's when he noticed the note. A quick scan only added a dose of confusion to his urgency. The frigid air reminded him he was clad only in a T-shirt and jogging shorts. He squinted, tugged on his ear lobe, and reread the note. *Why would Mom call me with an emergency and then leave?* he thought as the doorknob jiggled.

Kent caught but a glimpse of blond ringlets through the decorated window before the door eased open. "Hi, Kent," Sylvia said with a sad lilt to her voice. Her gaze, troubled and searching, held little of the light and laughter that had tortured his dreams since the day she left. She looked as fresh as always with glossy red lips that perfectly matched the red sweater she wore. And Kent would vow she'd lost more weight since Christmas. A twist of guilt stabbed his gut, and he hoped she wasn't starving herself on his behalf. Right now, her abundance of curves looked heavenly, and Kent wouldn't encourage her to lose another ounce if he had his say.

"Sylvia?" he breathed and felt as if he were sinking into the porch's wooden fibers. "Wh—what are you doing here?"

"I was. . .going to help your mother," she said and looked at his shorts.

Kent glanced at his scrawny ankles, protruding from the tops of the running shoes he'd crammed on without socks. All at once, he felt like a lanky twelve-year-old with his first crush. Sylvia wasn't the only one who'd lost weight these past few weeks. He'd barely been able to eat for thinking of her.

"You don't have a coat." She knitted her brows. "You need to come in," she added and flung the door open wide.

Kent embraced her invitation and stepped into the warm shop. The cold wind gave a final puff before Sylvia closed and locked the door in his wake. "I. . .don't know what's going on," she hedged and eyed him as if he were an odd phenomenon.

All Kent could do was stare back at her and resist the urge to haul her in his arms and cover her face in kisses. He shoved his hands into his flimsy shorts' pockets and reminded himself of the promise she made—a promise that she'd call if she ever changed her mind about him. Despite the fact that she was in town, Sylvia still hadn't called. That could only mean one thing: either she wasn't ready for the relationship Kent ached for or she was no longer interested.

"I just got in town this morning and called your mom. She sounded like she needed help here at the store, so I volunteered to come in today. She said she'd be thrilled to see me, but when I got here, that note was on the door." Sylvia nudged a curl from her cheek and placed the end of her pinkie between her teeth.

"Well. . ." Kent rocked back on his heels. "She called me and told me there was an emergency. She was so wigged out, I wondered if the place was on fire or something." Kent glanced around the immaculate shop as a hint of awareness tugged at his thoughts.

"I don't think that's the kind of emergency she was talking about," Sylvia said.

Kent cut a glance back at her and narrowed his eyes. *You look so good, Sylvia,* he thought. Instead, he said, "Do you think we've been set up?" Kent attempted to keep his voice light, but trying to hide the tremor in his words only deepened his tones.

"Uh. . ." Sylvia shrugged and gulped as if she were far from comfortable.

"You know, Sylvia," Kent began, ready to ask her if she might have changed her mind about them. But then he remembered her promise. *She never called me,* he reminded himself. *The last thing I need to do is open myself up to being hurt by her rejection.* After that knock-your-socks-off kiss in the Dairy Queen parking lot, her announcing that she was going back to Arizona had left Kent feeling as if she found him less than thrilling—despite her claim that she must do the Lord's bidding.

"Yes?" Sylvia finally asked, and her question reverberated with the hint of hope.

Kent peered to the bottom of her soul and encountered the faintest hint of longing and admiration, forever veiled in azure mist. He took a step toward her, and the aging wooden floor creaked with the pressure of his weight.

For a moment, he held his breath. The silence stretched into an eternity while Kent pondered how the last weeks had unfolded into a hollow existence. Out of desperation, he'd even gone out last night with the church youth director, only to realize he'd called her Sylvia when he said good night.

The longer he gazed into Sylvia's eyes, the more he felt as if he were coming under the hypnotic force of a wide-eyed princess who didn't know her own power. What a fool he had been to accuse her of purposefully trying to manipulate his children. Anyone who made light of the purity of her heart had to be the biggest oaf on the planet. Presently, her guileless gaze only heightened his awareness of her golden character and left him warmed and welcomed as if. . .as if he were coming home. At long last, after all these years Kent felt as if he had encountered the woman God originally intended him to marry. If only. . .if only she might agree.

Kent searched for something to say. But while his every instinct urged him to declare his love, his common sense reminded him about that phone call that was never placed.

Sylvia finally looked away and stepped to a display of designer pens, set in a freestanding glass display case with openings on opposite sides. Her spine stiff, she fussed with the rhinestone-crusted pens as if the security of the nation depended upon her decisions.

"So. . .how has Arizona been?" Kent stepped to the other side of the display and looked through the opening. Her fingers stilled upon a pen, and she gazed at him as if her heart were breaking. "Fine," she squeaked before a series of rapid blinks that did little to hide the moisture seeping from the corners of her eyes.

"What's the matter, Sylvia?" Kent asked, and couldn't deny that he sounded like a beggar, hopelessly smitten and groveling at the feet of the woman he loved.

"I. . .uh. . . ," she rasped and turned to a shelf laden with boxes of chocolate turtles.

"Why are you even in town?" he asked.

"Because. . .because. . ."

The railroad clock ticked off the seconds, and with every tick Kent suspected that perhaps Sylvia came to town for him, despite the fact that she never called.

"You never called me." The words tumbled out the second he

thought them, and Kent bit the end of his tongue.

"I was going to"—she sniffled—"earlier today, but. . ."

Kent stopped himself short of a shout. He rushed toward her and placed both hands on her shoulders. "But?" he whispered next to her ear.

She shivered, and he shamelessly hoped his nearness was the reason. "But—but your mom mentioned, uh. . ."

"Did she say something that upset you?" he mumbled and took the liberty of bestowing a gentle kiss near her ear. When she sighed and leaned against him, Kent moved his hands to her waist.

"It was about last night," she whispered. "She said you—you were—were—you went, uh, out, and I was afraid—"

"For two people who want us together so bad, my mom and my son seem to have a way of telling you exactly the things that will keep us apart, don't they?" He released a nervous chuckle and awaited her response. Head bent, Sylvia remained silent, so Kent rushed, "I *did* go out last night." When she stiffened, he continued, "But it would probably make you feel really good to know it's the only time I've been out with a lady since you left for Arizona and only because I was desperate for some way to get you off my mind. And we'll just say my date was really impressed when I called her Sylvia before dropping her off at her apartment."

A shameless giggle escaped Sylvia. "You didn't!" she whispered as if this were the best news she'd ever heard.

"Oh yes, I did." Kent nudged her to turn and face him. "I never even held her hand." He cupped her face in his shaking hands. "I really think she thought I was the dullest man on the planet." He grinned. "She seemed really relieved when the evening was over."

Sylvia's arms slid behind his neck, and Kent's hands slipped back to her waist. "These weeks since Christmas have been the longest of my life," she admitted with a nod. "I've done a lot of spiritual growing."

"Honestly, so have I," Kent said as he recalled those nights he'd prayed himself to sleep. "And I've kicked myself a dozen times for ever being so blinded by Tamala that I couldn't see you all those years ago."

"Don't beat yourself up over the past." She stroked the side of his face with a gentleness that left his knees unsteady.

"I know. . .what's done is done," he admitted, "and I *am* glad I have those two kids—just the way they are."

"How are they, anyway?" Sylvia asked.

"Ornery as ever." Kent buried his face against her hair and inhaled the simple floral essence, tinged with the hint of raspberries.

"I think when I married Tamala, it was all about satisfaction of my ego," he admitted and winced with the brutality of the bare truth. "She was a trophy for me, I guess. I was so fleshly, I couldn't see the godly woman right under my nose. Then, after we were married, I even ditched the call I felt God had placed on my life to be a doctor."

Kent turned down the corners of his mouth. "It was a decision I felt I needed to make for the family. But looking back, I know it was also another step out of the center of God's perfect will for me. If I could only hit the rewind button on my life and have the spiritual fortitude to see how real you were and how shallow she was." He rolled his eyes and shook his head.

Sylvia pulled away and took his hands in hers. "I can't say I was any godlier than you or anyone else at that time in my life. I think I worshipped you the same way you worshipped Tamala. And, well" —she shrugged—"you aren't the only one who's made career decisions out of the will of God. I never once prayed about leaving Arizona to come back here. When I came back home two years ago, God finally started breaking through all my dreams and brought me to a place where it was either you or Him."

"And?" Kent held his breath.

She gazed down upon their entwined fingers. "I died to all my plans for the future and finally told Him I'd stay single for life and work at the reservation until I die if that's what He wants."

A distant rumble of thunder attested that the east Texas weather pattern was up to its usual shifting tendencies. Kent looked out a window to see that the snow had increased by tenfold. And he would have vowed that some of those chilling flakes were now penetrating his soul. Perhaps he had misread Sylvia's intentions, and she had come back to release him forever.

"And?" he prompted again and didn't have the courage to tear his gaze from the window.

"And once I got all the way to that point, Kent, the Lord showed me that—that it *is* His will for us to be together. That is, if you—"

Without a word, Kent hauled her closer. Their lips merged into a confection of rapture strong enough to rattle the store shelves. He bestowed a breathless trail of kisses to her ear and whispered, "I've missed you so badly, I thought I was going to *die*. Never did a day go by that the kids didn't ask about you. Every time they asked, I just wanted to howl. And any time the phone rang, I held my breath, hoping it was you."

Sylvia settled her head against his chest and wrapped her arms tightly around his torso. "I've missed you, too," she admitted and then spoke the words he never expected. "Kent, I'd do anything in the world for you. I've got my master's degree now, and I'm sure I could land a good job somewhere. If I do that, I could put you through med school, if that's what you still want. You're still young enough that you could wrap it all up in just a few years."

A latent desire floated from the bottom of his soul—a desire to fulfill God's first call upon his life. *And what better way to do it than with God's first choice as his wife.* "You're a wonderful woman, Sylvia Donnelley," he breathed and then smiled. "But I can't let you do that—"

"But—" She lifted her head and challenged him with a wide-eyed stare.

"Unless you promise to marry me, first."

A radiant smile blazed from her spirit and illuminated her face with undeniable joy. "Now that's one promise I'll keep for life!" she claimed and nearly knocked him flat with another kiss that reeled his senses.

Epilogue

Six months later, Pete sneaked toward the steps of the town house his dad and new mom had rented last month after they were married.

"Pete! Whatcha doing up?" Pat's whisper floated from her darkened bedroom. Through the shadows, Pete detected his sister sitting up in the middle of the Barbie canopy bed Grandmom had given her for a going-away present. She'd given Pete a Monsters Inc. bunk bed.

"Go back to sleep," he hissed over his shoulder and stepped toward the stairway.

"But I want to know what you're doing!" she demanded.

"It's none of your bee's wax!" he countered.

"If you don't tell me, I'm going to scream!"

While the smell of Sylvia's double chocolate brownies tugged him downstairs, his common sense insisted he deal with the sister problem. He marched toward Pat's canopy bed, fists balled beside his pajama trousers.

Before they moved to live near the University of Texas at Austin, Grandmom had admonished both of them to behave for their father and new mom. "Your dad's going to be in med school," Grandmom said, as if Pete didn't even know that. "And Sylvia will be working hard! Don't give them any problems. You promise?" she asked like she was a judge or something. Pete had promised, and figured he'd done really well until tonight—when he simply couldn't stop himself from sneaking downstairs to steal another brownie before going to sleep.

"I'm going downstairs!" he huffed at his sister as if he were an overworked adult on an exhausting mission.

"Why?" Pat crossed her arms and glowered at him. But not even the glow of her night-light or the shadows could make her look mean.

"Because I need to. Now shut up and leave me alone." He nodded as if he were the final, nocturnal authority.

Her mouth dropped open. "You told me to shut up!" she hissed. "Sylvia says that's not polite. I'm telling on you!"

"You better not!"

"Fine, then, let me go with you, or I'm telling." Her bottom lip poked out like a pit bulldog, and Pete knew when he'd been whipped.

"Okay, then," he growled. "I'm going to get another brownie, and you can't make a peep. We've got to sneak past the den. That's where Dad and Sylvia are." He pointed his index finger at her nose.

Clutching her glow-in-the-dark prayer doll, Pat scrambled from beneath the covers and stood beside Pete. Her fine hair stuck out like a porcupine, and she smelled like that disgusting baby shampoo Sylvia made him wash his own hair with.

The faint sound of the late night news floated on the wings of the brownie aroma. Pete hoped something dreadful was happening in the world so his parents would be so focused on the TV they wouldn't notice two brownie thieves.

With Pat on his heels, Pete silently scampered down the stairway and paused only long enough to peek into the homey den. While the TV was certainly playing, neither his dad nor Sylvia appeared to be watching it. Instead, they were all slumped over on the couch kissing! Pete's stomach turned, just like it did at their wedding when Pastor Henderson said, "Now you may kiss the bride." For a few seconds, Pete thought he might even throw up.

"Oh, gross!" he hissed as Pat's stifled giggle gurgled forth.

Both Dad and Sylvia sat straight up. They stared at the doorway for a few seconds and then started scrambling around as if they were the ones who'd been caught at some mischief. Pete tried to slink into the shadows, but stepped on Pat's foot. She let loose a squawk that sounded more like a frog's croak. Pete then did the only right thing. He bounded back up the stairs without a backward glance.

"Don't leave me, Pete!" Pat's panicked cry floated up the stairs, but Pete never looked back. Instead, he ran into his room, hurled himself upon the bed, snuggled under the covers, and pretended to be fast asleep. He listened hard to see what became of Pat. When he heard only silence, he figured she'd made it to her bed just fine.

After a few minutes, soft footsteps entered his room and somebody who smelled like raspberries flipped on the lamp and sat on the side of the bottom bunk bed where he lay. "Pete?" Sylvia's kind voice penetrated his resolve to pretend to be asleep.

He opened his eyes and peered at his new mom. His Toy Story lamp cast a warm glow across the cluttered room and illuminated Sylvia's rumpled hair. Her lipstick was smudged around her lips like pink fur, and the rest of her makeup didn't look quite like it was all in the right place any more. Pete just figured that's what kissing must do to a woman. He curled his toes and wondered what she might be going to say.

"Pat told me what you two were up to," she said. "Do you have anything to say for yourself?"

"Uh...," Pete said and wondered whether he should tell the truth or try to get himself out of this one another way. After pondering the two weeks he had to do the dishes after his last lie, Pete decided he was better off to stick to the truth. Besides, his bigmouthed sister had already ratted on him.

He covered his head with the sheet and mumbled, "We were going to the kitchen to get another brownie."

"Thanks for telling the truth," Sylvia said and gently poked him in the ribs. "You can come out now. I'm not going to bite you."

Pete lowered the covers to below his eyes and watched his mom.

"I actually brought you something." Sylvia stood and stepped to the dresser, covered with a disheveled train track. She picked up a tall glass of milk and a brownie on a napkin.

His eyes felt as if they jumped out of his face. "No way! You brought me a brownie!" he exclaimed.

"Only if you understand you *have* to brush your teeth again when you're through," Sylvia said. "And this is not going to become a habit. Your dad and I just thought. . ." She tilted her head. "I don't know, we just decided our children really needed a brownie fix."

"I'd brush my whole body for one of your brownies," Pete exclaimed.

"Good," she said on a laugh. "Your dad is taking one to Pat, as well."

Pete smiled, sat up in his bed, crossed his legs, and accepted the unexpected treat. He chomped into the nut-laden masterpiece and gazed up at his new mom. "You're the best mother in the world," he claimed.

"And you're the best son." Sylvia settled beside him, draped her arm across his shoulder, and bestowed a kiss on his forehead. For once, Pete didn't think kissing was so yucky. As a matter of fact, that kiss made him feel as if everything was right in his world. He figured his dad felt the same way, too.

The Neighbor

Chapter 1

I knew you shouldn't have taken two weeks off work. You're so bored, you're already spying on the neighbors!"

Dr. Alissa Carrington jumped, her heart skipping a beat. She turned to face her best friend and dental office partner, Dr. Trena Selver. "Don't ever sneak up on me like that again! I almost had a heart attack!" Alissa carefully stepped down from the patio chair she'd been standing on to see over the cedar privacy fence.

"So, what's so interesting next door?" Trena asked. Without waiting for an answer, she climbed onto the chair and peered over the fence. "Ah ha! Now I know why you wanted to stay home instead of hitting the beach. He's gorgeous."

"Get down from there!" Alissa hissed as Trena dimpled into a flirtatious smile and waved. Grabbing Trena's hand, Alissa yanked her from the chair. "You've got this all wrong! I wasn't watching *him*. Police have been crawling all over that place since this morning. They're investigating the—"

"So you've started spying." Trena raised her dark brows. "FBI agent—forget this dentistry stuff."

Alissa, lifting her shoulder-length hair off her perspiring neck, inhaled the scent of her suntan lotion. "If you'd just listen. . ."

"Hello there, Frito," Trena said, bending over to pet Alissa's large gray mutt as he scurried under the fence via his recently dug hole.

Alissa rolled her eyes. It looked to her like Trena was the one who was bored. And when she got bored, it seemed she couldn't stay on the same subject more than two seconds.

199

"Would you listen to me?" Alissa insisted. "The guy next door is putting in a pool, and they dug up some human bones."

"What?" Trena's eyes widened, as if she'd seen a ghost.

"I said human bones. Dead people. Probably murdered!"

"And I thought you'd have nothing to do if you didn't go to the beach with me, but it looks like you've got plenty here to keep you occupied. With this kind of excitement, you could spy for a whole decade!"

"Very funny." Crossing her arm, Alissa watched Frito trot to the far corner of the freshly mowed lawn, and she wondered what she'd have to do to keep the mutt in his own territory. So far, he'd dug three holes to "escape" next door. He was obviously restless in his own yard, a yard Alissa meticulously cared for. Red geraniums, yellow roses, and tender dogwood saplings adorned the landscape, while potted ferns decorated her huge patio and the nearby glassed-in sunroom.

"Well, I'm leaving for the beach this afternoon," Trena said, dismissing Alissa's news for her own. "That's what I came to tell you. Cameron found out last night he could have this week off after all. So he, his parents, and I are heading out for Corpus Christi in about thirty minutes." She checked her watch, and then frowned at Alissa. "I was going to try to talk you into going, but I can see you're too enthralled with what's-his-face next door."

"Not with *him*. I was just curious about the bones."

"Right. Whatever you say." Trena rolled her eyes then frowned again. "But you need to be careful. The bones business is creepy!"

"It's not like it involves me or anything! Why are you always so paranoid?"

"I'm not. I'm just cautious. Well, gotta go," Trena said dismissing the topic as she was so apt to do. With a quick hug, she was off to spend the week with her fiancé.

Alissa stared at the fence. Should she go introduce herself to her new neighbor and apologize for her own spying and Trena's freshness? Trena always had been a flirt while Alissa was the serious one. Even in high school, Trena had been the cheerleader, Alissa, the valedictorian.

She stared up at the row of six evenly spaced windows that lined the back of her vintage 1920, two-story frame house. She should be repapering her bedroom, not worrying about what was going on next door. Hadn't the remodeling been her sole goal for this vacation?

Maybe she *was* bored. Perhaps her curiosity about the discovery next door had served the same purpose as lying in the east Texas sun the last two days. Procrastination. She was putting off the papering, basically because she'd rather be outside in her yard than stuck in the house.

She reflected for a moment longer, then brightened. The sun was shining! The red birds were chirping! And she was on vacation! With an impish smirk, which completely dismissed the wallpaper, Alissa grabbed her red swimsuit cover and wrapped it around her slender waist. The remodeling could wait. What was happening next door was far more interesting.

Barefooted, she picked her way over the cool stepping-stones that dotted the path to her rickety backyard gate, a gate that needed a fresh coat of white paint. Perhaps she'd paint the gate before papering her room. At least it would be an outside job. Accompanied by the protest of squeaking hinges, Alissa stepped through the gate, circled to the right, and stood peering into her neighbor's backyard.

He was bent over a mound of freshly dug earth, talking intently to the policewoman. A policewoman who seemed more interested in him than in the investigation. Trena had been right on one count—he was gorgeous.

Straight blond, sun-streaked hair touched the collar of his teal shirt in a casual yet attractive style. He needed a shave. And he wasn't much taller than Alissa. About five-eleven. Probably early thirties. Just Alissa's type. The type who looked like he'd be at home on a football field but would rather read or discuss horticulture while lounging around the pool in cutoffs. The type that made Alissa want to reach for her binoculars.

But was he a Christian? Dating a non-Christian had already gotten her into trouble once. For the moment Alissa pushed aside the thought. She didn't want to recall the painful memories, which often haunted her, especially not just before meeting someone new.

"Excuse me," Alissa said, nervously clearing her throat. He glanced up, stared at her blankly, and then smiled to reveal a row of white teeth. Alissa's throat went dry. That smile would probably stop traffic in downtown Dallas.

"Hi. Did you decide to come get a closer look?" he said in a soft, East Coast dialect.

So he'd seen her watching, just as she'd suspected. Alissa hoped her warming cheeks weren't as red as they felt. "Sorry about that. But. . .neighbors don't dig up human bones every day. And, um—"

"I'd probably have spied on you, too." His teasing gray eyes suggested a double meaning.

"My grandmother has always said my curiosity was going to get me killed."

"Let's hope not," he said, walking toward her.

As he neared, Alissa realized his excess stubble was actually the beginnings of a new beard.

"Here, let me get the gate." He reached for the metal latch.

"That's not necessary. I just wanted to introduce myself and apologize for being so nosey."

"It's quite all right. I don't blame you, really. The last thing I ever expected to do was find human bones in my backyard. This is really weird."

"I know. Makes you wonder about your house's former owner, doesn't it?" Alissa glanced at his sprawling red brick house.

"Yeah. Did you know him?"

"Just barely. I'd only been here two months when he sold to you."

"Ever notice anything strange?"

"No. But I stay so busy with my practice—I'm a dentist. Anyway, work keeps me busy, and I don't get to socialize much."

"Are Tuesdays your days off then?"

"No. I'm on vacation. My partner just left for the beach." Alissa broke eye contact, her cheeks warming again. "She's the one who waved to you."

The policewoman discreetly cleared her throat.

"Well, I guess I need to get back home. Oh, by the way," Alissa added as an afterthought, "I'm really sorry about my dog getting into your backyard. I guess I'm going to have to start keeping him indoors."

"It's okay. Really. He plays with Samantha."

"Samantha? So you have a family?" Disappointment stabbed Alissa. She thought he might have winced, but his next words banished that suspicion.

"Yeah." He shrugged his muscular shoulders and grinned. "I guess, if you can call a cat 'family.'"

Smiling, Alissa tried to hide her relief. "Frito always has been partial to cats. I think his mother must have been one."

Chuckling, he glanced over his shoulder toward the policewoman.

"Well, I—I guess I'll get back to my sunbathing. Let me know if I can help," Alissa said.

"Can you cook?"

She blinked. "Excuse me?"

"You said to let you know if you could help. It would really *help* me to have lunch with you." With a quirk of his left brow, his near-black eyes took on a teasing gleam. "That is, if you can cook."

"I can't. I'm a lousy cook." Alissa, her heart warming, dimpled into what she hoped was her most attractive smile. "But I'm the fastest dialer in Tyler, Texas. I could call for a pizza."

"Sounds good. Give me about an hour. I think it's good to get to know your neighbors. I'm Brad, by the way. Brad Ratner."

"Nice to meet you, Brad. I'm Alissa Carrington."

Chapter 2

An hour later, Alissa set the aromatic pizza on her antique dining table. She'd spent the last hour showering and trying to do something with her hair and makeup. Not that there was much she could do. It amazed her that she could completely rearrange somebody's teeth but couldn't get much more than a bronze lipstick on right. And her blond hair never did anything but hang straight. So what was the use?

Thankful for her naturally rosy cheeks and brown eyes and brows, Alissa made sure the back of her red T-shirt was tucked into her denim skirt. Then, with a flick of her fingers, she popped open the pizza box. If Brad didn't like pepperoni, she was in trouble. But Sherman had always liked it.

Alissa's hands stilled. Sherman. The very thought she'd fought to suppress. The same swordlike guilt, which always accompanied his name, seemed to pierce her soul.

"Why are you doing this to me?" he demanded. "How could you? Don't you know I love you? I thought you loved me!"

Alissa closed her eyes as the guilt blew through her being like tattering winds. "I'm sorry," she whispered to no one and wondered if she'd ever be able to forgive herself.

Sherman Devereauz, formerly one of Tyler's most prominent surgeons, had "conveniently" transferred his practice to Dallas immediately after Alissa had broken off their engagement eight months ago. To this day, Alissa wished she'd used more wisdom in her relationship with him. From the start she'd known he was an agnostic, at best. But his dark good looks and easy charm, along with her loneliness, had persuaded her that perhaps she could "change" him. As the wedding date neared, though, Alissa realized he wasn't going to change, that all her attempts to introduce him to Christ were in vain. She then envisioned herself taking her future children to church by herself, a trap she'd always wished to avoid. So she'd ended the engagement and vowed never to make the same mistake again.

The ringing phone broke into her reflections. Biting her thumbnail in anxiety, Alissa debated whether to take the call or to allow her answering machine to record a message. Her eighty-year-old grandmother hadn't yet placed her daily call, and Alissa feared this was it. Her phone conversations always lasted thirty minutes at the very least—thirty minutes Alissa couldn't spare just now.

Loyalty, however, forced her to pick up the cordless phone on the fourth ring. Her suspicions were well founded. "Alissa, are you going to take me to the church social tonight?" her grandmother asked before Alissa could say hello. "You know I don't want to miss it. Lila Dally is going, and she's taking that sweet potato casserole I gave her the recipe for. You know, the one with the pineapple in it? Anyway, she tells everybody it's *her* recipe. I just can't stand it anymore. I just can't! I'm gonna make those sweet potatoes and tell everybody it's *my* recipe. That ought to fix her up right and good. And another thing—"

The doorbell rang. "Grandma, I've got to go. But I'll pick you up at six thirty like we planned."

"That Reynolds man has gone too far this time. Do you know he actually asked me to go to the museum with him? And him an eighty-year-old man. Why, if he thinks I'm gonna start dating at this age, well. . ."

The doorbell rang again. "Grandma, there's someone at the door. I'll call you back." Alissa stared in consternation through the kitchen and toward the massive oak door.

". . .that Samuel Reynolds can just find himself another woman. I tell you—"

"Grandma, there's a *man* at my door. I've got a *lunch date*." Alissa knew that would do the trick. She also knew she'd pay for it later. Her grandmother would want every detail.

"A man! Well, why didn't you say so? You're already thirty years old, and it's high time you got another regular man friend. Wait till I tell your father. He'll be tickled down to his toes. Okay." The phone clicked.

With an indulgent grin, Alissa hung up. She'd never known her grandmother to say "good-bye." It was always "okay." Alissa rushed across her living room's rose-colored carpet toward the door, reaching it in the middle of Brad's third ring.

"I was beginning to wonder if I'd hallucinated our conversation," he said with a lopsided grin. Alissa, trying not to appear too eager, smiled. Faded blue jeans and a crisp white cotton shirt had never looked better. Add to that the hint of mystery his new beard gave to his smoky eyes, and the casual yet classy combination was almost too compelling.

Bells of caution sounded through Alissa's mind. *Don't get too attracted until you know more!* "Sorry 'bout that. I was on the phone with my grandmother—my father's mother. I think the house could be burning down around me and she'd just keep right on talking. Come on in."

Chuckling, Brad passed her, leaving a sporty citrus scent in his wake. "She's probably crazy about you."

"Yeah. I guess I am about her, too. My mother died when I was fifteen. Grandma was widowed shortly after that. Grandma and Father finished raising me together." *And God only knows how much I still miss my mother.*

"It's nice to have a family," Brad said, a dark shadow flitting across his eyes. But the shadow left just as quickly as he handed her a bottle

207

of cold soda. "I thought I'd supply the drinks."

"Thanks. Kitchen's this way." Having dated some of the tall, dark, handsome types, Alissa decided then and there that this guy made most of the dark handsomes she knew look like something Frito would drag up. Not that Brad was perfect. His brows were too heavy and his nose a bit too long for model perfection, but his physique made up for those flaws. *He must work out regularly*, she thought. His shoulders were too broad, his waist too narrow for any other explanation.

"Nice house," Brad said. Alissa glanced behind her and took a split second to admire the classic Queen Anne look she'd managed to accomplish in the last two months. "Thanks. I've had some work done on it. New carpet, new paint, new kitchen cabinets. And I'm supposed to be finishing my upstairs bedroom—wallpaper and maybe paint—but haven't had the motivation to start."

"It's this east Texas heat and humidity. It'll turn you into a regular lotus-eater."

"Yeah. You'd think being raised here, I'd be used to it. But July and August do this to me every year." Alissa opened the cabinet and grabbed two paper plates. "I'll serve you on my finest china."

"Good. I hate doing dishes. Mind if I get the ice in the glasses?"

"No, not at all. There's a full ice bucket in the freezer. Glasses are over there." Alissa pointed to the new oak cabinet beside her stainless steel sink. "So what did you find out about the cemetery in your backyard?"

"You've got that right. It is like a cemetery." The ice crackled as he plopped the cubes into tall glasses. "The best we can tell, there are two bodies over there. And the guy from the forensics lab says it looks like they've been there awhile. They won't know for a couple of months, though, exactly how long.

"That kinda gives me the creeps." Chills raced along Alissa's spine.

"Me, too."

"So are they going to question Mr. . . .what was the man's name who lived there before you?"

"Jenkins. Yeah. They're supposed to call him in today."

"Do you think he's responsible?"

"I don't know. He seemed nice enough when we closed the house deal." Brad set the glasses full of ice on the table, and Alissa poured the fizzing soda. "But then, that doesn't really mean anything."

"Yeah. Looks can be deceiving," Alissa said.

"The investigating officer is going to question our other neighbors. Maybe they'll know something. Man, the police and investigators have been crawling all over the place. Right now, there's not anyone over there. . . . But they'll be back."

"I guess this means your pool project's on hold then."

"Yeah. I'll just have to keep going to the YMCA for a while. I have to swim regularly—doctors orders."

"Oh?"

"I was involved in an—an accident two years ago." Brad, sitting down, made a big job of placing two pieces of pizza on his plate.

Alissa wondered if he was trying to hide something. He'd seemed comfortable when he first arrived. But the longer he stayed, the less comfortable he seemed, and the more tense his mouth became.

"Anyway, I've got a hip injury. And the swimming helps it." Brad's clipped words closed the subject and left Alissa wondering what had happened.

She took the seat across from him and helped herself to a piece of the steaming pizza. "I hope you like pepperoni."

"It's my favorite."

"Really? Mine, too."

"And they have something in common!" Brad said over a mouthful.

With a smile, Alissa bit into the spicy pizza. She hoped they had one other thing in common. "So, what do you do for a living?"

"I'm an—an artist. I work mostly in oils."

"An artist? Really? I've always admired people who can paint. I can hardly draw a stick man."

"I've always admired people who have the patience to go into the medical field. How'd you decide to become a dentist?"

"I guess my grandmother had something to do with it. She always encouraged me to make a career for myself. And when I had to have braces at twelve and realized what a difference it made in my looks and the way I felt about myself, I knew I wanted to make other people just as happy as I was. I'll admit there are some things about it I don't like. But overall, it's a great career."

Alissa started to mention her two-week missions trip to Africa last fall but stopped herself. Part of the reason she'd gone into a medical profession was to share her skills with those in need. She didn't feel a full-time call to the mission field, but planned to spend her life participating in mission teams every chance she got.

She couldn't help but notice how skillfully Brad had steered the conversation away from himself. Alissa also noted that he'd glanced at his watch three times in the last five minutes. He was trying very hard to feign politeness, but his readiness to leave was obvious. Oh well, this lunch date had been his idea, and Alissa would probably just chalk it up to a friendly neighborhood encounter anyway.

"It's hard to believe you ever had anything wrong with your teeth," Brad said softly. "You have such a beautiful smile."

Alissa, glancing up from studying her soda, encountered a mixture of agony and admiration stirring in his eyes. Her stomach tightening, she swallowed. This man was sending conflicting signals and managing to thoroughly confuse her.

"Thanks," she squeaked. "I guess beauty is in the eyes of the beholder, because—"

"I think I should leave," Brad said, then stood.

"Oh. . .well, okay." *You're starting to sound like Grandma.*

"Thanks for the pizza," he said, pulling his eelskin billfold from his hip pocket. "Here. That should cover the cost." He laid two bills on the table.

"No. Th—that's okay. I was g—going to order it for myself anyway," Alissa stuttered in confusion.

"I'll let you know what happens with the investigation," he clipped, ignoring her protest. With a swift turn he then rushed out of the house like a pack of demons was after him.

❧

Brad shut Alissa's front door, swallowed hard, and took a deep breath. *Well, you just made a one-hundred-percent fool of yourself.* If she just hadn't used Dana's favorite cliché: Beauty is in the eyes of the beholder. But that, coupled with his feelings of guilt, had been all he could handle. So he'd run. With shaking fingers, Brad rubbed the nape of his neck and slowly walked back toward his house.

He'd invited himself for lunch before he knew what he was doing. Brad couldn't remember being so befuddled by a woman since. . . "Since Dana," he whispered. And he wasn't ready to be involved with someone else. It seemed disloyal to Dana, disloyal to Kara.

A mistake. That's what lunch with Alissa Carrington had been. A huge mistake. And he'd never have made the date if she hadn't been so attractive. But there she'd stood in a red swimsuit wrap, no makeup, looking as hot and sweaty as he felt. Yet still she was a knockout, with hair the color of honey, eyes like brown velvet, a cute little pug nose, and a full-lipped smile that revealed a row of near-perfect teeth. Regardless of her looks, though, he couldn't even think of developing more than a passing acquaintance. He simply couldn't be disloyal to Dana.

Walking to his backyard gate, Brad stepped through it and scoffed at himself. He'd told her he was an artist. What kind of an artist went two years without picking up a brush? Brad had barely touched the fortune his talent had amassed. He had enough old paintings to keep the galleries happy for another year, but he wasn't producing anything new. What would happen when he ran out of the old stuff?

Samantha's meowed greeting from near the fence helped Brad push aside the disturbing thought. "Hey, Sam. Come here and I'll scratch your ears." Picking up the yellow-striped cat, he walked toward the huge hole in his backyard. Maybe the upheaval over these bodies would jar him back into his creative mode.

Then he saw it. Just a slight movement from the corner of his eyes, the kind of movement a quick glance might explain as harmless. But this time the movement wasn't harmless.

"Hey, you!" Brad yelled as a shadowed figure rushed from his massive patio window and through his house.

Chapter 3

Alissa stepped out of her front door and walked toward her Mustang convertible sitting in the circular driveway. Brad had been gone exactly five minutes. Five minutes! And Alissa now needed a fifty-minute drive that she hoped would help blow thoughts of him from her mind.

Her common sense told her to forget she'd ever met him. But something in her spirit seemed compellingly drawn to him. This feeling was different from any she'd ever experienced, different even from her initial attraction to Sherman. This was something akin to. . . perhaps it was compassion.

Sighing, Alissa walked across her landscaped front yard and told herself that the man was none of her concern. Yet, something about his pleading gray eyes haunted her soul, tore at her heart.

With another sigh, she fumbled for her keys in the bottom of her oversized leather purse. "Chalk it up to experience, Alissa ol' girl," she mumbled with a smirk. "Never have lunch with men with bones in their backyard."

The words had no sooner left her lips than a hard shove in the center of her back sent her sprawling to the sidewalk, her purse flying through the air. Her knees and palms felt as if they'd been doused in acid. She yelped with pain.

A dark-clad, masked person raced past her without so much as a backward glance.

"Are you okay?" a breathless man asked. Brad, bent over her, his eyes dark with concern. Had he been trying to protect her? Or was this just wishful thinking, hopeful longing?

Alissa, standing up, tried to regain her equilibrium and make sense of the last few harried seconds. "I think I'm all right. Guess I just skinned my knees and hands. Who was that? What's going on?" She turned to see the dark figure round the street corner two blocks away.

"I'll be back," Brad mumbled, before streaking away after the mysterious stranger. Yet Brad wasn't fast enough; the sound of a cranking engine and squealing wheels filled the air just as he reached the block's end.

Minutes later, he stood beside Alissa. "That person was just in my house," he huffed, his eyes churning.

She gasped. "Did he take anything?"

"I don't think so. It didn't look like he was carrying anything. But I didn't take time to look in the house. I just started the chase."

"Did you see the car?" Alissa glanced up the peaceful street in search of movement. But the only movement along the rows of emerald yards was a water sprinkler three doors down.

"No. Are you sure you're all right?" With a wince, she pulled aside her sarong skirt and examined her throbbing knees, now bloodied. Glad her thong sandals required no hose, she gingerly touched the red skin around the scrapes. "I think I'll live. It doesn't look any worse than the falls I took off my bike as a kid. I'll mend." Another wince, and she examined the heels of her aching palms.

Brad, however, didn't seem quite as optimistic. "Come on," he said, grabbing her arm. "I'm going to bandage your knees."

"No, really! I'm okay!" Alissa protested as he propelled her to his house.

"Don't argue. It's no use. If your knees get infected, I'll never forgive myself."

"You need to worry about calling the police. I can bandage my own knees. I'm a doctor, remember? Your having to do it is ridiculous."

But not half as ridiculous as the way you acted over lunch. Alissa didn't know whether to be glad for his concern or aggravated at his vacillating behavior.

His lips tight, Brad opened his beige front door and led Alissa into the spacious living room. *"Now sit!"* he commanded, nudging her toward a white leather chair.

She lowered herself into the chair's soft folds. "Okay. But call the police before you help me. And don't touch anything. Maybe they can find some fingerprints." She smiled to herself. Maybe all those old Dick Tracy movies would pay off after all.

Nodding, Brad turned toward the ivory phone sitting on a nearby brass and glass table. Alissa glanced around the room. Except for a thin layer of dust on the tables, the house smelled clean, looked clean. And it seemed to be an extension of his personality. Understated class. The fine balance of creams and whites gave the rooms an airy quality the vintage 1950 house lacked on it's own. Even the rows of ocean paintings lining the walls perfectly complemented the room's light décor.

She stood to get a closer view of the paintings. Each had its own personality. Each depicted the sea in a particular mood of upheaval or calm. And each held the same mesmerizing, illusive quality. . .the same sort of thing that stirred in the depths of Brad's eyes. They had to be his work.

So intent was she on examining the paintings that she didn't see the petite glass lamp table until she stumbled into it. With a quick downward glance, she steadied the porcelain oriental lamp before it could topple to its death. Then something else on the table snared her attention. A Bible. A worn Bible. But, it, too, was covered in a film of dust and had the name "Brad Ratner" printed in gold against navy leather. The presence of the Bible, once well used but now neglected, spoke volumes. And Alissa momentarily mused over the meaning, a meaning that added to Brad's mysterious appeal.

"Sit!" he commanded, hanging up the phone. "You can't escape. You might as well stop trying."

"I'm not trying to escape. I wanted to look at your paintings," Alissa snapped, his domineering attitude starting to annoy her.

"After the bandages." A coaxing, knowing smile tilted his lips as if he knew he'd gone too far with the commands.

Despite herself, Alissa returned his smile and resumed her place in the chair. The man could probably charm the stripes off a tiger. "What did the police say?" Alissa asked, hoping to hide the effect he had on her.

"The investigators are already on their way back. The office is going to radio them about what happened." He disappeared down the hall to return minutes later, carrying antiseptic gauze bandages and tape.

"You need to be warned. I'm a terrible patient. And if you put anything on my knees to make them burn worse than they're already burning, I'll scream."

Brad broke into an indulgent smile. "This is hydrogen peroxide. It shouldn't burn, little girl." Dropping to his knees, he began swabbing her wounds.

Had he just been flirting with her? Alissa wanted to shake her head to clear the confusion. One minute, he rushed from her house as if she was repulsive. And the next, he was flirting with her.

Regardless of Brad's strange behavior and her speculations about his faith, something bizarre had taken place in his backyard, a fact that Alissa couldn't ignore. Her curiosity began to whirl with unanswered questions. "Do you think that person in your house had anything to do with the bones in your backyard?" she asked, admiring the swift gentleness of his long, artist's fingers.

"Could be. But how? I mean, nobody knows I found the bones but you and me and the police."

"True. But I was curious enough to. . .to eavesdrop. Maybe one of the other neighbors did the same. Think about it. You have five candidates. There's me. There's the person on the other side of your house. Then there's the three people whose property borders your backyard fence but whose houses face the next street over. Any one of them could know that the bones were unearthed and that there was a lull in the police investigation."

"Good thinking. So would that mean one of the neighbors could be the murderer, not Mr. Jenkins?"

"Maybe."

"But what reason would he have for breaking into my house? The person could have just used the fence gate. But wait a minute!"

Brad looked up from Alissa's knees. "I came through the gate. Maybe the person entered that way but had to exit through my house so I wouldn't see him."

"Was your patio door unlocked?" Alissa glanced toward the door to see if there were signs of forced entry.

"Probably, I'm not the world's best at locking my doors. Besides, I was just going to be next door with you. I didn't think anything would happen."

"Do you think there might be something at the grave site that could incriminate someone?"

"Could be. I guess we could go look around before the police arrive." Brad placed the final piece of tape on her bandaged knees, and then took her hands in his to swab the scrapes with the cool peroxide.

Alissa, trying to deny the tingles working their way up her arms, finally decided it was no use. She reacted to Brad Ratner like dynamite with a short fuse.

"There. You should feel better now," Brad said seconds later. Seeming to carefully avoid eye contact, he stood and gathered the first-aid supplies.

"Thanks, I do." Then Alissa searched for something, anything to say. The awkward silence settling between them like a fog of unanswered questions didn't help her search.

"I'm sorry about the way I acted over lunch," he finally blurted to the gauze bandages.

"Oh, well, it's okay. . ." Alissa trailed off uncertainly.

"No, it isn't. I—I acted like a fool." Brad set the first-aid supplies on a nearby table and walked across the room to look out the patio window.

Speechless, Alissa stared at his back. She recognized the turmoil churning in him. It didn't take a world-famous psychiatrist to see that something dark and dreadful haunted this man's dreams, his every waking hour. Pain. She'd seen it in his eyes and identified with it.

Perhaps that was part of the attraction. A shared emotion. Hadn't she known the pain when cancer wasted her vivacious mother into a bony shadow? Didn't she have an occasional cry for what could have been? For how proud Harriet Carrington would have been that her daughter was now a successful dentist?

"I've got a very good explanation for the way I acted," Brad said tightly. Then, turning to face her, he ran his hand through his hair where it touched his collar. "But. . .but I—I can't tell you. . ." His voice trailed off.

"It's okay," Alissa said. Standing, she walked across the room to place her hand on his taut forearm. Covering her hand with his, Brad looked directly into her eyes. "You're a beautiful woman, Alissa Carrington. And I know we could be really good together—as friends. Would you be my friend? I can't offer anything else. But I need a friend right now."

Swallowing, Alissa nodded, and her heart palpitated with a mixture of disappointment and relief. So all he wanted was friendship. As far as she was concerned, he was the most attractive man she'd ever met. A combination of ruggedness and gentleness, of past hurts and hints of future happiness. Mere friendship. This had to be poetic justice. Isn't that what she'd told Sherman?

Sherman. The very thought of him, and her chest tightened. She'd devastated the man, had never seen a person so stricken as he was the night she broke off their engagement. Her honest explanation hadn't helped, had only made him angrier. "You're throwing me over for God," he'd yelled in bitter accusation.

If Brad didn't share her faith, though, his request for mere friendship was for the best. But then there was his personalized Bible, which showed signs of past diligent use.

In confusion, Alissa turned to open the patio door. "Let's go look at the grave site and forget lunch ever happened. We'll just start from here," she squeaked out with forced cheerfulness.

I should have known she'd do this, the invader thought. Lips twisted, hair disheveled, she stared at herself in the teak dresser's mirror. On the queen-sized bed lay the black pants, shirt, and ski mask she'd just removed.

Louanne thinks she's so smart. Just because that nosy Brad Ratner dug up her grave and she escaped, she thinks she can just come back into the neighborhood like nothing ever happened—like I never even killed her. Henry says she calls herself Alissa Carrington. But that's a lie. Nobody has that golden hair and wide-eyed innocent look but Louanne Young. And she must die again!

Chapter 4

Alissa peered into the shallow hole in Brad's backyard. Even in the summer heat, the thought of the wicked deed that had taken place here made her shiver. The smell of freshly dug soil, the reality of murder, and the hint of future danger cloaked the scene in a disturbing aura.

"And that's all I know," Brad told the television investigator. He had related the events that led up to his discovery of the bones.

Shortly after the police arrived, the television crew had surfaced, equipped with their "breaking story" curiosity and what seemed a million questions.

As the camerawoman scanned the yard landscaped in evergreens and ornamental shrubs, Alissa compulsively tried to step out of the camera's pathway, only to bump into an investigation police officer.

"Excuse me," she mumbled. She glanced up to see the camera aimed smack at her. *Oh, great!* Alyssa thought. *One more thing to explain to my grandmother.* After Emily Carrington viewed the evening news, she wouldn't be happy until Alissa brought her to Brad's backyard for her own inspection. Alissa wasn't the only one in the family with ample curiosity.

While yet another investigator cornered Brad, Alissa decided to take her leave. She'd fruitlessly answered a few questions about the person who knocked her down. When the police and camera crew realized how little she knew, they converged on Brad. Now she was simply in the way, a mere observer.

That was how she felt in relation to Brad, too. Their new

"friendship" was obviously going to be characterized by Brad holding her at arm's length. He'd hardly glanced at her since the investigators arrived.

With a sigh, Alissa turned toward the gate, only to glimpse a flash of white from behind the cedar fence spanning the back of Brad's yard. Then the sounds of metal against wood, and a resounding feminine howl, pierced the neighborhood's tranquility. Every gaze instinctively turned towards Brad's fence as low moans issued from the other sides.

"I'll see if she needs help," Alissa said, rushing from the yard. She quickly rounded the block and entered the woman's backyard, where she found her propped against the fence, gingerly rubbing her right ankle.

She wore an oversized red housedress that Alissa figured was an attempt to conceal her plumpish curves. Her bleached-blond hair was bound in a white cotton scarf, a scarf that hadn't stopped one of the pink sponge rollers from dislodging; it dangled between her eyes by a wisp of kinky, pale hair. Her lips, meticulously painted a neon orange, grimaced at the obvious pain ravaging her ankle.

"Are you okay?" Kneeling beside the sixtyish woman who smelled of lavender soap, Alissa noted the flimsy aluminum ladder lying in a twisted heap beside a row of climbing red roses.

"I think I'm fine. I was just—just tryin' to cut some roses when the ladder gave way and I fell and twisted my ankle," the woman whined in a heavy east Texas drawl.

Yeah, and I'm Peter Pan, Alissa thought. Nobody cut roses without shears, which were conspicuously absent. Alissa figured the woman had been spying, just as she herself had spied earlier. Biting her lips, Alissa stopped her judgmental thoughts. After all, she'd been no less nosy herself.

She bent to examine an ankle that showed no signs of injury. "Would you like me to drive you to a clinic? A quick X-ray will tell you if it's broken or just sprained."

"No, no, that's okay, darlin'. I don't think it's broken. All I need to do is maybe put it up on a chair."

"Elizabeth? Are you all right?" a raspy voice called from the white brick house's back door. Turning, Alissa encountered a woman as thin as Elizabeth was plump. Scrawny described her best. A dried-up scrawny prune with unkempt Lucille Ball red hair, and a crooked, wart-encrusted nose like the Wicked Witch of the West. Her deeply winkled brow creasing, she raced toward her friend.

"I was in my front yard when I heard you yell. But you sounded like you were inside. I knocked and knocked. When I didn't get any answer, I got worried and used the hidden key. What happened?" she gushed.

A flush crept up Elizabeth's neck to stain her smooth colorless cheeks. "I—I was cutting some roses and fell."

"Cutting some roses! I thought you left that to the yardman. What's gotten into you?"

As the newcomer bent over her friend's ankle, Alissa stepped back.

"Well. . ." Elizabeth seemed at a loss for an answer.

"I guess I'll go now," Alissa said, purposefully relieving Elizabeth from further embarrassment over her lie.

"Oh, um, thanks for coming over," Elizabeth said. "I'm Elizabeth, by the way, Mrs. Elizabeth Teasedale."

"Nice to meet you, Mrs. Teasedale. I'm Alissa Carrington. I'm the new owner of Mrs. Docker's old house."

"Yeah, we know," the newcomer stated.

"Sadie," Elizabeth gasped.

Sadie stilled as if suddenly realizing what she'd revealed. How did these two women know Alissa when she'd never even met them?

"Oh, I—I mean, nice to meet you," Sadie stuttered, her raspy smoker's voice seeming to scratch every stilted word. "I'm Sadie

Horton. My husband, Henry, and I live there." She pointed toward the sprawling, pillared mansion whose emerald-green yard ran to the block's end. Then, with a decisive turn toward Elizabeth, she hiked up her ragged, baggy jeans.

Alissa blinked at the incongruity. How did such a classless, brassy woman come to live in such an elegant home?

"Now you're going to the doctor, Lizzy. And no arguments," Sadie said.

Elizabeth, nodding mutely, offered no resistance to her friend's order.

"I really think that's the best idea," Alissa said.

"Thanks again, Dr. Carrington," Elizabeth said.

Figuring that was her cue to leave, Alissa wondered how Elizabeth knew she was a doctor. At the same time, she wondered if there was anything about her that the ladies didn't know.

"Everything okay over here?" a familiar masculine voice asked from the other side of the fence. Nodding, Alissa glanced up to see Brad peering over the cedar boards. She decided to inquire later about the slight slurring of his *r*'s. It suggested perhaps an East Coast influence and, like the man, spoke of culture mixed with down-to-earth casualness.

"Mrs. Teasdale fell from her ladder and hurt her ankle, and Mrs. Horton's going to take her for an X-ray." Alissa turned to the older women and made the appropriate introductions, although she fully suspected it was unnecessary—for the ladies anyway. If they knew Alissa, they probably knew Brad.

"Nice to meet you." Brad, producing his traffic-stopping smile, offered his condolences for Mrs. Teasedale's ankle. Then he lowered his voice to a whisper, and his eyes gleamed with conspiracy. "Oh, and just in case you haven't noticed, I seem to have a little problem in my backyard."

"Oh?" Mrs. Teasedale asked in obviously feigned astonishment.

The woman would starve as an actress, Alissa thought.

"Yes. The pool company dug up some human bones this morning. So don't be shocked if the police come around to ask you a few questions. They're going to be questioning the whole neighborhood, I'm afraid."

No genuine surprise or alarm registered with either woman, and only Sadie replied. "Thanks for the warning," she said, her eyes thin slits of contempt. Apparently she didn't appreciate Brad's humor. Turning her back to Alissa, Sadie began helping her friend to her feet.

"Are you sure you don't want me to help?" Alissa asked, taking a step toward them.

"No," Sadie said, as if to once and for all dismiss Alissa. Raising her brows, Alissa shrugged at Brad, who shrugged in return.

❧

"The top story this evening involves a bizarre finding which seems to have the makings of a late-night murder mystery," the TV news anchorwoman announced on the five o'clock news.

A smile twisting her lips, the murderer lifted the remote control, started the VCR tape, and increased the television's volume. She listened intently as the investigative reporter related the events, then grinned as the camera panned the yard to reveal Louanne standing beside her grave. Next, a brief interview with that nosy Brad Ratner.

She gritted her teeth. If only he had minded his own business, had never started that pool project, allowing Louanne to escape. Now she would be forced to murder Louanne again.

Reaching for her filterless cigarettes, she laughed and adjusted the VCR to rewatch the story she'd just recorded. It was only a matter of time, mere hours before Louanne would die once more. All she needed to do was crank up the little blue Mustang of hers. . .then whammy! The murderer slammed her right fist against her left palm. Maybe this time Louanne Young would stay dead.

"Alissa, I saw you on the news tonight. Why didn't you tell me about those bones next door? And that good-lookin' man! Is he the one you had lunch with? Do you think he'd let me see the grave? I can't believe it! Wait till I tell Aubry I saw the grave with my own eyes."

"Grandma, I don't think—" Alissa cradled the cordless phone against her shoulder and tried to brush her hair as her grandmother continued.

"Did you forget you had to pick me up in fifteen minutes for the church social?"

"No. I was headed out the door when you called."

"Okay." With a decisive click the line went dead.

Shaking her head, Alissa turned off the phone, grabbed her keys and purse, put Frito into the backyard, then hurried for the front door. Her earlier speculation about why Mrs. Teasedale and Mrs. Horton knew her identity had died shortly after she'd come home. If they were anything like her grandmother, then they probably knew her shoe size by now.

Alissa hadn't gone back to Brad's after leaving Mrs. Teasedale's yard. She'd come home to paint her backyard gate, and then puttered around in the flowerbeds until nearly time to pick up her grandmother. A quick check of her answering machine had revealed a message from Brad asking her to return his call and an odd message for someone named Louanne. The caller said Louanne was in some sort of trouble.

Smiling slightly, Alissa inserted her key into the locked car door, and then adjusted the hem of her red T-shirt. She ignored the call for Louanne and hadn't had time to call Brad back but planned to when she returned. Of course, they could only be friends, she told herself again. But that didn't stop the tiny spark of hope from igniting within, or the faint, undeniable thrill at the sound of his voice on her answering machine. *Maybe, just maybe*, she thought as she sank into the car seat and placed the key into the ignition. *But are you ready for another relationship? Look what you did to Sherman,* another voice insisted.

Trying to ignore the ever-present guilt, she snapped on her seat belt then fished through her cluttered purse to find her designer sunglasses. It amazed her that she could keep her closets immaculately clean while her purse usually resembled a pack rat's abandoned home. Trena frequently accused her of "repressed slob syndrome," and with a smirk, claimed that it went back to Alissa's childhood.

"Finally," she sighed as she dragged her black sunglasses from the bottom of her purse and put them on. She started to crank the engine, only to stop and adjust the rearview mirror. With everything in place, Alissa turned the ignition key, put the car into drive, drove out of her circular driveway, and began her journey up the hill in front of Brad's house.

Just as she increased her speed, though, a sleek, yellow-striped cat bolted from beside Brad's brick mailbox into the car's path. Alissa, her heart lurching, swerved to the right, and then smashed her foot against the brake pedal, which sank to the floorboard without resistance.

Chapter 5

The sounds of glass shattering and metal smashing into brick made Brad drop his ham sandwich in midbite. Only minutes before, he'd seen two children across the street playing catch in the vacant lot. Could one of them have chased the ball into the street and been hit? The little girl wasn't much older than Kara had been. She even had Kara's mahogany curls.

Had it really been two years already? It seemed like yesterday. But the torment, the pain, the misery Brad had experienced was enough to last a lifetime. If only he'd listened to Dana and stayed home that day. If only God hadn't allowed the tragedy.

A lump formed in his throat as his mind flashed images of Kara's limp little body lying dead in his arms, a crimson stain marring her T-shirt. That same fatal morning, she'd said, "Look at my new pink shirt, Daddy!" And he'd promised the T-shirt made her the prettiest little girl in the world. Would he once again cradle a dead little girl in his arms?

The answer lay on the other side of his front door. He hurried to the front door and reached for the brass knob. Brad's hand stopped. Could he face another tragedy? Even someone else's tragedy?

Grinding his teeth, he willed the fear to flee. The paralysis passed. And with a determined twist of the knob he rushed down his porch steps to see Alissa's Mustang enmeshed with what was left of his brick mailbox.

"Alissa!" he croaked. Only seconds before, he'd imagined cradling another dead child. But he'd never thought about the possibility of once again holding, sobbing over, the corpse of a beautiful woman. That possibility vanished, though, as he neared the car and Alissa emerged from behind the wheel.

"I'm—I'm okay," she stammered, a shaking hand covered her heart. "It's just. . .my brakes didn't work. I'm sorry about your mailbox." Tears brimmed her big brown eyes then splashed onto her cheeks one at a time, like fat raindrops taking their precious time to fall.

"Hey, it's all right," he soothed and rushed to her side. Before he knew it Brad had pulled Alissa into his arms for a consoling hug. He'd always said there was nothing more powerful than brown, tear-filled, feminine eyes. Unless, of course, it was the woman in his arms. Or the smell of jasmine perfume. His stomach felt as if he'd jumped from an airplane. And before he could experience any more emotional upheaval, Brad abruptly released her, only to have the jasmine scent linger with him.

Alissa, sniffling twice, produced a tissue from her pocket and wiped her eyes. "I guess I'm crying because I was scared speechless."

"Me, too," he breathed, noticing that the children must have gone back to their homes. "I was afraid someone had hit one of the children who were playing here earlier." Brad swallowed hard against the nausea creeping up his throat. "And then when I saw your car, I was afraid I'd—" He stopped himself short. Brad had almost said "I was afraid I'd lost you." Instead he said, "I was afraid you might have been hurt." He wondered what was going on within himself. Could this attractive dentist be weaving her way into his heart without his consent? His actions and words didn't match his claim of only wanting a friendship.

"Look at my car," Alissa groaned. "My '68 classic is demolished." Samantha yowled innocently from nearby and came to curve her way around Brad's legs. "And it's all because of that cat," Alissa said. "She ran out in front of me. I swerved to miss her, and then couldn't stop. Do you know who she belongs to?"

With an ironic smile, Brad bent to pick up Samantha. "Alissa Carrington, meet Samantha Ratner, my feline companion—and Frito's best friend."

"Oh, no! I just realized. . ." Alissa placed shaking fingers over her rounded lips. "If she hadn't run out in front of me, I probably wouldn't have braked until the next big intersection. Then I could have been. . ." She swallowed as what was left of the color in her cheeks vanished.

"Let's just be thankful you weren't," Brad said with more reassurance than he felt. "When was the last time you had your brakes checked?"

"I had the car serviced just last week. They were supposed to have checked everything. Transmission fluid, oil, brake fluid, and anything else that needs to be checked. I know absolutely nothing about cars."

"Then you know more than I do," Brad mumbled, hating to admit his weakness. His father was a mechanical genius, but that talent somehow skipped Brad, the firstborn, and went to his younger sister, Victoria. "My sister and father are the mechanics in our family. It's rather embarrassing when the college quarterback can't do more than add windshield wiper fluid without creating a total disaster, but his ninety-five pound sister can overhaul her car's carburetor."

Alissa, giving a final dab to the corner of her left eye, giggled. Brad adjusted his thin, black-framed glasses and began to relax for the first time since he'd heard the crash.

"I didn't know you wore glasses," Alissa said absently, her attention still focused on her crumpled car.

"I normally wear contacts," he explained, walking to the car's front bumper. "I'm slightly nearsighted—just enough to be annoying. I'd taken out my contacts earlier, when I went to the Y to swim, and hadn't put them back in." Brad didn't add that all the extra standing around because of the investigation had reactivated an old ache in his right hip. He'd explained to Alissa that he had to swim regularly because of an "accident"—if you could call a bullet wound an accident.

"Excuse me," a timid, high-pitched voice called from behind. "Did you need any help?" Brad turned to see a middle-aged woman of slightly plump build walking toward them. Her mass of short auburn curls framed an oval-shaped face, a face whose best feature was her deep-set, almost turquoise eyes. Whoever she was, she'd been a knockout once. But the beauty of her youth had been diminished by age and the dark circles under her eyes.

"I—I heard the crash," she continued. "I was in my backyard and thought I'd check to see if I needed to call an ambulance."

"Thanks," Alissa said. "But it looks like the only doctor I'm going to need is a car doctor." She waved toward the Mustang's crumpled hood before adding, "My mechanic runs a towing and auto-rebuilding service as part of his business; maybe he can tow the car for me."

The newcomer nodded. "I'm Claire Allen, by the way. Aren't you the dentist who bought Sarah Docker's house?"

Alissa nodded.

"I live right behind you, then."

"Oh, in the cute blue house beside Mrs. Teasedale?" Alissa asked.

"Yes." Brad couldn't miss the faint glimmer of disapproval that flitted across Claire's face like a fading yet turbulent shadow.

"I'm Brad Ratner," he said. "And I belong to the smashed mailbox."

"You're the artist then?" Before Brad could nod, she continued. "I'm sorry. I sound like twenty questions. If you haven't already figured it out, I don't socialize much. I'm an overworked R.N." She tugged the collar of her nurse's uniform for emphasis. "Otherwise, I'd have introduced myself before now. Anyway, both Sarah Docker and Whit Jenkins told me when they sold their houses. The six of us whose yards meet in the back had all been neighbors for so long that, even though we didn't see a lot of each other, we made an effort to keep each other informed." Claire pushed her auburn curls from her forehead.

"I guess I've met everyone now except the man who lives on the other side of my house," Brad said, his mind skipping from Alissa's accident to what had occupied it since that morning: Who placed the bodies in his backyard?

"That's Richard Calbert. He...um...he's a little different," Claire said cautiously. "Different, but very nice."

"Oh," Brad said, not understanding what "different" meant to Claire Allen but at the same time not wishing to sound nosey.

"What do you mean by different?" Alissa asked, apparently not caring who thought she was nosy. Brad covered an indulgent smile with his hand. He liked that in a woman. Curiosity. And plenty of it. With Alissa's inquisitive mind, he guessed her life would never be dull. She'd probably continuously ask questions that no one else had the guts to verbalize. Maybe his initial appreciation of her physical attractiveness had been brought about by this facet of her personality. Only a go-getter would spy over a backyard fence off and on all morning. Brad had seen her from the start. And what had begun in him as annoyance had turned into humor when he'd seen her obvious chagrin over her friend's blatant friendliness. Yes, Alissa was more curious than the average person but, surprisingly, she also was a bit shy. Just the right combination.

Dana had all the right combinations, too, an accusing voice whispered. Brad, his chest tightening, tried to ignore the taunting but knew deep within that the effort was hopeless.

"Well," Claire Allen continued in a lowered voice, "Richard's really not as strange as his—as he seems at first. He says he enjoys his job. Anyway, he makes decent money at it, they say. That's because he's so good at what he does. Maybe that's the strange part. That and the fact that it's odd for a middle-aged man. Most people in that profession are younger. But you'll know when you meet him, I guess, if you catch him on his way to work."

"Oh," Alissa said, sounding totally confused and in need of more information. Then she tensed and checked her watch. "For Pete's sake! I forgot my grandmother! It's six thirty now; I should have already been there!"

"I'll take you," Brad offered. "You can call your mechanic on your cell while I get my keys. Is there a chance he would tow it tonight and take a look at the brakes to see what happened?"

"Maybe. If he's not backed up with extra work. We're longtime friends—went to high school together. He usually makes room for me. I'm notorious for waiting till the last minute to have my car serviced, so his squeezing me in won't be the first time."

"Well, let me know if I can help," Claire said with a casual wave, and she walked back up the street.

Brad, waving to Claire, didn't voice his thoughts about Alissa's failed brakes. He did know enough about cars to understand that the brakes shouldn't have gone out if the maintenance check was done properly. Perhaps finding those bones had made him overly suspicious, but something about her brakes failing bothered him. Just an unexplained shadow of uncertainty nibbling at the back of his mind. Uncertainty, which he hoped, was unfounded.

Chapter 6

Y ou're late!" Alissa's grandmother accused as she opened the front door of her petite brick home.

"I'm sorry. I was delayed." Licking her lips, Alissa hoped her grandmother wouldn't sense she was hiding something. Alissa's brakes "betraying" her would weigh so heavily on Emily Carrington's mind that she'd worry about it happening again. So Alissa had chosen to keep the wreck a secret, and instructed Brad to do likewise.

"I'm with a friend. I hope you don't mind." Alissa said, diverting her grandmother's attention to the white Lexus sitting in the driveway.

Just as Alissa had anticipated, the diversion worked. "Is it a man?" Emily hissed, peering from the doorway through her fashionable wire-rimmed glasses.

"Yes. Brad Ratner's his name. You saw him on television."

"Oh! The cute one!" Emily giggled. "Can't wait to meet him."

Even though Alissa had little choice in the turn of events, she wasn't so sure her grandmother meeting Brad was the best idea. Emily Carrington usually exposed Alissa's men friends to a barrage of personal questions.

Despite the questions, though, Alissa was thankful that her grandmother's mind was still as sharp as that of a woman half her age. Not only her mind, but her appearance, too. She insisted on up-to-date fashion, including a bobbed hairstyle, tasteful makeup, and Chanel designer suits. With her discreetly tinted brunette hair, sparkling blue eyes, and soft complexion, she would pass for sixty-five by anybody's standards. And as Alissa's grandmother handed her the infamous sweet potato casserole, Alissa had to admit her pride in being Emily Carrington's granddaughter. Even if she couldn't have the mother she longed for, at least she did have Grandma.

"I'll put this in the car while you lock up," Alissa said, holding up the casserole.

"Okay."

"Don't be surprised by what she asks you, Brad," Alissa mumbled as she placed the brown glass casserole dish on the floorboard behind his seat.

"Believe me, I won't." An impish smile lighted Brad's smoky eyes.

Alissa, returning the smile, left the back door open for her grandmother and took the front passenger seat.

Seconds later, Emily plopped into her place and lost no time waiting for introductions. "Hi. I'm Emily Carrington." She extended her hand between the bucket seats.

Brad shook the offered hand. "Nice to meet you, Mrs. Car—"

"None of that Mrs. Stuff, now. I'm Emily."

"Nice to meet you, Emily. I'm Brad Ratner."

"I know. I saw you on television. And you're a lot better lookin' than Alissa's last man friend."

"Grandma!" This was going to be even worse than Alissa had expected, bad enough to scald her cheeks.

"Well, it's the truth," Emily slammed the car door for emphasis.

Alissa didn't even bother to look at Brad. She didn't need to. His muffled snickers told her plainly that he was probably dying of hilarity.

"The church isn't far from here, Brad," Alissa said, willing her voice to be calm even though her heart was pounding in something akin to panic. "Down this street. Now take a right. It's about five miles ahead on the left." She gripped the edge of the tan leather car seat as if it were a cliff over which her grandmother was about to push her. "And you have my permission to break the speed limit," she whispered from the corner of her mouth.

"What do you do for a living?" Emily continued as if Alissa weren't present.

"I'm an artist."

"Oh," she said in disappointment. "I thought maybe you were a doctor or something. Alissa's last man friend was. Made good money, too. But he just wasn't the right one for her. I told her that from the start. He wasn't a churchgoing man. Are you?"

"What?" Brad asked.

"A churchgoing man."

"Well, um, I. . .yes, I have been."

Alissa suppressed the urge to clamp her hand over her grandmother's mouth. The subject of church was obviously an awkward one for Brad, and Alissa immediately thought of the dusty Bible in his living room. A Bible that spoke of a devout past. What had altered his devotion?

"Good, because Alissa's a fine Christian girl. Do you know she even went to Africa last fall on a missions trip? Closed her clinic and everything, just to help those poor people over there with their teeth."

"Really?" Brad sounded genuinely impressed, and his warm glance looked it.

Alissa, on the other hand, was genuinely embarrassed. Once her grandmother started bragging, she might not stop.

"Yes, and she's planning on going back next summer," Emily continued.

"I'm sure Brad doesn't want to be bored with the details of my extracurricular activities," Alissa said, hoping to change the subject. Conversations in which she was the target of compliments always befuddled Alissa.

"On the contrary, I'm very interested," Brad said as he nearly leveled Alissa with his incredible smile.

She gripped the door's armrest and turned to gaze out the window at the city landscape mingled with majestic pines. Where would this acquaintance lead? Alissa had the expectant feeling of Christmas morning every time she looked at Brad, a feeling which had escalated into longing when he'd briefly embraced her after her accident.

"Do you make money with your artwork, Brad?" Emily asked.

"Yes." Brad's answer was laced with a chuckle.

"How much?"

"Grandma! You don't ask people questions like—"

"I do. Somebody's gotta look for you a good husband. Because let's face it, honey, you aren't doing too hot on your own."

Dismissing, or perhaps postponing, the money question, Emily clipped out her next query. "Have you ever been married?"

Alissa nearly choked. Emily hadn't asked Sherman that question until Alissa had been dating him a month. And she wasn't even dating Brad!

This time, though, Brad produced no mirthful snickers. His hands tightened on the steering wheel until his knuckles grew white. And silence enfolded them like the confining choke of death itself; the kind of icy, heavy silence that nobody, not even Emily Carrington, would dare break.

As the seconds ticked by and the car sped down the busy city street, Alissa waited breathlessly for his answer. She couldn't deny her own curiosity. She already knew he was hiding something painful from his past. Could it somehow involve marriage? And could this be the reason for his neglected Bible?

"Yes. . .once," he finally rasped. "She and my little girl. . .passed away two years ago."

"Oh, I see. I'm sorry, young man," Emily said discreetly, then changed the subject. "Have you checked on your clinic since you left Friday, Alissa?"

"No. I thought I might do that tomorrow. I need to check the voice mail anyway," Alissa said, wanting to applaud her grandmother. She had to give the woman credit for at least knowing when to end her prying questions.

"Don't you two worry about coming back to pick me up, now. I'll get that Reynolds man to take me home. He's been trying to get me to go for a ride in his new Corvette for weeks and weeks." She sighed. "Maybe if I go, he'll leave me alone."

"Mr. Reynolds is eighty," Alissa said as Brad pulled into the churchyard. "But he thinks he's forty."

"Forty!" Emily snorted. "More like sixteen! Do you know he actually thinks I'm going to date him?"

"Maybe you ought to think about it," Brad teased, his earlier tension vanishing. "It's a shame for an attractive woman like you not to have a boyfriend."

Alissa glanced toward her grandmother. Emily's face remained impassive. "You know something? I like you," she said then opened the door to get out.

Minutes later, after Alissa helped Emily enter the church kitchen; she sat in the car, rolled her eyes, and shut the door. "I'm really sorry about her. I'm afraid she's a bit on the pushy side."

Brad's smile proved that Emily's questions hadn't caused him any real damage. "I didn't expect anything less," he teased. "After all, you're rather. . .inquisitive yourself. I figured you had to get it from somebody."

"Please tell me I'm not as bad as she is."

"I don't know. . ." Brad put the car in reverse and eased out into the road. "Spying on someone across a privacy fence is pretty. . . um. . ." He mockingly glanced up as if he were searching for the right word.

"Nosy, I believe is the term."

Yes. As a matter a fact, you're right." Then, with a lopsided grin, Brad patted her shoulder and left his hand there several unnecessary seconds. Just long enough for Alissa to enjoy the effect. "But don't take it too hard. After all, something good came out of it. Without your nosiness we'd probably still be strangers."

"Oh, I doubt it," Alissa said. "You'd undoubtedly have introduced yourself when I demolished your mailbox." But would it have been so bad for them to remain strangers?

She could get accustomed—really accustomed—to having Brad Ratner in her life. And Alissa didn't think that would be wise. He obviously still had strong feelings for his deceased wife. What warm-blooded human being wouldn't after only two years? Especially with his little girl dying, too. What a tragedy! Alissa couldn't stop herself from wondering how they died. A car wreck perhaps?

He'd made it very clear, however, that his past was none of her concern. Deciding the smart thing was to avoid him from now on, Alissa inhaled the smell of leather seats and watched the neighborhoods, grocery stores, and mall pass by. Avoiding him might be harder than she'd like to admit, though, especially since she didn't *want* to avoid him.

"Now I guess it's my turn to be nosy," he said. "Did you think that Mrs. Horton—what was her first name?"

"Sadie."

"Yeah. Did you think she was a little. . ."

"On the weird side?"

"Yeah."

"I thought she was a lot on the weird side. And I don't think Mrs. Teasedale is far behind her."

"You don't think. . .nah."

"What?" Alissa, eyes wide, looked at him, waiting for him to vocalize what she'd speculated all afternoon.

"Well, about those bones. Somebody had to put them in my backyard. And Mr. Jenkins swears it wasn't him."

"But do the police believe him?"

Brad shrugged. "At present, they seem to have no hard evidence against him."

Alissa toyed with the hem of her T-shirt. "Do you know if they've questioned Mrs. Docker yet?"

"No. I've never met her. What's she like?"

"The 'Granny Smith' type. Wouldn't hurt a fly. Or seemed like she wouldn't hurt a fly. I only met her in passing at the closing of my home purchase."

"But it's not flies we're talking about, is it?" Brad steered the Lexus into Alissa's circle driveway.

"You can say that again," she said. Opening the car door, she peered toward Brad's mailbox and was thankful to see her car had already been towed. As usual, Tom was at her beck and call. "I'll be interested in meeting Mr. Calbert. If he's as odd as Claire Allen seems to think, he might be behind the bones. Did the police seem to have any leads on who could have been in your house?"

"No. But given my observations, they've narrowed it to probably being a female."

"Really? A woman?"

"Yes. Of average height and a slightly plump build. Either that or it was a man disguised as a woman."

"Or a thin woman who purposefully added some cushioning under her clothing." Alissa absently thought of Sadie Horton. Then she rolled her eyes. "Would you listen to me? A mere dentist, and I'm starting to sound like Alissa Carrington, private investigator."

"Yeah. And I'm no better. You just can't help but wonder, though." He took off his glasses and thoughtfully bit the earpiece.

"Well, maybe the police will find the murderer in a day or two, then close the investigation."

"For some reason, I don't think that's going to happen," he mumbled, as if his mind were no longer on the investigation.

His intense glance told Alissa exactly where his thoughts had traveled. It was the kind of mesmerizing, extended gaze that seemed to touch Alissa's very soul, incapacitating her. The effect verged on being hypnotic, almost as if she were falling into the smoky depths of his eyes. Then she was captive to a déjà vu feeling, as if their paths were destined to cross from the beginning of time.

But he only wanted friendship, and that was for the best. After all, Alissa wasn't sure she'd know true love if it bit her on the nose. She'd already devastated one man by mistaking human admiration for God-inspired love. She certainly didn't want to repeat that mistake, particularly not with a man as special as Brad Ratner. Alissa didn't think she could forgive herself for hurting Sherman, but she knew that she'd never forgive herself if she hurt Brad.

With a concentrated effort, she broke his disturbing gaze and turned to leave the car. "Well, um, thanks for the lift."

Chapter 7

That's right," Tom said after Alissa returned his call. "The brake fluid line was cut."

Her palms sweaty, Alissa sank to her poster bed and clutched her comforter. "Someone—someone wanted me to wreck my car?" she croaked as her gray mutt padded in to the bedroom to stare up at her in canine curiosity. Alissa had let him in upon arriving home, half for his comfort and half for hers. Still shaken from the wreck, she hadn't wanted to be alone.

"It sure looks that way. I think it might be a good idea for you to report this to the police. I'm not sure there's anything they can do. That is, unless you've seen anyone strange around your place today."

"No, I haven't." Alissa thought of the person who'd run from Brad's house that afternoon, then dismissed him or her. That person had been prowling around Brad's property, not hers. Her brake line could have been cut last night while she was sleeping. And she'd learned an important lesson; she'd make doubly sure from now on that she locked her car in the garage instead of leaving it in the driveway. Her father had often scolded her for forgetting to lock it at night. She realized now that she should have listened.

"Anyway," Tom continued, "at least the police will file a report. Then if it happens to someone else in your neighborhood, maybe a pattern will develop and they can find out who did it. Sometimes this kind of thing can be traced to a sick kid with a perverted sense of humor."

"Yeah. Okay," Alissa managed to squeak out.

"Are you all right?" Tom asked, concern filling his soft voice.

"Do you want me to call the police for you, or come over or something?"

"No. I'll be okay." She really wanted to say yes. But at the same time Alissa didn't want to give Tom any reason for false romantic hope. He was an extremely attractive Christian man who owned a chain of successful auto repair and body shops that stretched from Fort Worth to Austin. Yet there was simply no spark there for Alissa. She made arrangements for Tom's local garage to repair her Mustang, and was pressured to agree when he insisted on taking her to get a rental car the next day. A call to the police station produced a very sympathetic officer who, after a few questions, said exactly what Tom had speculated he might: Other than file a report, there was really nothing they could do at present.

Alissa then hovered over the phone, debating whether or not to call Brad. He'd requested that she let him know about her brake line, but that could wait until tomorrow. Besides, after her grandmother's pushiness, Alissa didn't want to give Brad the wrong idea and make him think she was chasing him.

So, in her desire for some human company, she decided to call her father who lived near Dallas, where he owned a pharmacy. She wouldn't worry him with the news of her brake line. The incident was probably what Tom had said—an impersonal prank.

"I hear you had a lunch date today," her father said after their initial greeting.

"Grandma didn't waste any time telling you, did she?" Alissa asked, flopping back on the bed to stare at the olive green and orange floral wallpaper with disgust. She simply couldn't put off wallpapering her bedroom much longer.

"No. And she filled me in about the bones next door, too. I was going to call you tonight, but haven't had the chance yet. What's going on?" he said, his kind, soothing voice immediately easing Alissa's nerves.

He was going to make a wonderful grandfather to Alissa's children. That is, if she ever had any children. An empty longing which she continually suppressed nearly refused suppression at that moment. The option of a husband and children didn't seem to be unfolding at present. *What about Brad?* a tiny voice asked, inviting Alissa to fantasize about the possibility. But there was no reason to daydream about the unattainable.

Taking a deep breath, Alissa related the day's events to her father. "And regardless of what Grandma tells you, Brad Ratner and I are just friends," she ended.

"Brad Ratner!" her father exclaimed, his voice rising half an octave. "Your new neighbor isn't *the artist* Brad Ratner, is he?"

"Yes, he's an artist. Why do I feel like you know something I don't?" Alissa asked, sitting up. Her father, although not talented artistically, had always pursued his esthetic tastes, surrounding Alissa with original sculptures and valuable paintings while she was growing up. She often sensed he was secretly disappointed that his daughter hadn't inherited her mother's artistic talent. Oh, she appreciated beauty in art. She simply didn't have the consuming love for it that her parents had shared. Alissa had always preferred creating beauty with her flowers rather than a brush. That was the reason she bought Mrs. Docker's big old house. It had an equally big old yard that she could landscape and relandscape to her heart's content.

"Alissa dear, Brad Ratner is one of this decade's leading American artists. As young as he is, he's virtually a child prodigy. His last painting sold for a quarter of a million in France. The man is not only filthy rich, but he's also an artistic genius."

"Oh, my word," Alissa groaned, recalling Brad's conversation with her grandmother. The she fell back onto her pillows and placed her left hand to her forehead. "Guess what Grandma asked him when we went to pick her up tonight?"

"There's no telling."

"She asked if he made any money with his paintings. Then when he said yes, she asked how much."

Don Carrington snorted. "Did he tell her?"

"No! I cut her off before she could push the issue."

"Well, maybe meeting her will shock him into picking up the brush again. Word has it he hasn't painted one stroke in two years."

"Really?" Alissa couldn't hide her curiosity.

"Yes. Do you remember hearing about that random mass shooting two years ago at a fast-food restaurant in New York?"

Alissa racked her memory for the story. "I must have missed that one."

"Well, some idiot went in at lunchtime and slaughtered fourteen customers because he was mad at the manager for firing him. Anyway, Brad and his wife and daughter were there—I think their names were Dana and Kara. Brad got away with only a bullet wound, while his wife and daughter were killed."

Suddenly, several things about Brad clicked into place, his slight East Coast dialect. His awkwardly telling her he'd been involved in an "accident" two years ago. His understated class—that elusive quality that suggested near royalty to her, even when he wore faded jeans. Then there was his tangible pain over something from his past. Now Alissa knew what that "something" was. No wonder he only requested friendship. The poor man was still recovering from the trauma of seeing his family murdered.

Could this be the reason for the dust on his Bible? Alissa remembered with aching clarity her initial anger at God when her mother died. She hadn't attended church for six months. Perhaps Brad felt the same way.

With a hard swallow, she vowed to honor Brad's request for a platonic relationship. As she'd sensed earlier, the last thing she needed to do was hurt him. That ruled out any romantic involvement because Alissa couldn't trust herself when it came to love. But she did know how to be a best friend. And she did know about turning to God in her pain, rather than blaming Him for it.

After another fifteen minutes of conversation, Alissa hung up with a promise that she'd introduce her father to Brad. She also felt much more at ease over her brake line having been sliced. Perhaps, as Tom had said, the cut was an incident hatched in the mind of some sick kid, and not an attack on her personally. With bones being unearthed next door, though, Alissa still had to resist the urge of looking over her shoulder every other second.

She couldn't believe the watch was gone. She held the black knit pants upside down and shook them furiously, hoping she'd overlooked the earth-encrusted timepiece, which she'd placed in her pocket yesterday. Nothing fell from the pants, however, but a few pieces of dried soil. And she'd already searched the house.

All the trouble she'd gone through yesterday to retrieve the watch—running through Brad's house in broad daylight, knocking Louanne down—and she'd somehow lost the very thing for which she'd gone to the graveside, the very thing which could incriminate her as the murderer.

You fool! Why didn't you check your pockets yesterday afternoon as soon as you got home?

It was her memory. Henry mentioned only last week that he was concerned about her, that her short-term memory didn't seem as sharp as it had been. She'd been so consumed with having seen Louanne and "fixing" her car that all thoughts of the golden watch that she'd compulsively buried near the bodies ten years earlier had vanished. And, after taking off the black pants, she hadn't checked her pockets.

A decade ago she'd been so careful to cover her tracks. Why had she given into that momentary, grief-stricken urge to rid herself of the watch? Luckily, the pool company's digging hadn't unearthed it. They'd come within inches. She grinned. Maybe this was one more example of fate smiling on her. No one had suspected her crime ten years before because of fate's willful cooperation.

The momentary smug smile turned into a rebellious scowl. Now the watch was gone. Fate must have turned against her. Furiously tugging the pants pockets wrong side out, she saw the hole for the first time. The hole was just big enough for the watch to have slipped and fallen to the ground. A frustrated shriek erupted from her soul, and she threw the pants across the bedroom to land on the row of crystal perfume bottles lining the mahogany dresser. Then, with an agile forward lunge, she violently raked the pants and perfume bottles onto the floor in a heap of shattering glass. Nothing was going right. First, Louanne didn't die as planned, now the watch.

Her momentary fury spent, she collapsed onto the queen-sized brass bed to stare at the ceiling. She must retrace her steps through the neighborhood. Maybe Richard Calbert would help her once more. After all, he'd assisted her when she buried the bodies.

Chapter 8

Trying to ignore the green wallpaper, Alissa slipped on her cotton garden gloves and left her bedroom. Yes, she was putting off the wallpapering project again. But today's weather was identical to yesterday's—not a cloud in sight. And the early morning coolness beckoned her to work outdoors. She planned to remove the boring monkey grass from the front flowerbed near her driveway and replace it with some pink geraniums. The weatherman had predicted rain for this afternoon. Maybe she'd start the wallpapering then.

Ten minutes later, her remodeling project forgotten, Alissa overturned shovel after shovel full of moist earth, then began removing the monkey grass from its flowerbed. For every clump she set aside, though, Frito created four or five clumps. He'd appointed himself her official "assistant gardener" when he was a puppy, and Alissa never denied him the joy of "helping" her.

"That mutt of yours is spoiled rotten" was one of her grandmother's favorite lines. It was the absolute, unadulterated truth, though. Alissa, tossing a new clump of monkey grass into the air, playfully tweaked the dog's ear before he ran around the yard in a frantic circle, the grass hanging from his teeth. He enjoyed the 6:30 a.m. coolness and the fragrant smell of dew-laden pines as much as she did.

As she shook the third large clump of grass free of soil, however, something other than dirt fell from the grass. Something heavy enough to make a metallic clink as it hit the flowerbed's brick border. Something, although caked in soil, resembled a very expensive, diamond-studded gold watch. Either that or it was a cheap fake a child had lost during play.

Picking up the watch, Alissa rubbed her gloved thumb over the face to dislodge some of the dirt. That revealed what she'd originally suspected. The watch was one of the most expensive brands available. Standing now, she wondered what she should do with it. Run a "lost and found" ad in the paper? Or maybe call Mrs. Docker? Perhaps the watch was hers.

"Good morning," a pleasant male voice called from her driveway. Turning, Alissa encountered a tall, thin jogger, probably in his late forties, who was wearing black-and-white running gear and a welcoming smile. His tan spoke of many hours outdoors, as did his sandy, sun-streaked hair.

"Good morning," she called back as he jogged into her yard to stop a few feet away.

"I'm Richard Calbert. I live two houses down. I saw you out this morning and just thought I'd introduce myself," he said through puffs of air.

"Alissa Carrington," she said, starting to extend her hand, only to stop with a wry smile. "I guess we'd better not shake. That is, unless you want to get your hands dirty.

The corners of his hazel eyes crinkled as his grin increased, and he grabbed her gloved hand and shook it firmly. "A little dirt never hurt anyone."

"That's always been my motto," Alissa agreed, wondering what Claire Allen found so weird about this man. He looked and talked perfectly normal.

"I'm sorry I haven't gotten around to introducing myself sooner, but I've been busy with my business. It keeps me hoppin'."

"Oh?" Alissa said, inviting him to expound on exactly what business he was in. Claire Allen had left no doubts it was something strange, at least in her eyes.

"Yes. I own a couple of flower and greetings shops. I have florists who do the arranging. I'm in charge of the greetings. Sometimes I'm a singing gorilla, sometimes Tarzan himself." He shrugged, his kind eyes twinkling with mirth. "It all depends on what the customers order."

"Oh yeah, I know you! I've seen your advertisements on television. You're dressed as a trapeze artist."

"That's me," he said. "One time. . ." His spontaneous laughter interrupted his words. "A couple of years back, someone had me dress as a ballerina for a gag. It was hilarious. Claire Allen saw me," he pointed toward Claire's house, "and I don't think she's gotten over it yet. She thought I was a tad bit on the strange side already, I guess. But that just pushed her opinion over the edge. Quite frankly"—he lowered his voice in mock seriousness—"I sometimes think she's a bit weird herself. Anyone who would raise goldfish so her cat can have fresh cuisine. . ." He rolled his eyes. "I've lived here fifteen years. They were all here when I moved in except for Mrs. Docker." He waved toward Sadie, Elizabeth, Claire, and Brad's houses. "Mrs. Docker bought your house ten years ago. Anyway, I'd thought for a long time that my only normal neighbors were Sarah Docker and Whit Jenkins."

Alissa giggled, her heart warming to this cheerful man. She could clearly understand how someone as serious-looking as Claire would think someone as lighthearted and chatty as Richard could be a bit odd.

"And from what I understand from the neighborhood gossip, you're a dentist, right?" he continued.

"Yes. It doesn't take long to travel, does it?"

"Not in this neighborhood. Sometimes I think Mrs. Teasedale and Mrs. Horton know my business before I do. For instance, yesterday evening when I got home, I had a message on my machine from Mrs. Teasedale about the bones in Brad Ratner's backyard. They've been highly interested because of Brad's fame as a painter."

"Oh?" Alissa began to wonder if everyone but her had prior knowledge of Brad's career.

"Yeah. Anyway, I think this bones business is kind of chilling, don't you?"

"That's an understatement. It's amazing to me that something like human bones could be unearthed in such a quiet neighborhood."

Alissa absently glanced at the earth-encrusted watch and rubbed the face with her thumb. "You wouldn't happen to know who this belongs to, would you? I just found it in my flowerbed. Did Mrs. Docker own a watch like this?" She extended it forward.

Richard, whistling softly, took it from her. "This cost a hunk of money. I don't think Mrs. Docker would have splurged on something like this. She's a widow on a fixed income, and besides that, she's eternally thrifty."

"I was thinking about putting an ad in the paper. I'm sure the owner would be glad to have the watch returned."

"Good idea. Incidentally, my brother's a jeweler, owns Calbert Jewelry downtown." Alissa nodded, recognizing the reputable name. "Why don't you take it by his place and have him dissect it and clean it up? He'll even appraise it for you. Then you'll better know what you're dealing with. You don't want to have the ad answered by some swindler who can take advantage of you because you don't have all the facts. I'll tell you what," he said, never taking a breath. "I'll take it to him, if you'll let me. That way, he won't charge you. He owes me anyway. I dressed up like a giant rooster for him last week. He'd wanted me to catch his salesclerk off guard and give her a big birthday kiss. I wound up chasing the poor woman down the street. Scared her to death at first, I think. Anyway, by the time I caught her, both of us, and a whole city block of onlookers were doubled up with laughter. So, like I said, he owes me."

"Okay," Alissa said with a chuckle, then immediately questioned her hasty decision. She'd only just met Richard Calbert. What if he were a swindler? She might never see the valuable watch again. Another glance into his hazel eyes swept away all doubts. If Richard Calbert were dishonest, then so was apple pie and motherhood.

❧

With a satisfied smile, she walked away from the large oak she'd been hiding behind in order to eavesdrop on Richard and Louanne's conversation. Louanne had never seen her watching from the yard's outer boundary, never known that Richard Calbert was once again assisting the person who'd murdered her. The person who'd murder her again, very, very soon.

❧

From his kitchen window, Brad watched as Alissa bade good-bye to Richard Calbert. He'd met the Calbert man yesterday after taking Alissa home. They'd pulled into their driveways simultaneously and had introduced themselves. Richard seemed nice enough—not quite as weird as Claire Allen had depicted him, not quite as nosy as Sadie Horton, Elizabeth Teasedale, or even Claire herself. He'd been only slightly curious about Alissa's accident as Brad briefly told him the details.

At the moment, though, Brad dismissed the thoughts of Mr. Calbert and concentrated on Alissa. He'd left the message on her machine yesterday evening because he'd wanted to ask her opinion about a painting. Later he decided that was foolish, perhaps a mere ploy for her attention. But he couldn't deny that his interest in his work, once a driving passion, seemed to be returning.

Something about Alissa ignited a need in his soul he'd considered completely dead. Perhaps it was her high cheekbones, her full lips, or her slightly square jawline, or maybe the combination of all three. But whatever the cause, the end result was the same. Brad had the undeniable desire to sketch her profile.

"Forget her profile," he mumbled, Brad really wanted to create a full-blown portrait of the woman enjoying her favorite pastime, her flowers. Giving into the compulsion, he raced to his bedroom closet, flung it open, and reached to the back of the highest shelf, where he'd stashed his sketch pad. Only yesterday he had wondered if he'd ever feel the creative urge again. Now he knew.

With a fervor he hadn't felt in two years, he flipped open the pad, grabbed one of his sketching pencils, and rushed back to the kitchen window.

In Brad's exultation, the pencil began moving over the paper as if of its own accord. This feeling, this experience, was exactly the same as it had always been. The heat of the moment; the intense force that refused denial; the churning within that sought release, a release only achieved with the finished work of art. Genius, some called it, but Brad called it creation.

Then, as Alissa's shoulder-length hair, captivating almond-shaped eyes, and cute pug nose flowed from pencil to paper, guilt flowed through his being. What was he doing? Had he lost his mind? What about Dana?

Every morning since her death, he'd awakened with her in his heart, in his mind. Blinking, he stared at the porcelain sink as a sickening realization seared through him; he hadn't even thought of her this morning. This morning, he'd awakened wondering what plans Alissa had for the day, hoping their paths would cross, planning an "accidental" encounter.

He tried to revive Dana's smiling face in his mind, tried to obliterate Alissa's. But he couldn't. He couldn't even remember what Dana looked like. The counselor had suggested he move to another city, start a new life for himself; had said a move might be the key to his recovery from that. . .that holocaust he'd witnessed. Could he, after two years, finally be recovering?

His upper lip broke out in clammy beads of perspiration, the sweat quickly moved to this forehead and trailed down his spine. But where did that leave Dana? And little Kara?

"No-o-o!" he screamed. Turning, he hurled the sketch pad toward the oak breakfast bar. Samantha, who'd been contentedly sleeping on one of the bar chairs, jumped and scampered into the living room, her tail straightened.

Brad wanted to run just as Samantha had, wanted to flee from the emotions which were tying his very soul into a knotted mass of confusion. He marched to the bar, retrieved the rejected sketchpad, and with new determination, ripped the offending drawing into four pieces. God might have turned His back on Dana and Kara in His "wisdom," failing to protect them, but Brad would never turn his back on them.

He'd decided yesterday that he must remain faithful to Dana. That decision stayed firm. Regardless of his emotions, regardless of Alissa's magnetic femininity, her mass of honey-colored hair, or her fabulous figure, he and Alissa Carrington would never be anything more than friends. Period! He dropped the torn sketch into the nearby trash basket.

The front doorbell's ringing seemed to finalize his decision. When he opened the door, however, he momentarily wondered if his betraying heart had conjured up its desire despite his head's persistent wish.

"I'm terribly sorry to bother you, Brad," Alissa said, her brown eyes pleading for understanding. "And I know it's early, but could you give me a lift? I had a call from a patient just now—infected wisdom teeth. If he weren't in excruciating pain, I'd wait on a taxi. Anyway, I could use a ride to the clinic as soon as possible. Would you mind?"

"I'd be glad to give you a lift," he heard himself say despite the guilt, the warning bells penetrating his mind. And once again, regardless of his fighting to keep it alive, Dana's memory faded from his thoughts.

Chapter 9

I hate to tell you this, Barry," Alissa said to the twenty-year-old Oriental college student after examining his teeth, "but it looks like your wisdom teeth are going to have to come out. Your gums are infected right now, though. That's the reason you're having the pain. I'm surprised you could even swallow. The swelling has even gone down into your throat."

"It wasn't really bad until yesterday. Then this morning, when I woke up. . ." He rolled his eyes to punctuate the pain.

Removing the blue examination mask, Alissa held up the X-rays for him to see. "These are really impacted. I could extract them, but you'll have less pain if you go to an oral surgeon and let him put you under anesthesia. While you're having the bottom ones out, I'd go ahead and have the surgeon take the top ones out, too." She pointed to the white teeth visible above his dark gum line as the antiseptic smell of her examination room seemed to support her diagnosis. "You don't have enough jaw space for them to drop properly. And you're just putting off the inevitable if you don't go ahead and have them taken care of. I'm going to write you a prescription for an antibiotic to get rid of the infection. Then I'll make you an appointment with Dr. Gardner for next week. In my opinion, he's the best oral surgeon in the area."

"Okay, thanks, Dr. Carrington. Oh, and thanks for coming in during your vacation. I'm sorry to have bothered you at home," Barry said, looking at her gratefully. "I—I hope I didn't interrupt anything, um. . .important." He glanced at the doorway meaningfully.

Following his gaze, Alissa reached for her prescription pad and saw Brad, arms crossed, watching from the room's doorway. His serious smoky eyes reflected something akin to admiration. Then, he looked down.

Barry must have noticed Brad's expression and assumed . . .only he knew what!

"Oh no, Barry, you didn't interrupt anything," she rushed, her betraying cheeks growing decisively warmer. "He's just, we're—we're just—this is my neighbor, Brad Ratner. He gave me a lift because my car's in the shop." If she sounded half as flustered and guilty to Barry as she did to herself, she'd probably done nothing but reinforce his assumptions. Brad's quick silent retreat didn't do much to lessen the impression, either.

Alissa, concentrating on writing the prescription, tried to pretend the situation didn't exist. And, with a hard swallow against the sudden lump in her throat, she attempted to regain her professional composure.

Why did Brad have to be so attractive? Even in his glasses, which he now wore, he looked like something out of a magazine. Well, maybe not quite that perfect. But close enough to make Alissa want to stand back and observe him in feminine admiration.

Apparently even Barry sensed the undercurrent of attraction Alissa felt for Brad. And if Barry could see it, what did Brad see? *Friends, friends, friends. We can only be friends,* she repeated to herself as she made the appointment for Barry's surgery, took the young man's payment, and bade him good-bye.

She and Brad had barely spoken on the way to the clinic. The atmosphere between them could only be described as strained, something Alissa didn't understand. Last night, she'd felt perfectly comfortable in his presence. Perhaps he wasn't a morning person, or didn't appreciate being disturbed so early. Or maybe, after being grilled by her grandmother, he'd decided he didn't even want her friendship anymore. But then there was that certain. . .light in his eyes when he looked at her, the same light that Barry must have noticed.

"I'm just going to check my voice mail and make sure everything's okay in the other examination rooms before leaving, Brad," she called into the waiting room.

"Okay. No rush," he called back.

There were nothing but routine messages in her voice mail. And as Alissa rounded the corner to enter the back examination room, what she saw hanging outside the window completely obliterated those messages from her mind.

"Brad!" she croaked, rushing into the waiting room. "Someone—someone—there's something in here. . ."

"What is it? Are you all right?" His eyes wide, he jumped to his feet and rushed to Alissa's side.

Alissa instinctively covered her eyes, trying to wipe the image from her mind, but it was no use. "Just—just go look," she breathed and pointed down the hall. "Last door—on the left."

Brad rushed to the back room with Alissa following at a more cautious pace.

"This is sick," he said seconds later as he stared at the window.

"I know. It looks almost exactly like Frito, doesn't it?" Alissa's lips quivered as she peered at the life-sized stuffed dog that hung by its neck from a white cord just outside the window. "At first, I thought it—it was him."

After the initial shock, the stuffed animal hadn't been what turned Alissa's stomach, though. The messaged taped to the window was what had sent her running in fear. A simple piece of notebook paper, that's all. But the words "You're next. Don't think you'll survive again!" meticulously cut and pasted from newsprint, had made her nauseous, made her nauseous still.

And the worst part of all, a snapshot of Alissa's car smashed against Brad's mailbox hung just beneath the words.

"Last—last night my mechanic said—said the brake line was cut,"

Alissa stammered in a quivering voice. "He seemed to think—think it was an impersonal prank by some kid. But—"

"There's nothing impersonal about this," Brad stated. "We need to call the police."

"But I want to go back home and check on Frito. What if they try to kill him while I'm gone?"

"Look," Brad said, turning to grab her shoulders in an intense grip. "As much as I love animals, Frito is only a dog. You, on the other hand, are a human being. You need to call the police now. This world has its share of sickos—people who kill innocent women and children without so much as a blink." His gray eyes deepened to black pools of despair as his fingers' tightening grip bit into her shoulders. "And I won't simply stand by while someone kills you. Do you understand?" he almost shouted.

Alissa stood speechless, as his gaze seemed to paralyze her.

Then, his fingers relaxing, some of the intensity faded from his eyes. "I'm overreacting, aren't I?"

Alissa nodded, understanding full well why he was overreacting. If, like her father said, Brad had witnessed his wife and daughter's murder, she'd probably have reacted just as strongly if she were Brad.

"You're right, though. I'll call the police. And when they leave, we'll go check on Frito."

"I'm sorry," he said, touching her cheek with the back of his index finger. "It's just that—"

"I understand," she whispered, slowly reaching up to cover his hand with hers. This time, however, Alissa felt no chills, no tingles from their close contact. Instead, she experienced a "coming home" feeling, a feeling which said her hand belonged, had always belonged, in Brad's. *Oh, dear God, is he the one?*

As the moment stretched, Brad's gaze traveled from her eyes to her lips, to linger there with naked longing glimmering like the faint flame of a newly lighted candle.

Then the tingles came, sweeping from Alissa's abdomen up her chest and on to her lips. Tingles. Or the conquering tide of desire long held at bay.

Then, a denying wind snuffed the flame from Brad's eyes; it was replaced by the determined set of his lips and a measured, backward step. "Go call the police," he said and abruptly turned away. "I'm going to check on the window from the outside."

❧

"You can think of no one who could possibly have a vendetta against you, Dr. Carrington?" the African-American police officer asked some thirty minutes later. "An ex-patient, perhaps?"

"No, no one," Alissa said, watching through the window as the policewoman liberally applied black powder on the glass pane. She'd taken several snapshots, then removed the stuffed animal and message. Now she was checking for prints.

"Well, unless Lieutenant Peterson finds any prints, there's really not much we can do. And it's not like it is on TV. Most of the time we don't find any prints."

"Yeah. That's about what I figured," Alissa said dully.

"I'm sorry," he replied. "But. . ." With a helpless shrug he stared at the report he'd been filling out. "You just need to be careful. Do you have someplace you could go to stay awhile?"

"Why?" Alissa shrugged and tugged on the hem of her oversized pink cotton shirt. "If this person is really intent on harming me, which, judging by the seriousness of yesterday's crime, I assume he is"—she gave way to an undeniable shudder—"then won't he resume his campaign when I come back? I can't hide the rest of my life. I've got a practice to run, for starters." She waved her arm toward the front office.

"I know it's difficult, but. . ." he trailed off, obviously accepting defeat when he saw it.

Alissa suppressed the tears of frustration stinging her eyes and stared out the window at the policewoman still dusting for prints. Brad, standing behind the policewoman, peered over her shoulder, his face full of unasked questions. He had barely glanced at Alissa since the breathless moment when he'd almost kissed her. Alissa hadn't looked at him much either. She knew in her head that their relationship shouldn't develop beyond friendship. Her heart, however, was another story. Her heart had wanted nothing more than to feel his lips on hers.

Chapter 10

Alissa didn't say a word on the short drive home. She couldn't. Her mind was focused on what she'd find when she opened her backyard gate. Frito hanging by his neck? He'd wanted to stay in the house when she left for the clinic, but she had forced him outside. Had she forced him into the jaws of death?

Seeming to sense her despair, Brad remained respectfully quiet. "Would you like me to go inside with you?" he asked as he slowly turned into her circular driveway.

Nodding approval, Alissa glanced at him in appreciation. "Would you mind?"

Brad's answer never came. Instead, he slammed on his brakes. "Do you know that car?" he shouted, pointing toward the red Mercedes sitting in the drive.

Because the vast array of trees and shrubbery partially blocked her view of the driveway, Alissa hadn't noticed the car until now. Her heart skipped in reaction to Brad's reaction. Then she relaxed. "Yes. It's Tom McDaniel. My mechanic. He promised to arrange for a rental car for me last night when he gave me the report on my car. I guess that's what he's here for."

Brad's tense expression vanished. "Sorry. I'm a little jumpy," he said as Tom unfolded his tall, thin frame from the Mercedes. "Did he tell you last night that your brake line had been cut?" He drove the remaining few feet of driveway, then smoothly stopped the automobile and turned off the purring engine.

"Yes."

"Why didn't you call and let me know?"

"Well. . ." Alissa didn't know exactly what to say. She hadn't called because, at that moment, she hadn't wanted to appear pushy. Hadn't wanted him to think she, like her grandmother, saw him as nothing more than matrimony material.

Tom, however, saved her from a reply when he gallantly opened Alissa's door. "I just drove up," he said, his ginger-colored eyes alight with a welcoming smile. "Perfect timing, huh?"

"Yeah. Thanks for coming," she said, tensely grabbing her purse and stepping from the car. "If you'll wait just a minute, I'll be ready to go. But first, I've—I've got to check something." Frito. Was her best buddy still alive?

Frito himself answered that question, though, when he raced from Brad's front yard with Samantha close on his heels. Alissa sank against the car, her eyes watering with relief.

Brad, now at her side, placed his hand on her shoulder. "Looks like you didn't have anything to worry abut," he soothed.

"Thank God." She dropped to her knees and whistled. "Frito! Come here, boy!" Alissa winced against the impact of concrete on her sore knees. Even the Band-Aids didn't cushion the blow enough to ease the pain.

"What's going on?" Tom asked.

"I received a nasty threat at the clinic," Alissa said, hating the words even as she said them. "Someone hung a stuffed dog that looked like Frito outside the exam room and left a message that said I would be next." Her deep breath shook despite her wish to control it. "Anyway, I was worried about what I'd find when I got home."

Frito, noticing Alissa for the first time, lowered his tail and ears, He completely ignored Samantha, who playfully attacked his right hind leg, and made a mad dash for the backyard.

Alissa forced a chuckle, and also forced her voice to a cheerful calm as she stood. "He knows he's not supposed to be out of the backyard.

He keeps digging holes under the fence. I had to discipline him last week for it. He's going to get himself run over."

"Alissa." Tom, ignoring her attempt at cheerfulness, placed a protective arm around her shoulders. "Why don't you stay with Mother for a few weeks? She'd love to have you, and the Florida coastline would probably do you good."

Brad's quick, perceptive glance took in first Alissa then Tom, and she felt the need to explain that Tom's affection was not reciprocated. But why did she owe Brad an explanation? She'd only just met the man, for Pete's sake.

"Thanks for the offer, Tom, but I can't run. Let me make sure everything's okay inside; then we'll go for the rental car," Alissa blurted out, wanting to change the subject. Tom's constant offer of assistance was painfully apparent. She'd thought when it started six months ago that her continued refusals would politely hint at her lack of interest. His tall, trim frame, boy-next-door auburn hair, easy smile, and financial security would probably be many a woman's dream come true. But not Alissa's.

"Oh. I decided to let you use my car," Tom said. "I've got the Volkswagen I can beat around in until I finish with your Mustang. The Mercedes is new and I'd rather you be in something I know is safe than take a chance on a rental car."

"But—"

"No buts." Tom extended the car's two keys to her.

"As far as that goes," Brad said evenly, his eyes a mask of something unreadable, something that may have bordered on a challenge, "Alissa always has a ride with me. She could even borrow my car, if she likes."

Tom looked Brad square in the eyes, a look much like a bull that's been defied by an equal match. "I don't believe we've been introduced," he said and extended his hand. "I'm Tom McDaniel, a longtime friend of Alissa's. And you're. . . ?" The greeting, although "proper" in form, sounded more like a territorial claiming of property.

"Brad Ratner." A tight smile. "Alissa's new neighbor and friend. I live right there." He pointed to his sprawling house. "So like I said, it will be no trouble for me to play chauffeur for a few days."

Alissa felt like a heifer being auctioned off to the highest bidder, a feeling she didn't appreciate. "Thanks, but no thanks to both of you," she said. "I'd rather have my own rental car. The last thing I need right now is to worry about getting a scratch on a Mercedes or whether or not my. . .chauffeur is home."

The muffled ringing of Tom's cell phone stopped him from protesting Alissa's decision. "Okay," he said, turning to the car. "But I still say you should leave town for a while."

"He might be right," Brad said, scowling at Tom as he answered the phone in the car. "Do you have a relative somewhere you could stay with?"

Exhaling, Alissa glanced at him, noting the glint of concern in his eyes, a concern also evident in his voice. "That sounds good, but what happens when I come back home?" she asked. "It would probably just start up again. And if this person is really after me, then how do I know he won't follow me out of town?"

"You don't, I guess," he said with resignation. "But I just don't want to stand by and watch—"

"That was the body shop here in town," Tom said, walking toward them. "I've got an irate customer who refuses to deal with the manager. So I've got to go." He looked at Alissa, his eyes beseechingly kind. "Are you sure you won't take the Mercedes? I really wouldn't mind."

"No," Alissa said in her most decisive yet most considerate voice. "A rental car will be fine."

"Okay. Well, I'll take care of this customer then be back to drive you to get a car."

"I'll take her," Brad offered quickly. "I'm not busy at the moment anyway."

"It must be nice," Tom muttered, his voice cloaked with the resentment of a possessive seventeen-year-old. "Don't you have to work for a living?"

Brad's jaws clenched, and Alissa placed her hand on Tom's arm. Tact wasn't one of Tom's better qualities, especially not when he was annoyed, and Brad obviously did annoy him. Alissa suspected, however, that the feeling was mutual.

"I'm sorry you can't stay, Tom," she said pointedly. "But I know how demanding your job is."

"Yeah. . .right," he muttered, his stony gaze softening as it turned from Brad to Alissa. "I'll call you later." And with that, he slid into his car, cranked the diesel engine, and drove away.

"How long did you say you've known him?" Brad asked.

"Since high school."

"Why do you put up with him?"

"He's usually not like this. He's really a fine Christian man."

"Well, he's the kind of guy that gets on my nerves."

Barely able to hide her smile, Alissa said, "I think he feels the same about you. . .um, would you mind going inside with me? I just want to make sure everything's okay before we go," she added, discreetly trying to change the subject. Part of her was elated that Tom seemed to evoke a certain jealousy in Brad. The other part, however, wanted to skirt the issue. Jealousy usually came equipped with romantic motivation, something Alissa wasn't sure of in her or Brad.

❧

"I'm going to have a banana on the way. Want one, Brad?" Alissa asked ten minutes later after she and Brad had glanced through the house, and, much to her relief found everything exactly as she'd left it. She'd also locked Frito snugly into the glassed-in sunroom leading onto her patio. No sense in taking any chances with his life. Alissa plucked a banana for herself from the ripening bunch on top of the refrigerator.

"No, thanks," Brad said. "I never have cared for bananas. Besides, m still full from breakfast."

"As far as I'm concerned, anyone who doesn't like bananas must e a space alien," she teased, not mentioning that the piece of fruit as her breakfast.

"I'm not so sure you're not the space alien," he parried. "I didn't now dentists stopped their vacation to see patients. That was really dmirable of you."

"Oh," she said, trying to formulate a practical reason for so readily lowing a patient to interrupt her free time. "Well, his family's been ay and Trena's patients since we opened the clinic five years ago. So I gured I owe it to him. Trena would have done the same thing if she'd een here, I'm sure. Besides, it didn't take that long."

"Regardless, it was still thoughtful."

Alissa, never knowing how to react to compliments, studied ne banana and searched for something to say. "Thanks," she finally queaked out. She really hadn't given the emergency dental exam any nought and was at a loss to think someone considered it generous.

"Uh. . .Alissa. . ." Brad paused awkwardly and rubbed the nape f his neck where his straight hair touched his white cotton shirt's ollar.

Her finger suddenly itched to touch his hair, to feel its softness gainst her fingers. Instead, she concentrated on nonchalantly peeling er banana and nibbling the sweet fruit. After today, she vowed to erself, she would stay away from the man because her mind defied aming when he was near.

"I wanted to ask you something," he continued. "Earlier, when we ere at the clinic and I got carried away, you said you understood why d reacted like I did. And I felt that you did understand much more nan I've told you. You know about Dana and Kara, don't you?"

She swallowed the bit of banana in a nervous gulp. "Yes." A dry ough. "Um. . .my father, he. . .um, he's a big fan of yours. A real art connoisseur. Anyway, when I was on the phone with him last nigh he told me about—about the shooting." With this explanation, sh felt just as nosy and prying as Mrs. Teasedale.

"Did he tell you I haven't painted in two years, then?"

"Um, yes," Alissa shamefully said to the drooping banana pe and then cautiously glanced at him.

One corner of his lips tilted in a smile—part force, part genuin "Did he also know the reason that I moved to Tyler?"

"No, he, um. . .he didn't go into that."

"Well, I'll tell you, then. It was an attempt to start a new li for myself. You know, to stop living in the past and create a 'brigl future.'" He waved his hand in sarcasm. "My sister owns a farm a hour from here. So I thought, why not?"

"Is it—do you think it's going to work?" Alissa had never felt s awkward, so stupid, in her whole life. What a dumb thing to ask man who's seen his family murdered.

"Who knows?" he said, a bitter twist to his mouth.

"Um, Brad, I—I don't want to pry, but. . ." Alissa nervously licke her lips as she mentally prepared her next words, words that woul answer a question and perhaps simultaneously give him hope. "We my mother died when I was fifteen, and I was furious with God for long time after that." She shrugged uncertainly and hoped she wasn prying. "I don't know if it will help you or not, but I finally realize that God was there to comfort me in my pain. All I had to do wa turn to Him."

"God?" he exploded, his eyes churning gray clouds. "I'll tell yo about God! I went to church my whole life, did my best to live Christian life, then He repaid me by killing my family!"

"Oh no, Brad," Alissa whispered. "God didn't kill them."

"He could have stopped it, and He didn't!" he yelled. "That's th same thing as killing them to me."

She stared at him in helpless silence, a silence that stretche between them like a great, gaping canyon. Yes, her words had answered the question his dust-covered Bible had raised. Unlike Sherman, Brad was a Christian, but he was struggling for his spiritual health.

With a sigh, Brad scrubbed his fingers through his hair as if he wanted to pull it out by the roots. "I'm—I'm sorry. I shouldn't have taken my frustration out on you. If it's any consolation, the last couple of days haven't given me as much time to think about the past. Between the bones in my backyard and all your upheaval. . ."

"I, uh, guess I have kept you quite busy, haven't I?"

"More than you know," he mumbled, his eyes growing very serious and then taking on that guarded wariness she'd seen at the clinic.

Alissa swallowed again as an undeniable attraction sprang between them. But Brad turned toward the living room. "I'm ready to go when you are," he said bluntly.

Frustration. Alissa had never felt it so sharply, so poignantly, as her stomach twisted into a tight wad of tension. Brad seemed to be making a career of saying and doing heart-stopping things, then cutting the moment short.

She placed the unfinished banana on the kitchen counter, took a deep breath, and grabbed a bottled water from the fridge. Alissa needed a long, cool drink of water to calm her nerves, and then she'd go rent herself a car. After that, she'd avoid Brad as if he had the plague. Forget his friendship business. Alissa wasn't prepared for the emotional hurricane in which he seemed determined to keep her.

The doorbell's soft chime punctuated her decision. The visitors who greeted her, however, momentarily erased all thoughts of Brad's contradictory behavior and replaced them with thoughts of intrigue.

Chapter 11

We just stopped by for a moment to welcome you to the neighborhood properly. We were afraid we didn't make the best impression yesterday and wanted to apologize." Mrs. Teasedale, again wearing her pink sponge rollers and bright orange lipstick, stepped into the foyer, with Mrs. Horton close behind. Both ladies stared curiously at Brad who stood beside one of the mauve, wing-backed chairs.

Alissa smiled in appreciation for the homemade bread Mrs. Horton soberly extended toward her. "Thank you. Would you like to sit down?"

"No, no, we can't," Sadie said, her rough voice much more congenial than it had been yesterday, her Lucille Ball red hair just as unkempt. "Henry's waiting in the car."

As she snapped the front door shut, Alissa sneaked a peek at the decade-old silver Cadillac purring in the driveway. The man behind the wheel was indistinguishable. Alissa was curious about the kind of person who'd marry someone like Sadie Horton, obviously not a man who pursued a woman of winning personality. Sadie, although attempting to act pleasant today, still appeared more brusque than neighborly.

"We heard about your accident yesterday," Sadie said. "How'd it happen?"

Mrs. Teasedale, apparently more inclined to display proper manners, elbowed Sadie in the ribs. "What she's tryin' to say, Dr. Carrington," she began in her heavy Texan dialect, "is that we wanted to thank you for coming to help when I fell off the ladder yesterday."

"How is your ankle, by the way?" Alissa asked.

"All better. The doctor said I just wrenched it, so it's only a tad bit sore." She flexed her ankle. "We came over, though, because we were terribly sorry to hear about your accident. We wanted to check in on you to make sure you weren't injured and wondered if there was anything we could do?" Although her words were right, her eyes depicted a lack of interest.

Elizabeth Teasedale seemed more concerned with examining the interior of Alissa's home than with offering assistance to an accident victim.

"Someone cut Alissa's brake line," Brad explained, walking up behind Alissa to take her right elbow.

"Really?" Sadie exclaimed sounding truly astonished. Or was that feigned astonishment? Something about that scrawny woman made Alissa's skin feel as if it were shriveling.

"That's terrible!" Mrs. Teasedale gasped, putting her fingertips to her mouth. Her nails were painted a bright orange and perfectly matched her lips. As with her condolences for the accident, her blue gaze wasn't on Alissa. Instead, she focused on Brad's hand as it gripped Alissa's elbow.

Alissa, trying to deny the tingles, purposefully pulled away from him. This was exactly the kind of contradictory behavior that was driving her crazy. One minute he almost ignored her, the next, he acted as if he had some claim on her.

"Do the police know who did it?" Sadie asked, her voice reminding Alissa of a bullfrog with laryngitis.

"No, not a clue," Brad mused. "They seem to think it's someone close by, though, because the person took a picture of the wreck, then left it for Alissa along with—"

Alissa placed the heel of her right sneaker on Brad's left foot. "They think the person may have been watching when the wreck happened, that's all." She didn't like the idea of these two strange women knowing all the details of her personal problems. Alissa swallowed, not wanting to take time to think about her next question. "Did either of you notice anyone with a camera in the neighborhood yesterday evening around six thirty or so?"

"Now look," Sadie said bluntly and rubbed the end of her warted witch's nose. "I'm going to tell you like I told the police last night. I don't know anything about anything. Not about the bones. Not about anything else that's going on. And I don't appreciate—"

"Sadie," Mrs. Teasedale hissed. "She was just asking. You don't have to get all bent out of shape."

"I'm just trying to keep you out of trouble. She must've seen you yesterday, or she wouldn't have asked."

"Seen her doing what?" Brad and Alissa asked in unison.

Mrs. Teasedale rolled her eyes to diminish Sadies's concern. "I was just—"

"It's none of your business," Sadie interrupted, grabbing her friend's arm. "Come on, Elizabeth. Henry's waiting." And with that, the two women left, or rather escaped, the premises, leaving behind the smell of Elizabeth's lavender soap and Sadie's cigarettes.

"Strange birds," Brad whispered while he and Alissa watched through a narrow crack in the door as the women climbed into the Cadillac.

"Yeah. Did you notice Mrs. Teasedale flexing her left foot when I asked how her ankle was?"

"Uh-huh. What about it?"

"Yesterday, she acted like her right ankle was injured. You don't think. . ." Alissa suppressed a shiver.

"If Mrs. Teasedale will lie about an ankle injury, she'll lie whenever she needs to. I think they know a lot more than they told us or the police."

"About the bones, you mean?"

"About everything."

"The police officer yesterday seemed to think that the person after me was perhaps a hostile ex-patient or something." Alissa closed the door as the Cadillac drove out of view and turned to Brad.

"Maybe, maybe not." Brad stepped away from her and crossed his arms. "The reason I was going to tell them about your message yesterday was because I wanted to get their reactions. I just don't trust them."

"Well, I don't either. But I didn't really want them to know all that's happening to me, either."

"Maybe they already know."

"I'd more easily believe they were involved in that bone business than in my troubles. After all, I just met them. Why would they suddenly want me—want me—" Her throat constricting, Alissa couldn't finish the words.

"Want you dead?" Brad finished, empathy softening his voice.

"Yes."

"I don't know. But I'd like to find out."

"What's that supposed to mean?"

"It means, my dear Watson, that sometimes in life we have to answer our own questions, do our own exploring." Brad thoughtfully picked up a roll of the teal and peach floral wallpaper that sat propped in the corner of Alissa's foyer. "And Sadie Horton was obviously, *very* obviously, trying to cover for Mrs. Teasedale just now. I'd like to know what she was up to when you had your wreck. I think I just might learn that a camera was involved."

"You mean that you're going to investigate them?" she asked incredulously.

"That's exactly what I mean. Wanna help?"

"Don't you think you should give the police a chance first? I mean they just started the investigation. You can't expect them to wrap it all up in one day, for Pete's sake." Alissa fumbled with the plastic wrap covering Mrs. Horton's homemade bread and gazed at Brad in worried apprehension. Everything with him was going faster than she had the nerves to stomach, and she didn't feel like "helping" him do anything. "Besides, what about all the people living across the road? How do you know they didn't do it?"

"No go. According to Richard Calbert, who, by the way, I met yesterday evening, those houses have all been built recently. So the residents are new. The forensics man said the bones have been in the ground awhile."

"But shouldn't you at least call the police before you start stirring up the neighborhood? Maybe the police are getting close." Alissa stiffened. What if the person harassing her was one of the neighbors? Would he or she become angry if Brad started nosing around, angry enough to actually kill her?

"Okay. If it will make you any happier," he said dryly, "I'll call to see if they've gotten anywhere."

She sighed and relaxed. "I think that's a good idea. Maybe the forensics lab has come up with something by now. Maybe even possible identities for the bones."

"Dream on," he said. "If you remember, they said it would be two months before they have a more exact idea of how long the bones had been there."

The phone's abrupt ringing startled Alissa into an involuntary jump. "Sorry. I'm just a bit on edge."

"Yes, and you've got every right to be. Want me to get it?"

"Would you? I'll go put up the bread; then we can go after the rental car."

"You aren't actually going to eat that, are you?" Brad asked, his hand on the white, cordless telephone located near the couch.

Alissa peered at the crusty, golden bread and remembered all the childhood fairy tales her mother had read to her about wicked witches poisoning gullible children with tainted cookies, gingerbread, or cakes.

Her mother had always ended those stories with a brief, loving lecture about taking things from strangers. Had Harriett Carrington feared then that Alissa's naturally trusting nature would lead her to trouble? Alissa's heart ached with loneliness only her mother could ever fill. How she wished her mother were alive to comfort her through this turmoil.

With a shiver, she then envisioned Sadie Horton's warted witch's nose and knew exactly what her mother would advise. "I think I'll trash it," she decided.

"Wise decision." Brad picked up the receiver.

Then I'll scrub my hands, she added to herself as Brad answered the phone. Minutes later, Alissa reentered the living room, the bread safely in the garbage can, her hands red from the scrub. Brad was still talking on the phone, or rather, being talked to. Then, with an indulgent smile, he slowly recited a telephone number and hung up.

Alissa groaned. "Don't tell me—"

"Your grandmother," he said with a smirk. "She was pleasantly surprised—no, thrilled—that I'm here. So much so that she said she didn't want to disturb you; then she asked for my phone number."

"And you gave it to her?" Alissa squeaked.

"Well. . ." He shrugged. "What was I supposed to do?"

"Okay, but don't come crying to me later. You've dug your own grave."

"Oh, come on, Alissa, she can't be that bad," he teased, still toying with the roll of wallpaper he'd picked up in the foyer.

"Don't get me wrong. I love her with my whole heart. But the woman should have been an international spy instead of a homemaker. Take my word for it, before she's through, you'll hear yourself telling her what brand of toothpaste you use, what size shoes you wore in the third grade, and your college grade point average."

Brad's spontaneous laughter was the infectious kind, the kind that reminded Alissa of music, the kind that brightened a room, or someone's life. "Oh well," he said in droll resignation, his eyes sparkling. "Maybe I'll find out the same things about you."

"She'll probably tell you that, too, whether you ask or not!" Alissa sank into the wing-backed chair and shook her head, wishing for a sudden North American collapse of all phone systems. She already wanted to die of embarrassment at the prospect of what her grandmother might tell Brad. And the woman hadn't even called him yet! Before it was all over, Emily Carrington would probably detail the whole story of her relationship with Sherman Devereaux, something Alissa feared would lower Brad's opinion of her. *But what does that matter?* she asked herself, refusing to admit just how much it really did matter.

"What room are you planning to wallpaper?" Brad asked, holding up the roll of paper, his eyes still alight with laughter.

"That goes in my bedroom. You wouldn't believe the olive green and orange stuff that's in there now."

"This will be a definite improvement, then. It's a nice pattern. You know, you really have a good eye for décor." He waved his hand toward the newly decorated living room.

"Thanks. Dad would appreciate your comment. I think he was always disappointed that I didn't inherit Mom's artistic ability."

"You inherited somebody's sense of style," he said appreciatively, his gaze straying to her hair then back to her eyes.

Alissa, her pulse increasing, wondered if he was only referring to the décor of her home. The faint flame in his eyes, the same flame she'd seen at the clinic when he almost kissed her, told her he was referring to her. As their gaze lengthened, Alissa felt as if she were drowning in a pool of utter confusion. One second she wanted to avoid him, the next, she wanted to be near him.

Despite her confusion, though, she knew avoiding him would be the most practical move. She didn't want to be hurt, either, and he was obviously still very devoted to his deceased wife.

Clearing her throat, she stood and purposefully broke their gaze. "I'll put the wallpaper back in the foyer for you," she said, not knowing what else she could say as he handed her the roll.

"Need some help when you start the job? I've always enjoyed wallpapering."

"Yuck! I hate it! I've been putting it off all week, actually." Alissa didn't want to accept his offer but didn't want to appear rude by rejecting it, either. So she decided to ignore it. "Are you going to call the police before we go?" she asked, hoping he didn't suspect her reason for the subject change.

"Yeah." Was that disappointment glimmering in his eyes? Or was it his own confusion? "Where's your phonebook?"

Minutes later, Alissa sat and listened intently to Brad's probing questions and vague comments of, "Yes. . .I see. . .no, I understand. . ." His casual shrug as he hung up seemed to support his earlier assumptions about the investigation. "They don't have anything much more than they did yesterday. There were some bullets lodged in the bones, so they're convinced it was murder. But they have no leads on identification. According to the investigator, they're studying the missing persons list but haven't gotten anywhere. And of course, they have no suspects."

"Did he say anything about questioning the neighbors?" she asked, crossing her arms while trying to avoid looking at him. *Avoid his gaze at all costs,* she told herself.

"I couldn't get anything out of him other than that they gathered no conclusive leads." He thoughtfully removed his glasses. "Basically, I don't think he told me anything that we couldn't get on the evening news."

"Maybe it's because they really don't know."

"Well, I intend to find out." Brad replaced his glasses. "And I'm going to start by questioning Claire Allen. She's lived next door to Mrs. Teasedale and Mrs. Horton long enough to probably give us all kinds of information. I want to know what Mrs. Teasesdale was doing yesterday afternoon that Sadie Horton was trying to cover up."

Alissa's curiosity piqued despite herself. "Frankly, I'd like to know, too, but I still don't feel right about nosing around like that."

Brad laughed indulgently. "You didn't mind sticking your little nose over my privacy fence yesterday morning."

"I know," she said to the antique floral print hanging near her front door. "But that was different. I was still in my yard. And—and nobody had threatened me yesterday morning, either." Goosebumps broke out along her neck and shoulders, and then crept down her spine.

"I know," Brad said, taking a step toward her, only to stop. "That's part of the reason I want to question Claire. I can't let someone—someone. . ."

Alissa looked at him despite herself and saw that his floundering words were only a reflection of the turbulence in his eyes. "Besides. . ." Alissa coughed dryly and examined her broken right thumbnail. "Claire Allen raises goldfish to feed her cat. And I think that's just about as strange as anything I've seen in Mrs. Horton and Mrs. Teasedale."

"Who told you that?" His voice sounded as strained as hers felt.

"Richard Calbert. This morning he stopped by and introduced himself. He said he'd thought for years that his only normal neighbors were Mr. Jenkins and Mrs. Docker."

"Now they've moved."

"Those were his exact words."

"Oh well, raising fish for your cat isn't a crime."

"It's just odd. . .it's. . .I don't know, it's. . .different."

"Well, as far as that goes, so is Richard Calbert. He's pleasant enough, I guess, but different."

"Yeah. But he's different in a good sort of way."

"Not according to Claire Allen."

Alissa thought about the watch she'd handed him that morning, and she hoped her instincts had been right, that Claire had been wrong.

"Let's go get your rental car," Brad said, walking toward the door. "Then maybe we can go visit Claire Allen." Alissa didn't miss how he automatically included her in his visit to Claire, even though she hadn't agreed to help him. Well, he'd soon learn that she was going to be too busy.

Chapter 12

S orry to just drop by, Brad," Mr. Whit Jenkins said, pushing up his small, wire-rimmed glasses with his index finger, "but I was wondering if I could come in for a moment?"

Brad opened his front door wider so the man, who looked to be in his late sixties, could enter. He'd only briefly met Mr. Jenkins when he purchased the house, but he'd instantly liked the short, gray-haired man and his straightforward manner; perhaps because he slightly resembled Mark Twain, one of Brad's favorite authors.

"Sure. Come on in." Brad smiled his welcome, wondering what Mr. Jenkins could possibly want. Brad had returned from taking Alissa to rent a car, had eaten lunch, and was preparing for his daily swim at the YMCA. But the swim could easily wait.

Mr. Jenkins waved his gnarled oak cane around the room as he entered. "Hey, I like what you've done with the house. Nice and airy. Jan would have liked it, too, God rest her soul."

"How long has your wife been dead?"

"Ten years. Ten long years. Cancer's what took her." He walked to the nearest white leather chair and sat down, his left leg stretched stiffly in front of him. The real estate agent had informed Brad of Mr. Jenkins' car wreck three years ago, and of the resulting prosthesis which extended to his left hip.

"I bet you still miss your wife."

"Oh yeah, I think about her every day. But I was fortunate to find another woman just as good to me as she was. Took me ten years to find her, but we got married last week. That's the reason I sold the house. She sold hers, too, and we bought another one together. One that's our house."

"Congratulations," Brad said, wondering if he'd ever find anyone as special as Dana. His mind instantly conjured up Alissa's image. Alissa, peering over his backyard fence; Alissa, surrounded by her geraniums and ferns; Alissa, her brown, liquid eyes infinite pools of compassion. Was it such a crime that he was so irresistibly attracted to her?

"Mind if I smoke?" Mr. Jenkins asked, pulling a worn teak pipe and a leather tobacco pouch from his hip pocket. Brad blinked as his mind came back to the present. "No, go ahead," he said, and went to pick up Samantha from her favorite sleeping spot in the bar chair. Tobacco smoke had never affected Brad much, but it always sent Samantha into a spasm of sneezing. Ignoring her protesting yowl, Brad opened the patio door and dropped her outside.

"The reason I dropped by," Mr. Jenkins said, creating a cloud of smoke as he puffed his vanilla tobacco, "is that I wanted to look at the place where those bones were found for myself. It's mighty strange to me that I lived in this house nearly thirty years, and part of the time human bones were in the backyard, and I didn't even know it!"

Did you really not know it? Brad wondered, and then dismissed the thought. He was growing suspicious of everyone. Surely Mr. Jenkins wouldn't be involved in murder. But then, you never knew. Brad had seen pictures of mass murderers who looked even more grandfatherly and nonthreatening than Mr. Jenkins.

"You're more than welcome to take a look," Brad said, standing. "I was going to put the pool right where your rose garden was, and that's where the bones were."

"I babied those roses for years, and then you came along and just dug 'em up, eh?" he teased, his hazel eyes alight with mischief as he stood.

"Not quite," Brad said, opening the patio door. "I actually transplanted them all along the inside of the privacy fence. See?" He waved toward the backyard toward the row of multicolored roses.

"Nice," Mr. Jenkins said, admiring Brad's work. "Those roses always drove Sadie and Elizabeth crazy, just crazy." He chuckled dryly, mirthlessly. "I'd hate for them to be done away with."

"Oh?" Brad said, rubbing the nape of his neck. He'd told Alissa he wanted to question Claire Allen, but maybe his questioning would start with Mr. Jenkins.

"Oh, yeah. We had a rose rivalry that went far past friendly competition." He walked toward the hole, and Brad followed. "It wasn't my fault, really. I was content to let bygones be bygones and go on with life, but not those two."

"They are rather. . .*different*, I guess is the word."

"*Vindictive* is the word." Mr. Jenkins puffed his pipe then removed it from between his teeth as he stopped at the grave site. "Believe me, I know," he said, studying the hole. "I lived beside them many years. We're even members of the same garden club. And the year my Snowfire beat out their Tropicana for the best rose award is the year I thought they were going to put me in the ground. Did you know they actually told the police they figured I murdered those poor people, whoever they were, and buried them out here?" He pointed to the roped-off hole. "Humph. If you ask me, they did it to try to poison my roses!"

"Do you really think they might have done it?" Brad asked.

"Ah, I don't know," he placed his pipe back between his yellowed teeth and took another puff. "They're kinda mean, those two, but I don't know if they'd actually kill someone. Besides, the police don't even have the identities of the dead people. Well, yesterday they didn't, anyway. Have you heard anything new?"

"No. As of this morning, they still had no identification, and I guess until they arrive at some, the investigation stays there."

"I guess. I've heard of these kinds of things stretching on for years. At least that's the way it is on TV."

Did he sound relieved, or was it just Brad's overactive imagination? "What do you think of the other two neighbors—Claire Allen and Richard Calbert?"

"Nicer than Elizabeth and Sadie, that's for sure. They both kinda stay to themselves, though. Always working. To tell you the truth, the only one of the whole bunch that I ever really liked was Mrs. Docker. She was like an older sister to me, especially after Jan died."

"Do you know if the police have questioned her?"

"Don't know. Haven't heard from her since she sold her house to that dentist a couple of months back. A real looker, that dentist. Never met her, but saw her coming and going some. Have you met her?" Turning from the grave site, he peered at Brad and adjusted his glasses.

"Yes, I met her yesterday." Had it only been yesterday? Why, then, did Brad feel as if he'd known her much of his life?

"You're not married, are you?"

"No. I—I'm a widower. Like you, I guess." For the first time, Brad was able to say the words without feeling as if his heart were being ripped from his chest.

"Well, it's a sad situation when you lose your mate, son. A sad situation. I spent many a night wondering why the good Lord would let Jan waste away with cancer.

"Yes, it's really bad. People just don't know." An unspoken bond spun its way between Brad and the older man, a bond forged of loneness and pain and confusion. For the first time, Brad felt as if someone really understood his situation, someone truly kindhearted. No, Mr. Jenkins could never have murdered two people and buried them in his backyard. If he had, then Brad's instincts were nonexistent.

"But you're mighty young still," Mr. Jenkins continued. "And that dentist is mighty good lookin'." A Santa Claus twinkle in his eyes, he winked and turned back toward the house.

The old man must be a mind reader, Brad thought as he smiled to himself. *Either that or your thoughts are completely transparent.*

Mr. Jenkins's visit stretched only minutes more. He'd obviously come simply to satisfy his curiosity, and with that done, he limped toward his nondescript blue sedan in the driveway. "Oh, by the way," he said, turning to face Brad. "I meant to ask you about your mailbox. What happened?"

"Someone accidentally hit it yesterday. No injuries." Brad instinctively glanced up and down the street, wondering if the person who cut Alissa's brake line were watching. He'd given Alissa strict instructions to call if anything else strange happened.

"That dentist better be careful," Mr. Jenkins muttered under his breath.

"What?" Brad asked, his brows rising in astonishment. How did Mr. Jenkins know Alissa was the one who hit his mailbox?

"Oh, um, don't forget what I said about that dentist." And with that, he hurriedly got in his car and drove away. Brad stood and watched as the blue sedan drove out of view. Had Mr. Jenkins actually suggested that he knew Alissa was the accident victim or was Brad's hearing starting to go? If Mr. Jenkins did know about the accident, then why did he ask in the first place? Could he be the one who cut the brake line?

Shaking his head, Brad shut the door. Why would Mr. Jenkins be after Alissa? They'd never even met. Apparently Brad had simply misunderstood him.

Dismissing the older man from his mind, Brad walked toward the trash can that sat near his breakfast bar. Only that morning he'd torn the sketch of Alissa into four pieces and thrown it away. But now, several hours later, Brad wanted to see it again. Fingers trembling, he removed the sketch from the wastebasket, smoothed it, and slowly lined up the ragged edges. Even though part of him wanted nothing more than to gaze at her image, another part of him still felt like a traitor, a cad.

After all, God had betrayed Dana and Kara, and Brad didn't want to likewise abandon them. But maybe there was some truth to what Alissa had said earlier. In reality, God hadn't killed them. That lunatic who pulled the trigger had killed them. Could God actually want to comfort Brad now?

"Oh, Alissa, I am so confused," he muttered. "One minute I want to pray, the next minute I don't think I can. One minute I want you in my arms, and the next I don't think I can even touch you." From the moment he'd met her, she'd affected him like a cannonball in the gut. He'd mistakenly thought his first reaction would fade, but it seemed only to strengthen, especially with someone like that Tom McDaniel practically pawing her. By her reaction, Brad didn't think Alissa cared much for Tom; or rather, he hoped she didn't care much. However, he couldn't deny that the idea of a rival had made his stomach twist in jealousy.

With a bewildered shake of his head, Brad gathered the tattered sketch and dropped it back into the trash can, a trash can he didn't plan to empty.

❧

A smug smirk covering her face, she stroked the earth-covered gold watch with her index finger and sat on the end of her bed.

Yes, Richard Calbert had been just as much help as she'd hoped he'd be. The watch had been so easy to retrieve from that dumb Louanne Young.

Now that all incriminating evidence had been removed, she could better concentrate on killing Louanne again without worrying about the police catching up with her. She picked up the gray wig lying on her dresser and began toying with its loose curls. Only that afternoon she'd removed it from the back of her storage closet, right where it had lain for ten long years.

"Don't worry, Louanne," she crooned, picking up the silver-handled hairbrush from her dresser. "I won't do anything rash." She stroked the wig aimlessly as she stared into the mirror, into her own glazed eyes. "You ruined my life slowly, and I've decided I'll slowly ruin yours."

Chapter 13

"M r. Calbert, this is Alissa Carrington, your neighbor." It was 9:30 a.m. Eight days had gone by since the attempt on Alissa's life. Alissa sat on the edge of her bed now, the telephone receiver in one hand, a roll of wallpaper in the other. She was finally going to tackle the dreaded deed, but she wanted to check with Richard about the watch she'd found first. "I'm sorry to bother you at work, but I was calling about the watch I found that you were going to take to your brother's jewelry shop. Has he finished with it?"

"Oh. . .the watch!" She heard him snap his fingers. "I completely forgot about it. I'm so glad you called. Just a minute, Alissa. . .Yes, those flowers are the ones going to Fifth Street."

Alissa listened as Richard dealt with the pressing demands of several deliveries. "Sorry 'bout that," he finally said. "It's a hectic day."

"That's okay. I understand. Listen, would it help you if I just retrieved the watch from you this evening and took it to your brother myself? I could always tell him you sent me." Although the watch wasn't an urgent matter, Alissa didn't want the situation to drag out until she had to go back to work. Then she might forget about it.

"No," he said quickly. "That's—that's okay. Like I said earlier—okay, thank you; come back, now!—sorry Alissa, one of my best customers is just leaving. Anyway, like I said earlier, my brother owes me. I'll take care of it."

"Okay," Alissa said, and with the appropriate good-byes spoken, she hung up while making a mental note to call him Monday. Alissa then stared at the atrocious olive green and orange wallpaper. The day had finally come. She'd spent the last week working in the yard, cleaning closets, shopping in Dallas with her grandmother, and avoiding Brad Ratner in general.

He'd left several phone messages for her that, after much thought, she hadn't returned. And yesterday, he'd even rung her doorbell, but Alissa hadn't answered. Her rental car was locked in the garage, so he couldn't have known that she was home. Basically, Alissa was sticking by her decision to avoid him. Not that it was doing her any good. All she could think about was sun-streaked hair, smoky eyes, and broad shoulders. He filled her dreams even, dreams in which she was always in his arms.

She had to admit that she felt downright mean for giving him the cold shoulder. But wouldn't the cold shoulder now be better than breaking his heart later? She'd already gone through that with Sherman.

But Brad isn't Sherman, a little voice whispered. *Sherman wasn't a Christian. And you never felt this way about him.* True, Sherman had never caused her heart to race, nor had he created the tingles she felt only at Brad's soft touch. And if Brad ever did kiss her. . .Alissa swallowed hard, knowing she would probably melt.

When Trena had called last night to say they'd made it home safely from Corpus Christi, she'd "innocently" asked about Alissa's gorgeous new neighbor. Alissa had been as noncommittal as possible, and Trena hadn't pushed the issue.

She'd explained about her wreck as she had to her grandmother, without mentioning the failed brakes. Alissa hoped the person had gotten the thrill he or she wanted at her expense and would leave her alone now. The peace of the last week seemed to support that hope.

Before Trena had hung up, Alissa drafted her into helping with the wallpaper.

The doorbell's ring now announced that Trena was unusually

punctual. Surprised, Alissa checked her sporty silver watch. "She's early, even," she muttered. For Trena, 10:00 a.m. meant sometime between ten thirty and twelve, not nine thirty.

Alissa trotted down the stairs and threw open the door, a mocking smile on her face. "So, Dr. Selver, I see for once in your life, you're on—" Her mouth fell open as she stared not at Trena, but at Brad Ratner. Brad, his hair slightly damp, his lips curled into a half smile, his left hand casually inserted in his jeans pocket.

"Expecting Trena?" he asked.

She gulped. "Yes. She's supposed to help me with my wallpaper."

"You haven't returned my calls," he said softly. "I've been worried about you. Is everything okay?" That wasn't the question his eyes asked. His eyes wanted to know why she hadn't returned his calls.

"Uh, yeah." Alissa could think of no convincing excuse for not calling him back. "I've just been. . .um. . .busy," she finally said. "Grandma and I spent the weekend in Dallas shopping, and. . ." And what else?

"Mind if I come in?" he asked.

"No. Of course not." Alissa opened the door wide, allowing him to pass her as she closed it behind him. What could he possibly want? She thought about the first time he'd come over and they'd shared a pizza. He'd been dressed much as he was now, a crisp white shirt, a pair of worn jeans, and sneakers. He'd also looked as good as he did now. Or did he look even better today? The past week of avoiding him had left her ravenous for his company. She hadn't realized that until now. *You never felt this way about Sherman*, the same little voice of only moments ago taunted.

Alissa immediately pictured her and Brad sitting on her favorite church pew with two tiny tots between them. Somehow she knew in her gut that Brad would be an excellent husband and father, and that despite his present spiritual turmoil, he would never neglect the spiritual well-being of his children.

"Would you like a soda?" she croaked, her throat dry.

"No, thanks. I really hadn't planned to stay that long," he said, following her into the living room. "I just wanted to make sure you hadn't received any more threats." The way his gaze roamed her face, her hair, and her lips said he'd simply wanted to see her.

Alissa's lips trembled as if he'd touched them, and she clutched the back of the nearby wing-backed chair as the trembling moved to her legs. "No, thank goodness. It's been a quiet week. I was just hoping that the person, whoever it is, has decided to leave me alone. Has there been any more news on the bones?" Alissa knew the answer to that question, but didn't know what else to say. The local television station was repeatedly running spots, asking for any leads to the identity of the victims.

"No. I haven't even been able to question Claire Allen. I've been over there three times, and each time she was gone. I thought I'd try again this afternoon."

"Oh." Licking her lips, Alissa nervously ran her index finger over the mauve chair's upholstery seam and searched for something, anything, to say. But her mind was as blank as the cloudless sky. The thick tension between them didn't help her, either.

Brad rubbed the nape of his neck then nervously crammed both hands into his jeans pockets. "Alissa, we need to talk. I—"

The phone's ring stopped him in midsentence. "I bet that's Grandma," she said, her relief obvious in her voice. "She hasn't made her morning call yet." For once, Alissa hoped the older lady would talk an hour. By then, Brad would politely leave. But did Alissa really want him to leave? Seeing him felt so good, yet it was also sheer agony. Alissa could never hold him, could never feel his lips on hers. He'd made that very, very clear.

She picked up the receiver, her heart pounding out hard, even beats. "Hello."

"Alissa? Tom here. I was just calling to tell you we're finished with your car."

"Already? It's only been a week!"

"Well, I'll admit I made it top priority. Don't want my girl to be without her wheels."

She cleared her throat and decided to ignore his blatant comment. "When can I pick it up?" Tom's advances were becoming more and more possessive, and Alissa dreaded having to bluntly tell him she wasn't interested.

"Anytime today. Or, if you're free tonight, I could drive it over and we could go grab a pizza and a movie."

Her first instinct was to immediately refuse. Then she thought of Brad, who couldn't help but listen. If he thought she were dating Tom, maybe he'd leave her alone. Alissa wouldn't be in the state of perpetual torment in which his presence placed her. With a quick glance his way, she turned to stare out one of the many windows lining her house's west wall and opened her mouth to accept Tom's invitation.

"No, I'm sorry, Tom," she heard herself say. "I think it would be better for me to just drop by sometime today." She simply couldn't go out with him. Not only would it be dishonest, it would also be using Tom.

"Alissa, are you ever going to go out with me?" he demanded.

She hesitated, not knowing exactly what to say, and fully aware that Brad heard her every word.

"This is me—*Tom*," he continued. "We went to the prom together, remember? Haven't you gotten over that doctor yet?"

"This has nothing to do with him," Alissa said evenly, not liking being pressured by anyone, not even a longtime friend.

"Well, why do I keep getting 'no thank you's,' then?"

"Tom, I um. . ." Alissa glanced at Brad again who now sat on the Victorian settee and scratched Frito's ear while mumbling to the dog. Maybe he wasn't listening after all. "I don't want to hurt your feelings," she said in a low voice, "but it wouldn't be fair for me to date you. You're my friend. And I can't think of you in any other way. If we were to start dating, I'm afraid you'd wind up getting hurt. Please don't be angry with me. I just can't."

"It's that Brad Ratner guy I met the other day, isn't it? I saw the way you looked at each other."

"You know I was turning you down before I met him." Alissa resisted the urge to whisper.

"Well," he continued, his voice thick, "if it's any concern of yours, you haven't kept yourself from hurting me. I really thought we could—"

"No, we can't. Tom, listen to me. There are probably women just waiting in line for you to ask them out. Am I right?" His silence answered the question well.

"I know one of them personally. She's in my Sunday school class. Carla Jamison. Do you have her number?

Silence again.

"That's what I figured." Alissa, as always, felt like Tom's elder sister, even though they were the same age. "Now call her."

The phone's click was his answer. Smiling faintly, Alissa hung up. Tom might be irritated now, but she had no doubt he'd get over it. This wasn't the first time he'd been angry with her. That was part of the reason she couldn't take his advances seriously. Their relationship really was, and always had been, more like that of a brother and sister.

"Exactly how many men a day do you dodge?" Brad asked, a sarcastic turn to his lips.

Oh great, he was listening. "I don't keep count," she said flippantly, his remark agitating her. "Would you rather I go out with the man even though I'm not attracted to him?" Alissa dropped onto the antique couch's corner, her agitation growing to anger. Who was he to point fingers? Hadn't he been toying with her ever since they met?

"Well, exactly what type of man are you attracted to?" he asked, matching her tone. "Since you've done such an excellent job of dodging me, too, I'm curious to find out."

Obviously, Brad was more disturbed by her not returning his calls than he'd let on. But that didn't keep the tension that had been building between them since their first meeting from exploding within Alissa like a fiery volcano of confusion, frustration, and disappointment. Brad Ratner, the only man to whom she'd ever been so strongly attracted, had the nerve to sit and ask her such a question. He was the reason she couldn't sleep at night. He was the reason she couldn't eat. He was even part of the reason she'd backed out on Sherman at the last minute. Even then, before she'd ever laid eyes on Brad, she'd been waiting on him, knowing that the right Christian man was out there—and he wasn't Sherman.

"If you want to know so badly what type of a man I'm attracted to, I'll tell you." She stood on legs shaking like a toddler's, and in her present state she no longer cared about hiding the truth. "The kind of men I seem to be attracted to are men who like to play games. Men who say they want to be friends then act like they want more. You know, Brad, the sensitive, artistic type." She went on, her voice rising every second. "The type who. . .who. . ."

Brad rose from the settee and purposefully walked toward her.

"The type who. . ." Alissa backed away only to have him increase his speed. "Who. . ." He reminded her of a tiger, a calculating, determined, gray-eyed tiger seeking his prey. She took three more steps backward, only to run into the living room wall. "What do you think you're doing?" Alissa croaked as he placed his arms around her waist.

"I'm going to do what I've wanted to do since the first time I saw you." His eyes narrowed to passion-filled slits as his breath fanned her cheek. "I'm going to kiss you, and do it properly."

Alissa gulped for the air that seemed to have left the room as her gaze was drawn to his mouth descending toward hers.

Tiny pinpoints of pleasure exploded through Alissa's chest, through her trembling fingers as they inched their way across Brad's shoulders to mingle in his hair. This. . .this was more than a kiss. It was a homecoming. It was what Alissa had been waiting on for years. It was right. Exactly right. And she knew now from experience what instinct had already told her. Brad Ratner was where she belonged, the one to whom she belonged.

He lifted his mouth to trail a myriad of tiny, fire-laden kisses across her left cheek and down her neck.

"Ah, Dana," he breathed.

Chapter 14

Alissa's spine stiffened as if she'd been struck by lightning. Brad's hands stilled in her hair. Slowly he pulled away to stare into her soul, his eyes churning, regretful.

"Alissa, I. . ."

She bit her shaking lips and blinked back the tears, not knowing which of the emotions whirling through her to express. The fury? The pain? The confusion?

Taking a deep breath, she purposed not to say something that she'd later regret. "I think you'd better leave," she finally choked out. Stepping sideways, she moved away from him. For the first time, Alissa fully realized why he'd insisted on mere friendship. A relationship with Brad would be hopeless. Not only was he still grieving his wife's death, he was still in love with her—a love Alissa now knew allowed no room for another woman.

"Alissa?"

"Just leave, Brad." Turning her back to him, she pressed her index finger between her brows. "And—and I think"—she took a quivering breath—"I think it would be best if we stayed away from each other. . .permanently."

Silence, the kind of silence that screams of high emotion, cloaked them like an icy winter's night. Brad said nothing, yet Alissa felt his gaze on her back, a gaze she couldn't bear to return. Without a word, he turned and walked out the door, softly closing it behind him.

Dashing away tears hot with sorrow, Alissa raced up the stairs to the bathroom and grabbed a box of tissues. A sob, low and mournful, wracked her body as she collapsed onto the bathtub's rim to rock back and forth like a soul lost for eternity.

She'd learned a lot in the last thirty minutes. She'd come to realize that part of the reason she'd broken up with Sherman was because she'd been waiting for Brad. At the time, she hadn't even known his name. But all the same, she'd been waiting for him. Marrying Sherman would have been more devastating than breaking their engagement. Soon after, she could have met Brad and known she'd made a terrible mistake. That would have been an unforgivable situation, much more unforgivable than what she'd opted for. She was suddenly grateful she'd prevented what would have been a disastrous marriage.

Alissa also now knew that she could love, could love with her whole being. She was certain of this because she'd made the worst mistake of all. She'd fallen in love with a man who could never return her love. The whole sad situation, so full of irony, produced a new spasm of sobs from the core of her being. Yes, Alissa knew love, knew it in its rawest, most painful form.

"Hello! Anybody home?" Trena's cheerful call rang up the stairwell. She never bothered to knock unless the door was locked.

Alissa rolled her eyes. *Great,* she thought as she grabbed a washcloth and began sponging her face in cold water.

"Alissa?" Trena called again.

"Up here!" Alissa patted her face dry with a fluffy scarlet towel, and a glance in the mirror told her the towel matched the redness of her stinging eyes. Clenching her teeth, she suppressed a new sob. Trena's arrival hadn't stopped the pain. She stepped into the hallway just as her friend, dressed in worn denim work clothes, topped the stairs.

"Ready to get to work?" Trena asked, her new tan bearing witness of her week on the beach.

"Uh, yeah. Almost." Alissa turned toward her bedroom and hoped

Trena hadn't noticed the tear seeping form the corner of her eye.

"Hey, what's wrong?" Trena placed a gentle hand on her friend's shoulder.

Alissa, wiping away the tear, squeezed her eyes shut. She wanted to tell Trena. She and Trena had always shared everything. But at the same time, the pain was so heavy, so intense, that Alissa didn't think she could bear to vocalize it. "PMS, I guess," she mumbled, walking into her bedroom.

"PMS? You've never had PMS in your life! Come on, what gives?" Trena plopped onto the end of Alissa's bed and crossed her legs, a matter-of-fact gleam in her eyes. "You ought to know by now you can't fool me. It's that man next door, isn't it?"

Picking up a bucket half full of water, Alissa didn't reply as she began sponging the old wallpaper. How did Trena always seem to know her thoughts?

"I figured something was going on last night when we talked on the phone. The minute I mentioned him, you clammed up." She tucked a strand of brunette hair behind her right ear.

Alissa dropped the sponge back into the water with resignation. "Okay. You're right. He's wonderful, he's a Christian, he's Mr. Right, and—and he's still in love with his dead wife," she blurted, her voice quivering.

"And you're in love with him?"

A quick nod. "Oh, Trena, I don't even know how it happened," she wailed. "I didn't mean for it to happen."

"Here, sit down. Let me have that bucket." Trena set the water bucket on the floor and drew Alissa toward where she sat on the bed and placed a supporting arm around her.

Within minutes, Alissa had told her friend the whole story, while Trena remained helplessly silent. "I never envisioned falling in love like this. I always thought it would happen slowly and painlessly."

"Not always," Trena stated flatly. "Look at Ruth and Boaz. Look at

Cameron and me. I knew I was going to marry him on the second date. Sometimes it just happens that way; you just know. Besides, you know I've always said that when you really fell, you'd fall hard and fast."

The doorbell's ringing cut off any reply Alissa could form. "I'll get it," Trena said, standing. "You need to lie down for a while."

"If that's Brad again, tell him—tell him I'm in Egypt." Alissa flopped back onto the bed, wondering how her peaceful life of only weeks ago had turned into one upheaval after another.

But the upheavals weren't over. For only moments later, Trena was back at the bedroom door, her face pale despite the golden tan. "Alissa, I think you better come downstairs. There's something. . ." She swallowed hard and suppressed a shiver. "There's something you need to see."

❧

Brad walked into his workroom, filled with the smell of fresh paint, to stare at the new portrait of Alissa that had evolved from the torn sketch. Of all the stupid things he'd ever done, Brad knew that calling Alissa "Dana" had been the most stupid. He wasn't even sure why it happened. He hadn't been thinking of her. His mind had been consumed with Alissa—her responsive lips, the smell of her jasmine perfume, and the feel of her silky hair. Even now, he couldn't get her out of his mind. Maybe he'd whispered Dana's name out of habit.

Brad studied the portrait. Alissa, on her knees near the flowerbed, her face tilted up with a ready smile, as if she were greeting someone she loved. If only that someone were Brad. He'd started and completed the painting two days ago, in what his mother called one of his "artistic frenzies." Those frenzies didn't happen often, but when they did, they usually resulted in Brad's best work. He had to admit, this qualified. Anyone who saw this painting in muted hues of blue, gray, and green would be struck by the intensity of the artist's emotion,

296

would immediately know the subject was loved.

Despite himself, despite Dana's memory, Brad's attraction for Alissa had escalated into the beginning of a love he couldn't deny. At the same time, though, the slight guilt remained. He'd never ceased feeling married, never stopped feeling like little Kara's daddy. Even though his head told him he was free to love again, his heart hadn't forgotten his pledge of fidelity to his family.

Perhaps that was the reason he had called Alissa "Dana." His heart simply couldn't let go. So where did that leave him? A bachelor for life?

Dear God, I've never been so confused. Please help me sort out this mess. A stunned blink. Brad suddenly realized he prayed, really prayed for the first time in two years. And the peace that followed flooded his soul as if God had actually heard him. Could Alissa have been right? Could God really want to comfort him?

But how could a God who allowed innocent people to die want to comfort those left behind? Wouldn't it be easier just to prevent the deaths? That assumed, of course, as Brad had heard all his life, that God really was sovereign.

With a resigned sigh, Brad turned from Alissa's portrait to leave the room. But a quick glimpse out the window lining the north wall stopped him where he stood. Claire Allen's blue-green Pontiac cruised past, then slowed to turn toward her house.

Brad, as he'd told Alissa, had tried to catch Claire at home several times the last week. Maybe today was the day. He wanted to ask her if she'd noticed what Mrs. Teasedale was doing the evening Alissa ran into his mailbox. Sadie had obviously tried to hide her friend's actions. Brad also wanted Claire's opinion of Mr. Jenkins. His feelings toward the old man had vacillated widely during the last week. One day he was sure the kindhearted Mark Twain clone couldn't have committed murder. Then the next, Brad pondered if he'd somehow misunderstood Mr. Jenkins' comment about Alissa hitting the mailbox, or if Mr. Jenkins did indeed have prior knowledge of the accident—and perhaps much more.

Maybe Claire Allen could help him. With one last, longing look at Alissa's portrait, Brad walked from the room.

❧

Alissa sat up straight as a foreboding sense of doom slithered through her. The last time she'd seen Trena this pale, this stricken, was at her grandfather's funeral. "What's the matter?" she blurted.

"Someone sent you a funeral wreath, Alissa. When I first saw it, I thought it was a mistake. Then I looked at the card." She swallowed. "There's a threatening message. . ."

Her heart pounding, Alissa raced down the stairs with Trena close on her heels. She'd thought only that morning that perhaps the person harassing her had given up his or her "mission." Now she wasn't so sure.

She halted on the last stair and gazed in breathless horror at the incredibly vast spray of red roses and baby's breath. Whoever sent the thing had spared no expense. It reminded Alissa of the rows and rows of roses, which had donned her mother's grave.

"Read the message," Trena hissed from close behind as if they stood in a mortuary. Licking her lips, Alissa forced her feet to descend the last stair and walk toward the symbol of death. Arms stiff, fingers trembling, she removed the small card from its envelope. "*Alissa Carrington*" was scrawled in block letters at the top of the card. At the bottom was a note that sent her stomach into knots: "*Too bad you won't see the flowers at your nearing funeral.*"

She tried to blink away the words, but they wouldn't disappear. The thinly veiled threat, she knew, was more than just a threat. Her failed brakes attested to that. Someone wanted her dead. Someone who planned to fulfill that desire.

Should she do as Brad and Tom and the policeman had suggested?

Should she leave town? Even though the idea suddenly sounded appealing, Alissa knew she wouldn't run. Putting her left hand to her throat, she collapsed into a nearby chair.

"This is sick," Trena whispered, staring at the wreath as if it were straight from Rappaccini's garden of poison.

"It isn't the first time," Alissa rasped. She hadn't wanted Trena to know, hadn't wanted her to worry. But now Alissa needed to talk.

"What?" Trena shrieked, the surprise obviously jolting her from her mortuary whisper.

"My wreck. . .when I ran into Brad's mailbox. Someone had cut my brake line."

Trena's dark brown eyes widened in horror.

"Then last week, someone left a threatening message at the clinic."

This time, Trena's mouth fell open. "What did it say?" she choked out.

Alissa briefed her on the details.

"Why didn't you tell me?"

"I haven't told anyone. "Oh"—she waved her hand—"Brad knows. But I didn't want to worry you."

"And your father and grandmother?"

"I didn't tell them for the same reason. Grandma would be beside herself."

"You need to call the police about the flowers."

"Why? What can they do? Advise me to leave town again?" Alissa's voice rose, and Frito, ears pricked, trotted into the living room as if he were curious about the excitement.

"It might be a good idea to go stay with your father awhile. I can take care of your patients."

"Forget it! I'm not running. How do I know this person won't resume his or her mission when I return? Or even follow me out of town?"

"You don't."

"And you know good and well you wouldn't run either."

Trena toyed with the bottom button on her denim shirt and didn't bother to comment on Alissa's declaration. "I leave town for one week, and your life falls apart," she mused.

Alissa snorted. "Don't flatter yourself into thinking you're the glue that holds my life together." Sometimes Trena's mother-hen attitude got on Alissa's nerves.

"I was just joking." Trena rolled her eyes. "Touchy, touchy, touchy."

"Well, wouldn't you be if—if—" She waved toward the offensive wreath.

"Okay"—Trena plopped onto the couch—"you have a right to be touchy. What florist is the wreath from?" she asked, changing the subject as she was apt to do.

Alissa had been so appalled at the message that she hadn't even noticed the name of the florist.

"Maybe we could call and see if they have a record of who sent it."

"Good thinking." Alissa glanced at the card she held, but the florist's name wasn't on it. She then went to the wreath, now filling the room with a heady rose fragrance, and looked at the envelope. "I can't believe this," she gasped.

Chapter 15

I was wondering if I could have a few minutes of your time, Mrs. Allen," Brad said, standing on the front porch of Claire's blue frame house. "I had a couple of questions I thought you might be able to answer."

Claire pushed her heavy auburn curls from her forehead and smiled. "Sure. Come on in. I've been out shopping this morning and have to be at the hospital in an hour, but I'll be glad to help you if I can."

Brad entered the homey living room cluttered with a neat array of knickknacks and filled with the smell of freshly brewed coffee. A twenty-gallon aquarium full of goldfish gurgled in the corner, and Brad remembered Alissa mentioning that Claire raised the fish for her cat. The lucky feline, a fat tabby, snoozed in a worn wicker rocking chair near the aquarium, his lips curled into what looked like a smug smile. By his plump appearance, Brad figured he didn't stray too far from his food source.

In seconds, Mrs. Allen had seated Brad in an outdated, brown plaid chair and handed him a mug of coffee she'd insisted he have. "Now, what was it you were wanting to ask?" she said, sitting on the edge of the couch, which matched his chair.

He politely sipped the rich liquid even though he didn't care for coffee. "I just wondered if you noticed anything, or saw anyone doing anything strange, the evening Alissa Carrington ran into my mailbox?" Brad hated to implicate Mrs. Teasedale and Mrs. Horton without first giving Claire a chance to mention them.

She thoughtfully stared at the bubbling aquarium, and Brad wondered how many hours a week she worked at the hospital. The dark circles under her eyes said she worked too long and slept too little.

"I don't recall seeing anything strange," she said, toying with the cuff of her white nurse's blouse.

Brad, clearing his throat, wondered what to ask next. He also wondered how long it would take him to starve as a private investigator. Probably about a week. "Um, did you see anyone maybe taking pictures with an automatic camera?"

"Well, now that you've mentioned it, I did. Mrs. Teasedale was in her front yard that day with a camera. I remember because I saw her when I came back home from talking with you and Dr. Carrington. I was in a hurry, though, and didn't notice what kind of a camera. Why?" Claire's thinly lined forehead creased.

"Oh, someone snapped a picture of Alissa's accident and sent it to her, and we were just trying to find out who it was." Even though his mind was whirling with what she had said, Brad tried to maintain a calm façade and casually stroked his new beard. There was no sense in getting Claire involved in problems that obviously were Elizabeth Teasedale and Sadie Horton's.

"You know, it's really none of my business, but Elizabeth and Sadie. . ." She hesitated and glanced at her hands, now clasped in her lap. "No, I'm not going to say that."

"What?" Brad set the mug of coffee on a nearby table and waited for her next comment.

"No, I really shouldn't. I felt awful the other day after I'd said what I did about Richard Calbert. He's really a nice man, and who am I to judge him?" she shrugged.

Sighing, Brad decided to go ahead and question her about Mr. Jenkins. He probably wouldn't get anywhere, though. Claire didn't seem to be the kind who enjoyed pointing out other's faults.

"Okay. I have one other question, and then I'll let you finish getting ready for work. Did you know Mr. Whit Jenkins very well?"

"Oh, yes, a delightful man. I always thought he looked like Mark Twain." She smiled.

"Yeah, me, too. He stopped by the other day. He wanted to see where the bones were dug up. It was the first time I'd had a chance to really visit with him."

"Well, if you visit with him long, you'll notice he's a bit . . .what's the word. . .clairvoyant, I guess is the best description of him."

"Really?" Brad's interest once again peaked.

"Yes, it's strange, really. Sometimes he knows things. I've often had the odd sensation that he could read people's minds. He says it's not that, that he's just a close observer of people and their expressions."

Brad wondered if this could explain how he knew Alissa was the person who demolished his mailbox. It would also explain why he hinted that Brad should become involved with Alissa. Perhaps Brad's facial expressions were that transparent concerning the woman.

Then a new thought struck him. "If he's so clairvoyant, why didn't he know about the bones in his own backyard?"

Clair twisted the worn silver band on her right hand. "Good question. Like I said, I'm not really sure clairvoyant is the right word. He's just—oh, I don't know, he just knows things sometimes. For instance, several years ago he had the feeling that Elizabeth and Sadie were trying to sabotage his roses. They were in a stiff competition at the local garden club. Anyway, he was right, because he woke up in the middle of the night to find those two—would you believe it?—pouring water on his bushes' leaves."

Brad's blank look must have spoken his ignorance.

"You don't water rose leaves, especially not in this humid climate. It gives them powdery mildew and black leaf, which can kill them."

"Oh." He thought of the many times he'd already doused the poor roses well, thinking their leaves needed a drink just like their roots did.

"Anyway, Whit chased them out of his backyard with his shotgun at 2:00 a.m."

"A shotgun?"

"Uh-huh. You've got to understand, that's the only thing those two would understand. They're what you might call obsessive. Once they set their mind to something, no matter what it is, they're bound and determined to do it."

Brad wondered if they'd set their minds to killing those people in his backyard, or to harassing Alissa. The fact that Elizabeth had been taking pictures the very afternoon of Alissa's accident was highly suspicious, and Sadie definitely wanted to hide the fact.

But why would they bother Alissa? They barely knew her.

Claire glanced at her silver watch, and Brad took the hint. "Well, thanks for your time, Mrs. Allen, I really—"

"Please, call me Claire," she said, standing. "I'm sorry I couldn't chat with you any longer, but like I said, I've got to get to work."

"I understand." With one last look at the unsuspecting goldfish and the smiling, fat tabby, Brad stood to leave. Looked like everybody in this neighborhood had his or her odd quirks.

The envelope trembled like an extension of Alissa's fingers as she stared at the florist's name.

"Who is it?" Trena asked, turning to prop her arm on the back of the Chippendale sofa.

"Calbert's Florist and Gifts," Alissa read.

"So?" Trena, brows raised, encouraged Alissa to explain her alarm.

"Richard Calbert lives just two doors down. I met him last week. He owns this flower shop."

"Are you suggesting he sent the flowers?"

"I don't know what I'm suggesting. It just shocked me. I was on the phone with him only this morning."

"Surely he wouldn't send flowers from his own shop. That would be like hanging himself."

"I know. Unless—unless—" The person who was harassing her was obviously close by, just as Richard was. Close enough to cut her brake line. Close enough to snap a picture of her wrecked car. Close enough to know she owned a gray mutt. "Unless he left his name on purpose to make himself look less guilty."

"Does he seem the type who'd harass someone?"

"No." Alissa swallowed. "He's probably not even involved. I'm sure I'm just overreacting."

"Well, let's call the flower shop and see if they have a record of who sent it."

"You call." Even though her head told her Richard Calbert couldn't be the one, at the moment she still didn't relish the idea of talking to him.

"Okay." Five minutes later, Alissa knew as much, or as little, as she'd known before Trena called. Calbert's Florist had no record of who sent the wreath. They had a record of a cash sale, but no identity of the customer. The clerk who took the money had been so busy she hadn't paid attention to the person paying the bill. And Richard Calbert had been working at his other shop when the sale was made.

"Well, at least we know it wasn't Richard himself now," Trena said, plopping back into her corner of the couch.

"I guess," Alissa said, less certain. "How do we know he didn't give someone the money to send the thing?" She sat on the edge of the sofa near Trena and stared at the card and envelope.

"We don't."

"I'm starting to feel like I should look over my shoulder every time I leave the house. I don't trust any of the neighbors anymore." The whole series of threats made Alissa want to sell her house and move to another neighborhood—the threats, plus Brad Ratner.

"Why don't we forget the wallpaper routine for today and go to the mall, then catch a movie? We can even stop and get your grand-mother. That oughta liven things up and help you relax."

Alissa nodded. "That sounds good." The idea of being cooped up inside all day with her wallpaper project no longer appealed to her. "I'll change while you throw that thing away." She pointed to the wreath.

"Do you think you should call the police first, though? Even if they can't do anything, at least they'll have a record of this. You never know, it might make it easier for them to catch him."

"You've watched too many Dick Tracy movies."

"That's like the pot calling the kettle black. If I remember cor-rectly, you're the Dick Tracy addict."

With a sarcastic smirk, Alissa walked toward the phone and once again dialed the police department's number.

The final blow. She couldn't wait to deliver it. Couldn't wait to feel Louanne's skull crack beneath the hammer. She lovingly stroked the hammer's cold metal head. Louanne's funeral would be very soon, and she'd be there in mourning, just like everyone else.

She had to seize the perfect moment, though. Louanne was probably now nervous enough to be on the alert. Well, she'd bide her time and wait, because one day, one moment, Louanne would let down her guard. Then it would be too late.

Chapter 16

I hope you're happy," Sadie Horton's bullfrog voice crackled over the telephone in angry accusation.

"Excuse me?" Alissa asked breathlessly. She'd rushed into the house as she arrived from work because of the phone's shrill ringing. Alissa had thought the call would be from her grandmother, not a disgruntled Sadie Horton.

"I said, I hope you're happy!" Her voice rose to emphasize each word with staccato clarity. "The police came and questioned Elizabeth and me again! Elizabeth was so afraid they were going to arrest her, it threw her into a spell with her blood pressure, and she just came home from the hospital today! And it's all your fault!"

"What are you talking about?" Alissa narrowed her eyes.

"I'm talking about you telling the police about Elizabeth taking pictures of her flowers the day of your wreck. She had nothing to do with your wreck you little witch. I tried to tell you that two weeks ago, but you wouldn't listen!"

Alissa steadied herself and tried to remain calm. "Mrs. Horton, I didn't even know Mrs. Teasedale was taking pictures the day of my wreck." But if she had been, Alissa realized, she could have conveniently snapped a picture of Alissa's crumpled car, then left it at her clinic with that hateful message.

"Well, somebody turned her into the police!"

"I assure you it wasn't me," Alissa stated. *But if I'd known, I would have.* This was probably what Sadie had been trying to hide the day she and Elizabeth brought the bread, and it made Alissa all the more suspicious of the two women.

"I don't believe you! Ever since you and that artist moved into this neighborhood, it's been nothing but trouble. Everything was going smoothly until. . .Henry. Don't you dare," Sadie yelled. "I mean it!"

Holding the phone away from her ear, Alissa looked at it in confusion. Then the line went dead. Apparently she could thank Henry for cutting the conversation short, a conversation which left Alissa's mind whirling. Who had known of Elizabeth taking pictures and reported it to the police? Maybe Brad had somehow learned of it. Alissa reached for the phone, then stopped. She couldn't call him. Even as much as she longed to hear his soft voice, she couldn't call.

He must have been out of town the last couple of days because until last night his car had been gone. Even though Alissa had tried not to notice, her gaze still lingered longingly in his direction, as if drawn by some supernatural force.

Five days ago she'd ordered him from her life. And the crying spell Trena had witnessed hadn't been Alissa's last. Saturday morning, her grandmother had greeted her with, "Why are your eyes so red? Have you been crying?"

Alissa had shrugged off the question and changed the subject. But Grandma had been mysteriously silent about Brad from then on, and Alissa knew she suspected all was not well.

Trena had been enormously sweet and cheerful at the clinic, but it hadn't helped the heavy loneliness that seemed to penetrate Alissa's soul, a loneliness that had dulled her eyes and numbed her heart. That, coupled with the tension of not knowing who was harassing her, left Alissa emotionally drained.

Was the person perhaps Sadie Horton? She'd just now seemed angry enough to make a physical threat. Trying to shrug off the abrasive woman, she quickly changed into work clothes and consciously ignored the bedroom wallpaper, which she still hadn't replaced.

Maybe tomorrow. She then grabbed a banana and headed outside. Her red and orange cannas, now blooming in the front yard, needed to be weeded. She hoped an hour of yard work would release the tension in her neck.

She'd been weeding only a few minutes, when a silver Cadillac purred into her circular driveway. Frito, sitting beside her, woofed once then promptly ignored the invader. Alissa didn't react so casually, knowing the car belonged to Sadie and Henry Horton. Had Sadie arrived to continue the accusations or to harm her physically? Alissa's mouth drying, her pulse pounding, she wondered if she should bolt into the house and lock the door. Although her thoughts were racing, her body was unresponsive, like heavy wood. She simply couldn't move. *Dear Lord, please protect me.*

The car stopped. Alissa held her breath as the skin along her spine broke out in cold gooseflesh. The Cadillac's door slowly opened, and a tall, thin, kind-faced man emerged from the driver's seat.

"Dr. Carrington?" he asked, closing the car's door.

"Yes." She swallowed, the first action other than breathing that she'd been able to produce since the car arrived.

"I'm Henry Horton." He slowly walked toward her; the anxious squint of his finely lined blue eyes suggesting regret. "I believe you were just on the phone with my wife?"

Alissa, still on her guard, stood and tightly gripped her miniature garden spade. If she needed it, at least she did have a weapon for her defense. "Yes."

"I. . ." He cleared his throat. "I just came to apologize for her behavior. Sadie sometimes gets carried away."

"It's okay," Alissa said, wondering if it really were. "I can understand why she's upset. But I promise you, I did not turn her or Mrs. Teasedale in to the police. I didn't even know Mrs. Teasedale was taking pictures the day of my accident."

"I believe you. That's the reason I came in person. You just moved into the neighborhood, and I don't want any hard feelings. Like I said, I'm sorry she even bothered you."

"Thanks." Alissa tried to smile. How did such a nice man as Henry Horton wind up with someone like Sadie?

"Well, I guess that's all I've come to say. I'll let you get back to—"

"Good afternoon," a familiar male voice said behind Alissa.

Jumping, she turned to face the reason for her sleepless nights. "You scared me," she said. Placing a hand over her heart.

He was tanner, his hair more sun-streaked than the last time she saw him. But his eyes were just as intense, just as kind as they were in her dreams, and his shoulders just as broad. His worn jeans and beige oxford shirt were still unable to camouflage his near-royal demeanor— a demeanor marked with an aggressive, protective caution.

"I don't believe we've met," Brad said, extending his hand to Henry Horton. Alissa, realizing she had been staring at Brad, made the appropriate introductions and tried to control the quiver in her voice.

All the time she wished there were a law against men being as attractive as Brad Ratner. How could she ever survive living next door to the man of her dreams, the man denied her?

"I was just leaving," Henry said, releasing Brad's hand. "But it's nice to meet you."

As the men exchanged pleasantries, Alissa noticed Richard Calbert jogging up the road. She waved in response to his friendly wave and wondered if he'd learned anything about the watch she'd found in her flowerbed. When he jogged back by on his return trip, she'd stop him and inquire.

Within minutes, Henry had driven out of Alissa's driveway to leave her standing in awkward silence with Brad and wondering why he'd come over in the first place.

"How have you been?" he asked.

"Fine. And you?"

"Fine."

She fidgeted with the hem of her stained white T-shirt. "I don't guess the police have learned anything about the bones?"

"No. They've finally given me permission to go ahead with the pool. The pool company is going to start construction again in the morning." He hesitated. "I. . .um. . .I know it's not any of my business, but what did Mr. Horton want?"

Alissa briefly told him of Sadie's phone call.

"I was the one who told the police about Elizabeth snapping pictures," he said, his gaze roaming from her eyes to her hair to her lips. "Claire Allen told me she saw her the day of your wreck."

"Well, Sadie Horton isn't a happy camper because of you."

"I figured as much. I'm just sorry she took it out on you. But I couldn't let that detail go by without alerting the police."

"Apparently they couldn't come up with anything incriminating, though, because they didn't arrest either woman. I mean, it's not exactly against the law to take pictures of your own flowers." Alissa's erratic pulse didn't match her calm words. She sounded as if she were carrying on a neighborly chat, when in reality a slow inferno consumed her heart. *Oh Brad, why do you have to be so unattainable?* Alissa wanted to wail the question from the highest mountaintop. Instead, she tried to avoid eye contact, a nearly impossible task, and prayed he'd leave before her traitorous body flung itself into his arms.

"I still don't trust those two. That's the reason I came over. I saw the Hortons' car, and thought. . ." He shrugged, the protective gleam still in his eyes.

"Thanks," she said to the nearby weeping willow.

"Have you had anymore threats since the note at the clinic?"

Alissa didn't want to tell him about the funeral wreath. After all, her life no longer included him. Therefore, any disclosure contradicted her request that they remain apart, and mocked the intimacy they could never share.

Brad rubbed the nape of his neck. "I'm no good at this. I might as well tell you, I know about the wreath."

"How?" Alissa blurted.

He sighed. "Trena. I had a message on my machine when I got home last night. I went to visit my sister for a couple of days. Anyway, Trena's worried about you and wanted me to keep an eye on things over here."

She rolled her eyes. "Great. If it's not Grandma, it's Trena. Sometimes I think the two of them are in league against me."

"Look, Alissa, Trena has good reason to be worried. And, well. . . so do I," he added softly, his eyes gray pools of fathomless pleading. "I. . ." He stepped closer and tucked a strand of stray hair behind her ear, his hand lingering. "I've been doing a lot of thinking. That's part of the reason I went to my sister's place. I wanted to think and pray and—and talk to her."

His sporty cologne filled her senses as she closed her eyes.

"Alissa," he breathed her name in near prayerful reverence, "I missed you so much." His other arm wrapped around her waist to pull her against his chest and hold her there as if she were life's most treasured possession.

And, dropping her garden spade, Alissa couldn't resist him. Couldn't resist that overwhelming feeling that Brad's arms were where she belonged. Couldn't resist the warmth that flooded her veins. His heart, pounding out hard, rapid beats beneath her ear, matched the robust beating of her own heart. And she knew she'd died and gone to heaven. . .until his lips brushed her temple.

The feel of his lips; that's all it took. And Alissa relived that moment only days ago when he'd called her "Dana." Was he now thinking of Dana as he held her close? The thought sent an icy blast through her stomach, an icy blast that gave her the strength to push him away.

The man seemed forever determined to twist her heart into

knots, and then douse her in cold disappointment. Well, Alissa wouldn't allow it to happen anymore. She was sick of his games. She'd told him to stay away from her last week, and she still meant it.

Clenching her fists, Alissa pressed her lips together with determination.

Alissa said, "Brad, I told you last week that we should no longer see each other—period. I meant it. I'm not interested in this on-again, off-again scenario you seem intent on replaying."

"But—"

"No buts." Alissa raised her hand to stop his words, and her heart felt as if it were being wrenched from her chest. "Until you decide whatever it is you have to decide about Dana, I cannot allow you to put me through an emotional upheaval every other day."

He opened his mouth as if he were going to retort, and then snapped it shut. His jaw muscles, clenching and unclenching, were the only evidence of his anger, for his eyes were masked in cold, gray mist. "Okay," he said, a chill in his voice. "When you want to listen, call me. Until then, I'll stay out of your way, your highness." With a mock bow, he turned and stomped back to his home.

Alissa let out her breath and suppressed the tears stinging her eyes, blurring her vision. A sinking sensation in the pit of her stomach hinted that maybe she'd been too brash in dismissing him again. He said he'd been praying. Did that mean he'd finally made peace with God? But regardless of that possibility, what she said was true, and her heart, now bruised and battered, couldn't bear the thought of him calling her "Dana" again.

As Richard Calbert jogged past on his return trip, Alissa forced thoughts of Brad from her mind, thoughts she knew would soon return. "Excuse me! Richard!" she called.

Slowing, he glanced over his shoulder then came to a halt as Alissa trotted to the road. "Sorry to bother you," she croaked, trying to control her still-shaking voice. "But I was wondering if your brother has had a chance to clean and appraise that watch."

"The watch," he said in resignation, his eyes shifting from Alissa to her house. "I was afraid you were going to ask me about that before. . ." He stopped short.

"Before what?"

Richard's eyes, the eyes that only days ago had been full of a friendliness that said, "Trust me," now filled with regret. "Before I found it. I cannot believe this happened, Alissa, but I seem to have lost the watch. The other day, after you called, I planned, honest I did, to take it straight to my brother. But I couldn't find it, and I have no idea what I did with it." He raised his long, lean arms in confusion. "I've turned my house upside down, my office upside down. I don't know what happened to it!

"Look, I'm terribly sorry. I know it will turn up sooner or later, though. I'm just so absentminded lately because I've been so busy at work that I'm sure I've simply mislaid it."

"Oh," she said again, the image of the funeral wreath appearing in her mind's eye.

"Did you ever find out who sent the wreath?" he asked, as if he were reading her mind.

"Uh, no. . .no, I didn't." *Was it you?* she nearly blurted. At the same time, she wanted to turn and run. Alissa didn't know who to trust anymore. Richard had promised her he'd tend to an obviously valuable timepiece. Now the watch had conveniently disappeared. He and his staff had also denied knowing who sent the funeral wreath. Did he really not know?

"It was probably just a joke." He smiled. "One time I dressed as a minister and delivered a funeral wreath—equipped with a crazy eulogy—to someone on his fortieth birthday. One of my more memorable deliveries."

"Yes. Maybe it was just a joke," Alissa said, her voice devoid of conviction.

"Well, I've got to run. I'll let you know when I find the watch!" With a friendly wave and a ready smile, Richard jogged on toward his house.

Alissa, wondering what really happened to the expensive watch, stood near the curb until he turned into his driveway. Then she glanced toward Brad's house to see Brad watching from his living room window. Her gaze lingered with his for several breath-stopping seconds. Irresistibly drawn to him, Alissa took a hesitant step forward. Then he dropped the drapes, and she turned toward her house, her eyes blurring.

What she didn't see was Brad's expression of fervent expectation as he opened the front door. An expectation that was immediately replaced by dejected disappointment when he found no one there.

Chapter 17

Alissa refused to think of Brad the rest of the evening. He'd consumed her thoughts since she met him, and even the mention of his name now brought floods of conflicting emotions. Should she have remained in his arms and been grateful for the morsels of his affection? He'd seemed angry and slightly hurt that she'd pushed him away. *It might do him good*, a stubborn voice insisted. After all, Alissa wasn't any man's plaything. She was a grown woman with feelings, a woman with emotional needs that only Brad could fulfill. Now she was back to longing for his touch.

"It's best not even to think about him," she told herself as she made herself a quick chicken sandwich. Completing that task, she decided the time had come to tackle the wallpaper. The old cliché, "misery loves company," truly explained how she felt. Nothing could make her more miserable than wallpapering. So why not heap misery on top of misery and do what she dreaded most, when she felt the most miserable?

Frito wagged his tail in hopes of receiving a bit of her sandwich, and she obliged him with the last of it. "Let's go demolish that olive green stuff and put up something with some style," she said, and the loyal mutt followed her upstairs.

The first thing Alissa needed to do was change out of her trusty gardening jeans and into a pair of baggy walking shorts. At least she'd be comfortable in her misery. Opening the spacious walk-in closet, she flipped on the light and turned to face the rows of built-in shelves that lined the closet's north wall. She'd claimed this extra space for her shorts, sweaters, and jeans stowaway shortly after moving in.

A quick scan of the shelves didn't produce the particular pair of shorts she was searching for, though—the khaki ones that she'd bought last summer. They were too big when she bought them, and that's the reason she liked them so much. Big equaled comfortable. Finally, after moving two pairs of blue jeans, she found them crammed into the left corner of the second shelf.

Alissa grabbed them and started to turn from the closet, when something caught her eye. A piece of folded paper, yellowed with age, was wedged into the shelf's far corner. Her curiosity heightened, she reached for the paper to unfold it and read the message scrawled in masculine script.

Louanne,

I've finally told her. Our plane for Australia leaves tonight. Be ready by eight.

All My Love,
Richard

Alissa blinked. The only Richard she knew nearby was Richard Calbert. Why would a note he'd written be in Mrs. Docker's house, and who was this woman named Louanne? It didn't take a brain surgeon to figure out the note was setting up a lovers' rendezvous.

Louanne. The name for some reason sounded familiar. She was sure she'd heard it mentioned since moving to this neighborhood. But when, and by whom? Nibbling her thumbnail, she wondered if Mrs. Docker would know.

Normally, Alissa would have shrugged off such a note as the leftovers of the house's last owner and trashed it. But the fact that Richard's name was at the bottom fanned her curiosity's flickering flame into a roaring inferno. Richard Calbert seemed too entwined with the strange things happening to her. Perhaps an explanation of this note might further reveal his true character.

She grabbed the phone book from her nightstand, looked up Mrs. Docker's number and dialed it, only to receive a recording. After leaving a brief message, Alissa hung up and stared in determination at the wallpaper.

❧

Brad sat in his living room, deep in thought. He'd suspected he'd blown his chance at a relationship with Alissa when he called her "Dana." Now he knew he had. His sister had simply shaken her head when he told her the whole story.

"You've just fouled up in the worst way possible," she'd declared. "You'll be lucky if she ever speaks to you again."

Even apart from the good counsel of his sister and time spent with his brother-in-law and nephew, the visit to their east Texas farm had done Brad a lot of good. He'd been able to do some soul-searching and, yes, to bring some closure to the healing process begun when he lost his family. That meant realizing he couldn't blame God for what happened. He still didn't understand why God hadn't prevented his wife's and daughter's needless deaths, and he probably wouldn't understand. But it was time to accept what had happened as he accepted God's comfort.

Alissa's words had brought him to this realization, a realization his sister had confirmed. Yes, Brad had finally resolved his anger toward God and asked forgiveness for it, and now felt a peace within he hadn't experienced since before the fateful day he'd entered that fast-food restaurant with his family. Now he knew he had to create a new life for himself.

These decisions had led to the painting that he now inspected—a dilapidated log cabin nestled at the base of wooded hills. Only weeks ago, he'd wondered what he would do to keep the art galleries happy when his old paintings were gone. Now he no longer had that worry. For that driving urge, that undeniable force which bade him to paint had returned with a new intensity.

Alissa. He could thank her for reawakening him emotionally and spiritually as man and artist. The irony of the whole situation was that he'd pushed her so far away, he didn't know if he could ever reach her again.

Brad rubbed the nape of his neck and stared out on the patio doors. Grinding his teeth together, he made an irreversible decision. First, he'd give Alissa time to cool down. Then he'd kill her with kindness, slowly wear down her defenses, and not take "no" for an answer.

Along with his emotional and spiritual healing, the trip to his sister's home had also resulted in a vague toothache in one of his left, upper molars. With a calculating smirk, Brad decided he should have a dentist examine his teeth immediately.

Two evenings lapsed before Alissa heard from Mrs. Docker, evenings in which Alissa had finally replaced the old wallpaper with the new. Staring at her accomplishment with satisfaction, she picked up the ringing phone in her bedroom and heard Mrs. Docker's kind soprano voice on the line.

"I called the other day," Alissa said, "because I found an old note in my closet, and was wondering if you might recognize it." She picked up the note she'd left lying beside the telephone and read it.

"Mmm. . .that doesn't sound familiar," Mrs. Docker said. "The only Richard nearby is Richard Calbert."

"That's what I thought."

"And I don't know anyone named Louanne."

Come on, think, Alissa urged. For some inexplicable reason, learning about the note had become of monumental importance to her. She knew she'd heard someone mention the name "Louanne" recently. If she could only remember who and when, she felt as if. . .she didn't exactly know what she felt. It was one of those sixth-sense sensations that her grandmother said Alissa shared with her mother.

"Let me think on it a few days, and I'll let you know if I come up with anything. It seems like I should know something, but my memory's not like it used to be, especially not since my heart attack last fall."

The real estate agent had explained that it was due to failing health that Mrs. Docker had wanted to sell her house and move into a retirement home. She now had a private apartment in assisted-living quarters where she had easy access to a nearby hospital.

"Okay," Alissa said. "Call me anytime. Do you have my number at the clinic?"

"No."

She slowly recited the number, then, after exchanging pleasantries, hung up. Maybe the older woman would have a memory flash tomorrow.

Tomorrow. Alissa thought about coming down with a convenient case of the black plague when she thought of her appointments for the next morning. Brad Ratner was first in line. The receptionist said he'd called early yesterday morning about a toothache and insisted that Alissa, not Trena, should see him.

Alissa didn't know what to think of this turn of events. The truth was, one second she wanted to avoid the appointment, while the next, she couldn't wait. Her head and her hurt pride told her to skip the country for a day, while her heart told her to enjoy every second of his presence.

❧

The next morning as she entered her office, her feelings were still vacillating between dread and happy expectation.

"Who's your first appointment? A regular?" Trena asked, entering to give Alissa her morning cup of coffee while Alissa ate her usual breakfast banana.

"No. A new patient," she said as noncommittally as possible and dropped the banana peel into the trash can beside her desk.

"I've got the Wilson kid." Trena rolled her eyes and sat on the edge of Alissa's desk. "Don't be surprised if we get serenaded by a chorus of screams."

"Dr. Carrington?" Molly Langford, their middle-aged, plump dental assistant, peered into the office. "Mr. Ratner is here. It's early, but I thought you might want to go ahead and get started, so I put him in the first chair."

Alissa swallowed and grabbed a breath mint from her drawer. "Thanks."

"Brad Ratner?" Trena whispered.

"Yeah."

"He's your first appointment?"

"Yeah. He says he has a toothache."

"Either that or a heartache," Trena said with a smug snicker and left for her own office.

Grimacing at her friend's back, Alissa straightened her freshly starched lab coat then headed for the inevitable.

❦

She'd waited long enough, and Louanne could live no longer. Tonight, the moon would be full, just like it had been ten years earlier. The perfect time for a murder.

"You should have been more careful, you double-crossing witch," she said to her reflection, and stroked the dull gray wig now resting on her head. "This time, I'll make sure you don't escape from your grave." With satisfaction, she picked up the nearby hammer and slammed it against the bathroom mirror, enjoying the vibration reaching to her elbow—the same vibration she'd feel when the hammer smashed Louanne's skull.

Chapter 18

Alissa walked briskly into the examination room, her spine stiff. "I understand you've got a toothache," she said in her most businesslike voice, a voice that hid the fluttering of her heart. Sitting down on a nearby stool, she looked Brad squarely in the eyes and attempted to act as if nothing had ever passed between them.

"Yeah. It's on the top left," Brad said, his eyes seeming to recount the moment they'd shared that blazing kiss. "I can't really tell which tooth it is. It's either the third or fourth one back."

She willed her face to remain impassive. "That's fairly common. When was the last time you had your teeth cleaned?"

"Three months ago." He looked as if he'd just told her he loved her.

"No cavities then?" she squeaked as Molly handed her a mirror.

"None."

"Have you eaten anything hard the last few days?"

"No."

His voice was as soft, as caressing, as hers was businesslike in the extreme. And Alissa wondered why he'd really come in. There were many other dentists he could have seen.

"Okay." She stood and covered her mouth and nose with a blue examination mask. "Let me have a look, and then we'll take some X-rays."

He opened his mouth obediently, his gaze never leaving her face. She purposefully concentrated on his molars as she examined them with the mirror and tried to still her trembling fingers. "Does that hurt?" she asked, pressing against his tooth with the explorer Molly supplied.

"Uh-uh."

"Okay, let's take some X-rays and see what we can find out." The dental assistant silently tended to the X-rays as Alissa left the room to check the time of her next appointment and regain her equilibrium. Minutes later she reentered, expecting to find Molly with the processed X-rays. Instead, she found Brad still alone. Alissa prepared to bolt back into the hallway. But Brad grabbed her hand before she could escape.

"Alissa, I'm terrible at this," he said.

"At what?" she croaked and tried to pull her fingers from his grasp, but he only tightened his hold.

"I do have a toothache, but I don't even care about that right now," he declared, and his little-boy smile made the room spin.

She stared at him in silence. "Then why did you—"

"I made the appointment because I just wanted to see you."

"You what?" Her voice rose in pitch, partly in professional incredulity, partly in feminine pleasure. "You could have. . ." She lowered her voice to a whisper. No sense in Trena and Molly and any waiting patients overhearing their conversation. "You could have walked about forty yards from your front door and done that."

"Yeah, if you chose to answer the knock at your door."

Alissa gritted her teeth as new irritation replaced the original pleasure. He was still up to his little games. Now he wanted to see her. By three o'clock he would probably barely speak to her, and more than likely he was thinking of Dana at this very minute. The very memory of his calling her Dana sent Alissa into a fit of fury. "Look, if you don't want me to find the cause of your toothache, then I have a schedule to maintain." She pulled her hand from his.

"Hey, I'm paying for your time." He stood and ripped the blue plastic bib from around his neck.

"Well, what did you want to see me for?" she whispered, her fists tight wads of tension.

"I just wanted to see you," he whispered, placing hands on her shoulders.

"Okay, you've seen me. Now go." She backed away from his touch. "I've already told you twice, and I guess I'll have to tell you again—"

"Look, I'm sorry for calling you 'Dana.' It was a mistake, a really unfortunate mistake."

"A mistake?" Alissa raised her brows. "No, I think you just spoke the name of the person on your mind, and it wasn't me!"

Brad stepped toward her, decreasing the number of feet between them to inches. "I think more than anything else, your pride is what's hurting," he said, his voice sounding relieved, his eyes sparkling with humor.

"Pride!" she hissed, backing closer to the room's corner. The nerve of the man! "Since when did you grow into such a mind reader? Besides, what if it is pride! How would you like it if I called you. . ." She started to say Sherman, then stopped herself.

"Sherman, you mean?" He once again narrowed the space between them.

"How do you know about him? No—don't answer that. I know how you know. My grandmother, right?"

"Bingo." Brad reached for her hand, but Alissa deftly sidestepped to cross the room.

"Look, we're getting nowhere with this, and I have patients coming, so why don't you just—"

"I don't care if she is with a patient!" a familiar female voice yelled from the hallway. "She's my granddaughter, and I need to talk to her. Now let me pass right now!"

"Oh, no," Alissa groaned and stepped into the hall to see Molly trying to corral Emily Carrington back toward the waiting room.

"Mrs. Carrington," Molly urged, "Dr. Carrington will be with you in just a few minutes. I promise. If you'll just wait—"

"There you are," Emily said, pointing to Alissa. "Tell this pit bull of yours to let me pass!"

"It's okay, Molly," Alissa said, crossing her arms.

With a smirk, Trena walked by, heading for the back examination room. "Having an eventful morning aren't we?" she mumbled.

"Just wait, you're next. And I'll be the one grinning when the Wilson kid gets here."

"I need a ride home, Alissa," Emily said, walking toward her granddaughter, determination glimmering in her clear blue eyes. "Can you take me?"

"Grandma, couldn't you call a taxi?"

"You know I hate taxis."

"Well, how did you get here in the first place?"

"Hello, Brad," Emily said.

Alissa glanced behind her to see Brad smiling indulgently.

"Hello, Emily," he said politely.

"I'll tell you how I got here." Emily continued, as if she'd not spoken to Brad. "That Samuel Reynolds talked me into letting him drive me to the drugstore. You know, the one across the street that gives the senior citizen discounts. Anyway, he got me in that parking lot in his red Corvette with its tinted windows, and do you know what he had the audacity to do?" She tugged on the lapel of her Chanel jacket, her expression one of near horror. "He put his hand on my knee and tried to kiss me, that's what!"

Alissa, biting her bottom lip to stop the smile, heard Brad's barely stifled snicker.

"So I told him, I just said, 'Samuel Reynolds, I never kissed but one man in my life and that was my husband.'" She shook her finger at Alissa's nose for effect. "'And if you think I'm going to start kissing men now, you're crazy!' That's just what I told him." Emily placed her hands on her hips in an indignant pose. "I've watched the evening news, and I know! You can get *germs* from kissing men!"

Staring at the toes of her penny loafers, Alissa pressed her lips together until they hurt. "Well, did you get what you needed at the drugstore?" she managed to choke out.

"No! I never went in! And now I can't even remember what I went there for! That's why I just want to go home!"

"I can give you a lift," Brad said. "I was about to leave anyway."

"Oh, could you?" Emily pleaded. "That would be so kind." She looked at Alissa. "He's a lot nicer than that Sherman character. I'll never know what you saw in him."

"We aren't through with our conversation," Brad muttered as he passed Alissa.

"As far as I'm concerned we are," she whispered, raising her chin in defiant determination. "Until you decide you're ready for a normal relationship—"

"Who says I'm not?" he challenged.

Alissa stared at him, not knowing exactly what to say. If Brad really were ready for a relationship, then that changed the whole picture. The question was: Could she trust him?

"Are you coming, Brad?" Emily called from down the hallway.

"Yes." He stroked Alissa's cheek with the back of his index finger, leaving a trail of tingles behind. "We'll talk tonight, okay?"

Swallowing, she hesitated. If she agreed, she might be stepping right back into his emotional hurricane. But if she turned him down, she just might be turning down the very man God had chosen for her.

Brad's eyes darkened in anxiety as the silence stretched between them and Alissa continued to deliberate.

"Okay," she finally said, and hoped she hadn't made a mistake.

His face relaxed. "Okay, then." And with a slow wink, he turned to leave.

Chapter 19

Brad knocked on Alissa's front door and waited, but no answer came. He glanced at his watch, six o'clock. Perhaps he was rushing in his eagerness to talk with her. He'd gotten her to agree to listen to him more easily than he'd expected to. Now if he could just convince her that he truly cared for her.

Knocking again, he tried to suppress the tiny fear that tugged at him. Alissa usually arrived home by now. *She probably had to stop at the grocery store or something,* he thought. Her Mustang wasn't in the driveway, so Brad walked to the closed garage. He hopped several times in an attempt to peer through the garage windows. Finally, he saw that the garage was empty.

The tiny fear slowly grew into stark apprehension. Brad couldn't explain it. The feeling was like some ominous, dark cloud that steadily descended on him and purposefully penetrated his soul. Perhaps he should go to the clinic just to make sure she hadn't had car trouble.

Turning from the door, he hoped car trouble was the only problem she'd experienced. After all, someone had already tried to kill her, and the funeral wreath promised another attempt. Maybe that was the reason for Brad's anxiety. But wasn't that reason enough?

With determination, he rushed to his Lexus. Something told him all was not well with Alissa. Something he could not ignore. He raced to his vehicle, whipped his cell phone from his belt clip, and retrieved the phone book he kept beneath the front seat.

꙰

She opened the storage closet's door an inch and peered into the clinic's empty hallway. The only person now at the clinic should be Louanne. She'd heard her tell her partner she was going to stay an extra hour to clean her office. The light from her office attested to that.

After warily listening for several seconds, she felt confident that, except for Louanne, the clinic was indeed empty. With a gentle push on the door, she stepped into the hallway and silently unlocked the back door, opening it only an inch. This would be means for escape after the murder.

She'd been waiting one hour for the staff to leave. Sneaking in at five o'clock had been so easy. She'd simply walked into the empty waiting room as if she belonged there, slipped by a distracted receptionist, and then crept into the storage closet. The rest had been a matter of waiting until the last "good-bye" was said. Louanne had told the receptionist to lock the doors as she left for the night.

She smiled. The doors were locked, but Louanne was trapped with a murderer.

Now the fun will begin. She lovingly caressed the hammer in her right hand and relived the moment she smashed her bathroom mirror. She couldn't wait to do the same to Louanne. Licking her lips like a predator, she continued her trek down the hallway. Like a prowling panther, she stopped just outside the office doorway and watched as Louanne, her back turned, inserted several books into their proper places on the floor-to-ceiling bookcase behind her desk. Louanne always did enjoy books. Too bad for her she didn't stick to reading them.

Her right eye nervously twitching, she adjusted the gray wig, raised the hammer, and approached her prey.

꙰

Alissa ignored the ringing phone. She never answered the phone when she stayed after hours, and she wasn't about to start now.

She placed the next to last book in the bookshelf. Alissa was notorious for removing books then forgetting to replace them. And her forgetfulness had created a growing stack she could no longer ignore. She'd also decided to straighten her office before going home.

Home. Where Brad waited next door to speak with her. Alissa wondered exactly what he would tell her. That he loved her, perhaps? As much as she longed to hear the words, she still had nagging doubts about their sincerity. Could he have gotten over his wife already, when only weeks ago he was still so obviously devoted to her memory?

These questions filling her thoughts, Alissa bent to retrieve the last book.

❧

She took another step, hovering behind Louanne and trying to decide whether to immediately slam the hammer into her head or call out her name. Wouldn't it be a terrible shock for Louanne to once more face her murderer? It would be terrible for Louanne, entertaining for her. Savoring the powerful moment, she finally decided to strike from behind and do it quickly. The longer she waited, the more likely she was to get caught. Besides, Louanne had been so naughty, she'd immediately know who hit her.

❧

Brad tried the knob on the clinic's door only to find it locked. "Good girl," he muttered. Relaxing, he took in the smell of summer pines and eyed her Mustang in the parking lot. The top was up and the doors appeared to be locked. Alissa was obviously taking no chances. His relief increasing, he pounded on the door with a force that ensured she'd hear him. "Alissa? It's me, Brad. Are you in there?"

❧

She lunged for Louanne, who, in response to Brad's call, stepped away from the desk just in time to miss the brunt of the blow. Her stomach tightening, she watched as Louanne sank to her knees after receiving the glancing blow behind her right ear. With the hammer heavy in her sweaty hand, she stood over her victim like a conquering mountain lion that has maimed an innocent sheep and prepares to make its fatal move.

"Alissa?" Brad's call increased in urgency as he continued to knock.

After a nervous glance down the hall, she wondered if she should complete her mission or run? Did she have time? With the front door knob rattling, the murderer decided to make her escape. She would be forced to finish Louanne's punishment later, perhaps tomorrow.

She then raced for the back door to move stealthily outside and run toward her car, parked two blocks away.

❀

Now frantic, Brad backed away from the clinic's doorway, took two purposeful steps forward, and rammed his sneaker into the door just below the knob. It popped open with a splintering protest.

"Alissa?" he called again, fearing what he might hear and at the same time fearing the silence. Brad rushed through the waiting room to see a light down the hall. "Alissa?" His heart pounding in his temples, he ran toward the ajar office door. What he found wrenched his soul.

His worse nightmare, he was reliving it all again, Dana, dead at his feet. But this time it was Alissa. Her body sprawled beside the desk. Her pale hair splayed across her equally pale cheek, a trickle of blood oozing from behind her right ear.

Brad couldn't move, couldn't breath, he couldn't blink. Was he forever destined to fall in love, only for it to end in death?

Her eyelids fluttering, Alissa groaned and slowly reached to touch the back of her head.

"Alissa," Brad croaked. Rushing forward, he knelt beside her to stroke her cheek. "Alissa, can you hear me?"

"Brad?" Another groan. This time, her eyes opened. "Someone st–struck me from behind. My head." She tried to roll onto her back.

"No, no, don't move." He didn't have extensive medical knowledge, but knew enough from college football to understand her need to lie still. "I'll call an ambulance."

"I—I think I'm okay."

He gripped her hand and gently kissed her cheek. "You're not okay until they say you're okay. Now don't move," he commanded.

❦

"You're going to be fine," the young physician said two hours later. "There are no signs of concussion, and the CAT scan looks fine." He went on to give her instructions for overnight observation.

Sighing, Alissa sat up on the edge of the emergency room examination table on which she had been lying.

"Do you feel like talking to the police?" Brad asked, pointing toward the middle-aged cop hovering near the waiting area.

"Yes." She gingerly fingered the small cut two inches behind and above her right ear. The only pain she suffered after the wound cleaning was soreness to the touch and a headache.

"You were very fortunate," the police officer said minutes later as Alissa, Brad, and he chose seats in the emergency room waiting area.

"That's what I keep thinking." She instinctively grasped Brad's hand as it closed over hers. He'd ridden with her in the ambulance, and she'd been grateful for his presence, was still grateful for his presence. He was like a rock, quiet and solid, exactly what she'd needed in her time of terror.

The dark-skinned policeman, whose nametag read R. BLACK-FOOT, wasted no time in his questioning. "Can you recount exactly what happened?"

Alissa glanced at Brad. "I was in my office, reshelving some books, when I heard Brad's knock on the clinic's front door."

"I take it the door was locked?"

"Yes. As I turned, I felt the blow—like something hard, maybe metal."

"Did you see the assailant?"

"No. I blacked out immediately—wait a minute. I did catch a glimpse of curly, gray hair."

The officer, scribbling in his notepad, never looked up. "Short or long? Male or female?"

Alissa blinked. "Well, it was rather fluffy, I think." She shut her eyes and tried to reconstruct what she had seen in a mere glance. "I don't know. I guess it looked more like a woman's hair, but it's hard for me to say. Then, the next thing I knew, Brad was telling me to lie still."

"It's a good thing you were there," Blackfoot said, glancing at Brad.

"A very good thing," Alissa added. Squeezing his hand, she smiled her appreciation into eyes that smiled back and held the glimmer of unrestrained affection.

The officer discreetly cleared his throat. "I'm going to have to take a look at your office. Do you feel like driving over there and letting me in?"

"Alissa, are. . .are you all right?" Trena, her dark eyes full of panic, rushed through the waiting area doorway and straight for her best friend.

"I'm fine," Alissa assured her.

"I wasn't home when Brad called." She knelt in front of Alissa to anxiously peer into her face. "He left a message on my machine, and I hit the ceiling."

"Just calm down. I'm going to be fine."

"Wait a minute! I'm supposed to be the one to tell you that."

"Yeah, but I'm not as high-strung as you are."

"What happened?"

Alissa quickly briefed her friend.

"I knew it! I had a strange feeling about leaving you at the clinic by yourself!"

"But I made sure the doors were locked. I don't know how the person got in."

"That's what we want to try and find out," Officer Blackfoot said.

"Could you let him into the clinic, Trena?" Brad asked. "I'd really like to get Alissa home."

"I'd like very much to go home," Alissa said. All she wanted was a long hot bath and a cup of even hotter tea. Facing the clinic right now held no appeal for her.

"Sure," Trena said. "I'll do anything to help. And just for the record"—she shook her finger at Alissa's nose—"I'm spending the night at your house tonight."

"No, I am," Brad stated emphatically. "I plan to camp out on her couch. That way, if anyone tries to break in, they'll have to get past me before they make it to the stairway. Besides, the doctor wants someone with her overnight. She's supposed to say up awhile then be awakened every few hours."

"Thanks," Alissa said, secretly glad for the protection.

"I think that's a good idea," Blackfoot said. "I wish we had enough manpower to have someone sit outside your house tonight. As it is, the best we can offer is a regular patrol of the neighborhood. But rest assured, we'll be watching."

"Good," Alissa said, wondering if she were safe anywhere. Somehow the intruder had noiselessly entered the clinic. *Could the same person be waiting for me at home?*

Chapter 20

I've looked through every closet and your attic," Brad said an hour later. "So unless this sicko is invisible, we're here alone."

Alissa sighed in relief. After a thorough search of the house's first floor, Brad had gone upstairs, and Alissa had sat with her gaze riveted on the stairwell. She'd never felt so vulnerable in her life, and hoped her assailant would be caught before it was too late. Who did she know with gray hair? That one clue obviously did not lead to Sadie Horton or Elizabeth Teasedaale. Perhaps the two women were simply bored and nosy and not in the least bit connected with Alissa's problems of late.

"I'm sure that monster would have killed me if it weren't for you," she said, wrapping her arms around her midsection in an attempt to feel more secure. "I never did get around to thanking you." A smile wobbled its way along her lips.

"That's what we knights in shining armor are for, ma'am." Brad, delivering another of his exquisite smiles, sat beside her on the Victorian settee and placed his left arm across her shoulders.

Alissa instinctively snuggled closer, loving the strength that arm represented, loving his masculine scent and, yes, loving him. Right now, she didn't care who he was thinking about. Alissa simply needed his touch.

"We knights are also available for hugging." He leaned forward to place his right arm on her waist, pulling her closer. His eyes, only inches from hers, beckoned her to respond to his embrace, an invitation totally unnecessary.

Alissa's heart palpitated in anticipation. Her breath, shallow and short, steadily increased in pace. And her skin tingled everywhere he touched her—her shoulders, her waist, and now her cheek as he gently stroked it with his thumb.

"And for kissing," he whispered against her lips.

Their previous kiss paled in comparison to the one that ensued. Alissa, wrapping her arms tightly about his midsection, responded with an abandonment which blocked out their conflict and filled her senses with Brad and Brad alone.

The kiss finally ended, only to have Brad pull her closer and desperately whisper in her ear, "Ah, Alissa, I'm so sorry. I feel like I've messed everything up between us. I—I know I've acted like a confused teenager, but can we just start again?"

Her throat dry, Alissa placed her head against his shoulder and reveled in the sensation of his warm breath on her ear. Right now, she'd agree to being burned at the stake with him. But a voice of caution whispered in the back of her mind. *How do you know he really means it? Tonight he calls you Alissa but what about tomorrow? Will it be Dana again?*

As much as she wanted to say "yes" to his request and ask no questions, Alissa knew she had to express her fears. They couldn't start over without completely clearing their past. Reluctantly, she forced herself to pull away from him and look into his pleading eyes. "There's nothing I would like more than our starting over, Brad. But I think we need to talk first, don't you?"

"Yes. I—I guess I'm rushing things, aren't I? Sorry." He wrapped a strand of her hair around his index finger.

"It just seems a little—I don't know—quick for you to want a relationship with me when only weeks ago you were calling me Dana." There. She'd said it. And even though she felt ungrateful for having voiced her opinion in the face of his honest admiration, Alissa felt better for having done it.

"It really hasn't been quick, you know. It's taken me two years to get over her." He stared across the room at Frito, who snoozed on the bottom stair. "What happened, I think, was that I met you at the very end of my grieving. Either that or meeting you shocked me out of it." He chuckled. "In the words of Whit Jenkins, you're 'quite a looker,' Dr. Carrington. And if you want the truth, I haven't been able to think straight since I saw you peering over my backyard fence." Brad, shrugging, toyed with the button on his blue cotton shirt. "I've just had some problems dealing with feelings of betrayal to Dana and Kara. See, just because they died, I didn't stop feeling like a husband and father."

"And what about God?" Alissa asked, hating to push the issue, but at the same time, needing an answer. "Where does He fit into all this?" As much as Alissa cared for Brad, she needed to hear him say that his relationship with the Lord was once again stable. Even though her heart told her he wouldn't shirk his family responsibility as a biblical husband, she still needed to hear his confirmation. She'd learned her lesson and learned it well, with Sherman.

"You were right, Alissa. God didn't kill my family. He allowed the tragedy, though. I don't understand why—"

"And you probably never will. There still are times when I wonder why He allowed my mother to die while she was still so young."

"I guess we're a couple of people who have lost a lot. But I also know we're a couple of people who God cares a great deal for. That's what I've come to realize all over again, that even though I was shaking my fist at God, He still loved me. I'm not saying I've 'arrived' spiritually. I still have a long way to go. But at least I know, and He knows, I'm back to giving it my best shot."

Relieved by his words, Alissa laid her head on Brad's chest. Yes, this was the man God had prepared for her. "That's what's so amazing about Him. He never gives up on us. I know it had to have been pure misery—what you've been through. Seeing my mother die was bad enough, but I can't imagine seeing her slaughtered. Do you know that even though it's been fifteen years, I still miss her? Sometimes I'm still tempted to get angry."

"I'm sure that's a temptation I'll have to overcome myself. But at the same time, I can't keep living in the past. I don't think Dana or Kara either one would want that. I've got a future to think about."

She pulled away to look into his eyes. "I don't expect you to forget about them, Brad. That would be inhuman. It's just—"

"I know. I'll never forget them. I loved them both with my whole heart, and a part of me always will. But I've still got to live today. I've got my painting. . .and you, I hope."

His last statement, so full of uncertainty, sounded more like a question, a question that melted all of Alissa's remaining reservations. For this time, she knew he meant it. "Yes, you've got me," she whispered, sealing her promise with a kiss.

❧

Alissa awoke the next morning to the smell of frying bacon and freshly brewed coffee. Stretching lazily, she smiled and reflected on the previous evening of promises made. Brad hadn't proposed, of course. They hadn't known each other long enough for that.

But the pledge was in his eyes, so full of love. Alissa would be content for now in the "getting to know each other" stage of their new relationship. And when Brad did ask, she'd answer with a resounding "yes." Chuckling, she thought of her father's shock when he would learn one day that Brad Ratner was going to be his son-in-law.

She arose, quickly showered and dressed, then headed down the stairs with Frito on her heels.

"Hey, sleepyhead," Brad said, greeting her with a ready smile and a soft kiss on her forehead. His hair, mussed from sleep, his shirt outside his jeans, his eyes, still drowsy—all this made Alissa look forward to the day she'd greet him every morning.

"It's early," she said, glancing at the kitchen clock that said six thirty. Too bad they couldn't spend the day together.

"Yeah, well, I didn't exactly have a king-sized bed last night.

"Was it too terribly uncomfortable?"

He shrugged. "Not too bad. But even if it had been a bed of nails, I'd have slept there. I'm still worried about you and this lunatic."

"You aren't the only one." Alissa caressed the scabbed-over wound in her hair as she recalled the three nightmares from which she had been awakened. "Thanks for checking on me during the night." Brad had followed the doctor's orders and awakened Alissa every three hours to make sure her slight head injury hadn't developed into something more serious.

"Anytime," he said as if he meant it. "Want some coffee? I made it just for you. I'm not a coffee person."

"Sure."

"Do you feel like going to work?

"Yeah. My head's not hurting, so I don't see why I shouldn't be able to."

"Well, in that case, I thought I'd go home and shower then come back to drive you in. Would you mind?" He took a blue mug from the cabinet, filled it with the aromatic coffee, and handed it to her.

"That would be great." Delighted at how comfortable Brad appeared in her kitchen, Alissa took the mug. "To tell you the truth, I don't relish the idea of driving anywhere alone."

Trena had called at nine o'clock the night before with news that the investigating officer hadn't found anything incriminating at the office. This hadn't surprised Alissa. Whoever was harassing her was adept at covering his or her trail.

"What time do you usually leave?"

"About eight."

"Okay. I'll be back at about a quarter till, then. I left enough bacon and eggs for you." He pointed to the stovetop.

339

"Thanks. This could get to be a habit." She smiled her most flirtatious smile and knew Trena would be proud.

"Who knows, it just might." With a playful tweak of her nose, he planted a kiss on her mouth, which pledged it *would* become a habit. "Lock the door behind me," he said as their embrace reluctantly ended.

"Don't worry. I will." She followed him to the doorway, retrieved the paper from her porch step, and shut the door behind him. Forty minutes later, she'd eaten her breakfast, fed Frito, done her face and hair, and then changed for work. A quick check of her watch told her she had twenty minutes to wait. Just long enough to read the morning paper. She settled into her favorite corner of the couch and began unfolding the paper.

But Frito had other ideas. With a demanding whine, he pawed her leg, then trotted to the back door, a look in his eyes that bordered on desperation. Housebreaking the mutt had been a near impossibility. But she had to give him credit; once he caught on he refused to do his dirty deed in the house.

"Okay, I'm coming." She walked through the sunroom, decorated with plants and wicker furniture, to open the back door. Just as Frito ran to his task, her doorbell rang. Expecting Brad, Alissa hurriedly shut the back door and just as hurriedly clicked the lock into place.

Chapter 21

On the doorbell's third chime, she opened the door to see Mrs. Docker smiling her greeting. The elderly lady, her gray hair styled conservatively, peered at Alissa through thick glasses.

"I'm sorry to bother you so early. But I'm picking up a friend for breakfast in thirty minutes. I felt like you'd be leaving for work soon, so I thought I'd just drop by and tell you what I remembered about that note you found."

Alissa didn't say anything for several seconds. She couldn't. She was too busy studying Mrs. Docker's hair. *Think*, she commanded herself. Was Mrs. Docker's obvious wig the same color gray as what she'd glimpsed in her office last night?

The elderly lady, dressed in navy double knit, waited patiently for Alissa to invite her inside.

Surely a senior citizen in her eighties wouldn't threaten someone's life. She lived in a retirement home because of her health, for Pete's sake. And all she wanted to do was tell Alissa what she'd remembered about the note. Maybe her story would explain Alissa's finding the name "Louanne" so familiar. Deciding Mrs. Docker was harmless, she opened the door wider. "Come in. Would you like some coffee?"

"No, no." She hobbled into the living room and seated herself on the couch. "Like I said, I can only stay a minute," she said in a high soprano voice that slightly shook with age.

Taking the chair opposite her, Alissa waited for Mrs. Docker to begin, and hoped she hadn't made yet another error in judgment as with Richard Calbert. Contrary to Alissa's original impression, he was apparently not trustworthy.

"I got to thinking after we talked, and it finally dawned on me about that note."

Alissa scooted to the edge of her seat.

"And?" she prompted.

"Well, shortly after I bought this house, Whit Jenkins told me about a terrible neighborhood scandal between the woman who owned the house before I did and Claire Allen's husband. His name was Richard, too, by the way."

"Oh?"

"Yes. It seems the woman who lived here before me—her name was Louanne Young—and Richard Allen were having an affair. Nobody knew anything about it until the two ran off together to Australia. Now here's the real twist. The plane they were on crashed over the ocean with no survivors. It was a terrible crash. Ten years ago, it was. I remember the media doing coverage on it for weeks." She patted the back of her gray wig. "Anyway, that's all I know. But I think that note you found was the very one that planned their rendezvous. Why I didn't see it for all those years, I'll never know."

Alissa's mind whirled with this news. "Well, it was actually stuck in the closet and rather hard to see." She stared at the phone as the reason for her familiarity with the name "Louanne" teased her mind.

"I never met Louanne, but Whit Jenkins said she was attractive. Blond hair, brown eyes, and thin-framed. I guess a whole lot like you. He said Claire was really devastated when she found out."

"Louanne had the same coloring? Are you sure?"

"That's the way Whit described her, 'course that's been ten years ago. I could have forgotten." Alissa's heart pounded in her throat as her mind finally focused on a recent memory. *You're in big trouble, Louanne.* The voice mail she'd received the day of her wreck! She'd shrugged it off as a wrong number, but maybe it wasn't. Maybe he person calling had intended the message for Alissa because she esembled Louanne, her husband's former lover. Claire Allen. Was he Alissa's adversary?

Her mind raced to the bones in Brad's backyard. Two bodies. wo people were supposed to be on a flight to Australia, a flight hat crashed with no survivors. Had they ever boarded the plane? Or ad someone murdered them before they had the chance? Was that omeone Claire Allen?

"Dr. Carrington, are you all right?"

"Yes," she croaked, her cheeks as cold as a tombstone. "I—I—it's ist that I think I need a drink of water." A drink of water and a tranuilizer. She had to call the police.

"Well, I won't keep you any longer. Like I said, I've got a breakfast ngagement, and I know you have to get to work."

"Thanks for—for stopping by." As politely as she could, Alissa ushed Mrs. Docker out of the house. She then securely locked the ront door and turned toward the telephone. But that was one phone all Alissa couldn't make. For standing behind the chair she'd just acated was Claire Allen, holding an automatic revolver. Claire Allen, vearing an ill-fitting gray wig. Claire Allen, her lips stretched in smug ictory, her eyes glazed in fury.

Alissa's heart raced in uncontrolled panic as cold sweat swept her ody.

"Did you think you could escape, Louanne?" she sneered.

"How—how did you get in here?" Alissa croaked.

"You're just as stupid as you always were. Your back door was nlocked."

Frito. She'd let him out and thought she'd relocked the door. How ould she have been so careless? Her lips trembling, Alissa inched oward the telephone.

"Stop!" Claire commanded, waving the gun for emphasis. "We're oing to talk, and then you're going to die again."

"Again?"

"Don't play dumb with me, Louanne. You and I both know you escaped from your grave. You can call yourself Alissa Carrington all you want, but we both know you're Louanne Young come back to life."

"Those bones in Brad's backyard—"

"Of course. Don't you remember me making you and Richard march to Mr. Jenkin's newly tilled rose garden?" It was so easy to shoot you both, while you huddled together beside that fresh dirt like two love-crazed teenagers."

"You're—you're confused. I am not Louanne." Her mind spun. Was this what it felt like to face death? This sinking feeling of finality, of the past remembered, the future denied?

Claire tilted her head back and cackled hysterically. "'I'm not Louanne,'" she mocked. "'We're not having an affair! Oh please, please, please, Claire, don't kill me.'" She sobered, her eyes as piercing as a deranged demon's. "You were a liar then, and you're still a liar!"

Alissa stumbled backward.

"I said don't move!" Claire demanded. "I'm not through talking to you."

Alissa stopped, but her heart felt as if it were going to jump out of her body.

"Do you see this?" Claire fumbled in the pocket of her black knit pants to produce a tarnished gold watch, the same watch Alissa had given to Richard Calbert.

Alissa gasped. "Richard gave you the watch?"

"That idiot?" She cackled again. "No. I took it from his car. I was watching when you gave it to him. That Calbert man is so helpful in his stupidity. The very night I murdered you and my Richard in Jenkins' backyard, Calbert invited Whit Jenkins over for dinner. So with Whit gone, his new rose garden was free for me to bury you in. The next day, Whit planted his roses on your bodies and never even suspected." She looked down at the watch. "I also buried the watch because—because I couldn't bear to wear it. I knew I had to retrieve it when your bones were dug up, but I made the mistake of dropping it in your yard."

Alissa thought about the person running from Brad's house the day she'd met him. That too had been Claire Allen.

"Do you know how valuable this watch was to me? My Richard give it to me on our tenth anniversary." A sob, slow and wretched, broke her words. "Right before he met you."

"Mrs. Allen, I am not Louanne," Alissa insisted, her voice quaking. "If you'll just listen to me. You need help—"

"Shut up! I don't need help. I'm the one who was smart enough to pull off a murder, and no one suspected. Do you know what I did after I buried you and Richard?"

Alissa remained silent.

"Do you know?" Claire shrieked.

"N—no."

"Richard was a pilot. I used his password to get into the airline's computers. Then I hacked into the boarding log for the flight and confirmed that Richard and you had boarded. That way, as far as the airline was concerned, Richard and you flew to Australia."

"Oh, really?" Alissa hoped her feigned interest would keep Claire talking.

"Yes. Pretty smart, huh? I was worried about Richard's and Louanne's families, though. I figured they would eventually wonder why those two lovebirds"—she said these last words with a twisted snarl on her face—"didn't write. Then the plane went down. Do you know how relieved I was?"

Alissa stared at her.

"Do you?"

"N—no."

"I was certain that fate had smiled on me. Then. . .then you escaped from your grave! Now it's time for you to die again. And this time, I'm going to fill you so full of bullets you won't ever escape your grave again."

"Please. . ." Alissa's eyes stung with tears, horror, of life denied. *Please, Lord, don't let her do it!*

An animal-like gurgling deep in her throat, Claire gripped the gun with both hands, pointed it at Alissa's forehead, and pulled the trigger.

❦

Brad heard the muffled gunshot as he locked his front door. And the same instinctive fear that had gripped him yesterday gripped him today. Alissa. The shot sounded as if it came from her house.

His heart felt as if it sank to his feet as he raced toward Alissa's front door. Had that maniac somehow managed to enter her home in his absence? He lambasted himself for leaving her and at the same time prayed his assumptions were those of an overactive imagination.

After bounding up her porch stairs two at a time, Brad skidded into the massive wooden door and unsuccessfully tried the knob. It was locked. He pounded against the door with both fists. "Alissa?" he yelled.

No answer. His desperation rising to new heights, Brad rammed his shoulder against the door only to receive a ravaging pain up and down his arm.

"Alissa?"

Another gunshot, it sounded like the explosive claim of death itself. This time, Brad was certain the noise came from her house. He also knew he'd have to take a different route into the house. Glancing toward the window to his right, he sprang into action. One swift kick and the glass shattered into a million fragments.

"Brad, no!" Alissa called, her voice full of surprise, fear, and something close to relief. "I—I've got the door."

"Alissa?" His heart stilled. "Are you all right?"

She flung open the door and stumbled into his arms. "Barely," she said, her voice breaking. Her lips quivering, she looked from Brad to the gun in her shaking right hand.

A moan, soft and pain-filled, floated from near the couch.

"Claire Allen," she said in answer to Brad's unasked question. "We need—we need to call the police and an ambulance."

"You shot her?" Brad croaked.

"Yes. But she almost shot me first." Alissa cringed. "If it hadn't been for Frito attacking her, I'd be dead." She spoke with as much calm as she could. "I'd put him out and—accidentally left the door unlocked. Claire must have left it ajar when she entered, and—and he followed her in, then attacked her from behind, just—just as she fired the gun." Another cringe. "Thank the Lord, Frito's impact knocked the gun from—from her hand, and the bullet missed me. I—I grabbed the gun and had to shoot. . .in self-defense."

Brad stepped into the living room to see Claire writhing on the floor, clutching her right thigh, and Frito growling only inches from her. "She came after you even though you had the gun?"

Her face pale, Alissa nodded then mouthed, "She's crazy." Aloud she said, "Get a towel from the kitchen and see if you can slow her bleeding. I'll call the police."

That evening, Alissa sat in Brad's dining room, feeling like royalty as he served her his own special pot roast, baby carrots, and scalloped potatoes. "I had no idea you were such an excellent cook."

"There's a lot you don't know about me," he teased.

"I guess I'm on a course of discovery, then."

"We're both on a course of discovery." He reached across the table to squeeze her hand. "I'm just glad you're still alive to discover."

"Me, too." Alissa rolled her eyes. "If it hadn't been for Frito, I'd have

TEXAS NEIGHBORS

a lot more than looks in common with Louanne Young. That dog was spoiled before, but as far as I'm concerned, now he can have anything his little heart desires." She sighed. "Poor Claire." Alissa reflected upon the pathetic insanity in the woman's eyes.

"Poor Claire? Poor Claire almost killed you. And she did kill her husband and his lover."

"I know. But it finally got to her. I don't think her conscience could let her get away with it. And when she saw me. . ."

"She became confused?" Brad, ignoring his meal, rose to circle the table and take Alissa's hand in his. "That seems to be the general trend around here, because the same thing happened to me. I haven't known which end was up since I first saw you."

Alissa stroked his hair. "The feeling's mutual," she muttered, her stomach fluttering with his closeness.

"You might as well be warned," he continued. "I plan to be a big part of your life from now on, probably forever."

"I don't expect anything less," she whispered against his lips.

A Letter to Our Readers

Dear Readers:

In order that we might better contribute to your reading enjoyment, we would appreciate your taking a few minutes to respond to the following questions. When completed, please return to the following: Fiction Editor, Barbour Publishing, Inc., P.O. Box 719, Uhrichsville, OH 44683.

1. Did you enjoy reading *Texas Neighbors* by Debra White Smith?
   ❑ Very much—I would like to see more books like this.
   ❑ Moderately—I would have enjoyed it more if _____
   _____
   _____

2. What influenced your decision to purchase this book?
   (Check those that apply.)
   ❑ Cover   ❑ Back cover copy   ❑ Title   ❑ Price
   ❑ Friends   ❑ Publicity   ❑ Other

3. Which story was your favorite?
   ❑ *The Key*   ❑ *The Neighbor*
   ❑ *The Promise*

4. Please check your age range:
   ❑ Under 18   ❑ 18–24   ❑ 25–34
   ❑ 35–45   ❑ 46–55   ❑ Over 55

5. How many hours per week do you read? _____

Name _____

Occupation _____

Address _____

City_____ State_____ Zip_____

E-mail_____

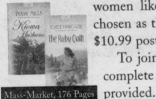